"The hospital is closed at this hour, mister Gamble. Leave or I'll call the attendants." A pure bluff. She was at a remote end of the Sanitarium's main building and there was little chance of anyone happening by.

"Purty late, missus Kellogg." He straightened, his pelvis thrust forward, his hands loose at his sides. "What if I told you I come just to see you?" A trickle of spittle leaked from the corner of his mouth. Ella could smell his whiskey breath.

"You're sickening." She glared at him. "You turn my stomach."

He reached for her abruptly and she quickly stepped back down the stairs away from him. He had to grab the bannister to keep his balance, but he grinned and said, "Whoops, whoops," in little teasing chirps.

Before she could turn, his fingers abraded her cheek like steelwool. It froze her power of motion. Her body shook so badly her teeth clattered. Then the hand became remarkably delicate in touch, a powder puff brushing her shoulder, moving lower. The buttons were being unfastened at her collar. The top one, now another.

"They any empty rooms around here?" Gamble sneered.

EMPIRES

EMPIRES

Robert E. Hencey

Published by The Miller Foundation

EMPIRES

TUNC · NUNC · POSTEA

"A seedling, a growing tree, and the promise of tomorrow."

Cover by Designworks.

FIRST EDITION / January 1996

Printed and bound in the United States of America.

For information address The Miller Foundation,
310 WahWahTaySee Way, Battle Creek, Michigan 49015

For Robert B. Miller, Sr.; it was his idea. And for Naomi; she stayed all the way.

Acknowledgements

For their help and encouragement, my thanks to Arthur Angood, James McQuiston, Norm Williamson, Jr., the staff of Willard Library, members of the Battle Creek Fire Department, Reta Thompson, Charles Eisendrath, Nicholas DelBanco, Bob and Al Miller, Matt Sutherland, Michael Barrett, Ross Kahler, and Melissa Paul.

A special note of gratitude to Eva Warrick, Barry Garron, Janice Young Brooks, and Lowell Erickson. They willingly contributed or wisely advised.

I am grateful to the many others who provided information, leads, and firsthand knowledge, but whom I've failed to mention. You, too, helped to write this book.

This novel is fiction but is based on real historical characters and events. Many of the comments, exhortations, speeches, personal letters, and courtroom pronouncements reflect the actual words of the speaker and are taken from authenticated sources listed below. Other sources include personal correspondence and diaries, as well as unpublished documents detailing the lives and businesses of the characters.

Biography of Charles William Post. A 23-page paper by the Verne Burnett Organization, 1947.

Collier's Weekly, December 1910 and January 1911.

C.W. Post: The Hour and the Man, by Nettie Leitch; Judd & Detweiler, 1963.

Ellen G. White: The Lonely Years by Arthur L. White; Review and Herald Publishing Association, 1984.

Good Health newsletters published by the Seventh Day Adventists.

Heiress by William Wright; New Republic Books, 1978.

Kellogg File, The; C.W. Post's Peaceful Paragraphs (Pamphlet of his address to The National Association of Manufacturers in 1913); The Battle Creek Enquirer, The Battle Creek Daily Journal, The Battle Creek Moon, microfilm editions; Willard Library, Battle Creek, MI.

Numerous books by John Harvey Kellogg including Neurasthenia, 1914; Plain Facts for Old and Young, 1882; The Natural Diet of Man, 1923.

Original Has This Signature, The, by Horace Powell; Prentice-Hall, Inc., 1956; as well as Mr. Powell's extensive collection of notes.

Science in the Kitchen by Ella Eaton Kellogg, 1892.

Selected Messages by Ellen G. White; Review and Herald Publishing Association, 1958.

Testimonies for the Church by Ellen G. White; Pacific Press Publishing Association, 1948.

White Lie, The by Walter Rea; M & R Publications, 1982.

PART ONE

Life should begin with ages and its privileges and accumulations, and end with youth and its capacity to splendidly enjoy such advantages.

Mark Twain

1

APRIL 1860

DOCTOR Millard Dunston stopped his buggy in front of Kellogg's two-story frame house on West Main Street. Through the rain he saw kerosene lamps burning in every window, thought the place looked cheery, despite it's owner's temperament.

The unpaved road was nearly a mud trough. Behind the house was a white frame barn full of livestock, bales of hay, and farming implements. Dunston considered moving the horse and buggy into the barn but the thought of slogging through the mud and then back to the house changed his mind. He guessed one of Kellogg's young'ns might do the job for him.

He opened the gate, walked through, carefully replaced the latch in its cradle, and picked his way along the gravel path toward the house, avoiding the deepest puddles. He stepped up onto the wooden boards of the porch as a splash of bright yellow light broke through the rain. It silhouetted a man's figure in the open doorway, a lean man of some size, but not big, five feet ten at most. His voice was powerful above the storm.

"I figured that was you, doctor. You coming in or staying out?"

The words rumbled like a rockslide, the way a fire-and-brimstone preacher might speak, or a hell-for-leather military captain. He was neither. He was a broom maker. Some who knew him would add that he was a good neighbor, ready to lend help or money when it was needed. They would also say he was a partisan of the church, strong on religion to an excess. Fanatical might be stretching the point, but not by much.

"I didn't ride out here to stand in the rain, John Preston Kellogg. How long's Angennit been having her pains?"

"Started four hours ago. I told John Harvey to say that when he come for you. Course, that was nearly an hour ago so it's been five now."

Dunston nodded noncommittally and entered the house and hung his hat on a wall peg in the cloakroom. A boy of eight years came forward from the adjoining room, stiffly, and took his raincoat. The boy's eyes were wideset above a sensitively shaped mouth. He padded along in thick woolen socks, no shoes. Behind him, in the dining room, brightly lit with several lamps and a fireplace, an armless rocking chair swung sharply where he had vacated it. Dunston saw knitting needles and yarn on the seat cushion and a nondescript fabric that was in the shaping.

"Doing your crocheting, Johnny?" Dunston asked.

"Ann Janette taught him," Kellogg said defensively. "Don't hurt a man to know how to mend his own clothes. Comes in handy."

"Didn't say it didn't." Dunston still concentrated on the boy. "What're you making?"

"Mittens, I think." The voice was soft, like beach sand on a mild day.

"Bit late in the year, isn't it?"

Johnny shrugged, looked at the floorboards. Dunston chuckled. "Good to get a jump on next winter. Right?"

The boy hoisted Dunston's slicker and looped it on a pegged rack by the cloakroom doorway. Other coats hung there, mostly woolen ones belonging to the Kellogg children.

"When Emuline come I told Laura and Emma to go up, keep out of the way less they was needed," Kellogg said. "John Harvey's down here, still drying out from being over to your place. He got soaked."

"No question, it's raining." Dunston chuffed like a dull explosion, eased onto a chair, his pancake-shaped hands spread flat on the scrubbed table top: stubby fingers, with nails long and stained, looking as if they belonged to a farmer or machinist. His vest and trousers were spoiled with brown splotches, different colors of medicinal powders, human fluids, and a few blots of unidentifiable origin.

"Business good, John Preston?" Dunston didn't really care. Just filling time. Broom making was a topic he looked forward to discussing about as readily as jumping off a roof onto a picket fence.

"Making a living." Kellogg looped an arm onto the fireplace mantle, pointed a knobby finger at his son. "You're already wet, go out and lead the doctor's animal in the barn. No point letting it drown."

The boy headed obediently to the cloakroom, put on ankle-high boots and lifted down his slicker.

"When you come back, go on up to bed. You got schooling tomorrow."

"Yes sir," Johnny answered, going out the front door.

Kellogg strode to the front window, pulled aside a thick brown curtain, peered outside, watching Johnny trudge through the muddy yard. He spoke to his own reflection in the glass. "I want Ann Janette to have the baby and be up and around taking care of things the way she knows how." He looked back at Dunston. "You see she stays well, hear me?" A coating of menace in his tone.

Dunston studied the toes of his shoes as though they were interesting instead of just scarred and dull.

"Doctors killed my first wife," Kellogg went on, "her too sick and weak to sit up and them bleeding her like you'd draw sap out of a tree..."

"I know, John Preston. You've told me that story ever time I come here. And ever time I remind you it wasn't me took care of your Mary. If it had been, she might have pulled through. Not saying she would, just saying maybe."

"What about now?" Kellogg walked back to the center of the room, glared down at Dunston. "With Ann Janette?"

"Oh, hell, man, put some rainwater on that damned short fuse."

"Don't curse under this roof!" Kellogg's hands became fists.

Dunston fired back, "Then quit goading me into doing it. Good Lord, I've delivered three of your brood, never lost a one, and Angennit never had a bad time with none of them." The doctor shook his head disbelievingly. "Why don't you sit down, John Preston, or make some coffee or go outside and cool off?"

Kellogg backed up against a chair, dropped into it. His mouth was twisted angrily, "I wish you'd learn to say her name correct instead of mushing it like you do." After a while he added, "She's waitin, doctor, been waitin for hours."

The following silence stretched into minutes. Dunston finally lifted out a thin chain with a pocket watch attached, noted the time, held the watch closer to be sure it was ticking, returned it to a pocket. He stood heavily, picked up his satchel and walked into the long hallway that ran the length of the house, ending at Ann Janette's bedroom.

2

"HELLO, Angennit."

Dunston looked around the room, surveyed it briskly, made certain the things that would be needed were at hand. The rainstorm slashed at the single window. A phosphorescent burst of lightning was followed by a crash of thunder that shook the house's frame.

He gave a slight nod of acknowledgement to Emuline Skipworth, which the black midwife returned. She sat in a rickety wooden chair on the far side of the bed, cooling Ann Janette's face with a damp rag.

"How you feeling?" Dunston asked the pregnant woman.

"I'm just fine. How is John and the children?"

She lay on her back, legs spread, a thin coverlet over her, her hair in a rope braid that trailed across the pillow. She wore no sleeping bonnet but had on a loose gown with a high buttoned neck and sleeves that closed at her wrists. Each arm was extended above her head so her hands could grip the railings of the iron bedstead. A mist of sweat speckled her forehead but no pain showed on her face.

"Don't worry about them, Angennit, they're getting along remarkable well." He dropped his satchel on the three-legged table by the door. "Emuline, what're them young'ns of yours up to these days?"

"Dey is sassy as ever, doctor Dunston." She gave a quick laugh. Eyes closed, squeezed shut in her thin black face. Flash of large white teeth, slightly protruded.

"They stay sassy, you know they're healthy." He removed his coat, draped it on the doorknob, and summoned Emuline to his side with a slight twist of his head.

Standing by the door, their backs to Ann Janette, Dunston asked the black woman in a whisper, "Has she emptied her bowels?"

"Jes a while ago I gives her a ennimy. She went good and I clean her all up."

"Emuline," he said in a mild, reproving tone, "I've told you an enemy is somebody who means to harm you. That isn't like an enema that you administered." He unbuttoned his cuffs and rolled up the sleeves. "You ought to try to remember the difference, even if it's just to keep me happy."

"Ennimy, bowels, bad peoples," Emuline made a scoffing grunt. "It all just shit to me, doctor Dunston. You know I ain't a eddicated talker, an I don' know why you think you gonna make me out one, an sides, folks knows what I means and dat's de important thing, ain't it?"

He grinned and turned to face Ann Janette. "We better have a look at our patient here."

"She been gettin the pains bout ever minute or two. I timed em by countin."

Ann Janette's moan lasted only a few seconds. Then she looked apologetically at Dunston. "I bet I sound worse than it feels. They're coming sort of fast but they don't hurt that bad. I don't plan to make any noise, don't want to be a crybaby, it just slips out."

He winked at her. "You and me are old hands at this, Angennit. We'll have it all done and over with before either one of us even knows it." He stood by the bedside and shifted the lamp closer on the side table. "Emuline, get that other lamp from the bureau and set it over here."

"Her water done broke a while back," Emuline announced while she carried the lamp to the table, placed it beside the other one. "Wasn't nothin unnatural in it. Jes blood 'n water like it post to be. I sopped everthing up in dem blankets dere in de corner. You wantin to see em?" She looked down at Ann Janette and assured her, "It all just like it ought to be. Havin a old baby ain't no job at all for womans like you and me, is it?"

"No need for me to see the discharge if you're satisfied," Dunston complimented her. He pulled his sleeves higher up to his elbows, kicked aside some stained rags on the floor, and lifted Ann Janette's hand, comfortingly. "We're going to move you to the edge of the bed, now. You remember? Just like last time." She nodded and another moan began, chased by a grimace that said I'm sorry.

"Help me scoot her around here, Emuline." He folded the coverlet away, let it fall to the floor. "Get her feet. Okay, Angennit, let loose of the bed, just kind of ease yourself down this way and we'll turn you."

She moved until she was positioned sideways on the bed, her feet at the edge, legs bent at the knees, gown tugged above the bulging stomach. Emuline pushed pillows under her head, then gripped Ann Janette's hands so when the final pains began she would have something to squeeze onto.

Dunston peered at the mouth of the womb, opened its lips deftly with his fingers, conducted his examination briefly with the detached concentration of a gardener deciding which limbs to prune from a prize rosebush. From his satchel he retrieved a needle and thread and a bottle of silver nitrate. He lodged the needle in the cloth of his vest so he could find it quickly if it was needed. He placed the unopened bottle on the table in easy reach beneath a lamp's glow. He ignored the dozen or so other vials of powder in the leather bag, the salves, gauzes, and the few instruments brought along in case the labor became a difficult one. He disregarded the containers of chloroform and morphine. This birth did not look like it would require either. The pocket knife he used to trim his cigars was deposited conveniently on the bedside table.

"Thank God we got some decent light here." The small talk was meant to keep her mind off any pain that gathered. "Some of these houses round town is darker than the inside of a butter churn with the lid on."

"Dat'd be my huse, but it's better'n no huse at all," Emuline said agreeably. "Dem old lard burnin lamps ain't good for much seein and dey sure smell awful when dey gets down to de las bit of lard. Now dese kerosene ones is jes bout the best I ever laid eyes on. I ever get me some money ahead, I goin to spend it on a kerosene lamp."

"You can have one of these," Ann Janette told her, pressing hard on her hands, holding back a groan. "You take it with you when you go."

"I thank you, missus Kellogg, but I couldn't..."

"Emuline," she said between clenched teeth. "I want you to have it." She released a heavy sigh, relaxed.

Dunston mediated. "Don't appear you got much say in this, Emuline. Besides, I don't want to hear any arguments over any lamps, understand? Might as well give up and shut up. We got more important business to do right now."

"I'll sho think on it, missus Kellogg." Then, to Dunston: "Yessuh, we got some work, doctor. We bout to has a caller."

She and Ann Janette were waging a tug of war, pulling at each other's hands to increase the contractions of the uterus and push the baby into the lower birth canal. As if to prove Emuline's prediction, Ann Janette's moan veered to a high-pitched shriek.

Dunston knelt in front of Ann Janette's open legs. He knew the womb was fully dilated. "Push, Angennit. Push. You know how we have to do it."

She cried again, shrill and prolonged. She pushed. She shoved against Emuline's strong arms, clinched her hands in pain and anger as if to break them. Push, Dunston instructed. She pushed. Her body was splitting. Push. She pushed, my God, she pushed. Something was bursting out of her, something larger than anything in the world, something so big and solid and relentless in its effort to escape that she knew it must be a nightmare thing because nothing real or earthly could possibly be so enormous, so unyielding. Push. Everything was pushing, feet pushing into bed, arms pushing into arms, belly pushing against that incredible, immense rock. Push, someone said, and she screamed, I'm pushing, can't you hear the grinding and the ripping because I'm pushing and that awful, awful thing won't leave, it wants to hold on too long, Oh God, it's too much to pass and I feel...joyous...joyous...Joyous. As ferociously as it began, it stopped.

THE back of the small head had come into view, chin tucked under, then the whole head emerged, then the shoulders, torso, and legs. In the last second of exit, the familiar gush of residue. Dunston stood aside quickly and avoided it, except for a spattering on his shoes and pants cuffs.

"You feelin okay, missus Kellogg?" Emuline asked.

Ann Janette nodded, the stretch of her face became calm. Emuline hurried around the foot of the bed and took the baby from Dunston, held it in towels and wiped the sticky glutinous veil from its head and body.

The doctor located a length of twine he had packed in a vest pocket, flicked off pieces of lint and crumbs of tobacco, tied it tightly around the umbilical cord. He picked up his knife from the table, clamped the flat blade between his teeth, sharp edge out. A squat, balding pirate ready to storm the royal barkentine. He opened the bottle of silver nitrate, held it in his left palm with two fingers, lifted the cord using his free fingers, sliced through the oversized vein like a butcher halving a sausage. Quickly he tossed the knife on the table, upended the bottle against a soiled forefinger, and daubed blackish powder on the end of the section that was attached to the baby. The entire cauterization took less than fifteen seconds. Dunston pried the tiny mouth open with thumb and finger, stuck the fingers of his other hand inside and expertly scooped out a choking glob of mucous that had collected there. Suddenly the baby gasped, then wailed.

"He's a fine boy, Angennit," Dunston grinned at her. He wiped his hands on a rag, dropped it to the floor. "Picked out a name for him?"

"Got a real good voice, missus Kellogg. Strong lungs, dey sounds like to me. Shore is his daddy's young'n, I'd say."

"John wants to call him Will Keith. I suppose that's what it'll be."

Dunston nodded approval. "You put Will Keith over in the crib to clean him up, Emuline. I'm going to check Angennit here and see if we did any damage that has to be fixed. We got one more thing to do." Ann Janette acknowledged with a swift closing and opening of her eyes, knowing what he meant.

She asked weakly, "Can I see John before I go to sleep? I'm very sleepy and I'd like to see him." Her voice was light and distant but she was still alert, fighting her tiredness.

"Of course, Angennit." Dunston patted her hand.

Kneeling down he made his examination. Finally satisfied, he stiffened his arms and lowered his weight onto the woman's stomach, mashing with his palms to separate the placenta from the uterus wall and remove it.

Outside the bedroom window, hunched on the narrow porch in the blowing rain, Johnny Kellogg turned away from what he had witnessed. On his knees, he scrabbled to the edge of the board flooring and vomited into the yard. After a few minutes he lifted his face and let the melting sky wash it clean. Finally, he stood up, pulled his raincoat tightly around him, went slowly to the front door and entered the house.

3

IN the town of Springfield in the state of Illinois, nearly 400 miles from Battle Creek, a boy woke up screaming.

He stopped when the cry reached his own ears.

He sat up rigidly on the tossed bed, listened attentively. No footsteps. Nobody rushed up the spiral staircase from the polished marble floor below. He hadn't been heard. Mild relief draped him like a warm shower. He didn't need mollycoddling by mother. He certainly didn't want any "dear boy" talk from missus Blainey, who kept house for them. Her pats and ooh-aahs always fluttered about him like the feather duster she never was caught without. He was too old for childish soothing. He was six.

Through the open window of Charley's room he scanned the hard-packed street below and, just beyond it, the house across the road, charcoal grey, its roof sprouting spiderlegs of trees against the plain white sky of late afternoon.

Less than six blocks away was mister Lincoln's house, on Eighth Street, just a short walk from Springfield's courthouse where he practiced law. Charley had seen the lanky, gangling man often. Rollin took him along a time or two when he visited "Abe," as his father called him. He had seen him on summer evenings when Lincoln used to sprawl in a caneback chair on his porch, big feet roosting on the banister railing like two tall skinny crows, a mix of people gathered around to listen to his views on everything from cabin building to state's rights.

Just the other day Charley heard his father say it was a shame Abe didn't have time any more for his veranda talks now that he was the Republican candidate for president. Charley had noticed placards popping out like moss in a shady place, nailed to gate posts, tree trunks, store sidings, all reading, "Vote for Lincoln and Hamlin, for Union and Freedom." No one listened hard enough as they passed that empty front porch on Eighth Street or they would have heard the muted, distant sound of Civil War bugles and gunfire.

Charley slid off the bed, moved to an overstuffed chair. He considered finding his brother, Aurrie, and drawing some pictures for him, but four-year old Aurrie was a nuisance, especially when he wanted you to draw only Indians. Indians shooting arrows, throwing spears, riding horses. And his other brother, Carroll, was good for nothing but stumbling into walls, howling his head off, and messing a dozen diapers a day.

Charley reached up to the desktop, randomly slid a book into his lap. A large, cloth covered volume with a picture of a capering animal on every page. A goat, cat, dog. A few words under each illustration. "Bob Cat plays the fiddle," or "Sally Squirrel dances a jig." Charley knew the words. In fact, he could read very well for his age.

He idly flipped the book's pages, gave it up to boredom, let the book lay dead against his legs. Around him were shelves of toys: wooden blocks, card games, bags of marbles, a croquet set missing some wire arches, a wooden wagon. A tenor banjo rested its fretted neck against the wall. He could pick out a melody or two on it, one note at a time. This convinced his mother he had great musical talent and she promised the household, "Charley will begin piano lessons on his seventh birthday." She had read of a piano that unfolded into a bed. The Cincinnati man who was working on it was quoted in the newspapers saying it would be ready to purchase very soon; he was trying to add a writing desk and chest of drawers to it. Carrie intended to buy one, with or without the desk.

Charley was eager to start the lessons. Music fascinated him. He had watched the band members read from the sheets of funny dots and lines when they played concerts in the town square, and it was a mathematical mystery to him, how they knew what they were doing. He wanted to understand it, understand the reason that guided its precision.

He scooted further into his chair, studied the line of the sun moving slowly higher on the wall, pursued immediately by smooth shadows that sucked up everything the light abandoned. A breeze sifted through the window screen. His eyes closed. He glided over into sleep.

The nightmare rushed back, the world turned emerald green, and geysers of white flame shot up from silent fields.

From the moving carriage, Charley could smell the sweet aroma of the locust trees. Whole stands of them at the edge of the prairie, on every side. The city of Springfield rested in the hazy distance, faded in the noonday sun like an old watercolor. The State House, with its wooden cupola and its portico supported by large white columns, hunkered at the city's center, dusty-looking through the gauze of space. It was regal and staunch and a bit potbellied, not altogether unlike the rustic, informal men who were elected to convene there to take care of the people's lawmaking.

Carrie said, "Rollin, have you noticed, all the houses we have passed have lightning conductors on their roofs?" Her small nose wiggled, rabbit-like, and she nibbled a thick lower lip.

"There is a reason, darling."

Charley squirmed. There again was that belief in a *reason* for everything. Oddly, now his father's words were clear, though he had been unable to understand them before. Must be a reason, he giggled without making a sound.

"They prevent the house from being struck by lightning. We have one on our roof, if you recall." Rollin made a snk!snk! noise in his cheek and flipped one of the mares with a light touch of his whip. The carriage picked up a barely noticeable increment of speed. "We've never been hit, either."

"I've heard of no one who has," Carrie responded.

"Of course not, darling. That is the purpose of lightning conductors." Rollin: confident, elegant, his black hair sharply parted, his wide chin sporting a Lincolnesque beard.

She scowled. "I mean I've never heard of *anyone*," nice little pause, "*anywhere*." She stressed the last word by stringing out its three syllables as far as they would go, giving them verbal strength they didn't own. Her straight, brown hair caught sunlight. "And there are hundreds of homes without lightning conductors." A geyser spewed red beyond a low hill.

"Stay with it, Carrie." Erastus' voice was squeaky, excited. Leaning forward, he slapped the back of the carriage seat. "Don't give ground. You're onto something."

Truman pulled his companion back into the cushions. "Leave them alone, Erastus. They can take care of their damned lightning rods without your interference." Erastus slumped in his seat, no argument, energy expended.

Charley's grandfathers were wearing dark wool suits and top hats and high starched collars like Rollin's that pinched up layers of skin. Each had side whiskers and a moustache the color of cotton. Charley was vaguely aware that neither Carrie nor Rollin had shown the slightest notice of the two old men.

Beyond a grove of timber on the horizon, at the edge of an unbroken plain of long, coarse grass, lightning skittered out of a mountain of blue clouds. It always was the signal for Rollin to halt the carriage. No one gave any instructions because everyone knew what to do. Charley's grandfathers climbed out of the carriage, slowly, achingly, but uncomplainingly. His mother waited for Rollin to alight and come around to her side and help her descend to the dry dirt road.

Finally, with the passengers lined up along the edge of the grass — grass so brightly green it actually glowed — Rollin gave Charley the reins, laying them across his lap, placing them between his limp fingers. Only now did Charley realize again that he was virtually helpless. He hadn't the strength to move the reins away. The leather straps felt like railroad ties crushing his legs. In his hands they had the weight of steel cables. He was immeasurably tired. He could not possibly step down from his seat unaided.

"Why?" his eyes pleaded. "Why are we doing this?"

"There is a reason." Rollin smacked the nearest mare's rump with his hand. The carriage lurched forward, both horses galloping, gathering speed.

Charley twisted around, peered over the jouncing seat. The effort drained his vitality completely. He saw Rollin and Carrie and Truman and Erastus all sitting down in the grass at the roadside, opening a picnic basket, spreading out a white linen cloth, and Carrie was parceling out plates of food. His grandfathers were trying vainly, toothlessly, to eat crisp fried chicken legs while Rollin laughed good naturedly at their sloppy efforts. Suddenly, in unison, everyone focused on Charley. They were becoming smaller and more indistinct by the moment as the carriage rushed him away from them. They waved merrily. He couldn't return the wave; he was too exhausted.

The mares were racing each other, their legs just blurred motion. Dust boiled away from the wheels. A mass of muscle and wood and frailty propelled at great speed. Mountains of advancing clouds. The carriage careened forward to meet them, reins flying free, flapping in the rising wind, biting at his eyes. Lightning split the horizon. The bulge-eyed horses, ears laid flat, were veering off the road, trying to change direction, carriage tumbling, leaving the ground, turning in the air, prairie overhead, lightning ripping upward, whirlwinds trembling the earth, carriage flaming, bursting hot around him, horseflesh sizzling, stinking, smoking, mares screaming, toothless mouths screaming...

Charley woke up to his own screams.

4

LEAVING his father's broom factory on Battle Creek's Main Street, Johnny Kellogg turned west on the busy boardwalk. He had put in three hours of sorting broom corn after school, worked his way through a full bin of stiff, golden grass. With a superb eye and a fast hand he had selected out the best of the eight-feet long, slender stems which would be converted into the sweeping end of hundreds of brooms. He had kept pace with the men.

Now he had thirty-five cents payment in the pocket of his full-legged, heavy trousers. Many of the other boys in school wore pants that stopped just a little below the knee, then gathered into a band and tied or buckled tight over long, coarse stockings. Johnny's trousers, similar to the ones worn by grownups in the factory, were an expression of compensation for being a regular working man. They were all the more conspicuous because of his diminutive size, but he didn't mind. They were a badge of some honor.

A nickel of his wages would go for candy, to which he was happily addicted. The balance would be put with other coins in a tobacco can he had cleaned and cached in the bottom drawer of his bureau. The money was used for whatever he needed, especially to pay his father for lodging, an arrangement that had been Johnny's own idea.

"FATHER, you've told me I'm a good worker, haven't you?"

"Yes."

"Am I as good as Thomas Gandy or Fred Defore?"

"Close. That's to your credit, being as they are full growed and you're not."

"I do as much work as they do? I mean, on the days I'm there all day, especially?"

"John Harvey, if you got something to get at, well, get at it. There's business for us both to tend to."

"Yes, father. You see, I was wondering, if I do as much as Thomas and Fred, and my work is as good, how come I don't get paid anything?"

They were standing in the factory office. A small room, cluttered with papers, order forms, record books, broom handles, a desk whose drawers and compartments bulged with receipts and invoices, a sturdy chair so smudged and blackened it looked as if it had not escaped a housefire entirely in time. John Preston moved his angular frame behind the desk as if to put its bulk between them. He rubbed his finger crosswise under his nose, thinking. Johnny was tilted onto his toes for extra height, both hands jammed deep into his trousers pockets, waiting.

"Big difference is, I don't have to pay for Fred's clothes and his food. I don't have to pay for Thomas to sleep somewhere, neither. And I surely don't give them men a handful of pennies for horehound drops or licorice. If they need boots, they buy them. I don't do it for them. You see what I'm pointing out?"

"Yes." A long silence. Then, "If I pay for all them things myself, I mean everything I need, would you make me a wage like you do the others?"

"I don't guess I know for sure, John Harvey. I'd have to give thought to it."

"Would you? I mean give thought to it?"

"Seems a big decision for you. We ought to mull it a while. But I suppose, if that's what you actual want, we might could try it out. See how it goes for both of us. Change it back if it don't prove sound."

AFTER several months, father and son became permanent employer and employee, landlord and tenant, to their mutual satisfaction. The arrangement had given Johnny a welcomed feeling of independence to work at a regular job, not just have boy's chores around the house. Manage your own funds, pay your own way.

He had a small reserve of cash. The reserve would be larger but he had dipped into it for eighty cents to buy a four-volume set of Farr's "Ancient History." Since the first day of school this year he had found in himself a growing, insatiable hunger for books. Lately it seemed neither the schoolhouse nor the town would have a sufficient supply. He devoured every page of every edition he could find, borrowing from doctor Dunston and anyone who was willing to loan. The book's subject wasn't of real importance. The printed word simply fascinated him.

He vowed to read the school's complete set of encyclopedias. His teacher watched him solemnly, doubtfully, as he went about the appalling task with an eagerness and intensity neither she nor he could explain. At volume G, going strong, she no longer questioned if he would do what he said.

Johnny still made the family's supply of soap and regularly fixed the family breakfast after his father or mother or Laura had stoked a fire in the four-lid iron stove. His favorite chore was to bake bread for supper. In that job he outshined Laura and Emma, though both sisters were so glad to be free of the task, their father claimed they purposely made a mess of things from time to time to ensure that Johnny kept his position as chief baker and cook.

Walking along Main Street, one of Battle Creek's two avenues of industry, Johnny listened to the din of hooves and wheels striking the cobblestone street, and the clacking of shoe leather against wooden plank sidewalks. He liked the racket. It gave him a feeling of being part of some big plan that generated activity everywhere you looked. His father was right: this was a town on the move.

He watched two unfortunate women go reluctantly into Dentist Robinson's office, glad he had no appointment. He saw and heard Brown and Thomas (of Dibble and Brown), in the doorway of their law office, loudly debating, in fine courthouse style, the question of who would go across to Purcell's grocery and buy cheese and crackers for an afternoon snack. A shuffling throng moved through the wide doors of Ramey's dry goods store.

Passing a meat market he whiffed the pungent odor of "fresh and salted," as the sign over the door proclaimed. A paint store, a tailor's shop. Several doctors' offices, all in a row as though needing the comfort of each other's presence in such an uncertain profession. One was named L.A. Foote; Johnny always thought it would be a big laugh if Foote only treated feet. Another grocer. Perry's Furniture Emporium where the air always tingled with the odor of furniture polish mixed with embalming fluid because one half of the store was an undertaking parlor. Then Bock and Peters hardware store, Collier and Wattles hardware, the Metcalf brothers hardware. No doubt about it, people needed lots of hardware.

5

SOMEONE shoved him. Its force sent him stumbling. A guardrail kept him from going into the street, but his head smacked into the upright post.

He looked back over his shoulder. Sammy Gamble stared at him, hands on his hips, face screwed up in a sour expression like he smelled something that stunk.

"Whyn't ya watch where yer goin, Kellogg? You damned near knocked me off the walk."

"You hit me, I didn't hit you." Johnny turned around, touched his forehead with his fingers, felt blood. The railing dug into his back.

"You callin me a liar, you little bastard?" Spittle came with the words. Half again Johnny's size, Sammy wore a cap pushed back on his head to make him look tougher, and strands of his greasy yellow hair splashed across his brow.

"That's what he's doin awright, Sammy, callin you a liar."

Lew Reesner was known as Loony Lew by the other kids. A puncher. Would hit anything near him, a fence, tree, horse. It was even said he'd wallop a girl if she got close enough, which none ever did. He grinned, wolfish, said: "You give us some money, we let you go."

With his back adhesived to the railing, Johnny said, "I got no money." The weight of silver was heavy in his pocket.

"He's lyin again, Sammy." Lew rolled his eyes until only the whites showed. "That's all the little turd can do. Lie. Tells you he didn't almost knock you over a minute ago. Now he says he ain't got money. He jist come outa his old man's broom place, din't he? He works there, don't he? He gets paid don't he?"

This line of thinking seemed reasonable to Sammy. "Why ain't you got'ny money? You get paid don't ya, moron?"

Tears burned behind Johnny's eyes. His forehead stung where it was scraped. People walking by ignored his glances, failed to hear his silent calls for help. One woman grumbled loudly to her companion, "I do wish these young churls would find somewhere to play instead of on the sidewalks."

Tears bubbled at the bottom of Johnny's eyes. With great willpower he froze them in place. He hoped to God they wouldn't run over. His throat was tight, corded, aching from tension. His side, where Sammy hit him, was sore and he wanted to touch it but he remained motionless. Finally, "I don't get the money ever day. Just once a week," he lied. "My father takes it home, he puts it away for me to save."

"Let's beat the shit outta 'im," Lew fumed, tired of the game, it going nowhere, nothing to be had from it. "This is wastin our time."

Sammy held out an arm of his ragged, filthy jacket. "Look at this. A big tear you put here in this sleeve. And here, your damned bloody head all over it. I'm sayin I'll skip it if you wanna pay fer some damage you done to my coat."

"Drag 'im in the alley over there and beat the shit out of 'im," Loony Lew raved and kicked the side of the building.

"Move away," an adult voice overwhelmed Lew's shouts. "Go on, you boys get the devil away, and I mean now!"

Frank Perry stood in the doorway of his funeral parlor. He wore a bloody apron from neck to knee and a white cloth mask over his lower face. Above the mask were grape-shot eyes, as stern as those of a falcon. He was six feet tall and looked like a grisly giant to Johnny.

"I said get, and by Gadfry I mean get!" He waved a long wooden ruler that had the likeness of a spanking rod.

Sammy and Lew leaped off the boardwalk, flew across the street, dodging between wagons, and disappeared behind Ramey's Dry Goods.

Johnny leaned weakly against the guardrail, too relieved to feel anything except gratitude.

"Thanks, mister Perry," he mumbled.

"You hurry on your way, too, Johnny Kellogg." Perry angled the ruler at him, sighted along its edge. "I don't want any more of that ruckus in front of my store, you understand?"

Johnny nodded and walked away with as much dignity as he could assemble. He passed a small grassy lot next to the furniture store. Near its center, stood a double-doored shed. One door was open and he could see squatting there like a spider the low, black hearse with its high slender wheels. A wooden, iron-tipped tongue protruded from the axle, lolling out onto the ground, no horses yoked to bring it to life. Fringed curtains on both sides shielded the wagon's contents from view. The driver's seat was elevated, cushioned, and unprotected from rain or sun. A dead man's carriage. Johnny hurried away from it, as if death could be denied if you didn't admit its presence.

He felt Frank Perry's peregrine eyes on his back all the way to the open door of Hart's Confectionary. That was when the candy message struck him, heaven sent, he was sure, and everyone knew you can't go against spiritual edicts. Even Sister Ellen White said so at the services. That's how she received her instructions, all those inspired do's and don'ts and personal rules and ceremonial unctions she passed along to the congregation so its members would know what God expected of each of them. Johnny entered the candy store whistling.

6

"WHY is Charley hollering, mama?" Aurrie asked.

"He had another bad dream," Carrie said.

She held Charley in her arms, seated on his bed. Aurrie twisted in front of the bed, curious because his brother was quivering. It reminded him of last summer when dada Rollin caught a fish and pulled it out of the water and it vibrated at the end of the line, the hook far down in its throat. When he put the fish on the grass at the edge of the small lake, its body was brightly colored, slippery, shiny, and rippling. Then dada Rollin struck it sharply above its eyes with a knife handle and after a minute or two its color went stale and dry.

"Why is Charley shaking, mama?"

"Don't ask so many questions, Aurrie Atwater Post." Missus Blainey flapped a washrag at the boy as she carried a basin of water into the room. "Your brother isn't feeling well. All this commotion is going to wake Carroll and we just put him to bed. You go outside and play." She swatted his pants with the rag, set the basin on the floor by the bed.

"I don't want to go out and play, I want to see Charley be sick."

"Go along, Aurrie, mother means it." Carrie released Charley, let him lie flat on the bed. She soaked the washrag, squeezed it out, laid it on his brow. He gritted his teeth and wished to hell they would quit fussing around him.

Missus Blainey took Aurrie by the arm, directed him to the door. "Please call me if you need anything, miss Carrie," she said, departing.

"I'm okay, mama," Charley urged, the washrag slipping across his eyes. "I was scared a little, that dream about granddad Eurastus and granddad Truman...and you and father."

She touched a hand to his cheek. "You don't have a fever, son."

"It's just the dream. It's scary."

"The same as always?"

"Different, mama, this time it was different, at least some." He pushed the cloth from his head, looked into her concerned, lovely, face. "Our buggy was turning over, mama, like it always does, and you're waving at me, everybody is waving from your picnic, with the white sheet and all the food, granddad Truman waving a piece of chicken, him and granddad Eurastus yelling words at me, they're far away but it's like they're right there with me, scary, and what they're saying is all mixed up 'cause they're shouting together..."

"What words? Do you remember, son?"

He propped on his elbows. "It was hard to hear them, they were far away but they seemed close, the buggy and horses made so much noise and I was coming out of the buggy, falling out of it." A blob of spittle popped at the corner of his mouth.

Her hand remained on his cheek. "Did you hear what they called to you?"

"Sixty. They kept yelling 'sixty', and 'no mares,' I think they mean the horses, their voices are high and screechy like Mrs. Blainey's when she's upset or spills something, they yell like they mean I should do something..."

"That wasn't in your dream, son," Carrie smiled, wiped his mouth clean with the rag and let it fall into the basin. She pulled him to her, smothered his words against her breast, clamping him tightly to stop his trembling. "You were hearing us in the room with you. Mrs. Blainey asked were you sick and I told her you weren't. I told her it was the nightmare again."

"But mama, that's different than what they yelled..."

"Listen to me, Charley." She held him at arm's length, looked into his begging eyes. "You heard 'sick,' thought it was sixty. After all, you are six years old, it is eighteen sixty, those numbers would be natural in your head, and you've had to listen to nothing but election talk and war talk out of your father and your uncles for so long, it's enough to give anyone the fright. It certainly has done me, anyway. When you were waking you heard me say 'no' to Mrs. Blainey and you heard the last part of nightmare: mare. You were already waking up and you heard some of our talk and it got into your dream."

She almost added, "Besides, you've never known either of your grandfathers. They died before you were born." Instead, she said, "That's all it was, son. See how simple when you know the reason?" She smoothed his hair back from his ears.

Charley stared at her a few seconds, nodded his head, signifying understanding. It sounded sensible but he couldn't quite make himself accept it.

7

HIS mistake, after the candy was eaten, was choosing to travel up Washington Street past Van Buren and Champion Streets, taking the long way. He wasn't eager to go home, not with his mother in bed, all wrapped up with the new baby. Just ahead of him appeared two hazards, but he noticed them too late to change his mind or his direction.

Sammy and Loony Lew crawled out from a row of hedges between two houses. They had finished smoking cigars stolen from the tobacco counter at Murphy's, and they picked this moment to leave the protection of the hedges. "Well, lookey, here. The little turd with the money."

"We was gonna come find you, asshole." Loony Lew punched the air with three snappy jabs.

At Johnny's left was a three-rail fence of flat boards that marked the length of someone's property. A frame house sat ten yards behind the fence. Both of its front windows were curtained, no light from inside, as though the owners were away. Not a sign of a rider or a wagon along the dirt street which was as forlorn as a cemetery at sundown.

Johnny was resigned to his fate. He tugged his hand from his pocket, palm up, thirty cents in it. Sammy snatched the offering while managing to pretend it was a distasteful duty. Then Lew hit Johnny in the stomach just at the bottom of the breastbone, boring into him with violent force. Johnny choked and Lew hit him again, in exactly the same place. Tears spilled into his eyes. He gasped for air, doubled over, slumped against the fence.

"You hadda sic old deadman Perry on us, did'n you?" Sammy bared his teeth like a dog. Johnny sensed hands were yanking at the buttons on his pants, the buttons of his suspenders. He heard them popping and tearing. "We're gonna learn you not to do nothin like that ever again."

Lew hit him a third time with that hickory log fist, digging deep, sending splinters of hurt ricocheting through him. He wanted to shout that they had his money, they should leave him alone, but he couldn't suck air into his flattened lungs.

Cold wind suddenly splashed his legs and he realized his pants were down. He could see them rolled around his shoetops. Hands yanked his underwear, pulled off the bottom half of his longjohns. They lifted him, spinning him up and round, off the ground, into the air. The fence tore into his spine as he bent backwards, his ankles shackled by trousers and underwear. Then he was over, falling to the lawn. His face pressed against the cool, wet leaves. He could see close up the remnants of last autumn's brownish dead grass. He heard his assailants drifting away up the street, their rowdy, twanging voices finally fading out of range. He raised onto an elbow, gripped the fence, hoisted himself erect. He looked across the lawn at the house beyond. A window curtain was pulled aside and a schoolmate, Jennie Rae Sumner, stared out at him. Her expression was bland, unreadable.

In the same instant Johnny realized he was naked from his waist down. The thought almost paralyzed him. Panicked, he jumped around in kangaroo hops, hauling up the longjohns and his pants. Then he whirled to confront the window, a challenge on his tear-streaked face.

He saw only the reflections of tree limbs and streaks of pale sky on the window glass. An adult hand deftly straightened the closed curtain, sealed it into place. For a moment, a peculiar thrill shivered over him. As he let himself out through the gate he gazed back at the window, wistfully, but it remained empty.

PART TWO

Do not speak of secret matters in a field
that is full of little hills.

Hebrew proverb

8

FEBRUARY 1891

A CONDUCTOR helped the three-year old girl down from the railcar's steps and onto the snow covered platform. She did not say thank you. Her circle-shaped face had all its features collected in a small center, and was perfectly fitted with a protruding upper lip that hid the lower one like an umbrella raised over a hat.

The traveler was dressed in a woolen coat of a bold plaid pattern. On her head a green wool cap covered her dark, straight hair with flaps that came down over each ear and tied in a bowstring beneath her chin. The coat collar was not turned up against the tearing wind but she raised a mittened hand to protect her eyes that darted over everything in sight with an odd mix of expectation and distrust. A simple black and white DEPOT sign over the doorway was blanked by crusted snow.

"Run along inside, Marjorie," her mother called from the passenger car platform. "You'll freeze standing there."

"I don't want to stay in this town, mother. I want to go home to gramma and grampa. In Springfeel."

"You know we can't go back to Springfield, darling. Please quit asking and go inside."

The woman who emerged from the railcar was indifferent to the wind, even as it plastered her coat to her body and ripped at her abundant hair. She took the girl's hand.

"'See, Winter comes to rule the varied year. Sullen and sad,'" she quoted from an almost forgotten poem.

"What's that, you say?" The conductor held his cupped palm beside a red-tinged ear to signify he hadn't caught the words.

"It was nothing," she called over the wind and the hiss of the train's steam. She smiled wanly. "Can you please see that my husband is brought into the building?"

He nodded with a mild sympathy on his face, touched his brimmed hat with the tips of two fingers. "Sure, ma'am, but you might find someone in the depot there could lend me a hand."

She escorted the small girl across the frozen platform to the warmth of the passenger station.

The station's empty interior was long and narrow. An iron stove at either end of the room, fat bellied, threw off heat in glowing circumferences. Brown-stained board benches, shiny with wear from seatpants and swishing skirts, were arranged in two rows down the room's center. A wall calendar was hooked next to a big blackboard behind the ticket agent's counter, the circular areas of its 8 and 9 in the 1891 had been carefully filled in by someone with time to waste.

One of the two doors on the side facing the main track swung open with a crash, followed by a blast of wind. A man jumped into the room as if he had been sprung from a coiled wire. He slammed the door shut, moved quickly to the nearest stove, removed black cloth gloves, let them fall to the floor, rubbed his hands vigorously to increase the circulation.

"Sonofabitch..." He sensed movement and color in the corner of his eye, then saw the woman and child watching him from the middle of the room. He coughed.

"Sorry, ma'am."

She smiled her melancholy smile at him. Her eyelids blinked five times, rapidly.

Friendly, he thought, relaxing a little, looking her over. The woman had features that were clean and sharp, accentuated by too much blonde hair piled too high. The wind had played hell with it. She was ruffled and creased and disheveled and her clothes indicated lack of money. Her tan coat was too light for the season and it hung on her like a shawl. Her figure was slim reaching to fragile, not much bigger around than the child whose hand she kept snugly enclosed in her own. Her shoes were scuffed on the leather, one heel leaning slightly. She would be better off with a pair of boots and heavy stockings, or at least some overshoes, he reasoned. She wasn't even wearing gloves. Still, he admitted, there was a touch of dignity about her.

The child with her did not smile. She glowered. So he looked to the woman again.

"Ferocious out there today, third storm this month."

The child said, "Dada would take me home if I ask."

"No, Marjorie." The woman's voice was sharp. "Daddy isn't able even to care for himself. You can't bother him with those things." Her hand came to rest gently on the girl's shoulder.

The girl pulled away, went to the window, planted herself there, her pouty profile crisp against the ice-caked panes.

The man thought, "That's a little missy not to fool with." He lowered the collar of his bulky woolen coat, then removed his hat which was jammed hard on his head to keep the wind from stealing it. His dark hair, slicked to the skull, showed first faded streaks of aging. He unbuttoned his coat, pulled it laboriously from his arms, tossed it onto a bench, then wiped melted snow from a thick moustache. A watch chain dangled from one vest pocket to another, stretching like golden embroidery across his ballooned stomach.

"I'm the ticket agent, ma'am. A. S. Parker. You visiting relatives?"

"No." Hesitation. Then decision. "I've brought my husband to Battle Creek for treatment at the sanatorium."

"Sanitarium, ma'am, not sanatorium." He emphasized the difference in the two pronunciations. "Doctor Kellogg likes everyone to use sanitarium, says it means something different from a sanatorium, though I'm not sure just what, but it's important to the folks up on the hill so that's good enough for me, and for just about everybody else, too." He showed teeth tinged lightly yellow from chewing tobacco.

"Thank you, Mr. Parker. I shall remember." She pronounced the word carefully, "Sanitarium."

He decided she was a teacher. That would account for her primness, her precision speech, and her visible lack of wealth.

The little girl remained transfixed by the window, turning her head only enough to glare at Parker. He made an overstated gesture of glancing around, seemingly confused. "Honey, your mama said you brought your daddy, but I don't see him nowhere. Don't suppose he got lost, do you?" He gave her his most jovial, stained teeth grin.

"He couldn't, cause he can't walk." Her expression did not change. She was totally spiritless.

"Well, now, I'm sorry to hear that, I truly am, I mean him being an invalid. That is too bad." He sucked in his jaws, concentrated on burnishing part of the floor with shoe leather. "I imagine you'll need a hand with him, ma'am? I mean, is he still on the train?"

"Thank you." Her eyelids fluttered. "I told the conductor I would try to find someone to help him move Charles into the station. It is gentlemanly of you to offer your assistance."

"Well, sure," he stammered. "Glad to be of some more use." He scooped up his hat and fastened it tightly on his head again, then gathered into his coat with grunts and prolonged sighs, displaying much more exertion than he showed getting out of it.

"I appreciate it very much, Mr. Parker."

He stuck his hands deep into his gloves, tugged at their throats to be sure his fingers were snug to the ends.

"You just stay in here with the little missy where it's warm and we'll have Charles inside with you before you can say how do you do."

He started toward the door, halted. "Uh, I ought to ask, your husband a big man? I mean, you see, I have this back trouble, not really supposed to lift heavy..."

Tears filled the woman's eyes. Blinking them back, she said, "You'll recognize him easily because he is a skeleton with skin stretched over. You'll think you're carrying a ten year old child."

"Yes. Well." He coughed. "We'll get him right on in here." He closed the door quickly behind him.

THEY put the stretcher on a bench by the nearest stove. The man's boots jutted from one end of the woolen blanket that was too short to cover him, his sallow face and stringy neck and thin shoulders protruded from the other end. The woman was right: he weighed no more than a healthy child. She tried unsuccessfully to maneuver the blanket around him so that it offered more protection. As she moved him, he groaned softly, a phlegmy expulsion of air, a cough repressed.

"He's just too long for covering up, ma'am."

"Thank you for bringing him in, mister Parker..."

"Park, if you please."

"...you've been very kind and I hate to ask you for another favor but I will because I must." She hesitated. "You see, mister Parker, we have to find a way to the sanitor...sanitarium. And, with the weather..."

"About the best I can do is get you a ride, ma'am, can't leave the station, but I can get a buggy if Norton's at his livery." He fidgeted with his tie, straightened it, tucked it flat into his green vest. "Streetcar won't be working, horses can't pull it up the hills in the snow."

"And would you be kind enough to call the sanitarium, tell them to watch for us? We will need help."

Walking to the telephone, he decided the man on the stretcher, unmoving, unspeaking, was probably a handsome cuss in his day. Thick dark hair and moustache, a block of bone for a chin, lips maybe a bit too rounded. He cranked the telephone, watched the woman cradling the man's head in her lap. She alternated her attention entirely between soothing his brow with brushes of her fingertips, and keeping watch on the little girl who was statue-like in front of the frozen window, staring at God knows what, since it was impossible to see through the layers of ice. Parker wished the woman had some decent shoes for this weather.

9

AS THE SLED plowed its way through Battle Creek's streets, the storm slowed, failed, stopped.

"We're gettin a break in the lousy weather. First time it's quit blowin, more'n two days and nights." The sleigh's driver added, prophetically, "Maybe you brought some fresh luck to our little city, lady. Best you keep them quilts pulled around you. People's ears and fingers get froze when it's this cold. Hell, have to have 'em amputated — you know, sliced off." He laughed a jackass bray, plucky with appreciation for his own humor.

The woman and the child peered curiously at the businesses and shops and houses, trying to ignore him, trying to absorb some message or greeting from this strange, frozen land that would at least allow them to endure it. How could such a remote, ice-burdened climate be beneficial to anyone's health or recovery? Doubt pricked at the woman like a pin that had come loose in an undergarment.

The gaunt man beside her was oblivious to his surroundings or the driver's diatribe. His glazed, gray eyes remained sightless without being blind.

Now that the snow had ceased, the child showed a glimmer of genuine interest, if not appreciation. "It looks like a picture," she murmured.

"Yes, it does. It reminds me of the painting grandmother has in her bedroom, the one with the little houses at the bottom of the winter hill, and smoke coming out of the chimneys."

"It just made me think of some picture I seen, that's all."

The driver turned three-quarters again on his elevated seat, talked over a hunched shoulder, "I always say life's a gamble and I got the right proper name for it. Name's Sam Gamble. Whether you like this town or don't, I'll say this for it, ever body thinks they's plenty to do here in the cold months, just ask, they'll tell you, sled rides, put up a snowman, that sort of crap, if you like it. Personal, I don't give a damn for it.

"We even got us a opera house if you go in for that hell-for-nothin screechin. Of course, we got another kind of house, about as noisy, specially on Saturday night, but a damned sight more fun if you know what I mean." A gusty laugh rolled out of him and vibrated his muscular shoulders.

Marjorie looked angrily at her mother, was about to say something, but the woman pressed the girl's hand to stop her. The child folded her arms across her chest, stared indifferently at the houses glissading past.

"Plenty goin on if your man likes huntin' birds or rabbits or some ice fishing."

"He's been ill a long while. He hasn't been able to get outside." Her eyes blinked, blinked, as if against the wind.

"Mmph. So I seen. Don't look like he's got the soup for much of anything." The driver expertly touched one horse's rump with the tip of a thick black whip to jog it away from the ruts. "Wait til it comes warm weather and things get green. You'll never find a more comely place than this town."

The child grimaced. The woman smiled weakly. She was at least happily surprised by the array of shops, offices, markets and other businesses along the way. The structures were mostly frame building, but several were brick, some were three stories high. She wasn't certain what she had expected, but it wasn't as much as she was seeing.

Her husband stirred, groaned, drew her attention, his eyes staring, not seeing. She touched his bleached face and was relieved to feel no fever. "Did you hear what he said, Charles? It sounds like a nice town we've come to."

The voice that answered was as grating as a metal file on an iron rod. "It better be more than nice, Ella, or I won't live to see another."

"What's daddy saying?"

"Nothing, sweetheart, he's just trying to enjoy our ride." She adjusted her husband's blanket. "You'll soon be in the hands of the best medical people in ten states," she told him. "This doctor John Harvey Kellogg will have you back to your old self in no time."

She held him tightly against her while she and the child watched as the sleigh traveled toward a colossal building that dominated the crest of a rise and rolled out beyond the horizon line. It was a woodframe Victorian-like structure. It gave the impression of being longer and higher and deeper than a chain of foothills on the Oklahoma plains. Repeated rows of windows and balconies and alcoves, and a startling number of tall chimneys brought to her mind a drawing in a book of a king's palace on some far away continent.

10

"WHO you suppose was in the sled?"

"Didn't notice."

Will Keith Kellogg spooned another mouthful of oyster stew. He sat squarely on one of the dozen revolving chairs that spanned the length of the counter from front door to rear. The glass window across the building's front was steam drenched. Red letters read backwards: RENID S'BBEW. Outside they read: WEBB'S DINER. Kellogg made drenching little noises when he ate, a sign of enjoyment, one that did not accompany every meal. When he came into the diner his stomach had been a cistern of scorching aggravation, as though he had gobbled a plate of red peppers. The oyster stew soothed it and tasted good. He paused between each bite to dab a cloth napkin across a thin, waxed moustache. His eyes moved constantly, taking in everything, giving back nothing. He was not a happy or optimistic man at age 31, though he would neither confirm nor deny it.

Behind the luncheon counter, Richard Webb, proprietor, wiped up coffee stains with a wet rag.

"Looks like they headed up to your place, Will."

"Not my place. Belongs to the doctor. I work there." Another noisy ingestion of oyster meat and thick cream.

Webb laughed. "I thought it belonged to the church, Will." His fleshy jowls jiggled and squeezed up around cheery eyes.

"Ask the doctor."

A snorting laugh. "He don't come in here too often. Fact is, he never comes in. Does he know you're here?"

Will twirled a piece of bread in the remaining juices in the bowl and soaked them up. He left two lumps of oyster meat to have last. "You trying to run off customers? Your questions annoy me. Takes the pleasure out of eating."

"Sorry, Will, just ribbing, I'm always glad to see you. I'm just a kidder, do it all the time, you know that." He shifted his large stomach, pointed it toward the kitchen, waddled away.

Will chewed the last crust of stew-sopped bread, moving his jaws slowly. Even if he regularly violated the doctor's rules by eating these "scavengers of the sea," he salved his conscience by doing as his brother instructed: he masticated every bite between his false teeth until it was literally ground out of existence.

"Want another bowl, Will?" Webb stood by his kitchen entrance.

Kellogg waved him away, completed his meal hurriedly now, gulping the two pieces of oyster he had saved, not enjoying them as much as he expected, feeling rushed to return to the Sanitarium and learn who was in the sleigh. If it was a new, important patient, the doctor would be howling for everyone to step lively and get the person settled in.

Will slid to his feet. His shortness always amused Webb. It was all in Kellogg's legs. Seated, he was as tall as the next fellow; standing he was five feet four.

As Will passed the cash register near the door he clicked ten cents on the counter, then took his hat and overcoat from a peg, pulled the collar high and the hat low, making sure its woolen ear flaps covered his ears. He opened the door to a gush of frigid wind and hurried into it, ignoring Webb's "Come back anytime."

11

"DAMN," Ella Kellogg said in her mind, allowing herself a wayward word on the grounds that it had biblical properties.

It was the sight of Sam Gamble in the Sanitarium lobby that caused her profanity. She wished she hadn't thought it, knowing Sister White would not approve.

The sleigh driver stood spraddled-legged as if an obstruction prevented him from standing normally. Back arched, hips slung forward, as brazen as if he owned the hospital. Gamble studied the ceiling, pretending to see it for the first time, not the hundredth. A cigarillo poked from his mouth, a dead, brown stump, no fire on it. The man's topcoat hung open now that he was out of the cold, and he arched himself sway-backed, flaunting his maleness.

At the Womens' Club tea a few weeks ago one member suggested that Gamble "puts a card in the window to try to snare the unwary shopper." All the ladies appropriately blushed, nervously laughed in the safety of their number, and Mrs. Graves, the president, changed the topic to the menu for the upcoming social.

The sound of Ella's shoes pecking the gleaming hardwood floor transposed into a muffled clicking as she reached the marble section where the entranceway spread out and up between great wooden columns like the chamber of a manmade grotto.

Gamble's eyes clung to her like resin. He always had admired the shapely, slender woman, her face masked with a cordial expression, even when troubled. Her dark hair was wavy and lay tightly against her head, leaving two large, well-shaped, pink ears exposed. He found something stimulating about those naked ears. A message, an erotic signal?

Her skirts swept the floor silently; an 18-inch waist-sash emphasized the roundness of her hips. Sleeves large and fluffy, ending above the elbows where a snug lightweight cotton of dark blue continued on to the frilled wrists. The dress fit high and secure at the neck and there was a row of miniature buttons down the back. She was tempted to dart behind one of the columns that towered twenty feet to the ornamental ceiling boards, let Sam Gamble deal with someone else, but there was no one else. It was one of those rare moments when activity was absent from the San.

Years ago, she had dubbed the hospital "San", a name that all but a few diehards accepted in place of the tongue-twisting "Battle Creek Medical and Surgical Sanitarium." No patients were loitering in the lobby; no influx of new arrivals. An aged man sat in the reading room off to the left, dozing in his chair, a book open in his lap, an ear trumpet across the pages.

The doctor himself was conducting a class in the gymnasium. He wouldn't finish for another hour. Of course, he would willingly come to the lobby in his skimpy loincloth, but he could not, having reluctantly promised Ella on that point. She was certain her husband would go naked down Main Street if it weren't unlawful.

Gamble watched her walk toward him, making it impossible for her to veer away or be casual in her approach. She felt as though she was wearing blocks of wood on her feet. Her stride seemed awkward. Had he noticed her studying him? She vowed to pray that night for forgiveness for her earlier thoughts.

"Good afternoon, missus Kellogg. You're bright and shiny as a new dollar. Musta had you a good night's rest, or maybe just a good night." He inclined his yellow head in a slouched greeting, the cigarillo clamped in his teeth. "Brung you some customers, one at least, and he's in sad shape." Gamble motioned with his grimy hat toward an alcove near the front door.

"Yes, I see them, mister Gamble. Thank you, I'll take care of matters now."

A woman and child sat on a bench just inside the waiting area. Beside them was a man in one of the San's caneback wheelchairs. When Ella moved toward them, Gamble edged intentionally but indifferently into her path. She eased back, keeping a constant space between them.

"Are you smoking that cigar, mister Gamble?"

"No, ma'am, I'm sure not. It ain't lit."

"Get rid of it, mister Gamble. Either throw it in the trash basket over there or return it to your pocket."

"Certainly, ma'am. I forgot I even had it." With an elaborate flourish of his arm, he pulled open a coat pocket with one hand, dropped the cigarillo into it.

"That new woman who come up. Her name's same as yours. Ella. About as far as the similarity goes, though. She ain't too much to look at. Not like you." No grin, just a steady stare which Ella could not match. "Little girl's name is Marilee, or Margie, or somethin. His is Charles. Come in from Illinois. Last name, Post, but he looks more like a broke stick."

"I'm amazed you didn't diagnose the man's illness and prescribe a cure while you were at it."

Now the stained-teeth grin. "You ought to try to break that habit, missus Kellogg, being sarcastic with them that ain't high stationed. It don't set well on you. Be kind to folks, they'll be kind to you, I always say."

His knowing wink brought a lump of indignation into her throat.

"Now listen to this, it's the best part. She tried to pay me for the sleigh with a pair of suspenders."

"What?" Unsure if she had heard correctly, interest perked, anger sidetracked by the absurdity of the offer. "Did you say suspenders?"

Gamble's moustache jumped as his face puckered into a sack of happy wrinkles. "Told me they was a special kind, nothin like them anywhere, keeps your pants up without heistin 'em too high twixt your legs."

Her scorn was reawakened, squashing any interest in what he had to say. "Mister Gamble I do not..."

"Said her old man invented them and he didn't deny it. She showed me how they work and by jingo they do a good job."

"You took them?" Curiosity defeated her disgust.

"Figured it was better than no pay. She looked like she might cry, blinkin her eyes like they need clearin. I didn't want her come in bawlin, me being kind hearted and all." He overlooked Ella's widening expression of incredulity, glad to be holding her interest. "I mean the little girl there, and her old man so tuckered he can't get off the stretcher. Besides, you'd have said I said somethin to her." He hurried ahead before Ella could reply to the accusation. "Me and one of your men had to lift him onto that wheelchair or he'd still be there on the floor like a rabbit been buckshot in the legs. Your man took off like a hound to find you but he didn't come back with you." He bit at a dirty fingernail, little snipping sounds like scissors at work. "Don't appear you got much help around today. Maybe you ought to hire some more people." Leering mouth, eyes grim. "I'd like workin in this hospital. Probly I could learn a few things." Silence. "From the little doctor." Silence. "And you."

"My husband will be glad to know you don't care for the position he was good enough to obtain for you." She wished she could make herself shut up. "Perhaps it was wasted effort for him to have interceded on your part. You better return to your job is my advice. Good day, mister Gamble."

The double front doors thudded open with reverberating echoes. Will Kellogg came in, closed the doors hurriedly, stomping snow from his feet while removing his hat and hurriedly unbuttoning his coat.

"Will," Ella Kellogg called, genuinely glad to see him. "We have a new patient. I need your help."

"Had to step out for a minute." Apologetic. Surprised and pleased to see the doctor's wife beckoning and agreeable, not upset at his absence.

"Our patient is over there, Will, in the waiting room. Just leave your coat and we will take care of his registration."

Suddenly, as if a cue had been given — all actors on stage right now — the area became alive with people. The nurse returned to the registration desk; two groups of four patients paraded toward the reading room, haranguing over a dietary point; two orderlies strolled into the lobby; and one of the San's army of maintenance men treaded down the hall.

Sitting in the waiting room with her small daughter and her immobile husband, Ella Post watched the man named Will scuttle forward and join the sleigh driver and the woman in black who, by her stance and arm movements, seemed to have authority over them both. Standing together, the trio reminded her of two seedlings beside a grown tree. At that moment, the tree startlingly uprooted itself, clamped a dirty hat on its wild yellow top, and strode away on pumping legs. The seedlings came forward to greet her after what had seemed an everlasting delay. The woman was serene and smiling; the short man was dusting snow from the legs of his trousers, looking queasy. Judging by the audible growls from his stomach, Ella believed he badly needed a bicarbonate of soda.

12

WILL Kellogg kicked solid chunks of snow from his shoes, then entered his house. The end of another fifteen-hour day. An iron-cased clock on the front room table rang cheery musical notes, thin and high. He counted the chimes. Eight. Must have missed one coming in, he told himself. It was nine o'clock, at least.

Ella — Puss — came into the narrow hallway at the far end where the kitchen was located. Plain dress, a shawl around her shoulders because the house got cold at night. She walked lightly toward him, arms outstretched to help remove the coat he was shrugging off, having difficulty, nearly too tired to pull his arms from the sleeves. She placed the garment on a rack by the steps leading up to the second floor bedrooms. Will flung his hat on a ladderback chair next to the rack.

"Are you hungry?"

"No. Ate supper in the dining hall." He noted the time again, nudged by the burning in his stomach. "Three hours ago. Maybe I could drink some buttermilk."

She put her lips quickly to his cheek, looked at him solicitously, their gaze meeting at the same level. They waited a moment in the quiet of the night house, the only sound a gaslight sputtering in the hallway, making wavering shadows against the flowered wallpaper. She reached for his hand, squeezed it gently.

He saw her through a haze of total fatigue; saw her tiredness, too, in the lines across her forehead, the ashen marks under her eyes. He viewed her dark brown hair curled close to that delicate, papier-mache head; the full mouth that he always thought so sensuous, though he never had told her so in their eleven years of marriage. He noticed for the thousandth time the narrow, upturned nose and the smooth, pale complexion that thrilled him to touch when they were courting. He saw her dark brown eyes magnified behind steelrimmed bifocals. He saw her and said nothing.

She touched his cheek where she had kissed him, then walked rapidly to the kitchen. Watching her go, he had an immediate surge of love for this quiet, undemanding woman, a trim mother of four children, three still living. Only Keith Kellogg, dead, sliding away at age four into some far place, holding his father's hand tightly, trying to stop the slide, then not wanting to stop it. Smiling pleasantly, saying "papa," and quietly releasing his final breath.

Will asked about the children each evening, naming them one by one, long after they were asleep and he had not come in time to see them. He still half expected Ella to tell him some amusing deed of little Keith's.

Last night, twenty-four hours ago to the minute, she had said, "Karl got a very good grade for his history test today. It's on the sideboard in our room, he wants you to see it when you have the time."

He had not looked at it yet. He wondered to himself if it was because he lacked the time, or because it didn't interest him so he made no time for it. It was difficult to compliment Karl. If it had been Len...

"And Beth tried to stay awake to ask when she would be old enough to go to school like Karl and Len. I told her you would explain it this Sunday and she dropped right off without another word." Reassuring him of his influence, at least in his own house. Then she had hastily said, "We must go to see Ann Janette soon. Your mother looks forward to our visits."

Now, in the unlighted front room, Will settled onto a nondescript upholstered chair near the window, feeling immediately the pleasant release of tension that is required to simply stand erect.

Snow twirled down from the roof, powdered across the window. Less than ninety yards north, the rows of lighted windows on the Sanitarium's ground floor glowed like rectangles of rubbed gold. Random lights dotted individual rooms on the upper floors, and he knew he could identify every one of them, give the name of the patient in each, how much they owe individually on their bills as of this week. It was small compensation to spend twelve years in a place and find that the only satisfaction was a knowledge of where each door and winding hallway led.

"Is your new office nice to work in?" she asked, carrying the glass of buttermilk. Embers in the fireplace cast a timid heat. "Would you like for me turn up the gas so there is more light?"

"Leave it dark. Eyes are tired." His fingers grazed his mouth, took the milkglass she handed him. He slurped at it.

"Office is a sham. Nothing like I asked for. Or need." Another drink, taking half the contents, leaving a thin white line just below the thin black line of his moustache. He drank the milk, put the glass on a table, licked away the residue from his upper lip. The milk was good in his stomach, neutralized the acid. He relaxed slightly for the first time all day.

Ella floated down onto the divan like a coverlet, barely indenting the cushions. Hands folded in her lap, face attentively turned toward her husband, she knew he wanted to talk about his day. She did not really care to hear it, especially the details, because the Sanitarium's labyrinth of services and products and happenings bewildered her. She could not fathom the growing number of disagreements between Will and his brother, a disquieting chain of events that threatened the orderly and decent way she believed life should be lived. Still, she listened respectfully to her husband's occasional reports, knowing he couldn't — or wouldn't — express those thoughts to anyone else.

"Cramped office. Sometimes it's like being in a coffin, Puss." She liked it when he used his special name for her, the one he gave her before they were married. "Window is so high up it's almost useless. Veranda stops the sunshine."

"But it is *your* office," she consoled. "You always said you wanted your own office and it is something few men your age can expect."

He continued as if she hadn't said a word. "Nearly fifty letters today. Five more than yesterday. Takes hours to answer them. People want rates, want to subscribe to Good Health, want to order a copy of this book or that by John Harvey. Billings and payments to do. Dozens of them. An insane patient got away today, so I had calls on him."

"Oh, in this weather. You'd think he would pick a better time of the year, wouldn't you?" Her voice suggested a scintilla of alarm even as she tried to make light of the topic. She had heard terrible things about insane people, and the asylums they were kept in. Her vision of such a person running loose in the San upset her, frightened her.

"Told John Harvey over and over, we shouldn't keep them. It'll come to no good. He never listens. On anything."

"Did you catch him?"

"Catch who, Ella?" Annoyed by the open ended question.

"The crazy person who ran away."

"Orderlies found him in the furnace room. Probably trying to get into the tunnels."

"He sounds smart to me, Will. He knew it was warm there."

He covered a tight-lipped smirk by smoothing his moustache, self-conscious about his false teeth, a condition he'd tolerated since he was twenty-two and his natural teeth had fallen out or loosened and were removed. Being on the road as a broom salesman every day, up to two months at a stretch, had meant little chance for good diet and nutrition. He'd endured sieges of diarrhea and dyspepsia by the time he was eighteen, both of which were symptomatic of his poor general health.

After a year of harsh living on the west Texas plains, brimming with the deception that the strength and freshness of youth lasts forever, he'd finally squandered his broom making skills and given his health an irreversible drubbing. Later, when he was nearly twenty and stayed mostly in Dallas, its green, fertile landscape reminded him of the lush countryside of Michigan and he felt almost at home. He recovered, but the damage to his system had been done.

"Something I meant to tell you about today, Puss. Forgot it."

"You'll remember. Don't try to remember and it'll come back to you. That's how it works."

"Really?" A disbelieving twist of his head, a bored lowering of eyelids. "Did you learn that from one of Elder Smith's sermons?"

"I didn't mean to sound know-it-all." Pain and apology washed across the translucent skin of her face, the frail bone showing through.

Sorry for his rudeness, he asked gently, "You been taking an afternoon nap? That's what John Harvey advised."

"I'm a bit tired now, Will, but it's late."

She said more but he didn't hear her. He was thinking about a man named King, a would-be broom maker in the panhandle state who wanted a monopoly on the business, hoped to make a fortune. King's drawback was that he knew nothing about broom making; his advantage was his membership in the Adventist church. He needed inexpensive, experienced help; Will was just what the doctor ordered or, more accurately, what the church Elder ordered. An aging John Preston Kellogg sent Will to Texas on a pointless pilgrimage. The man named King had failed anyway in the broom trade, despite Will's help.

Like the whistlecap on a teakettle, a valve popped open in his memory and he recalled what he'd meant to tell Ella.

"New patient today. Name of Post. Won't be around long. John Harvey says the fellow is nearly dead. Brought his wife and little girl along. They paid for the sleigh from the depot with suspenders. The man makes them. Or his wife does."

"I never heard of anything like that." Her mind swam at the wonder of it.

"Down on their luck. Woman dressed too light for winter. Man's boots cracked, run down. Little girl, though, frocked out for a queen's visit. They must spend whatever money they have on her."

"Is there anything we can do? I'd be glad to..."

"Not at my earnings, Puss. We have nothing to spare. We send money to mother every week." He turned his hands over on his knees, palms up, supplicating. "We'll always be poor. I don't want that to happen, Puss. I see Fred Gage at his father's company; Russell Hart's rich from his inventions; even Webb lives in comfort, horse and carriage behind his diner." He leaned on his elbows, head drooping. "Me and this Post fellow, we've got something in common. Bad stomachs and bad futures. Somehow, I don't like the man, and I hate seeing myself when I look at him."

Ella admonished, "We should count the Lord's blessings."

"John Harvey put the Posts in number twelve..."

"The charity building, Will?"

"Charity is twenty. Twelve is if you can pay something, just can't afford the main rooms." He snorted without contempt. "Post is paying with blankets."

"Blankets? Suspenders? Those are odd things to carry to a hospital. Is he a salesman?"

"Sold John Harvey on the blankets, didn't he? Stock left over from a former deal. His father is shipping them. Had one with him, wrapped in it. Good wool. Keeps us from buying more. Fair exchange, I guess." He snapped his fingers. "I remember what I wanted to say. His wife's name is Ella."

"My, we do have a lot in common," Ella Kellogg chirped.

Will frowned and his attention reverted to the San's lighted windows, like animal eyes watching him across the winter night.

13

"IT'S an enormous place, Charles. You can't imagine how huge it is, all the buildings and special rooms and a bakery bigger than Borden's in Springfield." Ella Post removed garments from their traveling trunks, put some articles on the top ledge of a three-cornered shelf, fastened others on hooks under the ledge.

Charles regarded his surroundings from the bed, his head on a folded pillow, a light sheet over his blue sleeping suit. Eyelids half open, held open by determination. Ella's voice, like every other sound — the wind, the hiss of the radiator — seemed far away and indistinct. A pleasantly painful sensation began at the base of his spine, ran like cold fire down each leg, dissolved everything in its path until it reached his feet where it evaporated in a small shivering numbness.

Their room was tight, clean, with a pair of wooden chairs, a miniature table. A square mirror with a paint smudge on it had been nailed near the door. On the lowboy was an embroidered scarf, a water pitcher and drinking glasses. The window had muslin curtains. Their daughter was sleeping on a cot wedged between the bed and the wall so there was only one way for her to crawl in or out.

"Marjorie loved playing with all the children at the Kellogg house, easily fifteen or more of them." Ella motioned a hand in an uncertain direction, indicating generally where the mansion was located.

"Would you...some water, Ella."

She hurried to the bureau, returned with the glass and held it to his lips while he swallowed, then lowered him again onto the pillow.

He gasped. "You see, Ella...other patients...*do* bring kids."

"Oh, Charles, I'm not sure. So many are the doctor's and missus Kellogg's."

Post's eyes widened. "Fifteen? Twins and triplets? That attendant said they've only been married…few years. Kellogg's our age…even if she's younger."

Ella's eyelids vibrated playfully. "They adopted them."

Post continued to stare in disbelief.

"Missus Kellogg — Ella, I mean — she insists I call her Ella, isn't it nice that we have the same name, she said they agreed before they got married never to have children."

"Idiotic agreement. She say why?"

"Mutual consent. The doctor maintains that having sex..." A tinge of red flowed into her cheeks. "...or getting pregnant, both drain away energies, I believe she called them 'vital energies,' from more important callings in life." She hastily lifted one of Charles' suits from a trunk and put it on a hanger.

"Fools. Maybe something wrong with one of them. Sick or operation." His throat was dry again, his skin hot.

Ella could hear his sharp wheezing and she wondered once more if this northern climate had been a wise choice.

"Well, when you are better and when you want to, I'll take you over the entire Sanitarium," she said with delight, convinced the sights would fascinate him.

"Saw enough today to suit me. Blood tests, breathing tests, strength tests." A huff of disgust. "I couldn't pull up the lightest weight on the machine. They poked, prodded, Ella. Thought I'd jump out a window. But didn't have the energy to crawl to it."

He was trying to jest with her, and she hoped it was a sign of improvement, but it couldn't be. Nothing good happens *that* soon.

An image, a fresh memory, trickled across her mind:

She was ushered into a magnificently furnished office by a white-suited attendant. A stranger looked up, kneeling in front of Charles who was slumped in an eighteenth century Louis Quinze chair. Her first thought: My god, I hope Charles doesn't throw up on that chair.

The stranger wore a black beard and a black suit. Under his nose a moustache spurted so thickly it appeared he had tried to inhale a house-painting brush and almost succeeded. He was questioning her husband: "Would you like something to eat, Charles?" but he was looking at her. She wished her pile of blonde hair had been more neatly combed and her clothing less worn.

When Charles gave a dubious bobble of his head to indicate he wasn't hungry, the stranger asked: "Something to drink?" The kneeling man continued to look at her, his exceptional peripheral vision also watching Charles.

Another fugitive nod. Eyes closing. She knew Charles would be asleep in minutes.

"I'm doctor John Harvey Kellogg," the stranger had said.

His voice was stern but had a fascinating baritone roll. He came to his feet in a sudden motion, seemed to fly across the room, locked her hand in his. She was amazed at his speed, even more amazed at his diminutive size; he could have stood beneath her chin. He had dark hair, shiny the way it would be if oiled, parted high and on the left. His nose was very straight, eyes soft, even sensitive, but dappled with fragments of granite. A man used to having his own way, she decided.

He escorted her to a massive, decoratively carved Jacobean chair. She quickly discovered that its paneled back and thin upholstery offered none of the comfort of the chair into which Charles had sunk.

"Perhaps Charles will sip this for you." He handed her a drinking glass half full of water and a curved glass straw. To the attendant he said: "Edward, wait in the outer office, please. See that the wheelchair remains at hand."

Suddenly he was taller. It took her a moment to realize he had stepped onto an eight-inch platform where his desk awaited him. Looking up at him she intuited that the elevation was a contrived advantage when speaking down to people.

Doctor Kellogg eased into a padded leather chair, its straight back and curved arms designed for posture. His desk lengthened out before him like the deck on a sailing ship. Crisply stacked papers and a bright silver inkwell with two fountain pens seemed lost on the expanse of waxed wood.

Ella had prodded Charles' lips with the drinking tube; he drew on it. She could almost feel the water washing grit from his throat.

"Now we're making progress," the doctor chanted, obviously pleased.

Abruptly, Charles interrupted her remembrances, pulled her back to their small room with its smudged mirror. "This doctor's wife who also has your name made quite an impression on you, didn't she?"

He wasn't interested in Ella's description of the Sanitarium or of madame Kellogg's aplomb or self-possession. But he knew, after the long silent journey, Ella needed to talk.

She put a finger to her chin and closed her eyes. "Missus Kellogg, I mean Ella, is intelligent and refined. And she has so much responsibility. She's in charge of the entire kitchen and the dining halls, plans the menus, makes up new foods to be served. She's almost running a hotel. But I like her. She just does what she pleases when it occurs to her.

"Hundreds of people are working everywhere. I never saw so much going on in one place, the patients doing things, too — walking, reading, swimming, playing checkers, digging and planting in the indoor gardens. I guess nobody just comes here to sit and relax."

When Charles didn't respond, she drifted back to that strange meeting earlier today. She wondered why doctor Kellogg had taken up their time in his office with that Granola story.

The bearded medical genius had perched up there behind his high desk, a shining example of supreme health. "Mister and missus Post, over four years ago, I added to the San's menu a product we call Zwiebach. A very special bread which is raised, sliced, then thoroughly baked into a brittle toast already highly dextrinized, actually pre-digested before it is consumed. Fit for any stomach, even yours I dare say." He had inclined his head toward Charles in a matter-of-fact manner.

"On one particular morning, I was preparing for my patient rounds, briefing my staff, when into the main hall flew a corpulent woman. She completely disrupted the briefing, flung herself across the room like a wad of dough, and plopped her immense body between me and my staff. Then she stuck her teeth out at me.

"There in her hand were her dentures and all the while she kept shouting, 'Look what your rock hard toast has done! My teeth are ruined.' I couldn't avoid looking because she was waving them under my nose like smelling salts. I discerned there wasn't a thing wrong with the canines, the bicuspids, the molars, but the two frontmost incisors were broken clean in half. Snapped as if they'd been struck a sharp blow with hammer and chisel. The woman was correct, her teeth were ruined."

"Oh, my." Ella's exclamation had been genuine, imagining the agony, forgetting the teeth were manufactured. Her eyelids blinked at least thirty times.

Doctor Kellogg smiled condescendingly. "She announced she would sue me, sue the San, sue the city, for a large sum of money she named on the instant. But as it turned out she settled for a paid up bill and a new set of teeth." He sniffed noisily.

"I immediately set to work to improve and save our Zwiebach. I experimented, my able wife pitched in, and we undertook a horde of tests. After weeks of searching we proved only that whatever we did to it diminished it, hurt its sweet flavor or made it harder to swallow."

He leaned down, picked up an invisible piece of lint from the rug, flicked it toward a hidden wastecan. "So, we took the only option left. We made tiny biscuits out of the dough, cooked them brown and crisp, ground them down to nuggets. Then we tasted them, expecting disappointment. They were marvelous! That little undersized biscuit did the trick. We had our Granola. Nourishing, and the patients love it. Best of all, it breaks no one's teeth. A complicated riddle, a simple solution."

ELLA. She heard her name. Charles was calling her.

"What did you and the doctor talk about after I was carted off?" He gazed at her from the bed.

"About you," she told him.

"He impertinent? Personal?"

"No. Why would you think that, Charles?"

"You tell him my nightmares?"

"Yes, I explained them to him."

"He say I'm crazy?"

"No, he thinks you are fighting nervous exhaustion. He wants to help you. He said so, very explicitly."

14

ELLA Post sat beside John Harvey Kellogg on the lounge in his office, humble, hopeful.

"Missus Post, your husband's condition is severe," the doctor said with great authority. "You hardly need me to point out the obvious. What I may add is our intention to do all in our considerable power to improve him."

"We heard so many fine things about your cures, doctor." Charles had been escorted away by the attendant an hour ago and Marjorie had gone to the kindergarten. "It may not sound complimentary but you are our last hope."

"Yes. Well," he grumped, "I suppose that is a compliment nonetheless." He watched her eyelids flutter as fast as a hummingbird's wings, thought how remarkable that they behaved as they did, seemingly without her control. "Dear lady, at the San we do not rely on healing waters, superb climates year round, or secret remedies brewed in pots in an underground laboratory. There are no miracle formulas concocted here."

His nose corrugated as though he whiffed an unpleasant odor. "Criticisms are made of us by certain, shall we call them, zealots of different persuasions. But our methods are tested by time and our patients are our stamp of distinction, healthy, reinvigorated people. Our critics continue to literally bury their mistakes."

Ella's eyes fluttered. "I don't think I know what you mean..."

"We espouse the principle of curing through natural means. We call it 'physiotherapy,' a big word for an uncomplicated and rewarding system. Our methods are scientific, precise, collected from around the world, not originated here necessarily, but organized at last into a useable system." He scooped up her hands, sandwiched them between his own. "At the heart of it, we strive to live in harmony with nature through diet and conduct. Pythagoras promoted a similar — though not fully developed course — more than two thousand years ago."

"You said Charles' dream, his nightmare, was important?"

"You have beautiful hair, my dear." Impulsively spoken when the thought occurred. "I've seen that fashion on recent trips to Chicago, but the local women haven't quite taken to it yet. I hope you don't mind my giving you a compliment." He released her hands, gently returning them to her.

Slightly unsettled at Kellogg's manner of catapulting to different subjects, she poked self-consciously at her billowing blonde waves. "Charles doesn't dream, doctor Kellogg. He has horrible nightmares and they jerk him straight up in bed in his sleep, soaked to the skin, quivering all over."

"Dear lady, the fact that he wakes himself at the crucial point each time is proof he is desperately working to protect himself."

"But waking doesn't make him well. For months he has been too weak to care for himself."

Kellogg again patted one of her hands which rested on her knee. He left his own hand on hers. His eyes were alight. His oiled hair was phosphorescent.

"My husband is convinced the nightmare is a prediction."

Kellogg sat away from her, his head drawn back on a stretched neck. His eyes dimmed and narrowed as if to see through rainfall. "A prediction? Heaven help us. We already have the famous Sister Ellen White in our midst. One oracle in Battle Creek is enough."

Ella tried to align his words, his actions, into a scheme. Nothing fit. But his assurance, his confidence, was as thick and tempting as fresh taffy.

Kellogg got up and walked to the window, talked into the gray light that had closed off the sunrays. "From among our twenty-four physicians I have assigned an attending doctor. He will prescribe treatments to be carried out by various expert staff members. Charles will undergo a provisional program of baths, exercise, massage, diet, rest. Each action will be recorded in his personal notebook and given to him for daily guidance." He turned. "I encourage you to read it with him, discuss its contents, question any item that is not completely clear.

"In the same book there will be a number of appointments set for special examinations in the next several days. I, as physician and chief, will have regular consultations with Charles and his doctor throughout his stay with us."

He pulled at his beard vigorously, jog-trotted past her to wait beside the office door, signifying the end of the interview. "Try to remember, Charles is being matriculated into a university of health and we will soon know much more about him than he knows of himself."

She crossed to the door he held open. Even while he admired the dignity she managed to display through her staunch posture, he noticed again how poorly she was dressed.

"You should consider a complete physical examination for yourself, too, while you are at the hospital, missus Post. Many things can be forestalled or eliminated if detected and treated before they become serious."

The brightness in his eyes reappeared. "I would be pleased to arrange your examination tomorrow or next day if you would like, willing even to conduct it myself." His face registered a minor tectonic shift. "To ensure it is done properly, you understand."

15

CHARLES thought, it's already the fourth day. Two days of tests and examinations completed. This morning an attendant waited in the hall for me until Ella put on a robe.

Then, into the wheelchair, down through those underground connecting tunnels, heat pipes and concrete walls, like an old dungeon. Up to the main building, out into the big lobby.

The attendant never stopped chattering. Pointless information: "We're going to get on the lift now, mister Post." Blasted jabberbox, I recognize an elevator when I see one. Drowsy. I let the feeling float over me like an underwater net. Let the damp cotton fill my mind.

We were in the hallway with doors, dozens of them. A different physician's name painted on each. Consultation rooms and examinations. Patients trickled in and out with the nurses, or sat on those drab black benches by the walls. Well-dressed people, overweight, in good spirits. Everybody was visiting like it was a club social.

The first room wasn't too inviting. Cold water pipes across the ceiling. One little window. Closed. Shade drawn to midpoint. Looked like another sunless day. An opaque glass on the top half of the door, turned the people into ripples when they went by. The room had a nice long table. They put a pad under me, must have been three-inches thick. Pillow was comfortable, too. The talking attendant went away. Good riddance.

The new attendant looked like a snowman, white trousers, white shoes, white jersey. I wondered why he cut off the jersey's sleeves. Stern face, receding hairline, muscular arms. That's why no sleeves, I decided, so he could show off his arms. He said his name was Sloan. First or last name? Didn't matter. Wanted me to drink another glass of water. Third one before 8 a.m. Off with the sleeping shirt, he said. Told me to be comfortable, going to give me a rubdown. Looked at me as if he was going to enjoy it more than I would.

Sloan probably thought my muscles were flabby. They were. My faculties were dead, too. That's how we used to describe our instructors at Illinois Industrial, those very words.

Ouch. Dammit, Sloan, I said, you're a little rough, anybody ever tell you? My skin is rolling up like old paint on a farm fence. No, Sloan, I can't lift my legs, maybe you didn't notice but I can't even walk. Of course I don't mind if you help me, otherwise I'll just lie here and go back to sleep if you let me. Ah, easy there, I'm not used to whatever we're doing, that doesn't feel too pleasant. Trying to cripple me?

My toes almost touched my forehead, then he let up and I relaxed and he started again.

Now sit up on the table, mister Post, Sloan said, and let's swing the arms. I'll help you, he said.

I said my arms are stretched out as far as they'll go, Sloan, with you turning me like a wheel. Yes, I'm breathing deeply. That's as deep as I can breathe, Sloan.

Turn over, lie flat, mister Post, he said.

A cold towel, scouring me like I was a pan, meant to remove whatever remained of the last traces of my skin. Then a warm soft towel. Better, I said. Much better. What are you rubbing on me? Lanolin and boroglyceride? And white vaseline? Keep my skin from chapping? *What* skin, I asked.

The blanket respected me, was satisfyingly sympathetic, all wrapped around me. I reasoned it must have been one of my own. Sloan said I could rest for half an hour. God, I was sleepy. Funny, because I just got up an hour ago, I was sure.

Moved to a new room, larger than the one with all the water pipes. I saw what could only have been a medieval rack. Sloan said it would strengthen my stomach and back muscles. I admit, it *was* comfortable, even tilted. 18 inches off the floor at one end. Glad my feet were tucked into canvas loops.

Grip the sides of the table, Sloan said, and pull as hard as you can. Breathe deeply. Always breathe deeply, he said.

I pulled as much as I can, I informed him. Why was he pushing on my stomach? That's too much pressure on my stomach, I said. You are shoving everything up to my chest.

But it's good for you, mister Post, Sloan said. Aids gravity to lift the abdomen and bowels and your other organs back into place if they are out.

It is hard to believe Sloan said that, but he did.

Breakfast in the dining room was a riot of hundreds of people, yipping like a bushful of bluejays. Most of them didn't even look sick. I was grateful Ella could join me, but I didn't feel like talking. Oatmeal gruel with lemon in it, a wheat biscuit, yogurt milk, walnuts. Fig bromose. God save me.

Teeth scoured, mouth washed with...what? Lye? Burned like hell. Then I went to a reading alcove and it was quiet, and no one pulled my limbs or splashed me with ice water. I was supposed to browse the books, pick out something I wanted to learn, prepare to do some work in. Gardening, carpentry, weaving, basket making. Jesus, cooking. I wanted to think about all the exhilarating choices.

Later they took me to a dimly lit room. The doctor himself came in and I suspected I must be in for an important bone wrenching. Let me explain, mister Post, this is a carbon arc lamp, he said. We control its heat by the regulation of the current through this rheostat, he said. The parabolic reflector and the lamp can be raised or tilted during treatments, he said. Its legs are equipped with rollers so the machine can be moved instead of our having to move you. We'll be applying heat to those joints and muscles you complained of during the morning exercises.

His gadget resembled a stove pipe with legs on wheels and a funnel for a head.

Perhaps, he said, solicitously, my incandescent light bath over here will amuse you. It's not ready for public display or use, but very nearly so. You may find its concept interesting if you think of yourself as privileged by this very preliminary viewing. The cabinet is wooden, four feet square, 54 inches high, and it has a 20-inch doorway to allow a patient to enter with space to spare. Every inch of it is planned exactly to my specifications, he said.

I told him the outside might be square, but the inside was *not* square. It resembled a bee hive.

That's right, mister Post, very good, the interior is octagonal, he said. The rows of mirrors inside are precisely one foot wide. I've placed vertical queues of lamps between each mirror, 48 in all, and arranged the circuitry so an attendant can control the groups or banks of lights by their own switches. It's safe, too. The conducting wires are double braided, insulated in rubber, then enclosed completely in conduits. All of the fuses and cut-outs are in a box at the cabinet's base, out of sight but easy to reach.

Then, whiff! he was gone as if the floor swallowed him. He had just wanted to order me grilled on each side for ten minutes under his carbon arc lamp and allow me to admire his electric bath box.

Sloan turned the lamp on. I knew the time had come to put me on a spit. When he tied a cloth over my eyes I asked if I got a final cigarette before the execution. Sloan said, is it too hot or too close? I asked, don't *you* know? It's *your* lamp.

Heat was relaxing. It could've lasted longer for my money. They took me out of the oven, flopped me on the table, hit me with ice! My God, Sloan, you are rubbing me with ice, do you realize what you're doing? I asked. He said yes.

Next, I had an erotically warm bath. When I showed I was enjoying it, Sloan took me out. We returned to the original room, same padded table, same pipes rattling and gurgling on the ceiling. Sloan rubbed me with road gravel. Acted like he was scraping rust off an iron plate. What is that stuff, Sloan? I asked. Salt, he said, moist salt. I might have guessed. They had used everything else except broken glass. When I grew sleepy they doused me with cold water again. Sloan said it rinsed away the salt.

In the late afternoon they finally let me doze off. It was a dreamy sensation and I remembered names I thought I'd forgotten. Ancient names. Hesiod, Moschus, Aeschylus. Old, old acquaintances from old, old books.

16

THE FIREPLACE was stoked with burning logs. Several electric wall lamps were ablaze and the light was brilliant in the library.

John Harvey went to his desk, opened the top drawer, removed a folded sheet of paper, took it to Ella. "I meant to keep this put away until tomorrow but you know I can't hold back gifts."

She opened the sheet. "A Valentine's Day poem. John, you've written me another poem." She read it, smiling at him between each line.

A dozen dear years have passed since we wed;
They are minutes, only minutes as they fly.
Though we're older and wiser it has been said,
A rare love like ours will never, ever die.

She finished the last of eight stanzas, gripped his hand, pulled him toward her and kissed his cheek. "It's beautiful. I will keep it with the others, my true treasures, besides you and the children." She refolded the paper as tenderly as if it were aged parchment and tucked it between the soft tangles of yarn in her knitting basket.

"I don't know how I ever managed without you." His eyes glistened with self-induced emotion. He was naked except for a loincloth.

"You did extraordinarily well before I ever came along, John. But I'm glad you don't think so."

A black woman entered the library carrying a silver tray on which were two glasses and a China pitcher of orange juice. She wore the uniform of female San employees: starched white cap and long bib apron over a white blouse buttoned to the neck where a small dark ribbon adorned the collar. She was one of a select few "coloreds" employed at the San or the mansion.

"Set those things here, Aurelia." Kellogg motioned to the enormous table before the desk, its surface obliterated by papers and books and magazines. He was not remotely embarrassed in the tiny garment which barely covered his privates. Aurelia saw him similarly undressed several times weekly, running up and down the stairs. She paid less attention to him than if he had on a swallowtail full-dress evening coat.

She found a level place to park the tray. "Would you like me to pour, doctor Kellogg?" Not reaching for the pitcher, waiting for his answer.

"Just leave it, Aurelia." Then, as she turned to leave, "Aurelia, we've been very pleased with your work, we both want you to know, and we intended to ask you if you'd like to assist missus Rumbault in caring for the green plants and flowers?"

Aurelia Skipworth nodded pleasantly and Kellogg added: "You understand, we could not release you from your regular duties, nor increase your salary — things being as they are, the need to put the San's earnings back into the purpose of the hospital as the church requires of us all, a fair and just obligation."

She smiled. "Ah'd be pleasured to help missus Rumbault."

"Good, excellent." He massaged his palms together, making small whistling noises through his nostrils. "I'll inform missus Rumbault tomorrow morning, first thing."

When Aurelia was gone, Kellogg said: "Fine woman, fine woman. I thought highly of her mother, old Emuline. All our family did, her helping mother with everything from laundry to birthing babies. A sad loss when that old colored died. I'm glad we could find suitable work for Aurelia."

He poured the juice. Tested it, brought Ella's glass to the table near her arm. He hip-hopped to the fireplace, moved back from its direct heat, hitched up his loincloth, went to the floor, rolled onto his back, did several leg lifts.

Seated on a bentwood rocking chair beside a bentwood table, Ella crocheted with a seriousness not often given to sewing. She refused to let herself observe her undressed husband. Brother Will referred to the loincloth as the "doctor's diaper," but never in the doctor's presence. His nudity troubled her tonight in ways she couldn't verbalize or deal with easily.

John Harvey sprang to his feet. He wiped his forehead with a hand-towel, brushed it across his beard, tossed it aside. It fell near Ella's feet but she did not look up.

"Post has convinced his wife that his nightmare is prescient," Kellogg blurted. "Balderdash. I'm guessing, mind you, but I think it will link directly to his illness, not a cause but a connection, one that has been with him since his childhood." He began running slowly in position, legs lifting high, knees nearly clipping his beard, adding speed, going nowhere.

It was uncommon for the Kelloggs to spend an evening in the library of their twenty-room Queen Anne mansion, though it was one of their favorite retreats. Normally at this hour, they were in the hospital's experimental kitchen, testing new recipes, new ingredients for foods, new durations of cooking time. Lately, they had toyed with trying to create paper-thin wafers or flakes, from cooked wheat grain. A few dubious tries, little or nothing learned. Tonight they were treating themselves by staying home.

Their estate, at Manchester and North Wood, was four blocks from the Sanitarium. The distance would be a problem during the winter, except for underground concrete tunnels that connected all of the Sanitarium buildings to each other, including the house. The seven-foot high tunnels, with their steamheat pipes and rows of coldwater pipes, doubled as walkways if the weather or the late hour demanded them.

The Kellogg mansion had been a belated wedding gift to Ella. Ten years in the coming. Made possible only after Kellogg's inventions and books began to fetch him large sums of money. Its wide, central hallway seemed to extend from the front door all the way to the state's Upper Peninsula. But it actually ended at the entrance to the pantry and double kitchen. It was a palace of chandeliers, mirrors, bookcases, and flower-laden tables (the blossoms grown in the San's greenhouses). A monument to pianos and tile floors and tall colonial clocks. A place where gold flatware, translucent china plates, and rows of drop-leaf dining tables were common. A home of elaborate meals, each with a dozen dishes made so deliciously from grains, nuts, fruits, vegetables, no guest ever noticed the absence of meat. At least, none ever mentioned it.

Even at this late hour, beyond the library doors a large staff was active, putting the last touches into housecare for the day. Three nurses routinely looked in on the dozen-plus children in the bedrooms upstairs, wards of John Harvey and Ella Kellogg. The adopted children were an unanticipated joy, made possible by the doctor's increasing income. He returned a generous amount to the hospital and the Adventist organization every month, but withheld enough for certain indulgences, including an amplitudinous family.

John Harvey twisted and bent in strenuous contortions, then burst into an alternating pattern of scampering and leaping as he dashed around the room. Each time he passed her on his winding tour of duty, he touched Ella's hair or shoulder with his hand and each time she reached to return the touch but he always had moved away.

"Post is fascinating for some odd reason I can't put my finger on." At that second, John Harvey's finger was marking its way down the crowded text of one of his dozen books on keeping the body fit. "He's more gambler than merchant, not afraid to take a chance on something untried, perhaps even reckless in that regard, which could account for his wasted condition. There is an engine running inside the man, you can hear it ten feet away, feel it throbbing. Sadly, it is killing him even while he sits talking to you." He slammed the book shut.

Ella lifted her head, stretched her neck, feeling a kink taking hold, crawling in to nestle back there, spurt its throbs up into her brain. It was that time of month. She let the needlework settle on her lap, rubbed a moist palm against the back of her neck.

"Sam Gamble was by today, crude and insulting as ever."

Kellogg skipped over to her, placed a hand on each of her shoulders, still running in a parody of travel, began massaging her neck. She gratefully surrendered to him.

He said pensively, "Missus Post is one for the books, paying off Sam Gamble with suspenders, probably blinking like a spinning wheel. I shouldn't talk, though, they are paying *us* with *blankets*." He squeezed her neck a final delicious time, then located the middle of the floor and began a series of toe touches, legs spread, arms alternating in arcs.

Ella closed her eyes, leaned her head against the chair's padded back. She silently berated herself for letting unrest and frustration insinuate themselves. She knew she should thank God constantly for the good fortune that was hers, spiritual as well as financial. Few employees at the San, including the doctor, earned more than a small salary. The doctor made these penurious conditions bearable by pointing out in staff conferences: "It is an honor to serve in a cause as humane as ours. If we are to be good stewards of healing and of the church's mission, we must be willing to donate time, skills, energies. We must make our own share of sacrifices." He had mapped himself a way out of the cage of low wages through a skein of well-paying enterprises connected to, but external from, the Sanitarium.

"He's uncouth and a lecher." Ella's tone was harsher than she meant it to be, nettled because her husband had not reacted when she told him

Sam Gamble came to the Sanitarium today.

Kellogg stiffened, arms rigid at his sides. "Who, Ella? Surely you don't mean Charles Post?"

"No. I spoke of Sam Gamble. He is despicable."

"Whatever he said or did, it isn't gainful to dwell on it, darling. You know he's a born trouble maker."

She gathered her crocheting angrily, whittling at it, the wooden needles clicking like battling beetles. Her words were mangled as they squeezed through her clenched teeth: "Innuendo, filthy suggestions." Caught up in the outpouring now, not caring if it was marbled with hysteria. "Always leaning back, showing off a...ah..." She couldn't say the word. Her pink ears tipped bright red and she gripped the crochet needles so fiercely they almost snapped. "A cigar smoking, whore-mongering sot."

Kellogg stared quizzically for a full minute, twined a strand of his beard around one fingertip. "I'll make a point of speaking to him when he comes again. Gamble gets a nasty pleasure from upsetting people. But he's more apt to leave you alone if you give him no notice."

Ella clinically inspected her husband, reviewed the diminutive figure — his muscular torso, arms, legs, slick and greasy with sweat. A slipperiness stirred in her belly, a jolt, a twinge, a muggy spasm of heat the thickness of oatmeal poured from a pan. It had been such a terribly long time.

17

ELLA Eaton. A woman from the east coast. John Harvey Kellogg, a man of the northern midwest. Sickness had brought them together. Ella's visit to her ailing aunt at the Sanitarium had been a favor to her mother. She had intended to stay only one or two days but the San's chief physician enlisted her as a volunteer nurse, and two days became two months. When her aunt recovered and went home, Ella suddenly had no reason to remain in Battle Creek.

"May I be so bold as to write you every now and again," John Harvey had ventured on the hour of her departure. "To keep you current on the Sanitarium's progress?"

And he did write, sometimes twice a day, always confining the letters to newsy items, only rarely hinting that it would be good to see her once more in person.

He engrossed himself in the San's labor as if he were ten people. Patients hotly argued that they had seen him at opposite ends of the

Sanitarium at the exact same moment. He was never ill, always in jolly spirit, ever ready to spew out an opinion or take a position on any topic you chose to ask about. But, late at night, when the town was moonswept, he would sit in his rented room and confess to the stars, as they pinned a dark blanket over the skies, that something was missing in his life.

Ella was gone back east and Will had married Puss. John Harvey had lost the two attentive listeners to whom he could unfurl his dreams and plans and think them aloud without apology. So he bought a train ticket, rode to New York state, and proposed to Ella Eaton, promising her poetry, music, money, medicine, purpose, and love forever.

The night of their wedding, John Harvey and Ella had come to each other, agitated and full of misgiving. They had groped with trembling fingers, shied apart in alarm, slept restlessly in their narrow bed in their single room and managed not to touch, woke with nerves ajitter, reluctantly moved together, parted, returned in dread and determination. In near panic, when daybreak tinted the ceiling with faded yellow streaks, they had moved as one, yoking, binding, encroaching, invading, finally fulfilling the ritual, if not themselves.

By the end of the first week, confidence and eagerness had replaced apprehension. There were no misgivings and they made love repeatedly, night on night, day on day, for nearly a month. They steamed the cold bedroom windows and lay in each other's arms and joked about the dripping window panes and sniggered uncontrollably. Their passion was followed by six weeks of anxiety as they waited for her monthly curse to start its flow. In its stead came dread and guilt and dismay. John Harvey anguished over his lack of restraint, impugned his own steadfastness, saw himself as irresolute and deficient, swore he would quit medicine to atone for violating his selfmade promise not to impregnate Ella.

They helplessly watched their fresh marriage shriveling like something delicate left unprotected too long beneath an August sun. But misfortune was not laying in ambush for them after all. In the second day of the seventh week Ella's period started. When she told him, they cried with relief, clutching each other like jubilant children. After their tears were finished, they pledged never again to provoke fate.

On Christmas eve, ten months later, there was a gathering in the San's main hall to sing hymns and pass out negligible gifts to the staff. Ella went home early, walking with several of the staff members who had early morning shifts; John Harvey stayed on to relate more anecdotes to the remains of his captive audience. An hour later, when he entered the single bedroom in the small house they had rented, he discovered Ella readying herself for bed. The skirts that had fit so tightly across her legs that her knees showed through, now lay on the floor in a mound of brocades, sash, bustle, boned basque, and petticoats. She wore only a white chemise. His resolve shattered like a porcelain doll's head struck with a tack hammer. Abstinence was abandoned. He pulled her against him and she felt him through the thin undergarment, their mouths crushing together with enough force to burst. Her body melted and oozed in vulnerable places. They fumbled for each other, gasped hoarsely as though their lungs were choked with gauze. Squirming, shoving. Obstructing without meaning to. Searching. Seeking.

And he managed to push himself away with a superhuman display of control, his face contorted by hunger, fear, but mostly determination.

"We can't," he whispered, and they didn't. Nor had they ever again.

18

DUNSTON was clothed in a white hospital gown under white blankets in a white room with white light filtering in through ice streaked windows. Kellogg was dressed in black, standing beside the bed, an inked exclamation point on a blank sheet of paper.

The old man coughed, pain riffled through his streaked eyes like water over gravel. He drew a shaking hand across his mouth to wipe away spittle. There was none there because he had no spare moisture in his body.

"I was thinking a while ago, Johnny, about how you told me all those times you'd never let yourself be a doctor. You couldn't stand the sight of blood. When you was a boy you sure could make some faces if I even mentioned it."

"Millard, I thought I'd be a teacher or maybe even a musician." John Harvey let himself be led into the familiar discussion. "I had many interests, but broom making and doctoring weren't among them."

"Something I want to say to you, Johnny. A word to the wise, you could call it, coming from somebody who knows."

Kellogg sat in the single chair, crossed his legs, hands cupping one knee. The only other furniture was Dunston's bed and a small bureau with a water pitcher.

"You and Will both got more of your daddy in you than your mother," Dunston began. "That's your loss, far as I'm concerned. Angennit was the only softening you had growing up. I think you got the best of it, a little more of her than Will."

"Millard, I don't have the foggiest notion what..."

"Dammit, that's because I'm beating around the bush and that isn't my way. I'll cut it straight like a good hickory switch. You're hardheaded and sometimes you got a closed mind about things. That comes from your daddy. Only time he'd listen to anybody except hisself was when the church called."

"You're tired, Millard. Let's postpone this..."

"Look at your own case, if nothing else'll prove it to you. Your daddy blamed medical men for everything bad ever happened to him, from a wart to a drought. Then Sister Ellen wiggled a finger, said let's make a doctor out of John Harvey, put him to work for the church, and your daddy couldn't bundle you off to school fast enough."

Dunston's breathing grew noisier. Kellogg leaned forward, monitoring, was waved away.

"Another thing, don't figure brother Will for being soft. He's tough as an ironwood tree. There's a hive of thinking going on behind that sober face. He'll put a scuttle of hot coals in your hip pocket, you don't watch him."

Kellogg smiled, discomfited. "Will's no threat to anyone. He's glad to have his job, happy for what he's doing."

"Keep your eye on Will. You push a thing too hard, it'll bend in all the wrong places. You look out for Sister White, too. She wields sin like a policeman's nightstick, can knock you to the ground with it."

"You're skinning them all alive today, aren't you, you old fox?"

Dunston grunted contemptuously, squinched his lips. "See what I told you about that closed mind?"

Kellogg's hand covered the veined, brumal hand of his friend. The fraternal harmony of the two men sifted into the walls like a pleasant aroma, perfume dabbed onto lace. A precious gift: talking with someone you don't have to worry will judge you hastily or unfairly, knowing he will not do that. "Well, you got one of your wishes, doctor Millard Dunston, because I certainly did what I never intended to do."

Doctor John Harvey Kellogg, more training than eighty percent of the nation's doctors. University of Michigan med school; one year. Bellevue Hospital Medical College; MD degree. Months overseas studying the world's most advanced techniques in surgery, developing a deftness with knife and needle, incisions and stitches so tiny, so tight, they were identifiable by other surgeons like a trademark. The "remarkable work of doctor Kellogg in Battle Creek," one Mayo Brother described the minuscule scar of an abdominal operation. Other physicians, veterans in the healing arts, raced to the San to learn from the young genius.

Dunston grumped, "What I actually want to know is if you'd let a dying man have a cigar. Food don't swallow easy, water's terrible. A smoke would taste sweet to me."

"We'll see." Kellogg stood up.

"That means 'no,' don't it?"

"Yes." Kellogg winked and closed the door behind him.

19

"It always is a pleasure to see you, Sister White," John Harvey greeted her at the Sanitarium's main doorway. He did not add, "Actually, among the worst possible ways I can imagine to start off my day."

In his office, Sister Ellen handed him her winter coat — a gray, weighty thing. She removed her woolen shawl. He laid it with the coat on the couch, guided her to the most comfortable stuffed chair. She was encased in a black dress, with only a hint of white collar and cuffs. Authoritarian attire for the church's unofficial but unchallenged commander.

In her lap, clutched firmly between fleshy fingers and thumb was a worn Bible, shreds of reference notes protruding at intervals from its ragged pages. Her thick half-puckered lips were plumped forward beneath a wide, oblated nose. Her ears were large and flat, reportedly the sign of a generous person.

"I am leaving soon...for Europe," she almost crooned.

Thank God, he thought, while saying, "Missionary work, no doubt." He sat opposite her.

She fired off a look of annoyance. "No other reason could justify the trip."

"Of course." Only in the presence of Sister Ellen did Kellogg's ordinary talkativeness dwindle to small utterances. When he was with her, his capacity for words temporarily departed. At such times, he sensed a remote relationship with Will's snipped style, but never inferred similar causes.

"John, our church has survived many embarrassments...has moved ahead in God's name to do His work." She smoothed a hand across her scalp-tight white hair, following it until she reached the hard-wrapped bun at the back of her head. The gesture was the sort a man might make when slicking down his hair.

"Our predecessors, mainly the Millerites...and worthies such as Joseph Bates...predicted the second coming of our Savior...Their intentions were good but their understanding of the Bible was wanting." Her voice drooped, then soared. "It was a foolish position for the church to take...The scriptures tell us 'No man knoweth the day nor the hour.'"

Kellogg listened to valuable minutes ticking away on the wall clock while work collected. He wondered how many more times he must endure Sister Ellen's exordium on how she found the Adventist egg, unprotected in the sin-scorched wilds, took it to her nest, guarded it and warmed it to hatching. He thought of brother Will's description of her, "a mulish case of denunciates and fulminates," and he smothered a smile.

"My very own people," she was saying, "and nonbelievers beyond our religion...doubted my early counsel...They refused at first to accept my visions...as messages from the Lord."

Her tempo was constant. The length of phrases were orchestrated to vary with the musical inflections that buzzed along just beneath the words. "I have traveled to Europe to establish missions...carried the Lord's word to far parts of the globe...Our schools educate the young...Our published works create streams of light around the world."

Kellogg could almost hear the seven huge presses running in the nearby Review and Herald printing plant. Never-ending activity, four stories of it churning away just across from the Dime Tabernacle at Washington and Main. More than 250 employees constantly cranked out millions of pages of books, journals, hymnals. Printing, folding, cutting, gluing, binding, wrapping. Shipping two million pounds of printed materials every year to twenty nations, the Netherlands, Germany, Sweden, France."The Divine Power works through many agencies, John...I am but one."

He mused to himself, "Religion tells us what we must do and must not do, but who tells the tellers? Each teller says God does, but in the end we have only the person's word." Such thoughts would have mortified Sister Ellen if he had verbalized them.

He often wondered how she might justify his father's pledge of $5000 to the church, virtually everything the family owned, donated to help start the Western Health Reform Institute. When the benevolent stockholders voted two years later to convert the Institute to a charitable holding, they all blithely gave up their rights to any profits from their soon-to-emerge Sanitarium. Kellogg reasoned again, his father was the Institute's treasurer at the time so it must have suited his sense of duty and sacrifice. But it impoverished the family. After John Preston died, most of the family fled the scene of financial ruin. Only his sister Clara

Belle and brother Will had stayed on in Battle Creek.

"My responsibility is like yours, doctor...We must follow what the Lord reveals."

"I'm afraid He reveals little to me, Sister."

"You would hear much... if you knew how to listen...It was allowed that I should know such things...as even the physician does not...Diphtheria is neither contagious or infectious...Salt is in no way a mineral poison...Sunbathing cannot harm you even if the skin blisters ...I will not allow you to embarrass us, John...This church found you, nurtured you, guided you..."

KELLOGG drifted away, remembering with a touch of chill that the hospital had only 20 patients when he had taken its helm. It teetered on bankruptcy.

He had ingratiated himself with Sister Ellen and her husband, Elder James White, had helped the ailing James to edit, write, publish church journals and periodicals, and in this way, and others, had endeared himself. The presiding chief physician of the hospital was released for incompetency, a charge he couldn't whip. John Harvey had instantly been installed. His first order had been for carpenters to build a raised platform to hold his oversized new desk. Then he went to work, dazzling even the most skeptical of his watchers, and delighting his few supporters.

He renamed the Institute a Sanitarium, capitalizing on Louis Pasteur's already famous "germ theory." He set up a training program for employees, put the staff through rigorous learning sessions. He searched nationwide for qualified medical men who would accept modest wages in exchange for opportunities to learn about a revolutionary health concept in the making.

The facility became a streamlined hospital while, in other designs, it took on the trappings of a first-rate metropolitan hotel. Incoming patients were greeted as guests, not persons afflicted. He insisted on examining each new patient personally, illustrating that "You, sir or madam, are a highly regarded visitor." There were rumors that he lavished a bit more firsthand attention on the ladies than on the men, especially where pelvic exams were involved, but there always are rumors of one kind or another about successful men, and John Harvey Kellogg was becoming successful.

He outlawed condiments, banned coffee, tea, alcoholic beverages, and all forms of tobacco. He initiated techniques of massage, light therapy, stomach and colon hygiene. He created foods, and prescribed fresh air sleeping, even in winter.

"Madame, roast them!" he told one lady whose two sons were listless, pale, unable to engage in normal running and playing games. "Roast them in the sun." Then he ripped open his own shirt, showering the buttons around the room like black raindrops. His tanned chest bulged. "I never miss a day of soaking in the sun. I even do my reading in the garden or on the veranda."

While the lady sat agog, he wrote out instructions for avoiding an overdose of sunshine and sent her on her way, grateful but too benumbed to thank him.

To another pair of patients, husband and wife, he determined that her shortness of breath was caused by her corset.

"You and I aren't trussed into one of these infernal boilers," he told the man, "and we breathe very well, thank you." He held aloft the corset he refused to allow the woman to replace after her examination. "But just observe the cruel wiring your wife endures so that you may parade her about town swelling at her top and protruding at her bottom, shaved to a pencil's width in her middle. In proportion to her height, a woman's waist is larger than a man's. They bear children so their internal organs have a good deal more work to do than a man's. It's natural they require more space in the body." He tossed the corset through an open window of the office while husband and wife quaked, believing him gone mad.

No subject was too delicate to assail, no patient's sensibility was too frail to shoulder the facts.

"Masturbation," he proclaimed during a lecture to the San's growing populace, "is heathen. Even after being solemnly warned, the masturbator will often continue this worse than beastly practice, addicted to it, ashamed of himself, deliberately forfeiting his right to happiness for a moment's mad sensuality."

He banned all meat from the San. All meat.

"The flesh of animals and fowls and fish were not meant for consumption by humans." It was a sermon preached to every new patient from the pulpit of elevated desk.

"Meat is man's greatest cause of constipation. One pound of beef or pork taken into your system will leave two ounces of residue that neither digest nor are absorbed into the body's tissues. It becomes a gruesome remnant that collects and rots and lodges in your bowels."

The hospital's new image drew crowds of ailing and world-weary people who sought Kellogg's magic elixir: his therapy of diet and exercise. Patients joyfully abandoned the providers of hacksaw surgery and the extorters of blood who often left the sick sicker and the dying dead. He added rooms to the Sanitarium; when he couldn't do that, he added buildings. He would have felt some extra pleasure if he'd known that even the stern, all-powerful Sister Ellen nervously admitted she could hardly keep sight of this lightning bolt she had loosed.

SISTER Ellen said loudly, "John, are you listening to me?"

He brought her into focus. "Of course I am, sister."

"The church has repeatedly risen...to expose the false curists...who tried to disguise themselves...in the shade of the reliable methods of the Adventists." Her face contorted as though a healthy belch would be welcomed. "Each time they were revealed for what they were: charlatans."

Kellogg said off-handedly, "I remember Elder James telling about a doctor Dye who devised a belt that gave off spine-jerking electrical shocks. It was supposed to restore lost manhood. More than likely destroyed some reproductive capacities."

She interrupted: "The church's methods alone have survived ...reliance on God's own pure water, fresh air...along with proper exercise, sound sleep, balanced nutrition...abstinence from alcohol and tobacco...the practicing of health first, not cures."

Each time he heard these preachments he maintained his temper while Sister White bestowed honor on herself for every discovery in the San's repertoire. He was beginning to truly appreciate the assessment made by Elder Canright before he quit the Adventist Church and moved to another town to become a Baptist. "Her visions," Canright said, "are merely the result of nervous disease, and a complication of hysteria, catalepsy, and ecstacy."

Sister Ellen leaned toward Kellogg and something ominous about her movement alerted his attention.

"I want us to discuss a master working calendar...Something I've been thinking about...a calendar of assignments, as it were...in the hall down below so it is easy to locate you, doctor...and ascertain the duties your employees are engaged in."

He was astounded. "Sister, we have close to three hundred people working here in any week. Thousands of activities every month. No calendar is large enough for such a schedule."

"Precisely why...one is needed," she said solemnly.

20

MARCH 1891

"HE WAS screaming like a wild man, we weren't sure what you'd want us to do..."

"You did the proper thing by calling me."

The intern's tenseness vanished, replaced by relief. It was a rash act to summon doctor Kellogg from his bed at four a.m. to advise on medical matters unless it was a case of life and death. But the doctor's interest in this recent patient had made the risk worth taking, better than having something go wrong and then be asked to explain why no one was consulted.

Behind the closed door to Kellogg's immediate left, just down the hospital hallway from the operating rooms, came whimpering noises easily mistaken for an injured canine. The physician intern had a notepad in one hand, pencil and stethoscope in the other; his street clothes hardly showed beneath a green smock. John Harvey had on a brown topcoat to cover his sleeping gown; shiny leather shoes on his feet, but no stockings. Kellogg touched his wireframe glasses, lowered his hand to a coat button, twirled it clockwise, worrying it nearly loose. A long thread hung from it, the button stuck at a forty-five degree angle.

"Did Post resist?"

"Not at all, sir." The intern shifted nervously from one foot to the other, jammed his pencil into the pocket of his smock but clutched it again, realizing he ought to be ready to take notes if necessary. "He held onto us like he thought we could save him from whatever scared him. We told mister Post's wife to stay in her room, stay with the little girl, you know, the sour little kid. It seemed to suit her."

John Harvey motioned approval, tugged at his beard, heard again the distinct whimpering beyond the door. "The man has had a fright which probably resulted from his recurring nightmare..."

"That's what his wife said, sir." Sloan, dressed in white, came out of the holding room shaking his head. "A sad case."

"We must help ease his discomfiture." Kellogg continued to pull at his beard, concentrating. His voice was faint, nearly a thought. "Ordinarily we would attempt to put him at rest, then quickly to sleep, but sleep brings on the very condition that upsets him. We have preliminary work to perform." Kellogg confronted the intern who reacted by tripping backward. "I ask you, doctor, what would you prescribe for mister Post?"

"The neutral bath?"

"Indeed, why not. It will put our patient into tranquility, and from there into a restful sleep. He should awaken fully refreshed. Sloan, you ready the tub. I want the water temperature at 94 degrees, not an iota off in either direction. Test it carefully. Keep testing throughout the treatment. Never let it range below 92 or above 96."

"I'll see to it, doctor Kellogg." Sloan disappeared again into the room, shutting the door noisily behind him.

"You're in charge, doctor," Kellogg said, gripping the intern's shoulder, looking up at him, shaking him gently as though to waken him. "Make certain your patient doesn't chill, that's critical. He mustn't chill. Sloan is to keep a Turkish sheet handy and wrap Post in it the very moment he comes out of the bath. You may want to start with a gentle rub but I leave that to your discretion, just be certain it is gentle, nothing vigorous."

"I understand, sir." The intern seemed ready to salute. Instead, he finally put his pad and pencil to use making notes.

"Monitor him carefully, doctor. While he soaks, the water will accumulate in his tissues and the cutaneous nerves will become saturated. The more the better, because it eliminates the movement of fluids in or out, neither themic nor circulatory reaction. At that point, when his nerve sensibility is lessened, his anguish will subside. Are you following me?"

"Completely, sir." Jotting more notes.

"Good. Now remember, his pulse rate will diminish, so check it regularly. His respiratory should not modify except to become easier, so stay alert for any undue changes. And for heaven's sake, before you lower him into the tub, examine the air pillow. We assuredly don't want him to drown."

"We'll follow every safeguard, sir, as carefully as if you were conducting it yourself." The intern lowered his notepad and gave John Harvey a serious nod of total dedication.

As an afterthought, Kellogg inquired, "Has Post been receiving the prescribed number of enemas?"

Without hesitation the intern answered, "I checked his chart when we brought him down. He is receiving twice daily, as you ordered, morning and evening."

Kellogg calculated the early hour. "Administer another immediately after the neutral bath." He tucked his eyeglasses into a coat pocket and walked briskly down the corridor toward the underground tunnels that would take him back to his mansion.

"IS DADA dying, mother?" Marjorie was propped on one elbow in the cot in their room.

"You know dada needs care, sweetheart. Sometimes he gets very scared in the night..."

"I do too."

"...but he isn't dying, Marjorie."

"He won't go away?"

"Only for a little while, so doctor Kellogg can help him, then he will be right back here with us." Ella sat on the edge of the cot, felt her daughter's small arms try to encircle her, squeezing tightly as if to squeeze out the screams that woke them both a while ago, before Charles was wheeled away.

"I want to go see gramma and grampa."

"We can't do that sweetheart..."

Insistently, "We can." Leaning her head back to frown at Ella, "I want to go home. I don't like it here."

"You said you met lots of nice children."

"I don't like them. I want to see gramma and grampa. This house is all sick people."

"Your father is one of them. That's why we came, so the doctors can make him well again. Would you want us to go and leave him here alone?"

Darkness hovered close and flat against the windows; a sneak thief ready to steal the lamplight at first chance.

"Wouldn't dada be sad if he couldn't see you tomorrow, Marjorie, or the next day or anytime? You know how he loves you."

"I don't want dada to be sad." She nestled her head against Ella's breast again, holding securely to her.

21

MAY 1891

WEBB'S restaurant door stood ajar to the glory of May zephyrs, chittering birds, a noontime sky of unblemished blue.

Will Kellogg was eating what was probably to be his last bowl of oyster stew for months. Webb had told him when he served it, "They're already out of season, can't get them in and iced down fast enough."

Will knew he was flirting with stomach poisoning, knew oysters were safe only in months with an "R" in them, but the long stretch to September was reason enough to take a chance. He sluiced a spoonful, rammed it into his mouth with a piece of bread. Then he saw Charles and Ella Post and their adult-child with the pouting, overhung upper lip, seated at a table a few feet away. His throat constricted, the food gagged him, panic swelled like the glob of bread he couldn't swallow.

He flattened two half-dimes beside his bowl, moved for the door, acting preoccupied with counting his remaining coins.

"How are you today, mister Kellogg?" Post, the cadaver, tipped a spoon in jaunty greeting.

"Hello." Will exhibited no friendliness, just feigned surprise. "When did you come in?"

"Actually, we were here before you." Post's voice was notably stronger, no longer confined to words bobbed out between gasps of air. "I thought your brother instructed patients against Webb's. We assumed it was a rule for his employees, too."

They had been here all along! Kellogg wondered how he could have overlooked the crutches, stacked like boat oars across the red wooden chair sticking out in the aisle. Or the essential wheelchair parked on the grass beside the building. He would have passed within a foot of it.

Will's mind, though, as he came to Webb's diner had been preoccupied with toting up the reasons for a better office, one that afforded him decent light and space. His concentration also was on phrasing and rephrasing a plea for a day's leave from work to take the family to a vaudeville show or a picnic at Goguac Lake. So he had sleepwalked right into Webb's restaurant.

Serves me right, he thought. "I would consider it a personal favor, sir, if you kept this between us."

"Keep what, mister Kellogg?"

"Seeing me here. In Webb's. It would only go against me with the doctor." Standing stiffly, arms at his sides, he focused on a point to the left of Post's well-combed, thick hair.

"Take my word for it, I don't intend to mention it to anyone, mister Kellogg."

"I'm in your debt. Good day."

"I want to ask a favor of you, too, mister Kellogg."

Kellogg stared down at the sleet-colored eyes of the man who'd cajoled John Harvey into trading medical services for blankets, whose wife walked the winter streets of Battle Creek with a wooden box strapped on her shoulders selling suspenders door-to-door for twenty-five cents a pair. The man was still as bony as a lake perch, and his face was a Halloween shade of putty gray, though he had sunbathed on the veranda an hour each day for almost a month. But there was a tenuous brightness about his mien that had been absent a few weeks ago.

Kellogg released the coins he was holding into a coat pocket. "What favor, mister Post?"

"It's in the nature of a privilege. A visit to your kitchens in the San to learn more about how the food is prepared." Charles Post paused, breathed deeply, quickly, as though he had run out of oxygen. A wheeze whined up from his chest but didn't seem to phase him. "The menus offer excellent fare and I'm eager to know the recipes."

Ella Post took little swallows from her glass of tea, giving all her attention to Marjorie who was spading her way through a thick slice of German chocolate cake. The woman's lack of interest helped to lower Kellogg's discomfort, as he stood by the table, out in the aisle, feeling foolish, vulnerable, and itchy all over.

Post said, "It is our first time in here, an excursion, an outing, I suppose. I think the doctor is wrong. The food is delicious."

"The doctor is often wrong." Kellogg shuffled both feet, moved away from the table. "He just never admits it. And there is almost no one to tell him otherwise."

22

NEARLY three hours later, in Burley's Tavern on Canal Street, a calamity of threats, laughter, boasts, profanity and profundity was in progress, soaked in a cascade of cheap whiskey.

Burley's scarred, wooden bar ran the length of the main room, taking up half of the interior. A dozen men leaned against it, gulping from mugs of beer that were weighty in the lifting, light in the lowering. Swilling jiggers of sour mash bourbon. Chewing. Spitting. The sawdust carpet, mushy brown around the spittoons, attested to bad aims. Like Webb's diner, the tavern's double front doors were opened to the afternoon breezes, so the usual fog of cigar and cigarette smoke was diluted with fresh air until both were about tolerable.

Sam Gamble hunched over one of the darkly gouged walnut tables that filled the remainder of the shadowy room. Behind him a crust-smeared window allowed a few wobbly strings of sunlight to worm through. He had been in the tavern for two hours. That amounted to eight drinks. He tilted his beer mug, was surprised to find it empty, rattled it on the table. "Burley! Beer an whiskey!"

"I hear you, Sam," the bartender shouted. "In a minute. Quit banging that mug, you break it you'll pay for it."

"Had my own saloon wouldn't come to this asshole place. The old man din't guzzle it away, I'd have my own. I coulda been like Burley, live good, have some money."

One of the regulars at Burley's passed Gamble, overheard him complaining. He paused, asked, "You want to have your own saloon, Sam, why don't you get it? Always sayin you'll do somethin big, whyn't you do somethin like start up your own place?"

Gamble spit on the floor. "You lookin to make trouble?" he snapped, and the other man moved on.

Burley carried a mug of beer and a glass of whiskey to the table. Sam had the fresh whiskey glass to his mouth almost before Burley released it, leaning back, swallowing the contents in one fluid move. Above the ridge of the glass he watched a man sauntering away from the bar and toward his table, walking a little sideways and taking longer to get there than he should. A grimy face was thrust out in front, belligerently, so soiled it would pass for a coal miner's. He wasn't a miner. He did odd jobs, piecemeal chores wherever he could find them, and part-time clean up at the Marvin's blacksmith shop on Canal Street and at the meat packing plant.

Loony Lew Reesner was forty-one years old. His head was totally hairless, bald of eyebrows and lashes, his skull ridged with scar tissue from a fire that trapped him in a second floor room in a tinder box flophouse in Detroit a decade ago. His squashed raisin eyes were embedded in doughy puffs of skin, one eyelid droopy and puckered, the result of a blow a long time back when a foolish carpenter struck him with a marking gauge while they argued right out there in the street, practically on the doorstep of Burley's place. Lew broke the carpenter's nose, jaw, and left arm at the elbow, then bit off most of one ear. No one had picked a fight with him since, though he had provoked a few.

"Buy me a whiskey?" The empty glass he carried was smothered in an oversized fist.

"Buy your own, Lew."

Lew pulled out a chair, unbidden, and sat almost delicately. "You ain't bein very goddamned nice to your pal, Sam. We're pals, ain't we?" His voice was devoid of good fellowship. He draped forward on his arms, his chin close to the table, letting Sam get a full view of the raveled skull, reminding Sam of who he was talking to. "Burley!" he shouted and slammed the table. "Whiskey here. My shit-assed buddy's payin for it."

"Dammit, Lew, you want to knock over the table, get your own." Sam drank some of his beer, gazed up from the pleasure of it, grinned lopsidedly at Lew. "Got me a idea or two. Tired workin for nothin, treated like a nigger."

"Who treat you like a nigger?" Reesner raised his head, genuine anger flushing his face. "You tell me who, I beat their face."

Sam reached across the table, hiccuped mightily, lightly touched Reesner's arm. "We been lookin out for each other long time. Didn't change when we growed up, did it?"

Reesner's head wobbled in agreement. A few flakes of sooty matter floated off of his cheeks.

"Struttin around for eight, ten years, acting like miss God Almighty herself."

Reesner had no idea who Sam was talking about but he didn't ask. He figured he would finally find out or he would not. Either way was all right with him so long as Burley brought a drink.

"Lookin to gobble me up, thinks I don't see." Sam's unfocused eyes were February stones. "Crookin her finger, 'C'mere, Sam, boy, I got somp'n for you,' cooin them big words to confuse, then warnin me off, thinkin I cain't tell her goddamned game." He drank and his moustache dribbled beer. "I was rich, or some church kneeling sonbitch, boots all shined, she'd come around me by now."

"That same damned woman got you all raw in the crotch, you been waiting how many years — seben, eight? Hell, you ain't never gone get it done. You both be too old."

Gamble stared out of tight slits crossmarked at the corners with wrinkles like well-healed stitches. "Gonna lay her down, give her what she been runnin from. When she hoots for more, you know what I do then?"

Lew's good eye rolled loosely in its socket. The barren lids closed slowly, flapped open sharply. "What?"

"Kick her stinkin ass right out'n my bed."

Lew's squeal of amusement was sharp enough to split fire wood.

As Burley placed Reesner's drink on the table, the two seated men were having a grand time, and he heard Sam say, "She take notice, damn her, have her call me *mister* Gamble, honey, sir. Can't join em, beat em, I always say." He belched loudly.

Sam hoisted his glass in a toast.

Loony Lew Reesner joined him. "Beat 'em. That's what you always say, Sam."

23

JULY 1891

WILL picked at the scabby paint on the front door of the small frame house, ground a chip to dust between his fingers.

"Peeling. Looks bad. You can bring a brush over tomorrow, Len. Scrape it, give it a good coat."

The eight-year old boy in shirt sleeves and knee pants wondered why big brother Karl didn't get in on this exhilarating chore. He told himself it was because Karl, the "imp" as father called him, did outrageous things. For punishment he was denied jobs such as painting doors on sweltering summer days. Len had learned a lesson he would never forget: impudence and rash acts might have their rewards.

But Len also remembered Karl pouring milk on the floor to feed a stray cat, and father raving about waste and messiness, then rubbing the boy's nose in the milk, right down there on the wooden floor, splinters and all. Impudence and rash acts also can have their penalties. He suspected, though, the trade-off was worth it.

Behind Len his three-year old sister, Beth, wrapped her hand around one of Ella's fingers, holding on with an intensity and strength both common and surprising in tiny children. Her attention riveted on a line of sand ants, a miniature flowing strand of two-way traffic and commerce. On the bottom step of the porch, ten-year old Karl scuffed his half-laced boot, its sole turned sideways, rubbing dark lines across the brittle paint.

When no one answered the next loud knock, Will opened the screen door, tried the knob. It turned, as he expected. Five people moved as a unit into the house.

"She's there, Will." Ella pointed to a rocking chair by the bedroom door.

He hurried across the empty center of the room, alarm swiftening his heartbeat as he glimpsed the old woman's head angled awkwardly onto her shoulder. She slouched in the chair as though all the bones in her clothsack body had been pulverized. Her mouth was slightly open. When he heard her steady breathing he himself exhaled a bleat of spent air. He knelt.

"She's asleep, Puss."

Ella joined him, Beth in tow.

He jostled the old woman's arm. "Mother."

Instant alertness flashed through thick spectacles hinged to her ears, immediate recognition in eyes that were wonderfully clear.

"Will. And Ella. I didn't know you were coming by." She sat upright, tipped the chair into delicate arcs of movement. With one hand she sorted and arranged strands of her finely threaded hair, while the other hand smoothed the front of a black wool dress, much too substantial for the season.

"Where's Clara?" Will asked, envisaging his sister, Clara Belle, frail at 100 pounds, mother of five, married to a cheerless and abstract man who couldn't find the right niche for himself in the work world. Clara Belle, the in-and-out companion of Ann Janette since John Preston's death ten years ago. The daughter now the mother, the mother now the child.

"Visiting," was Ann Janette's peremptory response.

"Mother, we came to see if you need anything." Will stayed next to her in his dress suit and black batwing bowtie, kneeling, feeling a cramp in his legs.

"Can't use up everything you and Johnny give me now." She peered into the shaded room, settled her gaze near the door. "Johnny isn't with you?"

"He couldn't get away from the hospital, Mother. He's very busy. The patients, the experiments, his writing..."

"The doctor lives farther than us," Ella rationalized too seriously. She went to the divan and sat near Ann Janette. "We're able to walk over in a minute or two."

Ann Janette braced herself out of the rocking chair, shook off Will's proffered assistance. She walked with her arms bent at the elbows, held waist high for balance. Going into the pantry that led to the kitchen, she said: "He hasn't been to see me for a while. Tell him I know there's not much pleasure in visiting an old woman but it's not enough excuse to excuse him. "While I fix some lemonade, you raise the shades, Ella."

Will knew that the invitation to lemonade meant hearing again how the entire family had caught measles during the killing epidemic of 1861 and his mother had used a wet sheet treatment to cure them. She had piled blankets on the kids, brought their measles to a head, next soaked the howling youngsters in cold, wet sheets for 24 hours in an overheated room, and then buried them again under layers of thick quilts. The deep red splotches appeared on cue, departed rapidly, and all the Kellogg kids recovered while hundreds were dying.

Ella opened the curtains, and used the same moment to release the boys into the tantalizing outdoors. They spun gratefully through the door, slamming the screen, bounding off the porch with high, daring leaps.

"Why did you do that, Ella?"

"They wanted to go outside, Will. They've heard your mother's reminiscences before."

"They owe their grandmother the courtesy."

Ella's sigh was weighted with submission. "All right, Will, I'll call them back, if that's what you want."

"It's done, Puss. Leave them."

He wandered to the door, observed his sons chasing each other through the heat waves of the empty field across the street. He questioned whether he had ever run carefree under a summer sky, played and skipped and cavorted so unrestrained. His stomach made a low, rolling complaint; bristlebrushes scoured its lining. Young people have it easy today, he thought; it is a pity they don't know their advantages.

24

THE Sanitarium estate lolled across three city blocks, patchworked with vegetable gardens, blossoming mulberry bushes, and flowers in colorful profusion — blue lupines, irises, pink phloxes, tiger lilies — perfuming the air, stimulating as a farm maiden's first kiss. The orchards were lusty with apples, pears, plums, grown to Brobdingnagian size. The vineyard sagged from brawny blue grapes, sweet enough to make jaws ache with expectation. There were two greenhouses, a swimming pool, and a bush-clogged park where deer, raccoons, rabbits, woodcocks, ducks and geese — even a red fox — came in the cool evenings to nibble the thick grass or drink from one of the fountains, emerging like vapory spirits out of the green walls, unafraid of the people near by.

Violin music floated high and elastically, the sustained notes flitting like a gathering of butterflies through the darkening woods and gardens.

"That will be doctor Kellogg serenading his patients," Post said from where he rested on a circular concrete bench.

"We should be in the hall, Charles. He truly expects the patients to hear his lectures, and he holds the recitals for their enjoyment."

"I can hear all I need to from here, lecture or violin."

Ella could faintly make out the distant strains of music, but could not tell a word of the doctor's oration, however strident it became. She was wearing a dress she cut and sewed during the winter months. Its bodice had blousy sleeves to which she had attached a fichu, or three-cornered cape, with ribbons at the shoulders. Charles told her she looked prim, neat, gentle. She had taken it as a compliment.

Post cupped both hands over the head of a cane, rested his smoothly shaven chin on his hands. Another cane was propped against his leg within easy reach. "Banty rooster Will Kellogg told me King Edward himself has ordered one of the doctor's electric light cabinet baths for Buckingham Palace." Shaking his head in admiration. "How in hell's half acre Kellogg figured out a use for incandescent bulbs before most people can pronounce the word, is beyond me. His mind is a race track."

He scrubbed his chin against his knuckles, still leaning down on the cane. More flesh had appeared on his face than was there a few weeks ago. He was no longer a cadaver.

"Ella, there is something about this town." Speculating, but convincingly. "Something about it I can't pin down, keeps sidling up to me like it's going to shake my hand, big and friendly, then at the last second it walks on around, avoids me. If you've ever chased a lightning bug you know how he disappears in and out of the bushes and you grab out and you'd swear you've got him until you open your fingers and there's nothing there.

"You've been patient and wonderful, hauling me around in that old wheelchair to the places I wanted to see and I adore you for it. I wish we could take a buggy, but the money..."

"You've heard no complaints," she volunteered pleasantly. "Look at the muscles I'm developing." She raised an arm and flexed it in a parody of a circus strong man, but he wasn't watching her.

Post's intuition told him that something urgent was accumulating. He had sensed it in the past, with the corn cultivator and the land in Texas, and it had nearly always been correct, even if not providential or profitable. But, one fact continued to elude him. He could not explain the engulfing presentiment that was in the very air, seeping into his pores. He hoped it might just be his health returning.

Post's concentration gathered new energy, crackled ahead like the impulses on a telegraph wire. He abruptly said, "Ella, you know, that Caramel Coffee at the San is about as remindful of caramel as a jar of warm pickle juice. Kellogg mixes burned bread crusts and bran and pours in a little molasses to sweeten it. Nothing unusual or very inventive about it except he's selling it faster than hot gingerbread on a cold day. Soldiers brewed practically the same drink in the war thirty years ago because they couldn't get real coffee."

Lamplights atop poles in the garden blinked on, sending golden circles floating down onto walkways and shrubbery.

"The lecture and musical festivities ought to be finished by now." He seemed suddenly aware of the time. "The indoors should be delightful." Ella assisted him up from the bench. He balanced firmly on both canes.

"That coffee thing has set me to pondering." His speech was sprightly. "I believe I just may have the start of the best idea that ever occurred to me."

25

AUGUST 1891

WILL was working in his shirt sleeves, cuffs rolled to the forearms, vest firmly buttoned over the hint of a protruding belly. He wore strong reading glasses, while assaying a full day's backlog on every corner of his desk.

"I'd like a word with you." Charles Post tottered in the doorway, supported by a cane in each hand.

Will detested interruptions. They intensified the load. He would have kept his office door closed, but the doctor insisted it remain open to ensure that no urgency or half-urgency went unattended because someone was too timid to seek entry.

"I'm scarce on extra time this morning," he said curtly.

"Can you spare a minute?"

Will flapped his hand like a glove being tossed away. "What is it about?"

"A way for you to become rich."

Kellogg laid his pencil on one of the many stacks of invoices. The cramped, cluttered office reminded him too vividly of his father's dim room at the old broom factory.

"So you have a way to make me rich? Interesting gambit. Calculated to gain my attention."

Charles eyed a wooden chair at the side of the desk. Kellogg motioned him into it. The chair was the only nonessential piece of furniture in the confined quarters, chosen because it was unpityingly cruel to the buttocks and discouraged long visits by patients or salesmen. Will believed Charles Post was both.

Post settled onto the hard seat, felt it resist his tailbone, hoisted his canes to a horizontal position across his lap. He might be, he realized, on the verge of raising serious questions about his sanity.

"I'll come right to the point and ask if your brother has considered selling the San's products."

"We <u>do</u> sell them. Patients order them. What do you think this stack of letters is?" He raised a sheaf of papers with envelopes clipped to them, dropped it, picked up another, "And this, and this."

"I know, mister Kellogg, they come from people who have stayed here, sampled the foods, followed their good sense and requested a supply be sent to them." Post placed his fingertips on the edge of the nearest stack of mail. Kellogg watched the fingers suspiciously. "These orders are a drop in the bucket. There are millions of people to add to your lists if they only knew what you offer."

"Mister Post, I can barely keep up with business as it is. You suggest we multiply it a hundred fold? Even if possible, which I doubt, I would say no."

"Build the volume, sir, and you can afford to hire men to do what you do. Increase the sales, increase the profits, and those profits can make you and your brother very rich."

Kellogg noticed the perspiration dotting Post's ashen face. John Harvey was right: this fellow probably would not be alive in another month, though he seemed to vacillate daily from improvement to ruin. At the moment, he looked half dead and he babbled like the inmates in the wing where the crazy people were kept.

Post knew he was being studied, tolerated it without comment, wanting the talk to go well.

"You're just trying to show us a way to make money for ourselves? No motive or gain of your own?"

"You know better than that, mister Kellogg. Don't patronize me. I'm sick, not feeble-minded." Seeing Kellogg's face twitch, Post reasoned he had hit a bruise. He pushed ahead. "I want to promote the products, make the Sanitarium's name a familiar one to every person who reads a newspaper or a magazine, wherever they live. For my service, I would draw a nominal salary. Furthermore, I would guarantee to recoup for you my salary, and increase *your* profits by at least thirty percent within twelve months or you would owe me nothing."

"Who will pay for this...advertising? I presume that is what you call it?" No amusement, just amazement at Post's presumption.

"The costs would be part of our overhead, from the first year's profits."

"I see." Kellogg scratched his ear, checked the wool of his sideburns, touched his waxed moustache as if to reassure it hadn't been misplaced. "The Sanitarium pays. I believe I fully understand your proposition. Let me restate. I want to get it correct. The Sanitarium will produce and package foods it has researched and developed. Granola, Caramel

Coffee, and so on. The San will also provide funds for advertising costs. And, the San will pay you a salary for promotional work. Is that the sum of it?"

"Yes," Post said, realizing how presumptuous the proposition sounded. Knowing where the idea was going. Downhill fast. He felt a dizzying loss of strength from the drain of the past minutes.

"For your part, you promise to repay your salary if our sales do not increase by how much? Thirty percent? Or was it more?" Will buttoned his sleeves, slid his glasses into a pocket. He stood up.

"I'm afraid I've offended you, mister Kellogg. You suspect that I bring nothing to the deal and offer even less if it fails." Post placed his canes solidly on the floor, drew his thin body upright. "I've worked out some details, done some calculations. If you'd let me present them to you, they wouldn't seem so reckless."

"I truly doubt that, mister Post." Staring up at him. "Even if it were so, my brother would never agree."

"Mister Kellogg, this idea is too obvious to be ignored much longer. Others are going to see it as I have. If you don't take steps, someone will."

"Meaning you? Alone?"

"Would you just approach the doctor for me? See that I get an audience with him?"

"You don't need me for that. The doctor is available to any patient. You could speak to him during his rounds."

"I've tried. He always is too busy, gives me flummery and hurries away."

"Ask his receptionist for an appointment. He never is punctual. But, eventually he will see you."

"I think if you spoke in behalf of the idea it would mean more, even if only to create a favorable atmosphere."

"I couldn't do that. I'm not persuaded by your proposal. It has an original ring to it, I'll admit. But, as certain as the sunrise, the doctor will say no. He refuses to turn his Sanitarium into a grocer's store. Or a choose-your-meal diner.

"You mean like Webb's?"

Kellogg switched off the wall lamp, then stopped in the doorway, his back to Post. "Are you trying to bully me? It is a pitiful strategy. Won't work a second time. I arranged for you to visit the kitchens freely. You did, again and again. I kept my part of our bargain. I'll do no more."

Post remained standing in the empty office for several minutes after Kellogg left. He bit his lip, mumbled aloud, "The little jackanapes has grit, I'll give him that, even if he is the most uncompromising stiffnecked bastard I've ever met."

Slowly, achingly, he followed Kellogg's tracks toward the caged elevator that would carry him to the second floor and the doctor's office. He was less disturbed by Will Kellogg's rebuff than by the occurrence of the old weakness in his legs, the chest congestion, insistent fatigue. He hoped it was temporary, along with the rotten weather.

ELLA Kellogg left her husband's office as Will arrived in the hallway outside. She touched his sleeve, detaining him.

"Don't bring John Harvey any problems today, Will. Doctor Dunston died this morning in his sleep. He had no opportunity to tell the old gentleman goodbye, as he wanted to do. He could use some cheering if you have pleasant news."

Her hand remained on his arm.

"All right, Ella." He was grateful he had discouraged Charles Post from coming with him. The doctor would have used Post's own canes to drive them both from his office. He looked steadily at her hand until she took it away from his sleeve.

"Tell Ella I inquired after her." She always said the same thing and it always sounded redundant to him.

He walked briskly into a large reception room, where a woman at the desk motioned him toward his brother's temple of privacy. To enter he had to open the doctor's *closed* door. The irony no longer chafed him.

26

"I AM NOT in the best frame of mind this morning so I don't expect this will take much time. I'd like a bit of solitude. I have only a few instructions for you."

Will Kellogg shifted from one foot to the other, waiting restively in the entrance of the doctor's water closet, fidgeting with his tablet and the folder of papers. "I can come back in a few..."

"Nonsense. Pull that chair over to the door. No point in wasting time when there is too little of it."

In the private lavatory that adjoined his office, John Harvey stirred languorously on a supremely designed toilet stool. A six-foot wooden cabinet embraced the stool on three sides, decorated with painted flowers and blossoms. It's padded arms let a person rest as comfortably as in an easy chair. It had a leather rack handy on one wall, stuffed with current periodicals.

John Harvey wore a heavy white undershirt that reached nearly to his furry houseshoes. He had breakfasted early, at around five-thirty instead of the usual seven o'clock, because he stayed awake after word came of Dunston's death. He would not eat again until six in the evening, knowing that two meals a day were sufficient for anybody, except possibly a laborer at heavy physical work. He had absorbed an enema a few minutes ago to induce one of two routine daily bowel movements, and it was having an effect.

"I'm sorry about doctor Dunston." Will sat in the chair he had placed halfway into the toilet door.

"Thank you, Will." John Harvey's face contorted from an internal reaction, then recomposed. "We'll speak of him in a minute."

Will looked away, abhorring the commission of secretarial and managerial duties while the doctor engaged in these personal callings. He fitted his glasses to his nose, opened his tablet to a clean page.

"First," the doctor began, "see Ella about getting someone to type the manuscript on fresh air sleeping. I completed it more than a week ago. It should have been typeset for next month's *Good Health* by now." Another facial contortion and a happy groan. "Be certain it includes my thoughts on sleeping with the head outside the window, or using a fresh air tube in winter to bring in clean oxygen."

Will Kellogg wrote reminders on his tablet. The doctor waited until the pencil halted before speaking again.

"Add this at the most appropriate place..." He dictated, eyes squinted in concentration, cheeks puffed while pondering the exact words he wanted, ignoring the notes in his hands. "Even in the harshest winter, a living room temperature of no more than 68 degrees is advised with adequate humidity." He inspected Will's face. "Should I explain?"

"If you think it's necessary."

"Very well. Take this down. In a warm atmosphere, the body naturally produces less heat; therefore, less oxygen is required, hence, less air. The result is diminishment of all vital processes. In a cold atmosphere, the intake of air into the lungs is doubled and energy is released by oxygen acting upon the body's tissues. In short, an unqualified benefit."

Will wrote speedily. He felt a mild swimming sensation in his head and, the topic and the moment seeming right for it, he asked: "May I open the window? Fresh air?"

John Harvey barely raised his eyes from shuffling papers. "Good heavens, of course. It should be open. Nasty weather today but the worst weather is better than stale oxygen."

After cranking loose the mullioned window and inhaling deeply, Will seated himself, pencil in hand. Another ensemble of orders and requests followed. He wrote down every word.

"Put the following regulation in all dining halls, kitchens, preliminary serving areas. Ensure that everyone understands there is to be no exception to its directive. Toast will not be — underline 'not be' — served in the dining room unless it is thoroughly dried and baked to absolute crispness. Underline 'absolute' and 'thoroughly.'"

Will indicated he would do so. The open window had revived his alertness.

The doctor smiled, dictated four more sets of instructions. Finally, he reached for the flush chain with one hand, used the other to tug at his beard, gripping its edges in his small fist like a wad of burned garden weeds.

"Enough for the moment. Wait in the office while I do my ablutions."

A HALF hour later, positioned at his elevated desk, dressed in his black suit and pure white shirt, John Harvey peered down at his brother whose comportment was rigidly attentive. Will had moved to a Jacobean chair, grudgingly. Its devilish construct was a test of endurance for the spine.

"Orange juice?" The doctor gestured to a pitcher. "Most beneficial to your health."

"No, thank you, I had breakfast at six o'clock. Before I came to my office."

"That's earlier than necessary, Will. I know you stayed late last night..."

"Nearly every night," Will thought.

"...to finish up some business, and it is appreciated, does not go unnoticed. I'm not insensitive to the fact that you have a family, your wife and children deserve more of your time."

John Harvey stood, hopped off the platform, scurried to the window, gazed through the light rain that speckled the glass. "Long constant hours of work have harmful effects, Will, can lead to disease, lowered resistance, shortened life. My advice is get more sleep, more sun baths, and put in fewer hours at your desk, spend less time in our testing kitchens."

"It's tempting, doctor. In fact, I intended to ask..."

"You had a nourishing breakfast? Ham and eggs and biscuits?" Continuing to look out at the rain.

"Such a meal would not meet with your approval, doctor."

Moving to the room's center, hands clasped behind him, John Harvey exercised his most intense bedside stare. "We must all — especially you, me, Ella, the San's regular employees — set the example. We cannot expect patients to adhere to our regimen if we don't practice it ourselves. We lose their trust."

"Of course." Staring back at his brother, wondering if this was prelude to a lecture.

"You haven't been eating at Webb's, have you Will, not after our last discussion?" Steady eye contact. Neither man inclined to break it.

"You made your wishes clear, doctor." At last, Will disconnected the stare, returned his gaze to the writing tablet, but did not write anything. His stomach boiled, an untimely griping, a thin high note that bubbled upward, then faded, only to start over again, in a similarly long squeal.

The doctor's expression was somber. "Remind me to prescribe something for your indigestion." He fluffed his beard with the back of his fingertips, bounded up onto the platform, resumed his seat. "Please see that doctor Dunston's funeral is a fitting one. Be certain there are flowers, a profusion of flowers. Don't arrange for a minister, he was not a church member, so I will deliver the eulogy."

Will scribbled, hearing his stomach's continued protest.

"Before I forget, I wonder if you can stay a few hours tonight, Will, and lend your assistance in the experimental kitchen? I'm very pleased with what we've learned about our dextrinized diet foods, and I'm encouraged greatly by the effects on patients. I'm fully convinced that one propitious day we will break the secret of flaking those wheat grains. Perseverance. It will pay off, mark my words. Tonight we'll take another try at the flaking. It will help to get my mind off Millard Dunston's death."

"I told Puss I probably would be late."

A grateful smile, another fluff of the beard. He rose and flattened his hands on the desk, head up, eyes fixed at a point near the top corner of the wall.

"You know, Will, there may come a day when people are no longer sick. Many animals never are; any veterinarian can verify that. The normal, usual, expected, and deserved condition of life is health. Sickness is logically expected to be found when abnormal, or accidental conditions occur. That is what we struggle with here, it is our principle duty. Sustained health would put us out of business, and I yearn for that fine day."

Will covered a yawn by lowering his head.

Applause startled both men, coming as it did from the partly opened door where Charles Post leaned against the jamb to support himself, his two canes looped over one skinny wrist.

"Bravo, doctor Kellogg. Inspirational." He hoisted his canes, slowly moved into the office. "I agree that health is a basic right of every human being, even if he or she can't afford to visit your marvelous Sanitarium. May I tell you about a sales idea I believe will complement your mission? Your brother has already heard it and, I openly admit, he turned me down. I hope you will be more farsighted."

27

SEPTEMBER 1891

"CHARLES is recovering, isn't he, doctor Kellogg? I mean you can probably see the improvement better than I can." Ella Post's eyelids were perfectly still. She was reposed, the natural crimson of her cheeks set off against her yellow, deeply piled hair.

Kellogg held his hand high to block the September sun. He believed for a moment the trees along the garden pathway were altering their colors even while he watched them. Yesterday they were green, now russet and ocher.

"I have a minute before I meet with members of my staff. I intended to confer with you later this week but this encounter is more convenient."

The wind fluffed Ella's hair. Unconsciously she tried to tame it, accomplished little.

"Have you noticed Charles becoming drowsy during the day?"

She signified no, then changed her mind, nodded yes. "He rests when he can, if that's what you mean. He still hasn't much strength so he tires easily from our walks. He is napping now, so I came into the gardens. Such a wonderful autumn day, though a bit cool."

Kellogg struck his hat steadily against his leg in a tapping rhythm, wishing he could return it to his head. "Does Charles ever mention rapid heartbeat? Pain in his left shoulder or arm? Headaches, backaches?"

Her eyelids loosened, trembled like willow leaves.

"I see. Tell me, have you noticed any mental confusion on his part, or occasional spells of despondency?"

"It would be peculiar if he wasn't occasionally depressed, wouldn't it, doctor? You haven't entirely cured him, you know." A little more tart than she had intended, but not by much.

Ignoring the mild jibe, understanding it, he said slowly, "I have diagnosed Charles' condition over these several months. Our tests bear out my conclusion and my associates confirm the diagnosis. Charles has advanced neurasthenia." He watched the colored leaves on branches that dipped and swung as if the air was water and they were seaweed. "Our efforts have not eliminated or corrected it. The simple truth is that he will not recover."

"What you say can't be, he is recuperating, anyone can tell. He talks of doing things, his mind is awake again for the first time in..."

"I am sorry, missus Post." He turned his total attention to her. "Charles is dying."

She staggered, her feet sidestepping in an awkward dance. He reached for her but she straightened immediately, firmly regained her balance. Her crimson cheeks had gone milky.

"Our work here, as I told you, is to help people find their natural state of health through natural means. We've never laid claim to miracles. Charles had every symptom of neurasthenia when he arrived. Though the disorders often subside and he seems at times to be recovering, his disease returns with increasing intensity. By the time he came under my care he was too degenerated for us to reverse his decline entirely. At best we've been able to halt it for short, intermittent periods."

"This, this disease you say he has..."

"Neurasthenia is largely a medical term for nervous exhaustion. On the face of it, it sounds almost ordinary, uncomplicated, as though a good night's sleep would put everything right. In reality, it is complex, interlaced with facets of the mind and body which we have been unable to plumb, even with all the advances of medical science."

Kellogg wished Ella Post would shift her gaze from him. He thought: she must finally blink, this woman whose eyelids can flutter for thirty seconds without pausing. But no part of her face made the smallest movement.

"The malady, missus Post, is often found among the educated classes, the so-called refined strata of society. Ironic, isn't it? As though developing the brain brings on the sickness, though that is not the cause, I assure you. Physicians, teachers, lawyers, professional men are more apt to contract it than, say, farmers or mill workers." He grunted. Smacked his hat against his leg.

"Many people, including some notable physicians, claim it is caused by overwork. Theirs is a gross simplification if not an outright falsehood. Never in all my years have I encountered a case of neurasthenia brought on by overwork. Work is purely physiological and any damages caused by it are repaired with rest and sleep, the best remedies for overactivity. Work is only dangerously fatiguing, missus Post, when done under unfavorable conditions or circumstances such as constant interruptions or undue pressures, such as one might endure from other people. I believe frustration more likely produces the disease."

"I don't care about all your suppositions, doctor. For God's sake, talk to me about my husband, not about this...this theory!"

The outcry was so unexpected it startled Kellogg. He frowned and his voice was tremulous. "Damn it, woman, it is important for you to know what is happening to Charles because it will intensify, and I intend to explain it to you, by jingo."

She directed her gaze at the path under her feet. Kellogg said more soothingly:

"His is not a hereditary thing, missus Post. You needn't worry about your daughter. I believe one might be born with a predisposition toward it, which accounts for the variables of intensity we find in different patients, but that is mere guesswork on my part."

The late September trees swooned. Their swaying limbs made a baleful sound. Ella was reminded of the night winds of winter, waiting. Her temples pulsed with soft pain.

"Are you painting the worst picture possible so that Charles' recovery, when it comes, will seem all the more marvelous as a result of your skills?"

"You're groping for reassurances I can't give you, missus Post." His voice was low, purposefully rich, his hat slapped dispassionately against his pants leg. "You must realize we've tried everything except bromides, hypnotics, and occult experiments, and those are not acceptable methods at the San..."

Her sharp glance was a silent scream of "Why?"

"...since the first two may induce equally grave conditions, nerve paralysis or total mental breakdown, and the third option depends on the supernatural for its solution."

Ella Post blinked rapidly. The wind mussed the edges of her shawl and tried to misplace curls of her wheat-colored hair. She was crying soundlessly. Kellogg offered his kerchief but she took one from her small purse.

"Then his nightmare..." she asked.

"Means nothing. Except to corroborate the presence of a predisposition such as I've described. I'm very sorry."

His arm was tired from shading his eyes so he placed his hat on his head. He noticed the trees once more — the reds, yellows, golds, browns. Yes, he wàs certain, they were green yesterday.

28

OCTOBER 1891

"I DON'T mind so much the suffering, but I hate the senselessness of it."

"Maybe its purpose is to make us think, mister Post, if you don't mind my saying so, to learn to solve our problems for ourselves."

Charles Post sat in the front room of the home of missus Elizabeth Gregory.

"Pain doesn't go anywhere, missus Gregory, except back to the pain. It snuffs your energy, crushes all desire to do anything except get through it."

It was a mid-October Saturday when the sun was warm and children across the neighborhood were rolling and shouting in the mountain ranges of leaves raked for burning. Soon the yards would be blue veiled with smoke and the air would sting a person's nostrils with a gingery tang.

"Don't you think, in its way, suffering can make us purer, mister Post?"

"If pain purified, mankind would have made itself perfect a long time ago. Hurting just makes us mean and vicious."

Shadows lay across the carpets and the round-edged furniture. A window was partly raised and a breeze moved the lacy curtains. Above the plain mantle of the fireplace, sunshine flashed from an oval mirror.

Ella Post was seated by a willowy potted plant that grew out of a metal bucket. Her range of vision covered both her husband and missus Gregory as they faced each other, him on the divan, her in a small stuffed wicker chair. The edges of their profiles were gilded by the window's backlight.

"Well, I've enjoyed our talk," Elizabeth Gregory said, "but you'll have to choose somewhere else to dwell. I can't provide rooms for you here."

"It isn't a matter of choice with us, missus Gregory," Ella interrupted. "We've been told Charles will not live out the year. We were strongly advised to find other quarters. It's that simple and dreadful."

"Missus Post, look around you, my house is not large enough as it is. I have five children. This is no place for boarders or I would take you, believe me." She was portly, gray haired, and had a dark mole at the corner of her mouth. From time to time she touched it, let her finger remain over it. Her dress was a black silk sacque, loose fitting, with wide sleeves, no lace or fringes or ribbons.

"Maybe if your youngsters could move in together for a little while, a few months, until I'm up and around again." Charles' voice had a mild whine threaded through it. He added hastily, "I'm not coming here to die, if that is what you think. Be assured, it won't happen. I need your help, beyond a mere place to stay."

"Oh, it will happen, mister Post, if you don't mind my saying so, death will come to each of us, you can be certain."

Cattle die and kindred die. We also die. The line of Nordic poetry limped through his memory. "I've endured a great deal, missus Gregory. It would take hours to tell you about it. For the past months I've lived on bean sprouts and yogurt and hardcooked bread, ate enough raw fibre to explode a horse, drunk enough water and fruit juice to fill Lake Michigan, soaked up enough sun to scorch that same lake into a desert. I've slept with the windows open in winter, exercised my limbs until they were numb, hobbled on crutches, canes, and done everything I was told to do."

He sighed forlornly, hands supplicating, eyes pleading. "Then I'm told, like an old Eskimo, go out and lie down on an ice floe and die and be done with it." Palms cracking sharply against his thighs, chin jutting grimly. "Well, missus Gregory, I refuse to accept the verdict, even if a hospital full of doctors is the jury. But if you turn me down, you may make their prediction come true after all."

Missus Gregory looked across at Ella. "Who did you say sent you?"

"Charles' aunt in Springfield, Illinois, missus Gregory. I don't think you would recognize her name. She is one of his mother's sisters."

"My aunt is a practitioner of your religion," he confided. "Friends in her church spoke about you and advised us to seek you out."

The older woman glanced around the room as if to reassure herself she wasn't hallucinating, searching for words to dissuade this persistent, damaged man who had come into her home on walking canes, leaving a wheelchair parked at the bottom of the front porch steps. He wanted lodging, treatment, and expected to delay payment for expenses until some undesignated date in the future when his wife supposedly would inherit a small trust fund.

"You said you own land in Texas?" She waited for Post's almost convulsive wag of head. "Then I must confess, I'm puzzled about your state of financial distress."

Ella explained. "It was an investment that didn't turn out as we had hoped."

"Cost us everything," Post admitted. "My parents too, lost so much." His voice wavered. "Almost everything they had."

"Does that trouble you, mister Post?"

He prosecuted himself for the millionth time. "It hounds me always. It never goes away for a moment."

Fingertip pressing the mole. "What do you know of Christian Science, mister Post?"

"I know it is my last hope."

"You're looking for a miracle."

"I'm looking for Christian help."

"You said pain causes people to become mean. Do you really believe that?"

"My husband isn't mean, missus Gregory, or vicious. He is just ill. Very, very ill."

Missus Gregory wondered if the Lord was testing her. Maybe. Maybe nothing of the kind. The Lord did not often send a dove or a blinding lightning bolt with a message anymore. She got up from her chair, went to Charles.

"I see no spiteful, vindictive man before me. You are not very convincing proof of your own theory."

"Give me time. I'm working on it." He smiled at her.

Not meaning to, she laughed with genuine humor. "What is it you really want, mister Post?"

"I've told you. A room for me and my family, and a chance to learn about the teachings and practices of Christian Science. They've been said to restore a person's health. I need that very much."

"What else is it you want?"

Montaigne's essay sidled into Charles' mind like a bright, shy child entering a room full of talkative adults. He saw a sentence on the printed page in absolute clarity, mouthed it softly: *"No wind favors him who has no destined port."*

"I'm sorry, mister Post, I didn't hear you."

Ella bent forward, listened intently. "Neither did I, Charles."

"I said I'd like to have an empire like John Harvey Kellogg's."

Ella watched Post in bewilderment. She had never known him to admit such an ambition.

"That's a very questionable aim for eternity, a thing entirely of this world." Missus Gregory's voice was slow and husky.

"I live in this world, missus Gregory, and I will for many more years. I want wealth, power, all the benefits and privileges that go with it. But I don't expect it to fall into my hands like an overripe apple off a tree. I am willing to work for it, to make all but the most unreasonable sacrifices to get it, perhaps even connive a little. I don't want to miss the gold ring and grab the brass one by mistake again."

He resettled on the very edge of the divan, his arms spilling across his knees, head up, concentrating his attention on Elizabeth Gregory. She was warmed by a sudden awareness that Charles Post was as handsome a man as she had seen, despite his drawn face and frail body.

"But in the same pursuit, dear lady, I hope I might bring about something good, some worthwhile progress to the gain of other people. Those aren't words to impress or sway you. If I get the chance, I'll prove them."

Feeling the intensity of his argument like heat from a bonfire she retreated to the window, noticed the wheelchair sitting dull and cold at the corner of the front porch just beyond the steps.

"In your estimation you truly believe that the earthly possession of an empire, as you call it, is worth aspiring to?"

"Every man yearns for it, and every man dishonestly pretends not to. I openly admit I want it."

Beyond the lightly drifting curtains, a carnival of red and yellow leaves swirled across the yard.

"And somehow I will have it," Charles Post said gently. "This town, Battle Creek, will see to it, with its mists and cool skies and deep snows and summer suns that caress like a mother's touch. It's the reason we came here." Voice failing, lips moving in mute expression. "It's the reason."

PART THREE

We boil at different degrees.
Ralph Waldo Emerson

29

MARCH 1893

"POST is working on a coffee drink. People say he took it straight from our formula, doctor."

"Don't let it worry you, Will, he's a salesman, not a medical man." Doctor Kellogg lifted an iron-stone bowl from a cabinet by the sink in the San's experimental kitchen. "Whatever he concocts won't go far without credentials, won't have the credence of our caramel coffee. Post will soon be out of business and forgotten."

He set the bowl on a table that looked like a butcher's block, worn smooth and silky from years of being scrubbed with borax.

Will filled the bowl with the contents of a pan from the stove, then fastened a wire strainer over the bowl's mouth and drained the liquid off the soaked raw wheat. He thought of the doctor's excitement those many months ago, babbling about an idea he claimed came to him in a dream. He had been instructed to go with John Harvey on a sunrise bicycle ride around the grounds. He did not own one of those two-wheeled contraptions that fascinated the doctor so much, and more to the point, he did not know how to ride one, so he'd agreed to trot alongside the peddling physician, notebook and pencil at the ready in case anything essential had to be recorded. So while one man breathed easily, legs churning on the wooden pedals, the other ran, breathing strenuously as they circled the Sanitarium's walkways for the fourth time. Will's feet hit the hardpacked ground with increasingly painful jolts as he sweated under his wool coat and vest, glad he hadn't worn an overcoat.

"Last night, I dreamt we might make wheat into very, very thin wafers," the doctor had announced, pedaling. "The impact of it woke me at four and I've thought about it every minute since. Good grief, Will, just imagine it, a wheat wafer, thin, chewable, digestible. A form to answer every objection against any other grain cereals we've produced. A flake. A flake, Will. It would be revolutionary."

"And you've a way to make this..." he hesitated on the word, "...flake?" Wisps of breath whisked away as he ran.

"I'm reasonably certain that if we boil the wheat, roll it out, mash it to a paperboard thickness, then crumble it after baking, we will have our answer."

Their first attempt had fallen apart before they could lift it onto the baking sheet. A year later, their eleventh try, they aerated some boiled grain.

It was a mess. They kept trying. Baked, it shattered into clods, heavy and thick as soaked clay. Boiled, it became a sticky, uncontrollable wad.

Now, attempt number eighteen. Will dumped the bowl, put the rolling pin on the soaked wheat, leaned onto it, using the wooden cylinder to mash the water-puffed grains, hearing their hulls crunch and shatter. He raised the rolling pin. Beneath it, and clinging to it, the wheat hulls were a debris of fragments and slivers, and the grain's interior was a porridge, impossible to smooth, no good for baking. When Will pitched it in the garbage tin at the back door, the doctor's face showed none of the frustration he felt.

Will's belly was burning and he looked forward to the glass of buttermilk Puss would give him when he reached home, but he refused to ask the doctor about his condition, not wanting a lecture on bad eating habits. He glanced at one of the open cupboards where a clock in an iron case with a statue of a deer on top was ticking quietly. Eleven fifteen. He hoped John Harvey did not start another test.

"Let's put these things away and get some rest," came the answer to his quiet prayer.

Together they carried utensils and cooking containers to a wooden sink. At sunrise, someone on the San's staff would scour and scrub and put everything back in its place.

"I paid the laboratory aide his fifty dollars, as you instructed, doctor. You now own the peanut butter mistake."

"It was a propitious finding, not a mistake. I'll admit patients haven't taken to it as I hoped they might. Still in all, it was worth the price, and it *will* catch on, I believe."

"The man burned that batch of peanuts," Will posited. "He shouldn't have been paid for a mistake."

John Harvey jutted both lips, adjusted his tie in the kitchen mirror above the sink. "He mashed those overcooked peanuts, I expect, in an attempt to hide them. It may all have been in error but he had the good sense to call my attention to an unexpected result. His judgement merited a reward."

Will retreated from the doctor's illogic, then said, "The peanut butter might be tastier if we *roasted* the peanuts. I would advise we try it."

"Steaming is healthful. We'll continue steaming," John Harvey said.

Will resurrected his earlier worry. "Post can steal the coffee formula from under our noses. We made it, but he could end up with it. He's started that health resort. An Inn. How could a man with no money come up so fast?"

John Harvey laughed lightly. "Stop worrying. There is no marketplace for what mister Post hopes to devise. We have difficulty getting our patients to use our own coffee substitute. Besides, the formula actually belongs to Ella, and she certainly isn't worried about Post doing anything with it."

"She should be."

"Will, it was *you* who recommended Charles Post be allowed to nose around our kitchens."

"No, I didn't recommend. I told you he asked if he could. You said 'why not?'"

John Harvey's mouth opened in a small yawn. "So what? Let Post play at his game a few months, his health farm, he will fail soon enough and pack his belongings and leave Battle Creek. A pity we did him a world of good, and his recuperation should be to our credit, but goes to the misguided ministrations of the Christian Scientists, as Post now claims."

A door at the far side of the kitchen opened slowly and Ella came in. Sadness eddied in her eyes.

"Ella..." the doctor began, eyebrows high with question.

She touched a finger to his lips.

"John, your mother died a few minutes ago."

CHARLES Post surveyed again the interior of the Dime Tabernacle, its endless rows of pews, the elevated stage down front with the huge triptych stained-glass window placed directly behind the pulpit for dramatic effect. He looked at the massive pipe organ in its alcove at the base of the stage.

"Quite a shrine," he whispered to Ella who walked ahead of him as they pushed along toward the front doors with the throng of other spectators and mourners. To a whiskered ancient behind him he asked, "How many people can it hold? Got a guess?"

"No guess to it. It was wrote in the Journal when it was built." The old man's beard and moustache moved and the words swept out dryly, like sawdust from a mill floor. "Takes three thousand in comfort. Probably two or three hunnerd more'n that was here, countin them up in the balcony and all them chairs in the aisles."

"The Adventists, I imagine," Ella said, leaning around her husband, "must be the top rung of the religious ladder in Battle Creek."

The whiskered old man glared at her as if she had spit on the floor but he made no reply. Post picked up the small talk. "I heard the building is named for the nickels and dimes collected to pay for its construction. People with money put in dollars, the children and poor put in coins."

The old man was annoyed. "They's a lot more to it than that."

Post said, "They probably named it the Dime Tabernacle because the Nickel Tabernacle would've been too hard to pronounce."

The old man grunted, then shuffled and pushed to get around them, tossing a glance that contained rattlesnake venom. He hurried down the outside steps and was gone. Post nodded to the Ordways, Barneys, Stetlers, Farleys, prominent families among the leading. Will and John Harvey Kellogg and their families, along with sisters Clara Belle, Laura, Emma, and brother Preston moved as one, marching in cadence. He edged in front of them, concentrating his attention on John Harvey.

"I'm sorry, doctor Kellogg, for your grief. Your mother must have been a wonderful woman."

"Thank you, mister Post." Clear gaze, no huskiness of voice, a man now accustomed to death, demonstrating a treestump stolidity that would have been mistaken for dullness in other men. He made a preliminary step forward, intending to go on, then hesitated. "Good of you to be here, sir."

The others passed without comment. Only Will looked directly at Post as if noticing a picture hanging askance in someone's house; bothersome, but not his to straighten. His face was crumpled with grief like a newspaper wadded, then smoothed out. Beneath his red-ringed eyes were half-moons of insomnia the color of loss.

30

JUNE 1893

JOHN Harvey Kellogg loved his Sanitarium but he delighted in those occasional forays that distanced him from the San for a week, not forgetting it, just letting it go to the back of his mind. Ella knew he never really shucked the business of diets and surgery and patients and publishing even for a day, because most of his travel time was spent with affairs that had to do with the San or one of its enterprises.

Today was different. A rare day. They had an early breakfast in their Leland hotel room in downtown Chicago, munching on foods brought along — graham bread, a variety of nuts, apples and apricots.

Now the rented buggy rolled along State Street, headed for the World's Columbian Exposition, so named in honor of Christopher Columbus in a monumental political gesture to the Italian population of Chicago. The morning was pure June, the climbing sun made slashes of crisp light between the shadows of buildings and topped the highest floors with a wash of brightness.

Ella still was imbued with the satisfaction, the glow of evangelism that was spawned by the visit the previous day to their fledgling medical missionary college out on Wabash. It could be said the medical college was chipped out of a diamond mine. It came in the form of a $40,000 gift finagled by John Harvey from the mine's owner, a Sanitarium patient he helped to recover from malaria and dysentery. Its doors had opened just this year in a neighborhood where store windows frowned morbidly inward on abandoned rooms; a neighborhood where food was a luxury pilfered from garbage cans in a better part of town; a neighborhood where children cried through the night from cold or hunger or dying. In the long, narrow room in the crusty old building, a current of wretched humanity flooded in each day for medicine, food, and a temporary place to rest. It had been rewarding to the Kellogg's to see their college's good work.

John Harvey hugged Ella to him as the buggy jounced along the brick street.

"Dear, I'm delighted we decided to do this, just enjoy ourselves today and catch a bit of the lighter side of life. Besides, it's proper and fitting after the good meeting with mister Perky."

"You truly think his machine will help you find the answer to your wheat flake, don't you, John?"

"It may, but it has many other possibilities as well." Embracing her tightly enough to bring a squeal. "When Perky met me at the train depot he could hardly throttle his excitement."

"He obviously thinks you can be of valuable assistance by testing and using..."

"Hah! He wanted to sell me an even dozen of his invention, that is what he hoped for at first."

"And you may buy them?"

"It's a novel device, mostly rollers. The wheat comes out between the grooves of the rollers in long strings. He refers to the product as shredded wheat biscuits."

"So he will have a shredding machine waiting when we return to Battle Creek?"

"It is virtually guaranteed. We even went over the details with his major stockholder, mister Harry James, a power figure in the City Gas Company. We were finishing up, had made our agreement, then Perky inquired very particularly as to how we market our foods, how we distribute them. I thought it was mere curiosity, but now, on reflection, I'm not so sure."

Ella knew he was battling with an unwelcome premonition so she said, "That's probably all it was, idle curiosity."

"You're right, dear, as usual." He polished his palms against each other and whistled at the driver: "Put some speed on, man, there's an exposition to be visited."

JOHN Harvey and Ella spent the rest of the day in a world of engineered art and ingenuity, an extravaganza that had taken six thousand committee members and three years of planning to bring together. Hundreds of miles of boulevards and lanes spanned out between dynamically shaped buildings, circled the topaz green and blue lagoons that twinkled across the Fairgrounds.

"This is utterly delightful, Ella. The buildings are from Olympus, look at the domes, the pinnacles," he said, arms outstretched, spinning his body like a pinwheel in a breeze, much to the amusement of more sedate passers-by. "I've never in my life witnessed such an array of electrical, industrial, artistic creations. Why, we could wander here for days, what an overwhelming testimony to the inventiveness of man."

"And woman," Ella amplified the praise.

Incandescent lighting everywhere. Gondola boats floated like leaves on the lighted water at the Grand Court. Fountains shot their colored streams 50 feet high. Colossal naval cannons and hydraulic presses weighing several tons loomed, and an intramural train, streamlined as if for a leap into outer space, propelled people in its shiny shell on its electrified center rail at breathtaking velocities of 25 miles per hour.

On the Midway, John Harvey cajoled Ella into entering one of the 36 glass-enclosed cabins of the world's first Ferris wheel. The circular frame grinded into action, overcame inertia, picked up speed, swooped its captives 265 feet into the air, up and around and down and up again, high above the panorama of buildings, miniaturizing them through distance, turning the spectators into drifting specks of color. At the finish of the ride, as she walked down the exit ramp on shaky legs, her fingers fretting the lace edges of her dainty parasol, she glowered, "Never again, John."

He laughed. "It was a genuine thrill, dear. I'm delighted you enjoyed it."

WHEN the Kelloggs left Chicago by train they were tired but refreshed. They heard none of the rumblings of the financial depression that was invading the city, stabbing even at the affluent areas where it had not been felt before. Jobs failing, businesses closing, money departing on swift invisible wings. John Harvey and Ella had their minds on the wonders of the Columbian Exhibition, the early success of the missionary college, and the work they had left undone at the Sanitarium. He especially anticipated the delivery of Perky's wheat rolling machine, a device that could shift the hospital's food productions into higher efficiency. John Harvey didn't yet know that the machine would never arrive. Its absence would slow his quest, but only momentarily.

31

FEBRUARY 1894

LEW Reesner and Sam Gamble weren't aware that the two whores were grateful the men were drunk. It meant less work for the working women, especially if the bastards passed out.

The room in Nellie's was no different from the other six on the same floor. Strictly utilitarian. An empty pitcher and a half basin of water decorated the rickety bureau. There was, of course, a bed.

Sam was sprawled on a mattress that had taken a lot of abuse in the interest of cushioning the women's tailends. He had donned the bottom of his longjohns when Lew and Flora barged in. He wasn't modest, just finished for the moment. There was no reason to get dressed. Both of his muscular legs were across Francine's skinny thighs. Her varicosed legs were like pieces of bleached driftwood dumped by the tide. His weight pinned her beside him on the stained, rumpled sheet while he took long swallows from a whiskey bottle Lew had brought along.

"Shit, Sam, you're too damned thirsty after workin so hard." Then, "Jesus, we could hear you two all the way down the hall." Lew giggled idiotically, leaning against the bed's railing, his shirt unbuttoned, nothing else on. He held Flora close with an arm around her, one hand fondling her saggy breasts. Every few minutes a prolonged yawn stretched her face.

Sam tossed him the bottle, spewing whiskey across the floor from its uncorked neck. Lew snatched the projectile in midair. "Sam, you can goddamn die of thirst next time I bring you anything." Angry, raisin eyes verged on mayhem. "Damned stuff costs too much you be throwin it away."

"Close that door when you go out. Me and Francine gonna get busy again in about one minute." He joggled his crotch and brayed with laughter. Francine examined her fingernails.

Lew arched over the bed rail, showed Sam his gabrous scalp, dull and red-streaked. He slapped Sam's naked foot, hard. "You gonna make like you got that little hotsy-tot from the hospital, ain't you? That's what you so lustful about, why you couldn't hardly wait to get here."

"Hey, what's he sayin'?" Francine raised up on her elbow, feigned jealousy, forgetting for a minute she was with cheap Sam who never gave a girl an extra dollar no matter what she did for him.

"Who gives a shit? Shut yer mouth." His hand covered her face, shoved her down onto the grimy pillow. Then, to Lew: "And you keep *your* mouth shut, too."

Lew's lips peeled like a coyote readying to snap. He liked scratching Sam's sore spot. "That was her you pertended not to see comin out Hoffmaster's dry goods yesstidy, weren't it? You was doin a good job of just about rubbin gainst her and actin like you din't know she was nowhere in town."

Flora shifted her weight onto one broad hip. "Come on, Lew, let's us go downstairs, get some sweet water to mix with that whiskey, what they is left. Sam spilt most of it." She did not want to return to the room with Lew. She wanted to get her two dollars, find the next customer. Flora didn't like the violent wiry man with his bald, scarred head and his puffy eye with the skin sloughed down, peering out like a snake in a rockpile.

"I didn't give her a nod," Sam's face was impassive. "Looked other way, let her know I ain't in no lather."

"That's pure cowshit! You start droolin soon's you see her." He scraped his bristly chin with a chipped fingernail while a thought cleared the hedgerows in his brain. "You spose them high minded women wash theirselves all over, you know, so they smell good wherever you touch em?"

"You won't ever know. Only female women you gonna get, Reesner, whores with no teeth. Me, I got higher aspersions."

Flora came out of her stupor, personally insulted. "Hey, piss on you. I got my teeth. Who you think you are?" Snarling, she pulled away from Lew. "I ain't standin around for that crap talk, tell him, Lew."

Lew's arm flashed around her waist, jammed her against him with an impact of hipbones and ribs that could fracture an anvil. Fright streaked up her neck like mercury in a July thermometer. "Shut yer mouth. I'm about ready to kick your ass out that window, watch you bounce on the street down there."

Francine rolled onto her side, broke wind. Her pinched, narrow face stared hatefully at the ceiling. "We going to do some more business, Sam, or not? I got to pee."

Her remark brought wheezy giggles from Lew. Flora joined in, trying to get on better terms.

"Damn you, Sam, lemme up or I'll do it on you."

He grabbed a handful of her tangled brown hair, pulled her against his chest. "Don't say anythin else, you hear me?"

Lew sniggered, hugging Flora now that she was almost back in good graces, her enjoying all of this because it killed time. "I'd like to see you poke that pink-ear woman, all I heard outa you for three years'n more. I think you're scairt of that little doctor fart of hern."

"Not scared of anyone, includin you, Reesner."

"You mean doctor Kellogg, don't you?" Flora blurted. "He's the only doctor you'd call a little fart, ain't that right?"

"For a whore, you're too goddamned nosy," Lew whispered. He shifted the bottle to his other side, and hit Flora with his calloused fist, the oversized knuckles digging into her face, splitting the skin, smashing the cheekbone and rebounding into the side of her nose, flushing her nostrils with a gusher of blood. She staggered sideways, tottered against the wall, folded up and slid to the floor, the discharge from her nose bubbling and running off of her chin onto her chemise.

Francine shoved Sam away, leaped off the bed, dodged a restraining hand by Gamble. The soiled bedsheet went with her, half wrapped around her. She screamed, "My God, the sonbitch tried to kill Flora, hit her hard nuff to kill her. You crazy sonbitch."

She knelt beside Flora, cleaning away blood with the sheet, helping her friend struggle to her feet. They moved awkwardly toward the door, Francine with an arm around Flora's shoulders, watching Lew and Sam with alarm bordering on panic. Easing out into the hall, Francine paused to hurl a threat: "Nellie's men will break ever bone in your dirty body, you crazy sonbitch."Lew headed for the door and she slammed it fiercely, retreating.

Sam was squirming into his pants. "That was dumb, bustin old Flora cause you was ticked at me. They'll be hell to pay." He plunged bare feet into his boots, snatched his shirt from the floor. "You better get your clothes cause them whores goin to have a bunch after us. We better be gone."

"To hell with them."

"We can get down the back stairs before they figure it out."

Lew giggled, threw the empty whiskey bottle on the bed, began buttoning his shirt. "Left my pants in the other room. I'll see you to Burley's pretty soon."

LEW heard the men on the stairs, then in the hall, then outside the door. Before they crashed into the room, he opened the door and grabbed the surprised, wide-eyed figure whose hand was already twisting the doorknob. He whirled him into the room by his coat lapels like two Gypsy dancers spinning around a campfire. Lew waited for the startled face to appear like a number coming up on a roulette wheel. His fist grazed the man's chin, brought a sharp, sickening click as a jawbone twisted in its sockets. Lew swung his other fist from down low, knuckles connecting at the side of the man's mouth, blood fluming, the head snapping.

That's when the other two men got into the fray. The first one slammed a numbing crash to Lew's temple, taking in the top of the ear, tearing it the way cloth tears. Lew's head rang like a dinner bell in hell and he knew instinctively the man was using a metal pipe or was wearing a steel band across his fist. He was sober now, the whiskey all shifted to malevolent, murderous energy. He bore in on the one who hit him, drove his fists into a too-soft abdomen. The man grunted in pain, falling to his knees.

The third man had maneuvered well for position. The cocked ballbat he carried now blurred through the air, connected solidly with Lew's arm at the shoulder. Lew swayed dizzily. A defenseless target. He saw the metal-encased fist coming at his eyes, closed them just before an iron jackass kicked him with enough force to fell a small tree.

It seemed to Lew he was lifted lightly and easily, allowed to float unimpeded toward the wall, landed like cotton fluff on the floor beside the bed, there by the open window where a cool and wonderful breeze drifted in from the street two floors below.

AFTER nearly an hour in Burley's tavern, Gamble was convinced Lew wasn't coming. Not that he minded. He'd had enough of him for one night.

He pulled in the delicious smoke from his cigarillo, thought to himself, Jesus! He hit Flora right in the goddamned face for nothing. Smashed her up good. The guy ought to be in John Harvey's sanitarium getting hisself treated. He's nuts.

In the street there was a commotion and a fire wagon hurtled by, its team of horses straining and blowing so hard Sam could hear them expelling air all the way inside Burley's saloon. The brass bell atop the wagon was clanging like the end of the world, the driver whipping his horses as if he was in a fairgrounds race while all the county girls were watching admiringly.

From where he sat, Sam could see the firemen hanging on the wagon's sides, waving and shouting at the people along the walks. Then Burley's crowd moved from bar and table to the dirt-streaked front window to watch, blocking Sam's view. A few men hurried out front for a better look, carrying their drinks with them.

"Fire at Nellie's!"

"The whorehouse is on fire, God Almighty!"

"Nellie's always was a hot place!"

Laughter.

Lew edged through the doorway, moving with peculiar caution between the men as they made a path for him. At Gamble's table he smiled out of his raw, hairless face. The puckered eye was closed and purple and pinkish. Blood was matted over the top half of one ear and there was a blue lump above the bridge of his nose. His left arm was as rigid as a wagon tree, jutting forward in a mock handshake. He sat gingerly in a chair, the way a cat lowers itself onto a rug.

"Nell's men caught you didn't they?"

"I got one of them bastards, busted the first one's jaw. Others come at me from behind. Had a ballbat, sonsabitches. Hauled me down the steps, threw me off the front porch like a bag o' beans."

Sam listened, sipped his whiskey, while Lew's open eye watched him thirstily.

"Broke my arm, can't move it. Don't hurt, though, feels like a old log hangin there."

"Hell, you ought to be over to Nichols hospital..."

"Walked up for a whiskey. If you'll get it."

Sam caught Burley's attention, motioned with his cigarillo for two drinks.

"I fixed them sonsabitches real purty."

"What'd you do, piss on Nell's winter tulips?"

Lew's useable eye winked and he slumped in the chair. "Found me some kerosene, dosed up the back porch, set it afire."

"Jesus, Lew." Sam leaned across the table, talking low, to be certain no one overheard. "Anybody see you?"

"I don't give a shit. The dirty sonsabitches hadda use a ballbat." Then, loudly to Burley, "You gonna bring us them drinks?"

At that moment two policemen pushed their way through the stragglers in the open door. They stopped and surveyed the room, slowly wended around the islands of worn tables like warships on a king's mission, shiny buttons and shields playing with the lights from overhead, catching and tossing them. Burley had stopped pouring Lew's drink, waiting now, watching.

The policemen's bowl-shaped hard helmets were white and contrasted with their dark, knee-length coats like snow atop two black gate posts. Both men had thick, drooping moustaches and tired, serious faces. The taller one leveled a billyclub at his target. "Lew, you set fire to Nellie's boarding house..."

"Boarding house?" Lew asked incredulously.

"Got five people seen you," officer Barnes said.

"Whores and Nell's boys."

"Sister White and doc Kellogg and his wife seen you, they was coming back from across town." Barnes paused, drew a breath as if hating to go on. "And reverend Doubleday and his missus, they seen you, too."

The other policeman moved his bulk noisily, purposefully. "Let's go, Lew. No trouble now, you're in no condition."

"Let him have a whiskey first, Barnes," Gamble entreated. "Then he'll go with you, no trouble."

"He's going anyway," the other officer said.

"How about it, Barnes?" Lew asked.

Barnes nodded and lowered his billyclub, motioned to Burley who had kept an eye on the proceedings.

Gamble snuffed his cigarillo under a bootheel. "You sure sneaked real quiet, didn't you, Lew? I always said you had a pimple for a brain."

32

HER heels clicked noisily on the rear stairs of the San's main wing. Patients and workers were asleep, only a few nurses on duty at strategic stations. The building was quiet, its deep corridors resonant with small echoes.

Before she had left the experimental kitchen and went down for a general check of the main desk, Ella had told Will to go home at eleven thirty, a half hour from now. John Harvey had looked in before eleven, dressed in his loincloth, drenched after a workout in the gym, saying he would be in his office if they needed him.

She climbed toward the second floor, keeping a firm grasp on the curving, brass-capped bannister to pull herself along. Her tired eyes were fixed on the placement of each foot on the polished stair immediately ahead.

"Better look up or you'll run into somebody."

Gamble's hoarse voice was an electric jolt, whipping her head erect, hurling lethargy away like a stone from a slingshot.

"What are you doing here?" Annoyed. Unsettled.

"Hey, now, that ain't no way to greet a friend. Everbody's got feelings, I always say. Don't pay to make 'em feel spit on." He leaned against the railing in an imperious stance, tight crotched pants, an unlit cigarillo in the corner of his mouth, wool cap haphazardly cocked on the back of his head.

"The hospital is closed at this hour, mister Gamble. Leave or I'll call the attendants." A pure bluff. She was at a remote end of the main building, far from the floor's central nightdesk and there was little chance of anyone happening by.

His bushy eyebrows hiked, pleating his forehead. "Purty late. You comin or goin?"

"Mister Gamble, I've been working with the doctor's brother in the kitchen. He'll be following along any minute, probably with doctor Kellogg."

"I saw the doctor a while back, come up these stairs in them little underpants of his, didn't even notice me. I figured you'd be along eventual."

He bared stained teeth, looking frighteningly feral. The first traces of panic perked into Ella's throat.

"I'm surprised little old Will's got time for anythin' more'n them bowls of oyster soup at Webb's. Must be a lucky man, and fast too, able to work next to a woman like you."

"What's this about oysters?" She hated to ask, hated wanting to know. "You say he's...Will is...eating at Webb's diner?"

"You find that interestin', do you?" When she did not respond he said, "You might be surprised what I know, could tell you, do for you. Might get all het up about things you ain't imagined for years, or never." He grinned through the scraggly, droopy moustache. "Cept in your bed at night in the dark, missus Kellogg."

The spell was broken. Her eyes flashed hard and merciless with more fight in them than she could have delivered.

"You've been drinking, mister Gamble."

"Some, but not too much." A hint of promise.

Gamble straightened away from the bannister, his pelvis was thrust forward, his hands loose at his sides. "What'd you think if I told you I come just to see you?" A trickle of spittle leaked from the corner of his mouth. Ella could smell his whiskey breath.

"Don't cause trouble for yourself, I assure you it would be severe trouble."

"My, how concerned and courteous we got. I'll be damned if you ain't learnin some manners. Tell me, when you and that spitball brother-in-law is working together, he ever try to grab you, you know, get his hands on you?" He reached for her abruptly. "Like this?"

She quickly stepped back and down, away from him. He grabbed the bannister to keep his balance, said "Whoops, Whoops," in little teasing chirps. Her heart was thudding in her chest and she felt sweat cascading under her dress as if she had just exercised vigorously.

"Please leave." The words squeaked out, her hand slid along the bannister as she forced her legs not to fold under her.

Gamble pushed himself upright, brought an outstretched hand around in a smooth motion, plucked the cigarillo from his mouth, pointed it at her, close enough for her to smell its sour odor. "Them pink ears of yours makes me think of all kinds of things about you. I 'spect you got other things prettier'n a man could dream."

"You're sickening. You turn my stomach. You're old and loathsome..."

"Hold up there, spitfire. I ain't but a year or two more'n that puff you married. I'm one helluvalot more experienced, though, specially in things that count."

His fingers abraded her cheek like steelwool. They formed a sandpaper cup around her ear, moved down across her neck. Her power of motion was frozen. Her body shook so badly her teeth clattered. The hand became remarkably delicate in its touch, a powder puff brushing her shoulder, moving lower. Revulsion gorged in her brain. The buttons were being unfastened at her collar. The top one, now another. Slowly, her dress parted as if in a fog-drenched dream, until she sensed rather than saw the stark lacy top of her petticoat revealed.

"They any empty rooms around here?"

Now his fingertips were prickly shoots of cat brier scraping her bare collarbone.

With enormous effort she wrenched her hands from the bannister, sped down the steps, tripping, her long heavy skirts tangling, hindering. She nearly fell, cleared two steps, three, four at a time, broke free of the stairwell, stopped to gasp air, holding the railing for support. She heard no sounds of pursuit. Her nerve tremulously crept back, bringing fresh anger borne of safety. She hurled a warning up through the gloom of the twisting stairway.

"Don't come near me again you filthy animal."

My God, she heard footsteps coming down. Gamble's boots rang on the wooden stairs. Panic sent her into new flight. She rushed along the corridor, through the empty side hall to another stairs, hurried upward, gulping oxygen, her mind not listening for Gamble, hearing only his shouted threats rolling behind her like a dark tidal wave.

"Bitch! Teaser! You say anything...I spread it you lured me...tempted me..." The voice faded, "...baited me."

Ella ran without direction, trying to escape. When she finally stopped, drained of strength, winded, there was only the muted clatter of pans and utensils being dumped into a sink in the experimental kitchen where Will was shutting down. She was in the brief hallway that paralleled the kitchen area, but she did not recall going there. Her hand shakily skimmed the several buttons that were undone at the top of her dress, came to rest on the last loose one. Her other hand found the doorknob, turned it reluctantly. When the door opened, and Will looked up from a low shelf where he was arranging canisters, she squeezed inside the room as though she were sleep walking.

"ELLA." An observation not a question.

"Sam Gamble just attacked me on the stairwell." Her voice sounded hollow and unfamiliar to her as though someone else was speaking through her. The door snicked closed behind her, a startling little noise in the stillness. "He didn't actually...I mean, he *tried* to attack me, but nothing...he's been drinking and he's out of his head. He grabbed at me..." She dropped the sentence futilely.

Will observed the open buttons of her dress, his disapproval swiping over her as palpably as if it were a hemp rope dragged against her skin. "I'll call for the attendants," he said without inflection.

"No!" The word screaked out of her in a fury, freezing his hand as it touched the intercom. She had to force control into her vocal chords, then she spoke quietly, hastily, running on too long. Head drooping, fingers over her mouth. "I don't want anyone else involved, it's terrible and it embarrasses me and I don't want others to know about it, so I want you to find him and order him out of the San." She paused for a breath, squeezed authority into her eyes, raised them to meet his. "Please do it this minute."

"Gamble isn't the sort I can just 'order out.' Not without help. Especially not if he's drunk."

She everted her strategy, went to a posture and expression of penitence. "You don't seem to understand. This horrid incident will be gossiped throughout the hospital if you alert half the night staff. Lies would warp the facts; disgrace John Harvey, me, all of us."

"I can't fathom your reasoning, Ella. Even if I could locate Gamble he most certainly would fight. That would bring other people on the run. And I'd only manage to get myself hurt."

She insinuated an emphatic note into her request: "You're in charge. You find him, make him leave." Growing malice tinted her voice: "John Harvey would confront Gamble without hesitation, if he were here."

"Then call the doctor."

"I can't. I don't want him to know."

Will answered resistantly: "You want *no one* to know."

"That's what I've been saying." The exasperation of it made her sick to her stomach. This man was an employee. Why in the world wouldn't he do as he was instructed? She straightened, arms stiff at her sides in a posture of command. "There's no need for this matter to go further. Please do as I've asked and take care of Gamble yourself."

"I said I can't, Ella. Besides, in all likelihood, he's long gone."

She felt the sharp, quick pain of tears prickling around the edges of her eyes. Her hand jumped to the unbuttoned lapels of her dress, crushed them together. "I never realized you were such a...a..."

"Coward?" he asked wryly. "How about 'sensible' or 'cautious?'"

She regarded him with what she hoped was visible contempt. His impudence was unforgivable, as raw as sewage. So she turned abruptly, fumbled with the latch, slammed the door after her.

THE next day, against her judgement, but giving in to a persistent wish to have the whole matter clarified, she went to her brother-in-law's cluttered little office. "Will, I acted foolishly last night," she said immediately. "I would appreciate your confidentiality."

"You have my word, Ella, your misfortunate situation will never be discussed by me. I will say nothing to anyone. Especially not my brother." He was in shirtsleeves, vest unbuttoned, reading glasses on his nose, ink pen in hand. "He might think I handled it poorly."

"So it's fear, not decency that prompts you."

"I'm a realist, Ella. You and doctor Kellogg see me differently." He removed his glasses, held them so tightly his hand shook. His eyes wandered the office, traveled its walls and corners. "To you I am a dependent, servile toady. Loyal to the San and its leaders at any personal cost. Maybe I am all those things, maybe not. But I am practical. Last night you were upset. You plainly had been through something very trying. I offered to do what I thought best. You wanted a different course of action. I think we should forget the entire event."

Her hands knotted into fists. She gave him a smile that stopped entirely below her nostrils. "How noble of you. I hope you enjoy your little minute of superiority."

He replied remotely, "Why do you attack me? I've done nothing to you."

"Nor *for* me, I might add."

"You see, Ella, how quickly the blame is shifted? I'm already at fault."

As she had done the night before, she left his office seething, and determined that John Harvey would hear about brother Will's patronage of Webb's diner. She also would tell John Harvey about Sam Gamble because she was afraid that he might physically harm her the next time. John Harvey could crush that possibility. She hurried down the hall, already forming the sentences in her mind that she would speak to her husband.

33

THE appendectomy was scheduled an hour ago. Doctor Kellogg hustled into the room with a jolly expression that belied the anger swimming darkly just below the surface. Brother Will had been directed to meet him here right after the operation and this time, the doctor swore, he would fire him, brother or not. "After the muddle he made with the peanut butter, nearly ruining it as a food," he muttered, "you'd expect he would be all the more careful. What he's done now is intolerable."

John Harvey strode past the nurse and the two assistant physicians.

"Hello, Arnold," he said to his patient. "you look fit enough for a bike ride with me this morning."

Arnold's answer was a spasm of facial muscles. He lay on his back on a table that was angled across the corner to maximize the light from both windows, each glazed with winter frosting. His lips rolled inward with pain. Kellogg rested a hand on the man's sheetclad chest.

"We'll have you well and pedaling that speedy two wheeler of yours in no time."

He removed the coverlet, pressed with a finger near the man's umbilicus, released the pressure abruptly, inspired a ululate of agony.

"Doctor Martin says you've been vomiting and having your share of discomfort in the lower right abdomen. He has diagnosed that your appendix must come out. I concur."

The second associate stepped forward, helped Kellogg to remove his coat and don a protective gown. "Your instruments are laid out, doctor. We boiled them thoroughly yesterday evening and dipped them in carbolic acid."

Kellogg studied the metal tray on which were clamps, scalpels, forceps, several with wooden handles showing imbedded streaks of discoloration from former operations. He walked to a metal table on which were three bowls of water. He peeled back his sleeves, grabbed a block of lye soap from a metal receptacle, worked up a dripping lather. He scrubbed his forearms ruthlessly, digging below the fingernails in the style of Schimmelbusch, the German physician devoted to cleanness.

A greenish iron radiator hissed heat into the room.

Before rinsing, John Harvey's eyes searched his hands for any centimeter of skin that had not been scoured, and his mind drifted momentarily to the irony of what he was about to do.

How far back in the past, he mused, did doctor Dunston convince me I could slice into the living human body? He remembered how Dunston's logic had harmonized with his own changed thoughts.

"Johnny, you're paying out a small fortune ever year to bring in them knife-and-saw men from Chicago or New York. And all because you think you was blood scared as a kid. That's barnyard manure. Learn to do your own surgery."

Kellogg dried his hands on a thick towel. He did not wear mask and cotton gloves. The mask frightened patients who already were under stress and the gloves interfered with the surgeon's touch.

"Nurse, you may begin the ether." To the patient he explained, "Arnold, we're ready. When you waken you'll be on your way to total recovery."

His hands were steady, as they should be because four other surgeries were scheduled directly after this one. He harbored no anxiety, the notion of the body's cavities were no longer repulsive or nauseating to him. He had performed 121 successive abdominal entries without a fatality, already a world record in a surgical category where one-in-six patients died from careless or stupid procedures.

When Arnold lay quietly, fully anesthetized, Kellogg said, "Titrate, now," telling the nurse what she already knew, telling her to let the ether drip only enough to keep Arnold asleep, just on the verge of waking. Routinely she waved a cardboard fan to blow fumes away from the operating table.

He held the scalpel deftly, as he might have held a pen for writing. He directed the scimitar-shaped blade unerringly to the selected spot, going through the layers of fascia, pulling the sticky muscles neatly apart while the assistants attached retractors to keep the muscles and tissues of the abdominal walls out of the way. In less than a minute from the time he had started the operation, he incised the peritoneum — that membrane cover of the vital organs — exposed the intestines, identified the inflamed appendix, and surrounded it delicately with a moist towel.

"Arnold is in luck this day. It isn't perforated."

The assistants acknowledged this information with a showy expression of relief.

"I will hold the caecum taut, doctor Martin, while you tie off the blood supply at the base of our little troublemaker with a ligature. The thread is there handy where you put it. Then I want you to cut off the appendix near the suture line."

"Me, doctor Kellogg?"

"Arnold is your patient, you correctly diagnosed his emergency, you deserve the privilege of ridding him of this wormlike little sac that is nothing but a nuisance." There was an easygoing rebuke in the tone, but it contained enough edge to stir the assistant into action. "When you're done, sear it with carbolic and invaginate the stump, tuck it lightly into the caecum. I will draw the suture snug and close the abdominal wall."

"Yes, sir. Thank you, sir." Eagerly and gratefully Martin took over from the San's chief physician and surgeon.

OUTSIDE the operating room, Will wondered why he had been summoned. His stomach burbled like a water bottle turned on its head. He decided not to borrow trouble by dreaming up catastrophes where there might be none. For instance, the peanut butter calamity still buzzed and stung like a wasp in his memory. He should have seen it coming. Tamper with the doctor's rules and you had to take your punishment if he caught you.

He couldn't deny he had roasted the peanuts instead of steaming them, had even added a pinch of sugar to lend some taste to the goo, after which, patients had actually requested it instead of avoiding it. None of those facts cooled the doctor's fury. He was blamed for ruining a perfectly healthful recipe, degrading it as a food.

"One more such incident," the doctor had muttered, his body trembling with contained fury, "and I will be forced to accept it as proof that you are dissatisfied with your employment and you desire to seek a position elsewhere."

Now, as John Harvey emerged grumpily from the operating room, Will decided it was not premature to worry. Will also was aware of Ella's presence, vaguely sensing her arrival off to the side of him.

"Oysters." The sound was strained through the doctor's gritted teeth.

Will's eyes widened with astonishment.

"Webb's diner. My God, man, how many times have I implored you, begged you, not to eat there? It reflects badly on me, my Sanitarium, if my own brother frequents that deplorable place."

"I don't frequent..."

The door to the operating room opened and Arnold, minus appendix, draped in white sheet, was wheeled out by the nurse. The two doctors followed their patient down the hall, having glanced at the Kelloggs, sniffed conflict, and declined to be witnesses.

"How many times have I threatened serious consequences if you again thwarted my wishes?"

Will's eyes lifted to meet his brother's. John Harvey's face was crimsoned.

"It will cause me pain to dismiss you." He clenched his fists, opened them, looked forlornly at Ella who remained silent, attentive, tracking every gesture by both men. "But the truth is, you insist on leaving me no alternative. Am I correct?"

Will removed his eyeglasses, folded them into a vest pocket. His gaze was on a distant wall. "You'll do what you believe is right, doctor. You always do."

Unexpectedly, a reprieve. "Just one more infraction, Will, and though you're my brother and I love you, I will release you from employment for the sake of the Sanitarium's reputation and the morale of the other workers. I've said this before. Now it's absolutely final." He sealed the point. "There will be no further familial advantages. Is that clear?"

"I understand, doctor." Will touched his upper lip, feeling for the waxed moustache which wasn't there because he had shaved it off several weeks ago so he would not lose valuable time grooming it each day.

"Was it Post who told you I went to Webb's?"

"No, it wasn't mister Post."

Quietly, "I have a right to know my accuser."

"I like you without the lip hair, Will. Makes you look five years younger." Doctor Kellogg put his hand on his brother's shoulder, jostled him genially, his acerbity gone, completely replaced by cozy companionableness. "Are you getting enough sleep, eating right, bowels in good order?"

Noticing Ella behind John Harvey, fiery color across her cheeks, her dainty bifocals hanging at her breast by a safety cord, Will said, "Another patient in the mental wing ran away last night. I was up late helping to find him."

"Yes, yes, I heard about it this morning. He hid in the swimming pool, I'm told." The doctor folded his arms across his chest. "We give those poor souls far better treatment than the asylums where they put untrained men and women of bestial demeanor in charge of humans who can't negotiate the simplest task for themselves." Shaking his head, he chuckled. "Besides, families pay well for our considerable care of their relatives."

Will mumbled something about having to get back to work and departed. He knew his brother's thoughts had already hastened to other matters. Walking away, he sensed Ella's eyes on his back, clinging there like leaches from the Yawger mill pond. He suspected she was disappointed that his punishment had not been more severe, more final.

"I believe that takes care of that, do you agree, dear?" John Harvey straightened his dark coat over his dark vest, pleased with himself. "I gave him a good upbraiding and an ultimatum."

"Yes, John, I heard." Ella's voice held no conviction.

SAM GAMBLE'S brain wasn't so blunted he failed to sense the men following him out of Burley's. He didn't even have to look over his shoulder, back along the damp street to catch them fleetingly framed in an occasional lit window. He knew they were there. He just couldn't figure out what they wanted.

They had come into the saloon an hour ago, four of them. Big bastards, especially the one wearing the high-crowned western hat. Sam hadn't recognized their faces, so he placed them as out-of-towners. They just circled a table at the elbow of the counter, sipped beer, said almost nothing to each other, but somehow kept him in view without turning their heads in his direction. When he left, they followed him outside.

It was nearly midnight and the street was empty. Sam displayed no surprise when their steps quickened and they came alongside and locked onto his arms, propelled him into the muddy alley between the tannery and the soap-making factory. The only light in the narrow passage seeped down from cold stars in the strip between rooflines. Less than eighteen inches of space separated Gamble from the man who faced him. The other two, one on each side, held his arms, but very loosely. The fourth man remained at the alley's entrance.

"Nell sent you, you tell her I didn't have nothin to do with that burnin. Wasn't even there when it got set, was in Burley's, you ast anybody..."

The man in the western hat hit Sam in the mouth with a truncheon or lead pipe, Sam wasn't sure which. He just saw a quick snap of forehand and then his lips split and his hat flew into the dark.

"Shit," he spewed blood, could taste it now, and the fear. His heavy shoulders squeezed up defensively but the hands on his arms clasped tightly downward, like the jaws of a jump trap. He was slammed against the wall, his head striking solidly on brick. A hundred fireflies flashed phosphorescently behind his eyes. A fist pounded his stomach, once, twice, with the force of a hard driven mallet. All the air in the world seemed sucked away by the moon. Hands released him like spoiled cargo. He thudded to his knees, arms outstretched for braces, but a short kick in his ribs flipped him sidewise.

He wanted to tell these men again that he had had nothing to do with the fire but he couldn't shape the words. Instead, from far away, as though coughed out of an abandoned railroad tunnel, hollow and ghostly, he heard a maddeningly slow voice: "You ever so much as say good morning to missus Kellogg, we'll give you worse'n you got tonight."

34

APRIL 1894

"AN offer? You rode all the way out from town to make an offer, mister Gage?"

"We did, mister Post. It isn't very far, is it, Katherine?" Fred Gage gestured to his wife, who rested beside him on the upholstered couch in Post's front room.

"My husband's belief is that business must be handled one person to another. No in-betweens or go-betweens."

Her voice was soft, unlike the Enquirer newspaper's rackety linotype machine she commanded with sinewy fingers. It was known that she could type a line, insert spacebands until it was correct, then move the entire line into the casting device and free her keyboard to pound out the next line, doing it so fast no one in the county could match her speed. She was equally direct in conversation

Gage chortled and his glasses tipped on the bridge of his nose, slid down a half inch. He sat forward. "It is well known you're working on a formula to make a coffee drink like the one over at the Sanitarium."

"No, not like theirs. It is undrinkable."

Gage removed his glasses, looped an airy circle with them. "When you're ready to package and sell your discovery, the Gage printing company is willing to print bags, labels, sales fliers, store signs, whatever you might need."

"Cash and carry?"

"We'll carry it," Katherine committed. "At least for a while."

"At what interest?"

"None," Fred Gage said, "for six months. Longer if it looks like you're going someplace."

Ella entered from the kitchen with a wooden tray of food and drink. While they ate candied nuts and ginger cookies, sipped ordinary coffee, there in the farmhouse-inn with the frontroom doors slid shut so no lodgers interrupted, Gage pointed out: "We Gages have taken risks before. We believe in it if the whathaveyous are right. We bought printing presses when we didn't know if we could keep them running or pay for them. We've put money behind city improvements, some of them ahead of their time but good for the city."

He set his plate on a side table, ran a hand through a tangle of hair. "I believe you'll make a go of it, Charles Post. When you do, I'll have me a first rate customer. You'll be obligated."

Post grinned. "What about the big ships in the harbor, the Kelloggs, the San, the Adventists? You may anger them. You know they accuse me of stealing their formulas."

"I think if you already had their formula and it was any good, you wouldn't waste time trying to find another one."

Katherine nibbled a cookie. "The Kelloggs have their own publishing house. Fred can't lose customers that aren't his."

The lamplight made hoods for Post's eyes. "When I'm ready, mister Gage, I will come knocking at your door."

TILTING sharply, wheels and axles shrieking, the buggy became airborne. Horses scrambled for a foothold, tangling their traces; fire crackled down from the sky, geysers squirted up from the orange hot earth. He was flung from the seat, rolling in the blistering atmosphere, arms flopping like broken wings of a shotgunned bird.

Charles Post sat upright in bed, moaning softly.

Ella stirred beside him, opened her eyes. "What is it, Charles?" Hoping it wasn't the nightmare.

"Just indigestion." He turned away so she would not see his sweat soaked face in the moonlight that leaked through the window curtains. "I'll go downstairs, take a little bicarbonate in some water."

"I can go with you." She laid aside the quilts to get up.

He placed his hand on her shoulder, eased her onto her pillow. "No need. I'm all right, just ate too much of your raisin cream pie. Go back to sleep."

He walked warily through the upstairs hall, glancing into Marjorie's room on the way. Satisfied that she was sleeping, he went quietly down the steps. The rangy farmhouse was alive with night sounds; its five paying guests snoring at various pitches in the wing of the house where they lodged; a tree limb scratching the roof; a wooden joist creaking; the hall clock's pendulum marking off man's idea of time's flow.

At the kitchen sink Post poured water into a porcelain pan, splashed it on his face. He opened the back door, flattened his hand against the cool mesh of the screen, letting the cold air swim around him, insinuating the loose cloth of his nightgown, refreshing his hot skin. At the yard's sloped ending, now bluish white under moonglare, the barn was an angular sculpture of light and shadow: peaked roof, paralyzed weather vane, shadowed double doors, black windows stamped out of bonewhite walls.

"Dear missus Gregory," Post whispered to the chilled darkness, "how patient you were with me, reciting your Christian Scientist's belief, the mind's power to crush mental boulders. You can change the world with that power, reshape it, you said."

His thoughts were fond for the woman who helped him find his lost health. On the third day after he had moved to her home, he had accepted the idea again that pleasure could be taken from a fine meal. In no time at all weight began to mold itself back onto his bones. His energy level zigzagged up like a mountain goat climbing a cliff, slow, careful, but ever upward. His hands grew steadier. It became easy to smile. The canes lost their imperativeness and he sometimes abandoned them when going from one room to another.

But, for the past months, after buying this farm, progress had slowed, and his trials in creating a coffee substitute had led nowhere, regardless of Fred Gage's optimism. Very little of Ella's trust fund remained after converting the house to an inn, and paying off a backwash of debts.

An ice-colored moon moved low in the sky, stretching shadows in soft streamers over the farmyard. He thought of Marjorie who never doubted for an instant that her father could do anything he set his mind to, and his spirits lifted a little.

Post was a ghostly figure in his white sleeping gown, the cold pushing through his body. He wondered if the answer to the coffee substitute would always stay just out of reach, like the town he tried to build in Texas? Like Battle Creek's mystical quality? Wondered if he was again attempting the impossible, pursuing an hallucination. He asked himself, why in the hell do men chase dreams of grandeur every day of their lives, then spend every night trying to hide in their sleep from other dreams that pester them with messages they don't want to hear? Is the prize ever worth the chase? He realized in the same moment, if Carrie had heard him she would have primmed her graying hair and said, "Charles, there is a reason for what we do, always a reason." Of course, she would be right.

After closing the back door, Post walked up the carpeted, wide stairway toward the second floor. "I guess the nightmares never go away," he thought.

A MURKY image appeared in the wall mirror, distorted by striae where the silver backing had fallen away. High-collared white shirt, black bow tie, suitcoat and vest of better fit than in previous years. Will removed the flat, narrow-brimmed cap, a sort of formal tam-o-shanter, noticed how very thin his hair was, bare brow rolling up from the frames of his glasses. "I'm getting old. And we are still poor."

"Don't pretend we're poor, Will." Ella said. It depressed her when he talked that way. She held an indefensible but deeply rooted belief that people who were not properly thankful for favors the Lord bestowed on them would pay a costly penalty. "It isn't true anymore, we may have been but we're not now. We're doing better than we ever dreamed, and I think your brother is very generous and very interested in your career." Her shrillness startled her. She quieted. "Mister Wandley down the street only earns twelve dollars a week. Gretta said he works sixty hours in the mill."

"Compare my hours, Ella. Mister Wandley earns more than me." He observed the two of them in the scumbled mirror and imagined they looked like an old oil portrait in blacks, grays, deep siennas. Across town a whistle screamed like metal shearing metal, the day's end for the millworkers.

"My gracious, you are manager of the entire Sanitas food company. I think that is very, very impressive, and the money is a blessing."

Will turned morosely to find her. She stood at the curtained window, her form indistinct in the gauzy light. She was looking out into the yard and he suddenly was terrified by the notion that she was dissolving into particles. He knew if he did not act, did not say something, she would disappear forever.

"My share of the profits are good, Puss. The doctor was wise to start Sanitas." Her form became distinct to him again. "The San's directors didn't like our experimenting with the different foods. At least this keeps the two businesses apart." He fished a paper from his pocket.

"Sister White wrote the doctor her typically blunt opinion." He held the sheet at arm's length. "She says, 'At a large outlay of expenses, doctor Kellogg has studied the processes for preparing healthful foods and has procured expensive facilities for their manufacture. It is proper that he be allowed to control a reasonable income from these products and thereby have the means to make appropriations for advancing the work of God as occasion may demand.'"

Ella acknowledged, "The good sister does make her expectations quite clear."

Will stuffed the paper away. "There is something about it that makes me feel queasy."

"You're just vexed because your brother said there would be no more salary from the San." Her tone was pleasant, making it obvious she didn't believe the request was unreasonable. She sat on the edge of a wood-frame chair.

Sucking his lower plate, squeaking it like a finger drawn tight against wet glass, he observed, "If business continues brisk, my salary is no loss, giving up fifty-four dollars a month."

"I should say not. You brought home three times that amount this month."

"Puss, John Harvey only agreed to the twenty-five percent of profits because he thought I was going to resign. He knows my work load. Bookkeeper, cashier, packing and shipping clerk. I'm errand boy, general utility man, scribe. It's hard work. And we're already making and selling a half-dozen foods."

"I have such trouble keeping up with all you do at the San and Sanitas, Will, and I only hear a small part, the part you tell me. I don't know how you balance so many things and not just get completely confused." She reached out to him, held his hand in hers. "If the doctor has agreed to sell Sanitas foods through the mails, not just to the San's former patients, you have made wonderful progress with him." She stroked his cheek in a single deft motion, smoothed some threads of hair by his ear.

"The San is still our first and best customer." He plucked a dab of fuzz from the rim of Ella's bifocals, noticing her moist eyes, the full-lipped mouth. He had an unfamiliar urge to kiss her. "Maybe Len will become a doctor. He sees for himself how John Harvey is admired."

"Karl already wants to be a doctor."

Will twisted a lip. "Karl is unpredictable. I would prefer if Len decided." His eyes bounced around the room, landing a second, then pushing off in the next leap like a wild creature trapped indoors. "Perhaps...both of our boys, Puss?" Voice hopeful, chin high and forward.

"It very well could happen, dear."

Down the street, a dog barked several times. Will's stomach screaked like a nail pulled from hard wood. He shared a look of disgust with himself in the streaked mirror.

35

NOVEMBER 1894

THE concoction Post was stirring would pass for thin blackstrap molasses. Its odor was agreeable, even pleasant. He crouched on a high, wobbly stool, his long legs drawn up with feet resting on the highest rung. Marjorie was with him, but she was looking out the front window of the barn laboratory through the glass runny with melting ice. It was nearly dark beyond the hill so she could only see undefined shapes of land and trees.

When he had rebuilt the barn into a laboratory the land was green and it was a grand view down across the sloping terrain to the road and beyond. He had hauled away the barrels, broken crockery, rakes and plows, the junk dumped randomly how many years ago? He cleared hay, moved horse stalls, covered the dirt floor with wooden planking, and tarred the wall boards against December gales.

When Post had toured the San's kitchens a year ago, under the tutelage of the little doctor himself, he had been impressed by the order and influence of Ella Kellogg on every aspect. She, alone, according to her husband, had created the recipes, trained the dietetic cooks, and attended to an awesome volume of details. Equipment and utensils were strategically arranged for the easiest possible access. The ice box had been moored as far as possible from the cooking stoves, in order to take advantage of the "cool side" of the room. And none of the ovens or cabinets had any fancy scrollwork because, Kellogg said, "raised patterns collect dirt." John Harvey had called attention to the tile floor, saying it was "impervious to moisture," and went to lengths to explain that the walls were painted, not whitewashed, "so steam does not affect them." Proudly he proclaimed, "All are Ella's doing."

"Well," Post admitted, glancing around at his own work place, "I may find my coffee formula but Ella Kellogg would have an epileptic seizure if she ever saw this crude little kitchen."

Earlier today the rural mail carrier had brought a large tan envelope scrawled with a Texas return. The news was good. Brothers Aurrie and Carroll had sold the last assets of the Fort Worth property. There was a check in the envelope. Not a lot, but enough. Added to last month's income — a couple of the farm implement patents bought by a smart speculator, nice check with a letter from his lawyer — and prospects had begun to look manageable. Ella said they turned a profit on suspenders; the girls they hired were catching on to the work and some mail orders were coming in. Even the LaVita Inn was operating at least at break even.

"I'm about to dig out the answer to old man coffee and I have a feeling we'll get it right this time, little sweetheart."

"I hope so, daddy. I'm bored. There's no one to talk to."

"You hurt my feelings, Marjorie. I talk to you."

She wrapped her arms around his neck as he bent into her hug. She felt the hot wetness of his skin against her cheek. "It's Christmas pretty soon, isn't it, daddy?"

"Yes." Charles said, pouring the dark liquid into a cake pan. His head felt weightless, as if it might float to the ceiling and stay there and bobble like a lost balloon. Nothing to eat since noon. He added finely ground barley to the mixture, was startled at the sight of hundreds of tiny bugs peppering from the sack. Then he refocused and recognized it was only kernels of grain.

He scooped the fluid into a wooden spoon, tasted it. The drink tasted faintly sweet, with a hint of chicory. It had none of coffee's bitterness, was delicate on the palate, unlike Kellogg's Caramel Coffee.

Ella watched from the side entrance, her blonde hair matted tightly under a wool scarf below which she wore a large, padded coat, good for warmth, but not pretty. When he noticed her, Post called to her.

"Ella," he proclaimed, holding the coated spoon aloft, "this is good stuff. A hundred times superior to John Harvey Kellogg's drink, but it just isn't quite right."

"You don't look like you feel well," Ella said. "I think you ought to rest while Marjorie and I finish here." She removed her coat, unbuttoned her blouse sleeves and rolled them up.

Charles carried the cake pan of liquid to the door, considered his longcoat drooped on a peg, decided against it. Outside, light flakes floated down, barely visible. He crossed the yard, going away from the barn, stopped fifty feet out and poured the black fluid onto the white crust of snow.

"Wheat and molasses. The right ingredients. Damn, I'm positive." Trying to reassure himself, sunk to his ankles in snow, oblivious of the wind that pierced his flannel shirt. "Moisten the bran oats with molasses. Start it roasting. Grind up the roasted grains. Now blend them together in a good mix. Boil for twenty minutes. The length of time is correct, of that I'm sure. There is no better way. Why doesn't it turn out right?" It was a one-way talk with the snowy field.

"Cook it more than twenty minutes, it gets overdone, burns. Cook it less time it's no good. Then it..."

The answer hit his brain like an electric shock. He staggered. Slinging the pan aside, he ran in long-legged strides back to the barn, burst through the door, startling Marjorie into dropping an armful of measuring pans, stunning Ella into an uncontrollable jiggle of eyelids.

"It's the stove, the damned stove," he shouted. "That's what's wrong, not the ingredients." He spoke so rapidly his words were a melded string of syllables. "The damned wheat's got to be raked, keep it moving or some of it burns, works against the molasses sweetener, kills it."

His wife and daughter stared uncomprehendingly.

"You have to keep it moving while it cooks, you have to roast it evenly. A long stove, that's what we need, keep the wheat moving, don't let it scorch. Listen to me, Marjorie, Ella. It's not what I'm putting in it that's wrong, it's how I'm cooking it. The stove. The damned stove, it's the damned stove."

SISTER Ellen White's office was on the second floor of the Adventist headquarters building. The room was skimpily furnished except for several shelves of books dedicated to works of the faith, and an 1895 wall calendar adorned on each sheet with Biblical quotations in old English typeface. Sister White's rolltop desk had seen better times. She wasn't bothered, though, by its splintered sides and unmanageable pull-down shell. It had served for two decades of spiritual writings and record keeping.

Sitting behind her desk, Sister White inclined her head toward her visitors. The sing-song cadence of her words bounced hollowly from the ceiling twenty feet above. "I hope, John Harvey...that you and Ella will accompany me...one evening soon to the Hamblin area...near Carlyle Street. The church...is considering a daytime mission there...a place where the workers and laborers...might gain respite from their toil." A small, foam-colored hand rested atop the frayed cover of her Bible.

"John and I will be very pleased to go with you, Sister White," Ella volunteered.

"Thank you, Ella. I knew...you would understand...The Adventists are engaged in holy warfare...striving to restore..the physical and spiritual health of those...who come seeking our aid."

"There can be no question about that, Sister White." Ella's dedication was pure gold, unmixed, unmitigated.

"And you, doctor, with your wonderful skills...your amazing talents, your brilliant mind...what do *you* say?"

"I'm not certain, Sister White, because I'm not certain what we are discussing, or even why you asked us here in the middle of the busiest part of our day." He took a chair near the desk, sat on the edge of its seat. "I hear 'holy warfare' and 'daytime mission', but do I hear another agenda, as well?"

"In part...But, plain and direct language...may be called for...You see, it remains my intention...that you and I should agree in full...on the administration of our Sanitarium...just as your good wife and I do...in matters of religion and faith."

"Surely we are in accord, Sister." His fingers drummed lightly on the wooden seat of the empty chair next to him where he had placed his hat.

"You know by now, John Harvey...I believe the physician must be...a messenger of mercy to the sick..."

"You'll get no argument from me."

"...bringing a remedy for the sin-sick soul...as well as for the diseased body."

"My feelings match your own."

"Let us see if we concur...on yet another point...The doctor is ever in danger...of forgetting the peril of the soul...He should stay alert to such failing...and speak in season the words...that will ever awaken faith and hope."

"Your wisdom is evident, Sister White." Fingers beating more forcefully on the chair seat.

Ella sensed her husband's impatience. "I believe Sister White is saying we must continue to practice economy in the administration of the San."

"Precisely, sister Ella. We must...live within our means and be...contented with a very small income...dispense it prudently, of course...rather than engage in ventures...and suffer sudden losses."

"That's meaningless," Kellogg said bluntly. "The San has had no such losses."

"John Harvey, you have studied much...but you have neglected the study of yourself." Sister Ellen was as calm as a curtain rod, her eyes resting heavily on the breast of his coat. He could feel their weight. "You would receive more strength by spending...one minute daily in meditation...pleading for God's pardoning love...than by hours given to scientific authors."

His fingers furiously romped on the wooden seat in a miniature drumroll. "Sister, you once told me that those who do not improve the talent the Almighty has given them will fail to reach heaven. Would you have me pray more and do less with my God-given talents?"

Her composure slipped a notch. "I have no desire to fight...not with you, John Harvey." She leafed backwards through an album in her mind. "Once a girl became mad over a trifle...and bore down on me at school...She threw a stone, breaking my nose...knocking me senseless...Faintness and dizziness have been...my constant companions ever since...I've never again breathed through this nose of mine. I've learned...to endure my misfortune and ugliness...but I have no taste for quarreling."

"Sister Ellen, my husband only wants what is best for the Sanitarium."

"Let our institution grow as fast as it safely can...but not in ways that cripple other branches of our great work...Our heavenly father is displeased with an avaricious spirit."

Kellogg rose slowly, walked to the door and opened it. "I'll put that thought on our master calendar, Sister. If we ever prepare a calendar."

She blanched, recalling that the calendar had been her idea. "I've had a warning vision of danger...if the Sanitarium's managers depart from the simplicity...which should characterize God's followers."

Kellogg put on his hat, extended an open hand to Ella.

"You'll do nothing to violate that trust...will you, John?"

"I wouldn't hear of it. Good day, Sister."

"I UNDERSTAND, mister Post, you have found your coffee drink formula. If that's so, congratulations to you."

"It will have you smacking your lips when you taste it, doctor Kellogg. I call it Postum."

"Postum. Yes, clever, most clever."

The two men were in front of the Battle Creek Creamery on West Main. Winter had temporarily taken a leave and the day was unusually bright. Sunlight burnished the streets except where left-over patches of soiled snow remained like suds from a dirty wash.

"And I understand you sell your Postum door to door from a, uh, pushcart?"

"Your information is accurate, as always, doctor, except I haven't been selling, just offering. The good people of our city don't seem interested in buying Postum. An attitude especially held by the grocers. They don't want to stock it at all."

"Give it some time. If it has quality, it will gain a place for itself."

"Then you don't object to what I'm doing?"

"It's not mine to approve or disapprove. The market place is open to any man who likes a good tussle with the odds."

"And you don't support the rumor that I stole your formula?"

"I've not participated in that rumor."

"Do you believe it?"

"*Did* you steal my formula?"

Post laughed enjoyably. "All right, doctor Kellogg, we have utmost faith in each other. Let's make a pact, arrange a cooperative deal in both our interests. I'll sell my product and your grain cereals at the same time, the same effort into each at every grocer's counter over the entire state. I'll have both our names imbedded in customers' minds from ocean to ocean by the end of this year. What do you say?"

"What I've always said: no." Amiable, even amused. "You must understand, I've developed a long list of health foods for the healing benefits they provide to my patients. I don't intend to commercialize them. I'm a physician, not a drummer."

"What does brother Will say about my offer?" Giving it one final chance.

"In all candor, brother Will doesn't like you, mister Post. I doubt he would embrace the notion of going into business with you." He spoke good naturedly, briefly clutching Post's arm in a well-wishing gesture. Morse and Shouldice, two businessmen, nodded as they passed, grinning knowingly at the cordial combatants.

"Then I suppose I must proceed without you?"

"I wish you much success, mister Post."

36

FEBRUARY 1895

FROM a hall window in the San, Ella Kellogg watched the snowstorm gaining momentum. Only when John Harvey and Will were nearly beside her in the hallway did she notice them and turn to meet them. Their faces were flushed and pulsing, their breathing came in quick huffs as though they had been running.

"Ella, we've chased through half the San looking for you." John Harvey grasped her arm and hauled her in his direction while he danced toward the nearest stairwell. "Come with us, please come right now, we've found it, hurry now, hurry along."

Her natural inclination was to draw back, but Will's words, "We can flake our wheat mixture," caused her to quicken her pace and fall into step.

When they reached the basement, but before they came to the tunnels that diverged out and away under ground, they went directly to a wire-meshed area with a concrete floor, a big sink, and several shelves of utensils.

"Watch this." John Harvey was cooing like a dove who had just found a fat grub. "We boiled the grain last night, cooked it the same amount of time as the last batch, but it was late and it was the final one, so we didn't dispose of it, we left it until today."

Will Kellogg lifted a heavy crockery vat from the floor, cradled it under one arm, reached into it with his free hand, came out with a wad of pasty, moldy berries. He surrendered the boiled wheat into a mounted wall container that resembled a large bread box but much narrower at its base than its top. Then he used a smooth wooden pestle to gently force the wheat through the box, directly onto a double set of rollers, about eight inches in diameter, two feet in length. As John Harvey activated a crank on the mounting mechanism, the two cylinders turned and the moldy substance went mushing onto the rollers like a loaf of rain-soaked bread.

"That wheat looks very bad to me, John. It has mold all over it."

"I know, I know. Please watch."

As the cooked, soft berries came out between the rollers each was...

Ella's hand shot forward, snatched up one of the thick pads.

"A flake. My god, John. It's turning to flakes! I'm astonished, John. I just don't understand..."

"Darling, it's simple. The one monumentally important step we never took was simply to let the soaked wheat stand after it had cooked."

She dabbed her eyes with a handkerchief. "But, John, if you let it stand and it gets moldy, what good..."

"I've already figured out the answer to that. We will allow it to set long enough to be thoroughly tempered, but no longer. We will build tin-lined bins for storage instead of those open crocks. That will eliminate the molding." He frowned. "But, even when we have our flakes we will confront one other obstacle."

Will said, "If the humidity is high, the flakes will become soggy."

"And if the day is sunny and hot, the flakes will dry too soon," the doctor added. "So, we shall bake them in a special drying oven where we can control those variables."

"Where do we have a drying oven?" Ella asked, still holding the large wheat flake in her hand as if it was a sacred scarab. "I'm not aware of one in the San."

"There soon will be. I'm shaping it up here." He tapped the side of his head with a straight finger.

IT had taken E.H. Herrick more than eighteen years to build up his business from a covered wagon full of pots and kettles he gathered regularly on Detroit's waterfront docks. When he branched out, adding some vegetables and sun-dried beef from farmers and hunters, he found his own combination for success. Now it was the largest wholesale grocery outlet in Grand Rapids, supplying foodstuffs and wares to half the retail stores in three counties.

Herrick stood behind the counter, leaning on his hands. He was nearly as tall as Post and had a narrow chin. His shirt cuffs were turned twice above his wrists, vest open.

A skinny clerk lethargically stacked cans of syrup on the shelves over the grain and flour bins along one wall. His head was tilted and an ear was cocked to be certain he missed none of the conversation between his boss and the gangly visitor. He liked to behold Herrick lowering the boom on a fast talking peddler.

"If your coffee drink is such a fine thing, why are you here in this part of the state trying to peddle to me, mister Pole?"

"Post, mister Herrick, my name is Post."

"Don't they have grocers in the big old city of Battle Creek? I'm asking because I know for a fact they do, some real humdingers, but I want to hear your excuse."

Post was tempted to quote Thomas Fuller: "Sour grapes can ne'er make sweet wine." He skipped the urge. His response was earnest and thoughtful. "The truth is, the grocery owners are good people but I'm a newcomer and haven't been accepted. They're cautious, maybe shy. They need some time."

"The merchants in Battle Creek are lots of things, but shy's not one of them. They probably figure they buy from you, Kellogg will put his spurs in them, isn't that how it is? What I hear you saying, you don't expect *me* to be cautious, that right?"

"Just the opposite, Mr. Herrick. The Kelloggs have nothing to do with it." He glanced at the lifeless suspenders both men were wearing, mentally vowed to leave two pairs of his own design with this grocer baron and his eavesdropping clerk. "I reasoned you might be more daring, maybe more able to see a good thing in the making. More willing to wager a little to win a lot."

Herrick scratched behind an ear, squinted at Post, weighing him, measuring and assessing him like a crate of produce. He had seen a legion of salesmen and gimcracks and "miracle foods" wash up on the beach, now forgotten, except for the lessons they had taught: buy what you can sell, not what someone tries to sell you, and be careful who you give credit.

"I supposed, mister Herrick, you didn't become successful by always following the wide, level road."

"I didn't get here by driving my team into a plainly marked bog, neither."

Herrick hefted the container of Postum from the counter where Charles had put it when he first came in. He turned the small carton in his long-fingered hand, slowly, the way he might have examined an orange or a peach. His voice was surly, as he read from the package, "A breakfast drink compound made of different parts of wheat and a small portion of New Orleans molasses." He looked sleepily at Post. "Not interested, mister Pole..."

"Post."

"...I already got too damned much of this imitation coffee stacked in the back room."

The clerk called from his ladder, "Can't sell it, nobody wants it, lucky if we get rid of ten packs a year."

Post scanned the clerk, a little surprised that he would butt in. The man was pale, had a bony face and wore a widebrimmed, curacao-colored straw hat.

"Claude's a hundred percent right, mister Pole." Said with such avuncular protectiveness, Post inferred the two men were related in some way. "I'm not interested in buying make-believe coffee. Fact is, it tastes like old rags boiled in ditch water."

Charles said simply, "Your customers will like Postum. They'll buy it."

"C'mere, I want you to see something. Claude, you keep an eye on everything."

Post and Herrick crossed the concrete floor, the color of old dirt. They passed under a row of electric fans suspended from the ceiling, floating in fixed silence, awaiting the heat of summer. Herrick pushed open a thick wooden door at the end of a corridor of shelves. Post followed him into a shadowy chamber that was piled with cartons and crates of merchandise stacked nearly to the raftered ceiling.

"See all them goods, mister Pole?" His arm moved in a semi-circle like a gate swinging shut. "Inventory, that's what you're looking at. Everything from shoes and saucepans to canned peaches and butter beans. I even got a player piano somewhere back in there I'd like to sell if I could dig it out. You know what inventory is? Inventory is my money tied up in something and I don't get it back until someone buys it."

Post said, "I appreciate your position, mister Herrick. My father and I once ran an implements store."

As though he hadn't heard him, Herrick kicked a barrel marked MOLASSES in red letters. "There's twelve of these and it's a slow sell. I got clocks, coffee grinders, tins of asparagus. So many bags of salt I'd have to look at the books to give you a number." The store owner leaned forward "You want to know what else I got horded away because no one but a fool like me would put one red cent into it?"

"Boxes of Caramel Coffee," Post answered calmly.

"About eight cartons of the stuff to be exact. Not a single package been sold in months. Proves I can't use no more." Herrick made a move to close the warehouse door and Post took the indelicate hint, followed him into the main building.

As the two men returned to the front of the store, Post asked casually, "What if I *guarantee* Postum will sell, guarantee you'll have customers asking for it by name, and you don't have to invest a thing, don't have to carry it as *inventory*?"

Herrick's left eyebrow skittered near his hairline. He straightened himself tall enough to look directly into Post's face. "I don't pay you anything for your, what you call it, 'Postum?' If it sets around 'til it turns to dust, I pay nothing?"

"That's right. But I can tell you, you'll sell out three cases inside of a week and order more."

"Mister Pole, you're stark mad. All I have to do is sell it or give it back to you in a week, no money owed?" Herrick snuffed noisily. "I won't go out of my way an inch to sell something nobody wants."

Post said nothing.

"One week?"

"Yes, mister Herrick."

Post put out his hand to seal the deal. Behind the two men, a can of syrup resoundingly hit the floor.

"You dent that can, no one'll buy it, Claude. It'll come out your wages."

Claude grimaced, eyes rebellious, and wagged his head. The straw hat slipped, he grabbed for it, lost another can. At the instant it slammed onto the concrete floor, Herrick took Post's hand, firmly shook it once, then let it go as if fearful he might have to keep it.

"Bring a carton in, mister Pole. One carton."

37

"LADIES and gentlemen, this will be a special evening for us, a celebration. No lectures tonight."

The San's large main room had the appearance of a convention hall on election night. Patients and attendants and nurses crowded into the chairs, standing in the enormous doorways, snugged around the great columns that supported the vaulted ceiling.

John Harvey looked at Ella where she was seated before the upright piano. She dutifully held a stack of music that included "The Mountain Maid's Invitation" and "I'll Love Thee Always," two favorites of hers. Their lyrics were tragic and romantic. She blew a kiss to her husband and he made a great show of catching it, to the howls of audience appreciation.

"Three days ago," he bellowed, "we discovered the process of flaking wheat grains, a secret of nature that has eluded us for many months, many years."

Six hundred hands crashed together in an uproar.

"Perseverance has its reward. After endless failures, we located the proper key to a tiny hidden lock. We opened the miniscule doorway and placed a lit candle in an enormous, heretofore darkened chamber of immense possibilities.

"Flaked grains," Kellogg shouted. "It will mean new kinds of foods, new ways of bringing healthy, tasty, cereals to your breakfast table, to the tables of all Sanitarium patients, now and in the glorious future.

"So our treat for you tonight, in observance of this long hidden, but now revealed scientific knowledge, is an evening of song and music. And, if I do say so, merriment for everyone."

The six-hundred-hand applause was sustained and genuine.

Doctor Kellogg pirouetted to the piano with the skill of a ballet dancer, seated himself with aplomb equal to a coronation, and took the proffered sheet music from Ella. His supple, well-trained fingers barely flicked the piano keys, but plucked a musical note from each, mingling them, blending and swirling them in a tide, wave on wave, washing over every listener, buoying each with song.

IN Will Kellogg's house, Ella and the three children, Len, Karl, Beth, circled the used piano Will had purchased a few weeks ago as a surprise birthday present for Puss.

Will was astraddle a revolvable stool, his hands searching out a halting rendition of "There's a Rainbow in the Clouds." Between stanzas he directed his makeshift choir with all the solemnity of an opera house conductor. Ella kept time by lightly thumping her foot on the floor, but the singing was being done by the youngsters, with a sort of humming-moaning assist by Will as he contributed a few intermittent words to the noisy rendition, reading the music lamely, and trying to deal more sweet notes than sour ones.

"What would anyone like to hear? I'm taking requests," Will asked in the broad manner of a stage performer. Puss laughed and it pleased him.

"Play the Salem Witches March." Karl pretended to shudder as if frightened.

"No, no, father," Beth dragged at Kellogg's sleeve, "Horseshoe Over the Door." Squealing expectantly, her blonde hair swishing like late summer hay.

"Never mind. 'Beautiful Dreamer.' For us, Puss." Will looked at his wife. She is tired, he thought, hit by the sight of increased lines that crinkled around her mouth and along her brow.

She adjusted her glasses self consciously. "I'm proud of you, Will. You said you would find a way to make flakes out of grain and you did. I don't know why you and doctor Kellogg were so taken up with it, but it seemed to mean a lot. So I'm proud of you."

"John Harvey believes he alone discovered it."

"But that isn't true is it?"

Will shook his head.

"The flakes are thick. Tough to chew. Flavor like baked newspaper. John Harvey won't let us add anything except salt. We're going to call them Granose. The doctor is already working on the patent. It will protect flaked cereals and our process for making them." His stomach complained familiarly, but he covered its gripes with aimless notes on the keyboard. "We'll make Granose in that barn up the hill behind the San. It's to be our factory."

"Oh, Will, the old animal shed on Brooks Street? It was supposed to be torn down. Surely..."

"We've cleaned the place up, Puss. Put in our big rollers. I think we're there to stay."

He suddenly hit the piano keys with such energy that he startled everyone to big-eyed silence. When the children realized their father wasn't angry, just invigorated, they rushed to catch up with the lyrics.

CHARLES Post backed up to the fireplace where dry logs burned with popping heat. His face was lifeless. He looked embalmed. He spoke dejectedly, the words sinking like clods of dirt in a pond.

"So I drove the team away from Herrick's store, on my way to the newspaper where the life or death of Postum was waiting. Walked into editor Willis Turner's office of the Grand Rapids Evening Press, told him I wanted to advertise and would pay when the product started selling, maybe a week or two. The man looked at me like I was a patent medicine drummer cozying up to his wife."

Marjorie asked the question on everyone's mind. "What'd he say, daddy?"

"He said flatly, absolutely no. Then he invited me to leave the same way I entered only more speedily."

The LaVita Inn's clients, five of them, were sitting in easy chairs, drinking coffee in the farmhouse's largest room, now converted to a lobby. They groaned in unison. Marjorie's small face tumbled and her pouty upper lip protruded a full half-inch.

A guest named Edmundson asked, "How could he turn you down without a fair chance?"

Another inquired. "Did he even taste your Postum drink before he ordered you to get out?"

"No, mister Simmons, he didn't. You know, Aristotle concluded man is a rational animal; he didn't say *every* man is."

"What will you do now? Try Lansing or go out of state?"

Ella's exasperation was as plain as a cockroach in the kitchen sink. "Why don't you tell it, Charles. You sound like doctor Kellogg threading out one of his boring stories."

Her scorn scurried past him, unnoticed. "I had a hunch while at Herrick's store," he continued, "so I borrowed an alcohol lamp from him before leaving. I went to the newspaper office with it and a package of Postum. It took a lot of talking but Willis Turner finally let me light up the lamp and boil some Postum there at his desk."

"How ingenious," mister Edmundson observed.

"When the Postum was ready for tasting I poured Turner a half cup. He sipped it, carefully at first, probably thought it might rot his tongue. Then he took a big swallow. The frown left his face and he told his reporters to try it. They wanted to buy a package from me on the moment but I directed them to Herrick's so he could learn how quickly customers would be attracted."

There was an audible sigh of relief from the guests, and even from Marjorie, who already knew the ending.

"Then you got what you went after, mister Post?"

"Yes, mister Edmundson. Full page ads in the Evening Press, up to $1000 worth, with no payments for four weeks."

He made a circle with his arms, like the band around a barrel. "Now, everyone come over by the piano, please. Marjorie, put on a player roll and crank it up. It's a damned good time to celebrate."

PART FOUR

Only in a house where one has
learnt to be lonely does one
have this solicitude for things.
Elizabeth Bowen

38

APRIL 1901

MOVING from the nineteenth century to the twentieth century left everyone in the nation a little winded, as if they had just come up from a five-lap swim underwater.

China was butchering foreign lords and missionaries. Italy's king was murdered. In France, a wild-eyed coterie of "Impressionist" artists flicked their teeth at critics who claimed they lacked skill in draughtsmanship, color, and composition. The Boer War in South Africa drug on. Germany's Count Zeppelin launched his huge, cigar-shaped dirigible. Not to be outdone, a couple of Americans named Wright designed a heavier-than-air flying machine. Sigmund Freud's *Interpretation of Dreams* was startling enough to be found on every book vendor's shelves.

In Michigan, Henry Ford had built a gasoline powered motor car and said he had ideas for making them faster and cheaper but refused to discuss what those ideas were. It didn't matter; Ransom Olds was already turning out plenty of motorized vehicles in his Oldsmobile Lansing-based factory.

Battle Creek kept pace with a speeding world. The city's population ballooned to 19,000, but no one was astonished by that number. If you asked any citizen on the street, the answer you'd get was: "Thought our town was bigger'n that."

"MISTER Kellogg!" Braxton howled above the pouring rain and rolls of thunder. "She took the lake path, goin over to town line. Probably will jump in if she don't get et up in the swamp."

Braxton was a giant in a thin white coat. He slung his head, throwing slabs of soppy hair from his forehead, popping them like a whip. He was breathing hard. He had been running and he was overweight and out of shape and the exertion had sapped him. He hadn't been an employee at the San long enough for the doctor to rebuild him.

"Don't these crazy people never run away on a night isn't cold or snowin or rainin?"

Will Kellogg, too, was dressed in a white jacket that lay on him like a soaked blanket. The men's hands were crisscrossed with scratches from thorns and branches, the knees of their trousers grimed from falling over clumps of wild plants, tree limbs, field stones.

"Edwina's a patient. Don't call her crazy." The irritation in his voice was only a reaction to the rotten task they had. "You take the lake. I'll go this way, over by the trees. One of us is bound to find her."

"Whatever you say."

"Braxton, if she's there, don't do anything. Talk to her quietly. Don't try to touch her."

"I know all that." Moving away, pissed off at this squat little man who had power only because he was the doctor's brother.

The wetness of the night seeped into Will. He shivered, squinted into the rain. Braxton was already well out of sight, on his way toward the lake. Now Will began a groping, slogging path across the field.

When he reached the wooded area, he called the patient's name twice, "Edwina!" and "Edwina!"

He recognized that she could be sitting behind a clog of trees only a few feet away. She would not respond. Nor could he be sure he would see her if he passed within inches. It turned out that Edwina was easy to find. She was standing by a spindly sapling not twenty yards inside the forest. Her white gown was a smudge of chalk against a drenched, black landscape. Her head inclined to one side, then the other, hearing all the woodland noises. She stared upward and the rain splashed in her open eyes.

"Will you come back with me, Edwina? There are people worried about you. You shouldn't run away."

"I was going to the lake and let it cover me up."

"Suicide is bad, Edwina. It's a coward's act." He walked closer to her, moving very slowly, not wanting to alarm her. "You're not a coward. You came here instead of the lake." Ransacking his mind for the phrases doctor Kellogg had told him were effective with runaways.

"I suppose so." She took a short step toward him in the drenched gloaming. "I really came this way to touch these trees."

"I'll take you home. To the Sanitarium." He reached out to her.

WILL'S clothes were pasted on him like a second skin, diaphanous and slimy. He had not changed them since returning Edwina Poole to the Sanitarium. He had simply grabbed his overcoat and went directly to John Harvey's house and interrupted the doctor's meal with several guests.

"Our circulars say insane persons are not received. We can't handle them, doctor. This evening we almost lost Edwina Poole." He dripped rainwater on the mansion's carpeted foyer.

"I disagree with you entirely, Will. The San is well suited to assist these persons. They are not insane; they have mental difficulties or disorders of certain extremes. We are, in truth, better equipped to help them than most asylums..."

"You should walk with them in a rainy field, doctor."

Ella's voice startled both men. "John, can't this wait, whatever it is?" She slipped into the hallway, sliding the dining room doors shut behind her. Her face was smiling through gritted teeth.

Will said glumly, "The trouble is over for the moment."

"Then, why disturb John with it? He has had a long, long day, not to mention performing several operations before lunchtime." She tugged her husband's arm in the direction of the dining room, frowning at Will. "I'd think you'd be more considerate of your brother's occasional moments of relaxation."

"You ought to stay out of this," Will said to her quietly, surprised at his own temerity.

Both John Harvey and Ella froze in position, open-mouthed. The doctor finally exhaled loudly.

"That will do, Will. I often overlook your impertinences where I am concerned because you are my brother, but in Ella's home you will treat her with courtesy."

Will cast his gaze around the hall. Gas pressed painfully under his rib cage.

John Harvey's fists opened and closed spastically. "We'll take this up tomorrow, Will, in the office, both of us composed and level-headed. Go home and rest. You are tired. That new son of yours, Irvin Hadley, must be keeping you up nights."

"Yes," was all Will could manage before he let himself out onto the porch and hurried away.

"John, I insist you fire him," Ella said.

He took her arm. "Tomorrow I'll straighten it all out."

39

JUNE 1901

"LISTEN to this," Fred Gage chuckled. He held aloft a copy of *Good Health* magazine. "Doctor Kellogg has a subtle way with words."

"I've read the piece, Fred." Joe Cox, editor and owner of the *Enquirer*, was putting away the day's receipts and cleaning up his desk in the newspaper's tumbled work area.

"What's he say?" Russell Hart snuffed out a yawn, leaned back in an unstable chair. He was a corpulent man, good-natured, and very wealthy from the sale of various inventions, especially a paper jogger used in printing shops across the country, including Gage and Sons.

Gage grinned. "What I been saying ever since Charles Post come to town. The man is a whale of a success."

"C.W.," Katherine Gage corrected her husband. "He's going by *C.W.* now."

"Millionaire can go by anything he wants to." Hart covered another yawn with a tap of his fingertips. "Last I heard, he was netting a million or more a year."

Fred began: "Doctor Kellogg says, and I am quoting, 'A peculiar sort of epidemic is raging in the vicinity of Battle Creek. A few short years ago a gentleman who had formerly been a patient at the Battle Creek Sanitarium and had thus become acquainted with the excellent cereal coffee substitutes undertook to manufacture a similar preparation. By ingenious and somewhat misleading advertising he has built up a large business in cereal coffee, shipping several carloads monthly to various parts of the United States.

"'Now there are a half dozen or more individuals who are likewise capable of knowing a good thing when they see it. There are six different factories in Battle Creek besides the Battle Creek Sanitarium Health Food Company, all engaged in making a cereal substitute for coffee.'"

Gage glanced up from the page, established that his listeners were listening. "This is the clincher. The doctor says, 'All of these companies are fighting like Kilkenny cats over trademark rights and space in the grocers' stores. Meanwhile, the Sanitarium looks on complacently, enjoying the skirmish.'"

Katherine walked to the front of the room, sidled up beside Fred. She had just finished cleaning up the linotype machine and was scrubbing her hands with a towel. "C.W. told you awhile back the Kelloggs were fit to be tied, didn't he?"

Gage agreed with a dip of his head. "Said the doctor was taking some stiff measures. Visitors being barred from the San's plant to stop the swiping of trade secrets. Post said a couple of ex-San people told him they had to sign affidavits, you know, legal promises, not to tell about any of the manufacturing processes."

"Question is, who's copying who?" Hart interjected, warming to the gossip. "After all, Post is supposed to have stole the San's coffee formula..."

"Adapted it," Katherine suggested.

"...and cornered the whole market. Then he put out that crunchy cereal..."

"Grape-Nuts," Joe Cox contributed.

"...right, Grape-Nuts, which Will Kellogg claimed was filched from their Granola formula. But the odd thing is, the Kellogg boys turned around and started making Gran-Nut and it looked and tasted about like Grape-Nuts. Gets confusing, don't it?" Hart extracted a watch from a vest pocket, listened anxiously to be certain it was ticking. "Missus Hart said supper at seven and that's right now. Cox, I bet your missus is there waiting. My wife will roast my own rump for the main course, we don't get a move on." He stood up abruptly.

"We're right behind you," Katherine assured him.

ON THE train that lunged and jerked westward to Battle Creek, were two travelers whose beliefs and views were as dissimilar as glass is from rock. Both had sprung out of the same volcanic eruption, but each had been formed through a different fusion. Sister Ellen White and Looney Lew Reesner had nothing in common, with the exception of an abiding interest in sin. She defined and deplored it; he chased it, enjoyed it and didn't give a damn about its meaning.

In the swaying coach car, the wooden floors shifted underfoot as the iron underframe and its two six-wheeled swivel trucks swung and lurched, and the faint light above the narrow passage blinked irritatingly. The two passengers stared at one another.

Lew was eating. "Had better at Jackson," he grumbled.

Sister White grimaced at the contents of the tin plate Lew held in his lap, wondering at the same time where she had seen this grisly man before.

"These are hard damned seats, ain't they?" he inquired of no one in particular.

Her look would have withered Elders in the church, but was wasted on Lew.

"I'm glad the weather ain't lousy, though, cause we can have them windows open and don't have to freeze our butts if we're away from that old stove down there..."

"I'm not in the mood for...conversation. Please leave me alone...Talk to whomever...you are sitting next to...but quit bothering me."

"They ain't nobody beside me, can't you see? I'm here by myself." Then, as it occurred to him, "Don't take it wrong, lady, I ain't tryin to get close to you." Thinking, Jesus, who'd want to? "I just ain't been out where I can talk to reg'lar people for a while..."

One of the elders, a stout man seated behind Sister White, hunched forward. "Whoever you are, sir, the good Sister White has asked you to leave her be. Please do as she requests."

Even as the woman's name caused blood bubbles to float behind his eyes, Lew spun around, color sweeping up from his neck to his ridged head. "You sit back, skunkhole, and stay shut or I'll stick this coffee cup right up your nose, handle and all."

Another elder rose beside Sister White's champion, looked over the seat at Lew, sat down without speaking. The threatened man silently withdrew.

"That's all right, Morgan...There'll be no trouble...I shall alert the conductor...the moment he comes through."

"Now wait, lady, hell, don't do nothin like that, it'll just bring on trouble..."

"You have already succeeded...in causing trouble."

"...and I don't want none. I had me plenty of that the last five years, not lookin for more. Didn't mean to flare up to your friends, it's a old habit, one I'm workin to break. No disrespect, just tryin to be friendly on a long ride and like I said, ain't no one sittin over this side of me to chew the fat, no one next to you, neither."

In spite of his ferocious features, the pleading in his voice drew her interest and she studied him quickly, deciding whether he was sincere.

"You're right, ma'am, not to eat this slop. Ain't fit for humans." He dropped the plate of food clatteringly to the floor, kicked it under the bench in front of him. So this is Sister White, he mused. Ain't that a corker?

As the train began to slow for its stop in Albion, the diminished sounds of wheels and engine gave way to the more immediate racket: Snores, giggles, hacking coughs, sneezing and, — mercifully — further back, much further back, the squealing cry of a baby with colic.

"You would be well advised...to avoid the harmful foods, sir...among them beef, or any meat...and those caffeinated drinks...like coffee...are dangerous to you. Take my word...you'll feel better, live longer...if you forego them...in favor of vegetables, nuts, well baked breads...and the like."

Her expression, Lew noticed, had turned from sour ice to lukewarm leftover beer. Inwardly he grinned, delighting in his undimmed ability to convince a person of motives he did not share. He had learned two very helpful things long ago. The first was that people got chummier when they became convinced that you agreed with them. The second was that most people who considered themselves educated or worldly would go to lengths to prove they were completely indifferent to a person's deformity or ugliness, would even feign unawareness of it. In Lew's case, that was akin to not noticing that a couple of bumble bees had speared your arm.

Within minutes the train rattled out of Albion and Lew said, "You wouldn't be the Sister White who is pretty big in the church there in Battle Creek, would you?"

"I work...in the Adventist cause...Through the church, our publishings, missions...in other countries as well as the Sanitarium, of course."

"Now that's somethin, ain't it?" A note of exuberance, a large grin. His raisin eyes glittered. "I always heard about you, never had no chance to meet you. Proud to do so. Name's Lew Reesner. I'm on my way to Battle Creek, too, ain't that somethin now, meetin you like this."

"You have folks in Battle Creek?" she ventured.

"Got none. They're dead." Before she could say she was sorry, he continued. "They wasn't much. No big loss, you know what I mean? My old man was a hire-out for work honery cuss. Used to beat hell out of me with a tree limb big as your two thumbs. Walloped me near ever night when he was in town. I think he did it just to prove he was tough. If he'd lived about two more years, I'd put a knot in his tail. I was gettin to be about as big as he was." Lew twisted sideways and hung one leg over the arm of the seat, out into the aisle. "I was twelve when he got killed working on some bridge job down by Fort Wayne. Wagon full of logs rolled off on him, mashed him flat."

Now she said it: "I'm sorry."

He put what he hoped was a sorrowful expression on his face. "Ma took to bed right after that with some kind of sick. I hadda wait on her hand and foot all the time. She died about a year later. I gotta tell you, I was glad she went. I sure didn't want to spend the rest of my life doin for her." He swung his foot lazily in the aisle and anyone passing by had to turn sideways to edge through. No one, though, who glanced at him said anything.

Sister Ellen watched the green sloping hills and sundrenched trees. She spoke as if to them. "When my husband became ill…I cared for him for many months…ministered to his every need…I didn't mind."

Lew almost purred. "Well, now, that just shows the Lord's difference in folks, don't it, sister?"

Despite herself, she smiled. "I fear we...got off on the wrong foot, mister Reesner...You say you are traveling...from Jackson to Battle Creek?...You've been away on business?...I could swear I know you...from someplace." She pressed the back of her hand across fleshy lips as if to seal them like the flap of a handbag. "I didn't literally mean swear...you understand?"

Jesus, he thought, that whining up-and-down voice of hers could drive you to murder, you had to listen to it very long.

"I could lie about where I been, Sister White, but I won't. I been servin time in Jackson..."

"The prison?" More an exclamation than a question.

"That's what it is, all right." He sensed that the elders behind her were sliding forward to the edge of their seats, so he angled his head and shot them a grin that sent them scooting backwards, riveting their attention on the window and its run of scenery.

"You see, Sister White, I burned down a whore house. Some folks seen me do it, told the police. The judge give me five years."

Her hand stayed pinned to her lips. Her voice was noticeably higher and had a catch in it as though the words had to jump over a little fleshy barrier in her gullet. "Even if someone did...identify you...the judge should have given you...a medal. You did the town...a service."

Lew made no reply. He was thinking about his prison cell, eight-foot long, four-feet wide. He had paced it off a million times. He was thinking about how he had missed being able to buy a whiskey when he wanted one. He was remembering the grimy, sweaty months in the wagon shop, making buggies and wagons for gents on the outside to sell for a lot more than they paid the prison. And he was thinking about how he could repay Sister White for helping to get him sixty months in prison.

40

JULY 4, 1901

LEN Kellogg, eighteen years old, knew sadness that filled him like helium pumped into a dirigible, except that it changed instantly to lead and sank to the bottom of his stomach. He told himself the reason was the spangled exuberance of the day. Firecrackers and flags and a parade were signals that summer was finishing its business, was already packing its valise, had a ticket in hand, would soon be waiting on the platform to leave town.

Beth was restless beside her brother. She grumbled, wishing she had gone with Karl who was on his way to Goguac Lake where the festivities had begun. But Len couldn't hear her complaints above the din of a passing musical group and the chatter of hundreds of people who lined both sides of Main Street, watching the good old Fourth of July parade thump and clang past. The crawling line of carts and wagons was strewn with colorful cloth, draped with banners and bright fabrics.

It was a lengthy parade, strung out for five city blocks before a flickering sea of hats and opened umbrellas. Streams of children squirted out of the crowd like sweet marshmallow creme, tossing happy shouts at the bright, chalky sky. The parade passed and the horse racers moved their mounts to the starting line.

When Hannah appeared beside Len she did not speak, nor did he turn to look at her. He just knew she was there.

"Woot you like to go to the lake, Beth?" Hannah flashed white teeth between thin, well-shaped lips. She held the little girl's hand gently in her own as if it were a bird's egg.

"I told Len a hundred times I wanted to." Beth's sullenness was offset by the yellow glow of her blonde hair.

"The horse race was about to start." Keeping his eyes on Hannah's lavish smile, he thought to himself how much whiter was her snowbank hair than Beth's.

"You were supposed to take care of me, anyhow, Hannah," Beth accused. "Mother told you to."

"I could just now get to here, darling. Your mama had me to do a thing or two for her first. Your little baby brother was acting up." Her smile intensified at Len, eyes defiant. "Maybe wanting attention on his self." A quick laugh.

Hannah and Beth, both of them squealing happily, hurried toward the Kellogg buggy parked beside the school. Len willingly went along.

THE weather was exactly what everyone had hoped it would be. From the water's blue-tinged edge to the dense groves of trees and beyond, the earth rippled with people, bright pennants, streamers. Kids of every size and mischief zipped like field mice in meadow grass. Balloons bobbled and floated, rose and dipped in flurries of glossy commotion. Cottages and camps along the shoreline were splashed with paint and draped with bunting resembling colorful crayon drawings on a child's tablet.

Four or five orchestras — including the Galesburg brass band —

played with uncommon energy in makeshift pavilions of white planking that were decked out in red-white-blue cloth. On Picnic Island, in the lake's center, Surby's double-decker resort hotel was fancied up with soft drink stands, open tables of food, and lines of firecrackers strung high across the front lawn so a battery could be set off every few minutes and then replenished while another was popping like corn. Rented rowboats from Surby's docks had a waiting list of a hundred names. Ferry boats transported crowds from the mainland and returned with others in a steady zig-zag pattern.

"MARJORIE, you stay close with us, I don't want you getting lost in this crowd."

"Mother, it's only Goguac Lake, not Central Park."

Marjorie was thirteen, had already traveled to more countries than most adults would visit in a full lifetime, and had been tutored by her father in the serpentine ways of business and commerce. Her face, yet oval and always with the pouting upper lip, was more mature than her mother's.

Her mother's simple, direct way of viewing the world continued from beneath fluttering eyelids. Ella was awed by the wealth and power brought to their family through the expedient of a powder that mixed with water and became a coffee drink. Belying their riches, her dress and shawl were plain, almost colorless.

"Father, must I stay with you and mother? My friends are at the dock. They're taking the ferry across to the island." An imploring look that said the answer was already known.

Charles (C.W.) Post seemed to have grown larger than life. He towered when walking, his glance was capable of crushing, though it rarely did. He smiled down at Marjorie. "Go on, but don't fall overboard. You'll ruin your dress and none of the boys will want to be seen with you."

She laughed sharply. "If I did fall over, it wouldn't be because of any boy, and I wouldn't need them to help me out, father."

Marjorie darted away toward the boat dock and C.W. smiled after her. "Think she'll make an impressive company owner one day, Carroll?"

"White City will be there for her when she's ready," his brother answered, referring to the name given to the Post empire's immaculately clean factories. Carroll was shorter than Charles by two inches and younger by five years. He had light brown hair, parted in the middle. His expression was forever pleasant but masked a sharp, driving talent for dealing with details and doing any job with dispatch. "We're operating around the clock, nearly 500 workers, not to mention the downtown projects."

Ella's attention was on Marjorie hurrying away from them. A nervous tic twitched the edge of her mouth. She didn't hear Carroll's praise for Charles.

"Don't fret about Marjorie, dear," Mollie Post said, taking Ella's arm in her own. "C.W. has made her into a totally self sufficient young woman. I'm going to ask him to do the same for me if I live long enough." Carroll's wife was heavyset and cheerful. She had red hair, a broad nose, and a gentle mouth, enjoyed her friendship with Ella and was flattered by her own position as favored "aunt Mollie" to her niece.

"I've advised Ella to get out more often, do more things, travel a bit." Charles' gaze was far out on the lake, languishing close to the distant shoreline. "We can afford it."

Ella's face was pouchy around the eyes. "If I didn't know better, I'd think he is trying to get rid of me."

"Nonsense," Mollie said. "C.W. is just so very busy, like my Carroll. I hardly see him since he started at the plant."

Carroll replied, "There is always more to do than we get done, Mollie. With profits of a million a year, we can't let our guard down for a minute, too many others trying to move in, cut away our market."

Ella said, "That's balderdash. An alibi for the simple, well-known fact that Charles has outgrown me. Isn't that right, darling?"

Post said nothing, refused to look at her.

"None of it is surprising when you remember that Charles always wanted a son, has never overlooked the fact that I delivered him a daughter. Entirely my fault. I must have picked up the wrong invoice. Isn't that the right word at White City? Isn't that how you place an order? Don't you use an invoice?"

Charles said frostily, "An invoice is a list of goods already shipped, Ella."

"Come, dear, let's get some lemonade." Aunt Mollie gently nudged her companion's elbow.

Carroll waited until the women were beyond earshot. "Not going so well between you two is it, brother?"

"Not for some time," Post said simply. "Odd isn't it, I've made more money more quickly with a manufactured product than almost any man in history. The Post family can buy anything any of us want. I have it all, or so it would appear, and everything is unraveling. 'Wealth is well known to be a great comforter.' How did Plato know? Was he a pauper? I can't remember." He received a shrug of inchoate understanding from Carroll.

"It's going to get better, C.W. I mean, all the pressure from starting La Vita Inn, the Company, the hotel, all those downtown constructions. Lord knows it's enough to put a couple on edge."

"Brother, I've drawn imitators from all over the nation, would-be hot-shots tramping into Battle Creek every day, each with a scheme to do what I've done. But most of the so called cereal companies aren't even producing a product, they're just selling stock and leaving town again, the money in their pockets. But I still..." He let the sentence falter, tired of it.

"They don't last, C.W., because they don't have your genius for sales, for marketing."

"Forget the flattery, Carroll."

Post walked aimlessly in a direction opposite to the one Ella and Mollie had taken. "If you want to survive in the market today, you have to file your advertising directly with the consumer, place it before her, and if she approves of it she will force the patronage of the dealer."

"It worked with Postum and Grape-Nuts," Carroll gloated, keeping pace with his long-legged brother. "We do spend a penny or two on advertising, C.W., but it sells, oh, how it sells." From memory Carroll recited: "Postum will improve your health and it's cheaper than coffee. Coffee kidnaps your health. Postum is the pure food drink, with a rich, Java-like flavor, gives you better nerves, less biliousness, better digestion, a clearer brain, steadier heart action..."

Charles laughed, drawing friendly smiles from several people around.

"...and it is absolutely free from any harmful ingredient. An army of former coffee drinkers now uses Postum." Carroll swirled his hand in the air, finger extended, and concluded in a shout: "There is a reason!"

C.W.'s mood was buoyed, "If I do say so, the ads in New York Mystery Magazine were effective."

"They were revolutionary at the least. Spot cash," Carroll said, "spot cash to anyone whose original testimonial is used by us in Postum advertisements." He hushed his voice. "Lord almighty, we were swamped by the entries. We paid out several hundred dollars but we bought some marvelous ideas."

"The Bible was indisputably right about one thing," Charles observed, continuing to doff his hat to passersby. "Riches maketh many friends."

"These people admire you, C.W. You're doing some splendid things for this city and most of the people appreciate it. They're buying Grape-Nuts, even if the ads did draw heavy fire. They're telling you they don't care, they still like the product and nobody can cast a slur on it, not in Battle Creek."

Charles said dryly, "Do you suppose the cereal ever *did* really cure anyone's appendicitis or tightened their loose teeth?"

"Maybe. Quite likely."

"Or did away with their malaria or tuberculosis?"

"People claimed it did."

"For a prize, Carroll, for a prize."

"THERE'S the famous mister Post strutting his stuff."

"We're here for pleasure, Will." Puss's reminder was gentle, plaintive. She pressed his arm to move him toward the concession stands along the main walkway, pushing the cart ahead of her with baby Hadley in it. "Please forget about business and the San and cereal flakes and everything except having a good time today. The children have looked forward to this for weeks."

"I'll put that splendid advice in the form of an official order from chief to manager," John Harvey crowed as he and Ella joined Will's family. "Today we relax. Tomorrow is time enough to take up the battle of the store shelves with mister Charles Post."

"C.W.," his wife corrected. "He prefers initials to a name, now that he's someone to be reckoned with."

"I'm so glad our paths crossed," Puss beamed to Ella, trying to divert the talk to inanities.

"Yes, so am I. How are you and the little youngster feeling?"

"We're quite all right," Puss said unconvincingly.

"She does too much," Will injected coolly. "She should take things slower. We've hired that Swedish girl, Hannah Peterson. Hannah is supposed to do the housework. Help with Beth and Hadley. But Puss doesn't want to overwork the help." He shrugged in disbelief.

"Come in next week, Ella," John Harvey patted her shoulder avuncularly. "I'll have doctor Michaels give you and Hadley a thorough checking if *my* schedule is full. Your color looks good but Will tells me you're tired most of the time. I don't like the tone of that. We should make a few more tests."

She agreed without enthusiasm, nuisancing the bright-buckled strap on her handbag.

"Let's all go over to the grandstand," John Harvey expounded, getting into the spirit of the day. "We're meeting George Willard. Come along, you'll have a fine afternoon."

Will sucked his false teeth. His darting eyes found no acceptable way to decline the invitation. His face sagged into dismal folds. He wondered why sovereigns think everyone else considers it an honor and delight to be in their royal presence.

"C.W.," Will's sourness seeped into each word, "makes me think of a cutworm."

"Discussing mister Post, were you?" Doctor James Peebles intruded into the circle of Kelloggs, unwelcomed, but unaffected by snubs. He earned a living by selling medical lessons and diplomas, as well as nostrums and medicines, through a mail-order institute. His barn-size beard and shoulder-length hair were ivory white.

"How are the Sanitas wares selling? That Gran-Nut you put out, isn't that a steal from C.W. Post?" Peebles chortled.

"If anyone stole something, *he* did," Will challenged "It was our formula."

Peebles shifted languorously to gaze down at Will. "If you've tasted the two, you'd know they are about as similar as porkchops and pig's knuckles. One's good, the other takes some getting used to. That flake you've got out," Peebles said, "it's lumpy. Too thick. Uneatable."

"Thank you for your opinion." John Harvey was already weary of Peebles' overbearing presence. "Granola and Nuttose and Maltose and the Toasted Wheat Flake are faring grandly. I wouldn't concern myself if I were you."

"I'm just gossiping, John, just passing the time of day. Don't mean anything by it."

"For your information, our Caramel-Cereal..." Will began.

"You mean your version of Postum?" Peebles continued.

Will's face blazed anew. He stalled an answer long enough to fill his lungs for a shout. "Post walked out of the San with that formula. Everyone knows it."

"Next you'll say I stole it," Charles Post remarked affably. He and Carroll pressed into the eye of the group, acknowledging the ladies by tipped hats.

Will turned to his brother accusingly. "Father always warned us. Throw in your lot with a thief, you'll get robbed."

Post's friendly expression died. He started toward Will Kellogg, his gold handled cane rising like a club.

ON PICNIC Island, Len Kellogg and Hannah Peterson strolled away from the food tables, the parasol-covered chairs, and the colorful croquet games dotted like flowering plants on the hotel's lawn. They held hands, arms swinging easily, him looking disinterestedly into the trees, she glazing the path ahead with her liquid watchfulness. They pretended to be headed nowhere in particular.

"You are sure your mama don't get angry wit me because Karl is taking care of Beth?"

"She won't know. Karl's not a tattler. Beth won't say anything as long as she has fun."

The hem of the woman's percale skirt tickled the ground. When the wind struck its folds, the cloth was smoothed against her thighs and across her flat stomach. He watched her and wanted her. On impulse, he pulled her against him, tried to kiss her mouth. She averted her face, let his lips burrow into luminous hair. Her body stayed firmly molded to his. She felt him wanting her.

"You tolt me you would not try to do these things if I agree to go with you away from the others."

He stood back and hooked his thumbs on his belt. His eyes stroked her high bosom and rounded hips through the loose dress, made over from one of Puss Kellogg's garments.

"You think I'm not much of a gentleman, don't you?"

"Sometimes, no, but mostly I think you are. I think also you are a normal man with maybe too much yens."

She reached for his hand, drew him along through the trees, toward the lake. They picked their path around fallen limbs, clumps of wild plants, a tortoise edging its way to the water.

When she halted, her breathing was rapid. "You are a beautiful man, with your bristly moustache and your so pretty eyes." The words clipped, slightly twangy. "Them's just some of the reasons I love you, Len Kellogg."

"If you do love me, Hannah, why can't we..."

"Ho, no, I won't be trapped by no cage of sweet words. My mama tolt me about such talk."

A string of firecrackers erupted, a distant sound, like tree branches breaking in an ice storm, accompanied by childrens' shrieks and screeches. Len grasped Hannah's wrist, felt its female strength, stepped close against her, his arms banding her waist. He kissed her, his mouth grinding hers, bringing a small grunt of pain low in her throat. He burrowed at her, forcing his mouth further inside hers. At last, she clutched him, returned the kiss, sucking him deeper into her. Gasping, they parted.

"When, Hannah?" His voice was as dry as attic dust.

"When we are married, Len. I have tolt you."

"We marry," he said between intakes of air, "father would ride me out of town on a rail. You have no idea how furious he gets. He wants me to go to college, be a doctor like uncle John. Karl is already studying medicine." He sighed, puffing his cheeks, tossing his head in confusion. "You'd think one of us would be enough. Other times he tells me I should follow him in the food company, learn about it. He talks like we've got our own business. Even if we did, we'd have to compete against uncle John. It wouldn't seem right going against him."

"So, Len Kellogg, *you* think about what is *right*." She shook off his grip, backed away from him, blue eyes now scratched with thin blood-lines. "Well, my mama would kill me and then die herself if I shamed her. So, marriage is right. The other way is not right."

"What if I say I will marry you?"

"I would say yes I will marry you, too."

"And my father would fire you from working in our house."

"Your mama would not let him. Besides, I would be in the Kellogg family with mister Len Kellogg making me a house and bringing a pay-check ever Friday so we would not have to ask no one for anything. It would not be right if I take wages to help your mama and to watch little Beth and baby Hadley. I would just do it."

He explored her earnest face. "Well, Hannah, I guess I shall just have to marry you."

A trill of giggles burst from the surrounding bushes. Len hurried to the edge of the clearing, parted the branches. Kneeling in the foliage were three girls about Beth Kellogg's age.

"You've been snooping, you little twits." Furious, he waved his arms. "Get out of here. Get!"

"Don't wave your arms at me, Len Kellogg." Standing up, holding her ground, one of the girls glowered at him. "I can be here if I want to. You don't own this island."

"Marjorie Post, you're an actual pain in the ass. Scram before I stretch you across my knee and spank your bottom."

THE THREAT in Post's eyes could have uprooted fence poles.

"Either call me a robber to my face so I can knock you winding or keep your remarks to yourself."

"I don't have to accuse you of stealing. There are enough others in town who say it." Will could hear the dry scraping of his tongue on his false teeth. He couldn't remember ever being in a fight.

"Hold on, C.W." Carroll clasped his brother's shoulder as Post bristled and moved toward Will Kellogg.

The outbursts drew Ella and aunt Mollie back to the growing cluster of people.

"What is all this, for heaven's sake?" Mollie asked, addressing Carroll, her eyes huge, her cheeks as red as her hair.

"There has been some misunderstanding," doctor Kellogg interjected.

"Let the big man rave on, doctor." Will's hands were shoved into his coat pockets. A defenseless posture. "He wants a fight. Uncouth. Him and Sam Gamble should team up."

"By glory, that's the final straw." Post tore his sleeve free once more, glaring over John Harvey's head. "You want a punch in your sour face, Will Kellogg, right here or over there behind that cabin?"

Carroll begged, "Please, C.W., let it be."

"I won't become a common brawler just to suit you," Will sputtered. He heard baby Hadley crying behind him and wished Puss would take the child away.

"Charles, come away," Ella Post beckoned as she and aunt Mollie worriedly moved out of the crowd.

"You are a yellow dog, sir," C.W. shouted.

Will Kellogg said wryly: "Just remember what a yellow dog does on a post."

C.W.'s jump was hampered by Carroll who had a firm two-handed hold on the coat sleeve. At that instant, Post unexpectedly found himself facing Fred Gage who had stepped in from the sidelines.

"Glad to locate you, C.W." Gage's eyes were bulbous through his wire rimmed spectacles. "Thought you might like to go over to the grandstand with Katherine and me. They've got some sort of big whoop-ti-do planned with a few speeches to praise our city's outstanding citizens. You're no doubt one of them."

Post staggered. His face was colorless. He seemed unmindful of his surroundings. Then awareness drifted back to him as effortlessly as a hawk sailing on a wind current. "Probably a good idea, Fred. I don't much like speeches, unless I'm making them, but if I stay here I may get hauled to jail for doing mayhem."

Abruptly, he turned and headed toward the concession stands with Fred Gage.

"CITIES change. Some for better, some for worse."

Joe Cox paused so the crowd could soak up the profundity of his comment. Around him on the platform sat the chief of police, a circuit court judge, a state senator, and George B. Willard, editor of the Battle Creek Journal, the Enquirer's formidable rival.

"Cities only change when someone or some event makes it happen. Cities aren't creatures who wake up one morning and look in the mirror and decide to do their hair differently," Cox bellowed. "Let me tell you, friends, Battle Creek is changing."

Between orations, steamboat whistles blew, bands unleashed rousing melodies, and sky rockets lifted off in streams of color. The celebration and speeches went on into the night.

A STREETLAMP filtered light through the rainfall, lacquering the horse's back with silver. C.W. Post was parked alone in his carriage on a narrow street at the rear of the Post Tavern. Anyone walking by would believe the carriage was empty, would have had to inspect it to discover Post inside. His coat collar was pulled high, and he wore thin black leather gloves. His eyes were washed pale, as if the rain had diluted their color. They roved the scene around him.

No breeze stirred, so the raindrops fell straight down like sand through a sifter.

Post had delivered Ella and Marjorie home an hour ago after the weather doused the celebration at Goguac Lake. He had mumbled something about going for a ride to relax and Ella had said nothing, just guided her daughter away toward the house.

"Do you know what money gives you?" he asked himself now, seated alone in the carriage. His horse followed the sound of his voice, looked back at him through one sad eye.

"Money means the privilege of saying any damned fool thing you want to without being contradicted. That is, if you pick your audience with care. Money means no voice ever is really heard in your presence except your own. Money means it becomes harder to learn anything because everyone tells you that you already know it all. Money means you can afford to be ignorant enough to believe all that crap about your own infallibility."

A smile formed, then dissolved away like a good intention. "I must not have enough money yet to have earned those sacred rights of the rich and powerful. Mayor Cox, our stalwart editor, said not one damned word about the Post Tavern Hotel, or the theater. I'm surprised he bothered to mention the carton factory or Carroll's name."

Under the shelter of the carriage roof, his imagination pictured the Tavern. Nearly a block long, six stories of red brick, with more than 120 windows on the front face alone. Impeccable furnishings, each apartment a miniature palace with private bath and telephone.

Carroll had exclaimed when he first saw it, "This hotel can stand shoulder to shoulder with the very best in any city."

Post's mind crossed the street to the northwest corner of McCamly and Main, scaled Battle Creek's first real office building: the Marjorie Block. Seven stories tall. Brick, white concrete, with oval windows at the top and layers of decorative cornices. Rows of big double windows across all four sides. He thought of the current construction project next to the plant: 600 houses, landscaping them, putting in trees, gardens, shrubbery, the Post Addition.

"So mister Cox of the *Enquirer* spent time on almost every business in the city directory except mine." The rain started to slant and some of it blew onto his face. He ignored it. "Even praised Bromberg's jewelry store, as if Battle Creek doesn't have five or six dozen jewelry stores. Named John Harvey Kellogg as the citizen of the year, rattled off the doctor's enterprises, every one of them, down to the least. Hailed the doctor as a genius, masterful businessman, heaven knows what else. But not a word about me."

He licked the rain from his lips. "Maybe I'd feel better if I were like John Harvey Kellogg: unaware that the universe doesn't revolve around *me*. Even Ella and I have worn out our interest in each other. We both know it. We've known it for a long time but neither of us admit it. Sometimes, when she instructs me about something, I just want to ask her, who anointed you the big mediator in life? She probably wants to ask me the same thing more often."

Lightning sizzled behind distant buildings. A rumble of thunder. The rain increased. Post turned the buggy homeward.

41

AUGUST 1901

"I WILL be leaving your employment in six months, doctor."

Will Kellogg wiped his hands on a greasy rag, flung it into a barrel of refuse by the moving oven in the Sanitas plant. He stood up from the clogged roller he had been cleaning. Shelves, a dozen of them, one beneath the other like ladder rungs, jiggled toasting wheat flakes along a full length of revolving belt, dumped them onto another shelf where they traveled in the opposite direction. Heat shimmered around the two men, humid enough to swim in.

"Will, we're making profits, and your work is important. I pay you handsomely, more than $7,000 last year just from Sanitas. Think about what you're giving up. And consider the question of loyalty."

"I built your new building, doctor. Begged and borrowed $50,000 of financing." The factory whirred loudly, steadily. Up and down the area, men removed trays of wheat grain from bins, rolled noisy carts of ingredients across the uneven floors while workers with oil cans and wrenches patrolled the machinery. "The plant is producing at capacity." Will gestured at their surroundings. "There is my idea of *loyalty*."

"It's your factory, though. I didn't authorize its financing, Will. Don't forget that fact." The doctor stood regally in dark suit, white shirt and black tie. He was immaculate.

"It's one reason I'm leaving." Will unrolled his soiled shirt sleeves, buttoned them, smoothed down the hair around the crown of his head where only random strands remained. "You've loaded me with the debt of the Sanitas factory..."

"I lease the building and equipment from you at a fair price. A good business arrangement. You're not losing a penny."

"But it's my debt. I'm responsible to pay it off."

"A cautionary consideration you would be wise to remember. Our partnership is valuable to both of us. Something else is rankling you."

"All right, doctor. At your bidding and on your sole decision, we have sat by and watched Charles Post get rich. He has reaped a king's fortune. He's selling products we worked years to develop." Will's voice quaked with frustration. "I've hoped you would come to your senses. Challenge Post, and others, with our own products. But your answer remains 'no.' It's senseless. I won't be bound any longer by such obstinancy and shortsightedness."

John Harvey used his handkerchief to sop sweat from his head, patting it against the skimpy hair on top. "I see," was all he said.

Will's soiled thumb and forefinger, massaged the bridge of his nose, left greasy smudges. "Last week Edwina Poole hung herself in her room. It wasn't five months ago she ran off to Spring Lake. Would probably have drowned herself then. I found her that time, but it didn't make any difference after all. She still hung herself. I told you over and over we shouldn't keep mental patients. I tell you now, I'm tired of it all."

Doctor Kellogg took three mincing steps away from the oven, toward the stairway to the lower floors, then wheeled around. "You've had a fine paying job, brother, a job most men in town would give their big toes for. You've had the prestige of the San behind you, and yes, the name I've established. Not only do you receive ten percent of Sanitas — our Granola, the toasted wheat flake, Maltose, our Gran-Nut, the entire line — but I'm giving you twenty-five percent of the profits from our publishings, the medicines, all my surgical and exercise apparatus..."

"Giving?" Will's body jerked as if he had touched the hot oven. "You make it sound like a gift."

"You earn your way, for heaven's sake, I didn't suggest otherwise. I'm just telling you what you have to lose." He smiled entreatingly. "I provided Len a job, didn't I? A watchman, a very responsible position."

"I'm going on my own at the end of this year, doctor," Will said dully. "I'll stay with you that long if you wish. Help you get things in order for the new man."

John Harvey fidgeted impatiently. "Perhaps Ella was correct when she advised me we might all be happier if you worked elsewhere."

Will's face was grim. "Then she finally will get her wish."

LATE August broke heat records, topping 104 degrees for three straight days. Lawns died rusty brown. Summer trees became deep autumn relics, their leaves cracked and brittle.

In that wilting month, Irvin Hadley Kellogg, eleven months old, died of an infectious disease. He was buried near his grandparents, John Preston and Ann Janette, and the older brother he had never met, Will Keith. And, within a few days, Len Kellogg and Hannah Kristina Peterson, recently of Sweden, were wed as abruptly as a hiccup, to the dismay of Len's parents.

ELLA sat lumpishly at her kitchen table, wearing a bib apron over a black mourning dress. She was separating ripe red currants from unripened ones in a cardboard box. Across from her, by the open door onto the back porch, Len and Hannah were ready to bolt if they must.

"Your father is too mad to speak about what you've done, Len. We've barely grieved little Irvin Hadley into his final rest and you foolish children do this...this..." Unable to find a suitable word, Ella snatched up another handful of currants. Her eyes leaped at Len's, then drifted back to her work. "How could you disobey his orders? And you,

Hannah, after we brought you in, treated you like one of our family."

"That's what she is now, mother," Len said off-handedly.

Ella's emotions confused her. Unable to sort them like spices or berries, unmindful of the heat that squashed the room, she poured the selected currants into a pot of boiling water and stirred them with a wooden ladle.

"Hannah and I are eighteen, mother. Not exactly children, even if you think of us that way. I'm working. So is she. I'll explain to father, tell him how it will be all right."

"We did not mean to go against mister Kellogg's wishes. I tolt Len we should ask permission." Hannah's eyes were a little frightened.

"Your father doesn't want to speak to you, Len. He wanted you to be a doctor. Your marriage has shocked him badly. It was hasty and uncalled for."

"We luf each other, missus Kellogg. Don't that mean something?"

IN the last week of the eighth month, after eleven unbroken days of hundred degree temperatures, a brush fire of rumor was kindled that C.W. Post and his very attractive new secretary were often seen strolling the grounds of White City at odd hours, she taking notes, he dictating letters and memoranda. Word had it that she was the only secretary he asked to work late with him, though he employed dozens. And it was well known that Ella Post was away on another of her relentless trips to foreign countries, leaving Marjorie behind to oversee the house and the staff at the La Vita Inn. The question was: who was overseeing mister Post? It made for racy gossip.

42

DECEMBER 1901

POST Manor. Elizabethan, ivied, all stone, gables, and glass. The reception hall was wide, carpeted, and adorned with beamed ceilings, bronze statues, suits of armor and gold-framed original paintings. At the top of the ample staircase, C.W.'s office was to the left, nestled beneath one of the gables and over the porte-cochere. There was a fireplace, built-in bookcases, carved pedestals, and busts of famous Romans — Hadrian, Seneca, Marcus Antonius. Behind a six-foot tall Oriental screen was a dark, paneled desk, turned to catch the light from the windows. The screen also shielded him against intruders during business hours.

C.W. sat down in his leather chair, resting his forearms on the desk's marble surface.

"Several trivial things first, miss Young. I believe we're nearly caught up on Postum Cereal's business for the day but a few other things require attention. We'll go to the larger issues a bit later, they will take more time to think out."

She nodded understandingly, moved the dictation pad into place on her lap; her hand hovered with pencil ready.

"Make a note reminding me to do an article on cooperative banks. I'll send it to the bigger newspapers." He tapped a silver letter opener against his chin. "Those building and loan associations are laudable, should be encouraged. They give the man of moderate means a chance to own his own house at a cost he can endure, makes him save some of his income by having to purchase shares in the co-op."

"My father says your Post Addition is an even better idea. More directly helpful."

"Don't be misled. Post Addition is no charity gesture. I want our workers to be national examples of pride, thrift, and character. They must care about themselves and their children's health, the conditions they live in, and they must have a chance to show they care. Homes with roads and utilities, plenty of green trees, and yards where kids can play. The price of each house is exactly what it costs to construct, but not one penny more." He laughed. "My, how I do ramble."

Gazing directly into his eyes, she said, "My father claims there is widespread respect for you around the factory."

"Your father's a good worker. So is your brother, George. I'm sorry their coal business failed, but it brought me two of my best milling department employees." He switched topics. "Please let me see that bill of lading from the railroad. You brought it in?"

"Of course," she said, taking the document from a folder and handing it to him. Their hands met as he reached for the receipt. The touch sent a static spark, and they both drew back sharply. The paper fell to the floor. The office seemed suddenly too warm and too close.

"The point I want to make in my article," C.W. began anew, in a voice that sounded alien to him, "is that a man may be an investor and not a borrower in a cooperative, but a borrower must be an investor. Does that make sense?"

"Yes, sir." She picked up the bill of lading and put it on his desk.

"The last few days I've had Christmas on my mind," C.W. heard himself say, hardly able to believe his course had meandered so far. "I've always felt Christmas is a holiday for northern climates. Michigan is perfect for it. I mean, with snow and all. And I love Christmas candy, miss Young. Do you?"

"I'm a juvenile about it," she said huskily. "Mother and I make sweets for weeks and weeks before Christmas. Last night it was butterscotches. In a day or two we'll do the peppermint drops and orange straws. At the end it will be the maple creams — they're my favorite — and the chocolate caramels." Her face had a dreamy look. "The aunts and uncles and cousins come in on Christmas eve, and we put up mistletoe and have music and fix more food than we should."

"It sounds beautiful," Post admitted, carefully edging into her dreaminess.

"You and missus Post and Marjorie are invited to come by. You can taste all of the..." She hesitated, blushed. "How forward of me."

"Not at all," he said quickly, and felt a startling hunger in his chest. "If missus Post returns from her visit to Great Britain, we may come around."

"If not, you and Marjorie are most welcome." Her gaze intertwined with his; her heart pumped so loudly she knew he could hear it. "But there *is* a condition."

Post stared at her, waiting.

"I have a first name," she said. "It's Leila."

43

FEBRUARY 1902

"I got me a plan, burn down that goddamned San," Lew boasted.

Sam Gamble, flat on the cot in the corner of Lew's shack, acknowledged the announcement. "What for? You'll just get caught, sent back to Jackson."

Lew sipped coffee from a dirty mug. On the table before him were remnants of bread, cheese, and five hard-boiled eggs, two of which he had bought at Burley's, the other three he had stolen when Burley wasn't looking.

"Them Kelloggs and that crazy Bible-spoutin Sister, they put the law on me, got me jailed. I ain't ever liked that squirt-assed doctor, then I met the high-falutin Sister White on the train and by God, I didn't even like her as much as I don't like him. Burn down the San, make 'em both pay."

Gamble rolled over, faced the ceiling, eyes closed. "Do what you want, just leave me out."

"Bullshit. You livin here off'n me, me puttin up with your whinin and you actin like you're a hunnert and ninety years old, and I ask for some help on this and you think all you got to say is no thank you." A light flashed behind Lew's bleary eyes. "Besides, you could put his sweet woman in her place. She snubbed you plenty. It was her got you beat up, remember?"

Gamble wearily clumped his feet from the cot to the floor, forced himself to a sitting position. The gorged muscle of chest and neck and bicep that had been his pride in earlier days was startlingly missing. He grasped the edge of the cot, propped himself with unsteady arms.

Lew massaged his naked head vigorously, then gobbled a hard-boiled egg, some of the rubbery yoke dribbling onto his lap. "What's the best way to get in there without runnin into all them goddamned doctors?"

Sam made a mental tour of the San, remembering its hallways and corridors and stairwells from the days when he delivered ice or went there to catch sight of missus pink ears. The effort at thinking increased his headache. "I'd go in through the tunnels. Maybe from the fieldstone building out there where they got the lab. Better yet, the nurses house. They never was too good about keepin doors locked."

Lew nodded. "That's the way we'll do it, then."

"I tole you, don't figure on me. I'm sick."

Lew slung the remainder of the egg against the shack's plank wall. "Damn you, you'll help if you're dyin or dead," he screamed, both eyes yellow with rage, one glowering under the folds of its damaged lid. "We burn it to the ground and you're with me, show me how to get in. Strike the matches for me if I tell you."

Gamble's arms bent and he teetered onto his side, lying on the cot. "I don't know if I can, Lew. Jesus, I feel awful."

"Have some of this, old pal. Fix you right up." He ransomed a bottle of liquor from under the table.

When Sam accepted the offering, just holding onto it, not drinking, Lew shambled to the door, gazed out at the unexpected February thaw. The railroad tracks at the end of the gravel yard glistened like snail trails under sooty skies.

"We'll do it tonight." He wiped his hands on his coat. "Yessir, doctor Kellogg, we'll come to see you tonight."

AT the Post Tavern the Posts had consumed a sumptuous meal, were finishing off with cups of Postum, the men lighting up cigars, Marjorie digging into a parfait glass of cherry tapioca.

"What are you writing on the tablecloth, Carroll?" Mollie stretched her neck, tried to read the words upside down. "Don't you know it will ruin the fabric?"

"C.W. can take it out of my salary. I'm listing the companies that've started a cereal business around here since C.W. did." He blew a torrent of cigar smoke into the air.

"How many you have, uncle Carroll?" Marjorie asked.

"Eleven, honey. There's Ralston, although it's more like a branch since it's really out of St. Louis. Cero-Fruto there at McCamly and Liberty. I don't think they'll be around much longer, though. They're in bad financial trouble. I.W. Fell's doing pretty good with his Mapl-Flakes; he claims it keeps your bowels open, stops bad breath, gets rid of gas, eliminates insomnia and puts rosy cheeks on your kids."

Post said, "I think Fell has been reading our ads."

Enjoyable as the meal had been, pleasant as the company was, Charles felt jittery, discontented. He closeted a vague desire to get up and leave the hall and go...where? He wasn't sure.

Mollie asked, "Charles, when is Ella returning from London?"

Marjorie skewered her father with a look.

"She wrote a while back, before Christmas," Charles said, "but I don't remember her mentioning coming home. Soon, I imagine."

Post moved away from the touchy topic. "A labor leader came in last week, told me he could get workers for us under a dollar an hour. If we went along with his union, that is."

"And you showed him the door, I hope," Mollie suggested.

"I told him there was no earthly reason our workers would join his union and send their money out of town to stir up strikes and violence in other parts of the country."

"It has been terrible lately," Mollie lamented. "Killings, bombings, injuries, my, my." She finished her Postum, dabbed at her mouth with a napkin. "Charles, I see where the famous Andrew Carnegie is giving New York City a gift of five million dollars to build libraries. Are you planning to go and do likewise?"

"I'd appreciate it if you'd say nothing about me leaving Battle Creek." He knocked cigar ashes into a big glass ashtray. "It's far from certain I will move. I'll content myself with doing my part to help turn Battle Creek into the best little city it can be. I want to repay this town for what it's given us."

"By leaving?" Mollie's eyes twinkled.

"The east is where the center of commerce is, it's where we need to be represented. The better Postum cereal does, the more it will mean to Battle Creek."

"Like it does for missus Young, daddy? The coat and necklace you gave her?"

Mollie immediately began to search for a waiter to order more Postum. Carroll coughed as though choked on cigar smoke, bending over his knees, napkin at his mouth.

"It is *miss* Young, Marjorie. Not missus. She isn't married."

"But you are. To mother."

LOONY Lew cracked the lock with his crowbar, hesitated, listened. The night was cruelly cold and his breath was visible in small frosty clouds. Finally, he pushed the broken door of Brandenmeyer's Hardware and went inside. When his vision adjusted to the dimness he saw a cash register on top of the nail counter, a weight scales and wrapping paper rack, buckets, pans, graters, tin funnels. Harnesses were strung on the walls above wooden kegs of nails. Rolls of fencing, were lined up like fat silver soldiers at attention. Pitchforks and shovels dangled on hooks, carbide lanterns hung from spikes on the wall. He moved with care, testing the floor ahead of him with each step. It took him five minutes to locate the cauldron-shaped drum near the rear of the building. Kerosene.

"DOCTOR Kellogg is becoming quite daring with his advertising, isn't he, Will? I've never seen anything like this with the Kellogg name on it." In her front room, Ella referred to the latest issue of Good Health magazine draped across her lap. She resettled her glasses and read aloud:

"A gentleman whose baby lay at the point of death, starved and poisoned by cow's milk, learned by accident of Malted Nuts. He made haste to obtain a supply and this fat-and-blood making food snatched the child from the jaws of death. That story is on a level with Penny Dreadful booklets. Is it true or did John Harvey make it up to sell Malted Nuts?"

"I don't know, Puss." Will worked at a makeshift desk, a converted library table, reviewing the week's receipts for the Sanitas plant. "I think C.W. Post has scared John Harvey. My brother is reacting."

"Karl wrote he has no intention of getting married yet. He will definitely be a doctor." Ella was referring to a letter received today.

Will removed his glasses, scrubbed his eyes with balled fists. "One out of three." She knew he meant Len and himself, the losers.

"If you do decide to start your own cereal company," she began, flustered, searching for something of comfort but choosing wrongly, "are you trading a certain job for an uncertain one?" Adding lamely, "And the burden of more work than ever?"

Lord in heaven, he thought, she is frightened I might fail at what I do. She's afraid I'll drive us into bankruptcy. She believes I only exist in the shade of my brother.

Will's stomach boiled. He closed the ledger books. "When I leave the doctor next month, I won't go back, Puss. I give you my word."

THE Post Tavern apartment was spacious. Excluding the bedrooms, it contained two sofas, eight fabric-covered chairs, four wing chairs, a fireplace, floor-to-ceiling windows, walk-out doors and a balcony, two matching Regency oval tables, a Duncan Phyfe library table, a wall of bookshelves, and enough lamps, mirrors, and original paintings to outfit five or six Battle Creek homes. A 16th century Ispahan floral rug covered the front room floor in golds and mulberry.

Marjorie walked across the expanse of the room in the darkness. Her bedroom door was open, a black box behind her. Charles' door was shut but a glow of lamplight outlined its bottom edge. She listened until she heard the rustle of papers, then she turned the latch without knocking.

Charles Post looked up. "You should be asleep, little sweetheart."

"Can't." She came into the room. "Are you busy?"

He shoved some papers aside, leaned into his slat-back chair. "No, but it would probably be better if we waited until morning."

"It's morning now. It's four o'clock."

"You know what I mean, smarty."

The upper lip protruded delicately. "Can I ask you something, daddy?"

"Certainly." He sipped amber liquid from a teacup.

"What are you writing?"

"Notes, an update for 'I Am Well.' Uncle Carroll thinks it should be reprinted and put in the Grape-Nuts boxes once more." He displayed a battered example of the small booklet produced eight years ago. "People still write us for copies."

"I liked the part about the Yogi who could climb a rope that stuck up in the air."

"I never actually saw it happen, sweetheart. I only heard about it. Is that what you wanted to ask?"

"No. I wanted you to tell me why mother doesn't come home."

"I tried to tell you at dinner."

"Isn't she lonesome?"

"I think everyone is, Marjorie, some time or another." He emptied his teacup. "Please go back to bed. You need sleep and I have work to do."

"I miss her, I miss mother. Sometimes I feel as bad as I did when you used to be sick and I didn't get to see you for a long time."

He looked across the room at his daughter. He realized she would soon be a grown woman. He told her again, softly, to go to bed.

She stood up. Her stiff-backed stance reminded him of Ella.

"Daddy, what's all the light by the Sanitarium? Come and look."

Post went quickly to the window, his robe winging behind him like a flying jib. The predawn sky above Battle Creek was vivid orange and red — shifting, polarizing, vibrating in live patterns.

"My God," he exclaimed loudly, causing Marjorie to jump. His hands contracted, fingernails chiseling the flesh of his palms. "My God," he repeated, "The Sanitarium is burning!"

44

SAM entered the Sanitarium's first floor hall from the basement tunnels. Directly opposite him was the pharmacy. An attendant was carrying out a shiny tray of medicants, saw Sam, took in the filthy clothes, the unshaved face and bloodshot eyes, reddish saliva stains on lips and beard.

"What are you doing here?" He demanded. "This area is closed."

Sam's mouth moved but he said nothing. He just slanted himself against the basement door, propping it closed.

"Are you a patient, mister?" The attendant had no way of knowing, since the San's main building alone was six stories tall and had nearly 300 people sleeping in its rooms. Holding the tray of medicines, he was uncertain whether to go back into the dispensary with it or hit the nearest intercom and call for assistance.

"Need help." Sam's voice was an ossified sigh.

"What are you saying? Speak up, man." The attendant shifted the tray into one hand. The glass bottles on it clinked musically. "What is it you want?"

"Help me, damn you." A cold savagery showed in his eyes and he stood up straight, preparing for — what? His arms were unreliable, no strength in them, his legs infirm. "Fire. Call firemen. Burning."

Convinced at last that the apparition was a mental patient, the attendant's free hand searched behind him until it clutched the pharmacy door handle. He eased the door open, edged inside, placed the tray on a counter by the entrance. He guardedly watched Sam and blindly explored for the telephone, fingers scurrying along the wall like an insect. At that moment, Sam pulled open the basement door. Roils of smoke billowed and swirled from an underground eruption. Flames darted behind the smoke, hot and searching. The attendant suddenly felt the swollen heat pulsing beneath his feet as if the floor were on...

"Fire." Sam said in a frothy exhale.

"Holy shit." The attendant sprang out of the pharmacy in a leap, running down the hallway, racing for the alarm box, screaming the warning Sam had already given twice: "Fire!"

THE hydraulic elevator rattled to a stop on the third floor. Its door clanked open loudly, hollowly in the stillness. Sam looked both ways along the empty hall, saw closed rooms, electric wall lights, occasional chairs for patients to rest and talk with friends or other patients. A cough ground out of his throat. He put a shoulder to the wall, choked off the desire to clear his lung passages, settled for a few muffled exhalations.

After several minutes he walked woozily to the end of the corridor where another hall intersected. From there he could see the nurse's station near the geometric center of the building, as it was on each level. Uncertain what to do, he hesitated, then heard the faint banging of a broom or mop handle striking a bucket. He lumbered toward the noise, going the opposite direction of the nurse's station. Ringlets of smoke sneaked across the top step of the stairway entrance behind him and wiggled across the floor like snakes.

Aurelia was stacking cleaning tools in a large storage room laden with push brooms, dustpans, feather dusters, buckets, shelves of linens and towels. When she noticed Sam, she stared unbelievingly.

"What do you want up here at this time of night?" she asked defiantly.

"Place is on fire," Sam managed to say. "Missus pink ears got to get out. Go get her out." Then he gave way to a spasm of coughing that drove him down onto the floor.

Far below, the fire had eaten its way out of the basement, into the pharmacy, and was racing up the main stairwells. Thick smoke already was pouring out of vents in the roof.

LESS than two minutes after the alarm had sounded in station two, horses were rigged to steamers and hook-and-ladder wagons and hose wagons, reins dropped from the ceiling, a fireman stomped a trip lever, spring-loaded doors burst open, and the wagons shot out of the station house, boilers pouring smoke, steam whistles ejecting clouds of shrill moisture. Wagons also were on their way from firehouse one, several blocks away.

Chief Plato Weeks arrived minutes after captain Vern Fonda. Both wore the groggy faces of men rousted from their beds. Weeks stepped in front of a man in a nightgown who was running across the lawn, cradling a porcelain bedpan in his arms, a wild look on his fear-mottled face.

"Is the fire still below the first floor?" the chief asked. The man glared back in utter confusion, then loped off without answering. "Send some men inside to recon, Fonda. Have one of them get right back out here to me." The captain moved on instruction, not needing the chief's other comment: "We have to know what we're up against."

Patients and nurses and doctors were scurrying out of the building like mice exiting a barn where the weasel had come to hunt. Patients were dressed in robes and hospital gowns. Some were pushed in wheelchairs by attendants; others rushed along on their own motor power, forgetting they were supposed to be ill, even immobile. Every fire escape was a writhing spinal column of human flesh moving in agonizing slowness down the body of the wood-frame structure.

Along the front and side streets of the building, firemen attached black rubber hoses to cast-iron hydrants. The fabric reinforced hoses were spun like giant skeins of yarn from enormous wheels mounted on hose wagons. Steam pumpers, with vertical boilers and coal-burning stokers roaring at inferno pitch, were brought into place to boost hydrant pressure to 1500 gallons per minute. Three wagons outfitted with chemical extinguisher tanks, each brimming with a soda-acid-water mixture, were positioned strategically by the battalion chiefs. The chemical wagons' 24-foot extension ladders would take a man and hose only to the second floor. No higher.

INSIDE the building, near its center, the fire trailed up a service stairwell, met no resistance, pushed from below and sucked from above by the updraft. Steps, banisters, walls, all wooden. Plenty of fuel to feed the hiking flames, keep them straining for more. Within minutes, flames scaled the entire back of the building and the heat could be felt eddying through the corridors on drifting currents of dying sparks and bits of ashes. All wiring had burned out almost at the start and the electricity was shut down, but an eerie orangish glow gave the impression of hundreds of lamps. Torrents of water and chemicals thudded against the front walls like a tropical storm.

AURELIA knelt by Gamble. "You got to stand up. I can't carry you."

Sam's head lolled, he oozed spittle. His breath was harsh. "Got to get her out," he nearly wept the words.

A bunched bathrobe appeared in the doorway, naked hairy legs emerging from its hemline. A white hand clutched an open box of matches. In the other hand a lit match, as if there wasn't enough fire in the building. Behind the flickering face were three other people, half-shadows, drifting, shifting splotches in the dimness.

"I'm a patient. Where's the goddamned stairs?"

Aurelia coughed, fanned the smoke with her cloth. "Other way," she gasped. "Fire escape, take it, safer."

The match fizzled. White hairy legs retreated, pursued by three vague specters. The smoke gulped them all.

Using a broom for a crutch, Aurelia finally put Sam Gamble on his feet and ushered him into the hallway. Her throat stung as if quilled with pins. "We're all right, we get the end of this hall, there's a window. Fire escape." She yanked on Gamble's right arm, helping to support him. He was coughing uncontrollably and though he was a stick-man compared to his former self, he seemed to her to weigh five hundred pounds.

The heat had suddenly intensified to shock level and the smoke was a sealed cocoon. People were shouting very far away. Smell of burning wood everywhere and the stench of blistering lead paint.

There was a rush of air and flames. It barreled around a corner or out of a room — Aurelia couldn't tell which — struck them, reeled them backward, tumbled them to the floor, breaking their hold on each other. Instantly the fire retreated and smoke expanded into the hall, grainy and smothering.

Aurelia stayed flat on the floor, discovered she could breathe there. "Where are you?" she asked, squawking the words into swirling black wool. She reached out, found nothing.

"Where are you?" she called again.

She wiggled across the heated floorboards, crawled atop a cotton dhurrie rug, almost cried with relief. It was the only rug of its kind on the third floor. Its design and fringes and position informed her that the fire escape was twenty feet ahead. In her mind it was twenty miles. The doorways on both sides of the hall were glowing and making horrible cracking sounds.

OUTSIDE, Weeks and Fonda knew the Sanitarium couldn't be saved. It was burning as if made of paper. The front of the building was a single torch, and a high wind was fanning the flames into greater frenzy. They battled now to minimize the loss in any way possible.

"Keep chasing it," Weeks shouted through his megaphone in a voice emptied of hope, then muttered, "Thank heaven it isn't snowing."

His words were lost in the roar of a falling wall and roof at the pharmacy wing. Bright particles spewed fifty feet into the sky. The flaming fragments drifted onto the roofs of frame houses along Harbour Street and ignited the shingles.

At the main building's north end, four people jumped from the crumbling porch roof, clothing afire, to land in outstretched blankets that were quickly rolled around them to stifle the fire. Crunching and groaning, the San's cupola slid away, toppled, a meteoric globe that plummeted to the ground. A detachment of firemen near the entrance barely escaped being smashed under it. A brick section of the front wall loosened and shattered in a cascade of stone, belching outward, tripping a fireman on the ladder rungs as he scrambled down. He pitched the water hose into space, was flung after it, screaming as he fell, hitting the ground a full story below. At the same moment, the entire back wall was transformed into a molten mass, sliding earthward in terrifying slow motion. The atmosphere was alive with burning brands, hurled by the wind.

Lieutenant Shaw materialized out of the yard's turmoil. "Chief, it's caught the hospital, too."

He pointed across Harbour Street where flames were leaping out of the other facility's upper windows. The roof was a stretch of fuming wood. A woman jumped from a fourth floor window, her white gown floating around her like butterfly wings. She crashed onto a roof two floors down.

Fonda ordered some men to follow him, signaling three wagons to shift to the hospital with their hoses. "Put a ladder on that roof where the woman landed. We have to get her off of there."

SAM sensed he had been left behind, was curious why he didn't care. He knew he could never climb down the fire escape even if he could find it. His lungs were seared, his thorax busted open, he was sure, from some kind of pain worse than anything he had ever felt.

His smile was grotesque, a parody of the stretched, silent scream from a tongueless victim on an Inquisition pyre. For a fraction of a steaming moment he wondered if missus pink ears had made it to safety. Then he realized he didn't care about that, either.

A nearby wall collapsed with the sound of a freight train roaring from a cavern. Confetti of sparks, twirling like swarms of drunken fireflies. Intense heat curled hairs of wood on the floorboards. Something was sizzling, frying. Smoke wrapped Sam Gamble tightly in a fleecy shroud. His lungs leaped and jerked. He felt panic. Horror. "Lew, you no-good sonuvabitch," he tried unsuccessfully to shriek.

A starburst of nerves erupted with brutal pain. No air. Blinded. His brain's oxygen clamped off. He quivered into numbness. Consciousness slipped, was gone. In the same instant, the floor shattered, pulled apart, fell, taking him down with it.

AT six a.m. the winter sun was yet hidden but the world was a myriad of noises and streaks of dancing light — all children of the fire. Sounds of splintering, breaking, popping; spitting embers, bursting wood and glass; creaking, groaning walls, swaying, falling; horses whinnying and stamping where they were tied beyond the fire's perimeter; thumping of pistons and clanking of linkages in the connecting rods of the pumpers, making the ground vibrate while flames swelled, receded, growled anew. And there was the low murmur of the crowd, a wordless anthem hummed by a stunned, confused chorus.

Beneath the waves of smoke, distant from the worst heat, near the very middle of the crowd, was Charles Post, fully dressed in tie and hat and topcoat. Beside him, Marjorie, Carroll, Aunt Mollie.

"How dreadful, Carroll." Mollie held tightly to her husband's hand. "I can barely believe it."

"What's gone and what's past help, should be past grief," Post quoted Shakespeare, but was swept with an odd sort of remorse anyway.

At the front of the crowd, where faces were highly illuminated with streaks of flickering colors were Will Kellogg, Ella, Len, Hannah, Karl, Beth. The flames reflected from Will's glasses and Ella's — four small mirrors in constant, jerky motion. Will's hands were smudged with charcoal from helping people down the fire escapes.

"Are your hands burned?" Ella's face was tear grimed.

"No." Will looked at his palms as if they belonged to someone else. "They're not burned, Puss. Just dirty."

"You helped a lot of people off of them escape ladders, mister Kellogg, you and my Len. We were worry't about you being hurt but we was proud of you, too."

"Hush, Hannah. We weren't in danger." Len squeezed her waist suggestively, pleased she had noticed his heroics.

"Oh, Will," Ella cried, "there goes the rest of the wall."

Nearby, Joe Cox wrote rapidly on a pad while Russell Hart talked to him in an unrelenting flow of words.

Further along, Ella Kellogg stood surrounded by San employees, including Aurelia Skipworth, all motionless and dumbstruck. Mouth slack, shoulders drooped, Ella tightened her coat, feeling its warm wool, and she wondered, "What will John Harvey do when he comes back tomorrow? This will kill him."

Only a few feet from her, Sister Ellen White was grouped with a dozen or more church elders and deacons. Loudly she singsonged, "I prophesied this would happen...The catastrophe...is God's signal to us...He is displeased."

PART FIVE

Young people are fitter to invent than to judge.
Francis Bacon

45

MARCH 1906

A DEEP fright, a pointless kind of fear, but prickly and real, occupied part of Will's mind. It was a fright that huddled down in his gut and scraped with a clawed finger to remind him that it didn't mean to go away.

Fear of failure.

The scare was bunched inside him with a strange mate: cool-headed, lighthearted joy, his throat and chest pinched by elation.

If he had his way about it this was the last time he ever would walk the length of the Sanitarium's north porch to meet his brother. A too familiar walk. He could detail the stones and bricks and tiles on the walls and flooring of the huge ionic porch. He knew every detail, crevice, every crack, as if he had put each in its place.

His heels rang on the slabs of artificially tinted stone. The sunlight sifted through rounded archways and painted the opposite brick wall orange, turned a row of windows to reflective white. Thirty wheelchairs lined the brick wall, each with a female patient, eyes closed, facing the sun, all bundled alike. Doctor Kellogg's famous wheelchair brigade taking the cold air cure.

Will smiled inwardly. He could almost hear John Harvey instructing: "Breathe deeply, ladies, very, very deeply. Unload your congested viscera, enrich your blood with vitalizing oxygen. Breathe deeply."

Will entered the lobby. It was immense and as brightly lighted as if it had no roof. All of the sky seemed to enter its big windows and plated doors. Even after these four years of maintaining the rebuilt San for John Harvey, it still unnerved him when it swallowed him. Today, though, the thought of leaving it forever was a giddy sensation of release, as airy as the cliff high ceilings.

A heavyset woman in a nurse's white uniform behind the reception desk asked, "Can I help you this morning, mister Kellogg?"

"Inform my brother I am in the lobby. We have an eight o'clock meeting."

Will walked on toward the glassed partition at the end of the lobby. As he passed the ornate registration desk, he noted the tall cabinet clock. It told him he was ten minutes early. He stopped at the flower and plant garden in the center of the floor, looked around at the tall marble columns entwined with vines. Then he moved on to stand in front of a broad, plateglass partition. Beyond and beneath it was the Palm Garden, a glass-domed South American jungle stocked with ferns, air plants, orchids, orange and rubber trees. Down in the artificial, humid heat were banana trees growing tropical fruit in wintery Michigan in the month of March.

He thought: the doctor got everything he wanted in his new Sanitarium. Even those jaded, worldly-wise, immeasurably bored New Yorkers who come expecting what? — a log cabin and outdoor privy? — soon lost their pose of mild contempt and were caught gaping at the majestic size and surroundings.

"Fireproof, Will," that is what John Harvey had proclaimed. "Solid, unflinching fireproof." He'd stood in the lobby, almost where Will now waited, and held out both arms as though inviting the place to jump into his embrace like a dog.

"Nothing can destroy this Sanitarium, not fire, wind, frost, or floods. It is permanent. Iron and marble and cement, basement to roof. And it's all automated, with fresh air ducts and heating ducts so the air goes where it's called for, straight to where it's needed."

It was a fact. The new San was far better than the original model. It had a chapel, two swimming pools indoors, two more outside, and a surgical ward with every known antiseptic precaution.

Will thought of how quickly the doctor had lined up financiers but had, in the end, cajoled him into staying on as an employee and a fund-raiser. "You see, dear brother, while we have ample cause to celebrate the offered support of several well-to-do individuals, no one of them has suggested he will foot the entire cost. Furthermore, I would not want just a *single* backer even if one was available. That capitalist would virtually own the Sanitarium, an untenable prospect. Therefore, we must draw from a variety of sources, and keep the San a corporation."

John Harvey's mood had dampened instantly and he had frowned. "The rebuilding is only part of the story," he said. "The institution also has $245,000 in other debts. In actuality, we must find a total of three-quarters of a million dollars."

And, they had.

Will clicked open his gold pocket watch. His reverie had eaten up the spare ten minutes and more. His stomach purled. He spoke under his breath:

"Well, John Harvey, I don't have to linger while you play the laggard any more."

He shut the watch, adjusted his hat. As emphatically as a judge's decree he strolled toward the grand entrance doors. When he passed the reception desk the nurse asked:

"Are you leaving before the doctor comes, mister Kellogg?"

His face was stern, his lips barely moved. "Tell my brother if he wants to talk to me, I'm in my company's office." An afterthought, "Advise him to call ahead."

The pawing fright was yet with him, scratching his insides, adding to his belly's murmurs. So, too, the feeling of exhilaration remained, but it had become dominant. Will exited the Sanitarium building and quickly left its grounds. On his way along Washington Street he halted at the door of Webb's diner. Without hesitation he went inside and ordered three eggs up, six strips of crisp bacon, and a platter of buttered toast.

FOR once in his life John Harvey's tardiness to a meeting was for good reason. He was on trial.

The courtroom: his office in his home on Manchester. The witness chair: his leather seat behind a desk nearly as wide as the one in his former Sanitarium office, but not elevated on a platform. His defense attorney: himself.

The prosecutors: two ancient-looking men who were dressed almost identically in black longcoats, holding black hats in their hands. Each had a bearded face and brushy, overhanging brows. Side-by-side on a Victorian love seat, they peered at the doctor and leaned forward at the same angle in a sort of dual hunch. They were no relation to each other. Only their religion and their purpose this morning connected them.

"Brother Amadon, Brother Bourdeau, may I send for some refreshments? Juice or milk, perhaps? Have you breakfasted?"

"It may seem early in the morning for us to wake you." Elder George Amadon's voice was feathery, even delicate.

"Not at all." John Harvey's tone was generous. "I stopped my work at the San just after one o'clock this morning, took three hours sleep, then was awake and working again."

The soft voice continued: "A young lady opened the door for us and said 'Papa will come soon.' You have a large family, I might guess. It is a blessing."

"Ella and I had no children of our own, as you may recall, so we gathered a goodly number of homeless youngsters and made them our family."

Elder Bourdeau's resonance was the opposite of his companion's: grating to the ears. "We came to determine where you stand in regard to the Sanitarium and other matters."

Kellogg shifted his eyes from Bourdeau to Amadon, searching for explanation.

Amadon said, "Every week we have a gathering of the elders. At our last meeting we learned from Brother Foy that he had a most disturbing interview with you and you were not pleased with him because of his attachment to the Tabernacle's people. He said you remarked that you did not think you would voluntarily withdraw from the church but you would be rather pleased to have the church drop your name."

Before Kellogg could object, whispery phrases supplicated:

"Nothing would please us more, brother Kellogg, than to have you tell us we have formed a wrong view of your position."

"Brother Foy," Kellogg sighed, coloring, "is a man whose conduct has been circumspect, at best. I often hear he does things which are not good for the institution, for the San. I have kept him on as an employee because of his Godly life and good influence. My talk with him, which has most certainly been reported to you inaccurately, came because of a remark he himself dropped, saying he had no confidence in the religious standing of the Sanitarium or its work. He told me that the Lord and the General Conference brethren were not in sympathy with the Sanitarium, more specifically, my leadership of it. The claim amazed me."

Bourdeau's head moved affirmatively. Amadon only raised his shaggy eyebrows, sadly.

"What of your book?" Caressingly, accusingly.

"*The Living Temple*?"

"That is exactly what brother Amadon meant," Bourdeau skirled like an angry bagpipe.

Kellogg bent forward, made a temple spire of his fingertips.

"After my book was condemned by the Conference I was flabbergasted. The views I put into it I had already stated at the Conference, with all present to hear and critique, including yourselves. Not a word of disagreement reached me. My sentiments were published in the *Bulletin*, and I preached them at camp meetings. Afterwards, sister White read the report of what I said and she declared, 'That is right.' I sent the book's manuscript to her nearly a year before publication and I never received one line from her criticizing it."

"Do you believe there is only one life, God's life?" Amadon moistened his lips.

"What you mean is: am I a pantheist? I am not. If I were, wouldn't I be out worshipping the morning sun or talking to the trees? If I've made errors, I only ask to have them pointed out and I will correct them."

Bourdeau waved a bony hand. "What of the document dated two days after the fire? It was sent to you as a written demand not to rebuild the Sanitarium in Battle Creek."

"I never received such a document, sir. I never knew it existed until it was published nearly three years after it supposedly was sent to me. The building was finished by then. That entire maneuver was nothing less than a scheme, an outright fraud to discredit me." Kellogg appeared to be relaxed but hidden within his deskwell his left leg jittered as though taken with palsy.

Bourdeau's eyes were mummified: cold and crumbly. "We intend to bring the Sanitarium into unison with the instructions the Lord has given."

"Gentlemen, I don't interfere with the way you manage your church, so, wouldn't it be reasonable and fair if you showed the same courtesy toward me and my San?"

"*Your* San?" Bourdeau scoffed.

"I built it, sir, made it what it is."

The elders exchanged sickly glances.

"When I came to the San, its rooms were empty, it was losing money. Today it is world famous, filled to capacity. There are waiting lists of people wanting to get in, famous people, influential people, paying patients as well as those with little or no money." John Harvey's declaration grew to lecture pitch and pace. "You should wish such success for your church.

"There are careless charges that we are robbers at the Sanitarium, but no one points out to us what we have robbed. They say we have spies around the country. I am aware of none. My book, they say, is not orthodox. When the claim was made we boxed it up. The remaining copies are sealed away in the basement of the sanitarium.

"Still the lies continue about me, stories that I own a house of prostitution downtown and allow the doctors in the Sanitarium to seduce the nurses.

Sister White even wrote that my book taught free love doctrines. She openly libeled me after earlier approving the book.

"If this church endorses the campaign of the General Conference — its reliance on fraud, deceit, and misrepresentation — then I say, when they drop my name from the lists I shall accept it as release the Lord has given me from any further responsibility to them. I am, though, ready to make restitution if the claims and accusations are pointed out to me. I am sick of the damaging rumors being encouraged."

Bourdeau growled contemptuously, "You could not possibly carry on the Sanitarium without the General Conference."

"Brother Bourdeau, brother Amadon, we know people go to Sister White with schemes they want to carry through under her endorsement. They get the old lady's approval and then stand up and say, 'See, the Lord has spoken.' But the Lord hasn't spoken; it is only an old woman, as interpreted by those who would use her to their own gain."

"Then in this matter it is Sister White versus John Harvey Kellogg."

"It isn't any such thing, brother Amadon."

"What pray tell do you call it?"

Kellogg picked up a pencil, tapped it methodically against the edge of the desk. "It is Sister White versus the facts."

The pencil's clackety-clack was of little notice to either of the old men. Watery sunlight reached through a window and lay gently on the wallpaper and sparkled off the face of a wall clock. Nearly an hour gone by, John Harvey thought. I will have to apologize to Will, maybe even send him some garden vegetables from the greenhouses.

"The people who work here sacrifice much in the cause," he argued quietly now. "We are trying to maintain the only Christian medical school in the world, the only one the world has ever seen. The men and women receive little compensation; after a day's work they study nights, evenings, mornings."

"You did ignore the Testimony instructing you to build a smaller hospital after the other burned down," Amadon rejoined. "You were asked graciously to assign the Sanitarium to the General Conference."

"The General Conference has demonstrated it knows nothing about running a hospital."

"Then your answer is 'no'?" Question and fact bundled into one utterance.

Bourdeau cleared his throat. "With me, the question has converged on the point of the Sanitarium by-laws. In them, you stated your conviction that the work of the Sanitarium is not to be sectarian or denominational."

"I said members must believe in the fundamental principles of Christianity."

Bourdeau narrowed his eyes under drooping brows. "It is a great great question in my mind, then, that our Seventh Day Adventists who started the institution are not mentioned at all in the incorporation or the by-laws which you and your board prescribed. How can the Adventists be known as the persons who control the Sanitarium?"

"They shouldn't. They aren't. They never were." Kellogg held the old man's baleful stare. "Brother Bourdeau, the denomination did not establish the institution. A private corporation did. People put money into it and it was owned by them. They were all Seventh Day Adventists but they didn't include the church in the articles of incorporation. It was distinctly understood and stated by me when I took charge, the institution would be nondenominational."

"But, the money to operate..."

"The church never appropriated money to it, and the tithe was not appropriated to it. It was done by individuals in the same way you would run a business, but working all the while *with* the denomination, *for* the denomination."

Bourdeau slapped his leg angrily and stood up. Amadon, too, got to his feet.

Finally, Kellogg rose. "I tell you so you can carry my words back to the others, this is a medical institution and it will not be run with an ulterior denominational purpose."

Both men put on their hats in unison, turned as one toward the door. Amadon wet pale lips. "Thank you for your time, doctor. You'll hear from the Conference after it has deliberated."

JOHN Harvey knelt in front of Ella. "I'm sorry, my darling, but I told Amadon and Bourdeau the truth last week."

He wanted to reach out, touch her, soothe and calm her, but was unsure if it was the thing to do. Ella cried quietly into her handkerchief.

"You wouldn't have wanted me to lie to them, would you?"

Her face was covered by both hands and he was surprised to see how worn and scraped those hands had become. We are getting older, he thought. Too quickly. We are no longer young, and I have broken her heart by not capitulating before the church elders.

"When did you hear?" he asked.

"This afternoon," she snuffled. Her hair, tightly stretched above pink ears, was fringed with gray.

"You are still a member in good standing, Ella. It's not as if we have both been turned out."

She gazed through round spectacles that sat high on the bridge of her narrow nose, cheeks shiny in a flow of tears. "I'd love you no matter what they accused you of doing, John. But what will we do without the church? What will become of our San, of us, of everything we've worked for?"

Kellogg sidled onto the seat, avoiding her folded knees, and put an arm around her. "Grand things, my darling, grand things. The San has yet to see its finest days, I assure you."

46

"MAY I have your carriage sent around, mister Post?"

C.W. touched the man's chest with his cane. "Lawrence, how is business today?" Post was wearing a top hat and cape.

"Same as last week, sir. Post Tavern has no vacancies."

"Good. Keep it that way. The carriage is already waiting."

Lawrence Montgomery smoothed the thick, straight black hair above his ears. His manner was familiar, easy, not at all servile before his millionaire employer. "Missus Post isn't accompanying you, sir?"

Carroll answered, "She probably just isn't in the mood for speeches and ceremonies tonight."

"I trust she is well." Cheerful. Considerate. Thoughtful. A perfect hotel manager, which was why C.W. hired him.

"She is well," Post smiled. "Just a headache."

On the street, an apparition in fetid clothing mashed his ragged cap tightly onto a hairless head, then did a weird skipdance as if afflicted by uncontrolled muscle contractions. C.W. and Carroll watched the act with amused disdain. Montgomery stared disquietly.

Loony Lew finally spoke while keeping his good eye on the three men. "A minute of your time, mister Post."

Carroll said, "C.W., I'll handle this."

C.W. eased around Montgomery. "I'll see what this gentleman has on his mind." He walked thirty feet down the street, his cane marking the way, Lew following.

"I come to tell you somethin 'bout Will Kellogg's cereal factory."

"What about it?" Post stopped, gazed into the distance.

"It's gonna get burnt down." Lew waited for a response, got none. "Troublemaker's got it in for them Kelloggs."

"Why tell me? Why don't you tell the Kelloggs?"

Lew hacked up a gob of spittle, sent it sailing into the street. "They wouldn't say hello to me if I was handin out hunnerd dollar bills on the corner down there, but I hate to see anythin bad happen to anybody, so I thought you ought to know what the boy told me."

"What's this trouble maker's name?" Post asked.

Lew studied a while. "Didn't give me his name," he said at last.

"I suggest you take your information to the police chief. It's of no value to me." C.W. turned away.

Lew quickly skipped in front of Post. "I waited, thought you might be grateful, knowin a thing like this. Might be to your gain."

"I see." Post removed a dollar from a leather wallet, handed it to Lew, then walked hurriedly to his carriage.

Loony Lew glared after him. "That's all? A goddamned dollar?"

"He had a cock-and-bull story about the Kelloggs," Post told Carroll, standing by the carriage. "I think it was a trick meant to get a handout. He couldn't possibly know anything. Yet, if there's a particle of truth to his ranting..." He trailed the gold-handled cane clemently along the side of his neck at his hairline. "Tomorrow, when you get to the plant, I want you to telephone Detroit, talk directly to Lauhoff. No one else. Set up a contract to purchase all of the water-cooled rolls he can manufacture over the next eight months."

"All?" Puzzled. Wondering if he had heard correctly. "We planning an expansion I didn't know about, C.W.?"

Down the street Lew continued to cuss and stamp his feet like a man with his pants full of red ants. A few strollers stared at him and crossed to the other side of the brick-paved avenue.

WHEN aunt Mollie opened the apartment door, hotel manager Lawrence Montgomery waited there, smoothing his thin moustache with a manicured finger. Surprised to see her, a quick blink was his only reaction.

"Yes?" she asked, drawing out the word into a long question.

"I heard from mister Post that missus Leila is sick with a headache. I wondered if there might be anything she needs? If so, the hotel will assuredly provide it...a doctor, something from the pharmacist, cold refreshments..." He ran out of offers.

"I'll tell her. Thank you."

Mollie started to close the door when Leila called from inside: "Ask mister Montgomery to hold my husband's carriage. I've decided to go along after all."

WITHOUT introduction or preamble, C.W. set aside his meal and went to the microphone. Behind him, a huge banner had one word in white letters blazoned against a blue background: "POSTUM." Those seated nearest him in the cafeteria hall stopped eating and began to applaud, Postum employees, including anyone who had ever worked for the company. Eventually, every table joined in. The clapping continued until Post successfully gestured it down to silence.

"What a wonderful group you are. No one who ever lived could ask for a finer work force, a better army of friends." He raised an arm to forestall another round of applause.

"I'll begin with a reflection on the history of the Postum Cereal Company." He launched into the familiar story. "At the start there was me and Marjorie and an old shed where we tried to dig out nature's secret to a simple little formula. God smiled on us and we found it.

"One unnamed rival with the initials WKK did his best to steal my ideas, said I was all cat, mostly wild." Audience laughter rolled up and down the hall. He wound down the tale, became pointedly serious.

"But that isn't what I came to discuss. Tonight I am going to take up a personal subject. I know it isn't considered good taste to speak about private or domestic topics in public, but it is time. I'm going to say it briefly and candidly."

The hall was quieter than a desert canyon in midday heat.

"When we were barely out of our teens, the first missus Post and I were married. Ella and I soon found we had made a childish mistake, both lacking mature judgement in the choice of a partner for our lives. We kept our high esteem and regard for each other, but as far as making a home together, well, that was another matter. Our parting was inevitable. If you'll allow me the literary license from Greek mythology, there were times I felt as if *A dreadful sound troubled the boundless sea. The whole earth uttered a great cry.* I imagine Ella had similar misgivings as often as I. She is contented today with things the way they are. She has a very sizeable income; she is certainly able to indulge, without limit, in her craving for travel.

"My daughter, Marjorie, has been a pal to her father since her baby years, and not too long ago, while I was trying to care for her alone, it was apparent she should have someone with her during the weekends and at day's end when she came home from school, a companion to see she was well looked after. Leila Young was my private secretary. Her schedule enabled her to come by our home to be with Marjorie in the evening hours. She became a rather regular member of our family. I had the chance almost daily to see the traits of a gentle, womanly character. My affection for her grew and, as you know, we were wed. If I have recently done anything wrong by taking Leila Young into matrimony it is only that I have married a poor girl, a girl who earned her living as a secretary." He paused, allowed himself a bright smile.

"But, enough. I regret only that the Postum company has grown so large I no longer personally know every person who works for me. Well, tonight I'll stand here until it thunders, if it takes that long, because I want to shake hands with every one of you. Please do me that honor, come up to our table. And honor me, too, by meeting my wife, if you have not. Leila. Missus Post."

47

JUNE 1906

C.W. had purchased the house at 285 Maple Street for Marjorie the year before. She had not lived in it long enough to scuff the parquet floors in the cavernous entrance hall or even to christen the ballroom with a good party, and Marjorie enjoyed hosting a good party, everyone knew that. She was in there and out before the dust settled on the gold wall-lamps, moving to Washington, D.C., to be closer to C.W. and within commuting distance of New York, the chosen center of the Post empire.

"You didn't even come to my damned wedding, father."

"You know the reason, Marjorie. Your mother would have stayed away if Leila and I attended, she said so and she meant it."

"That's bullshit."

C.W. drank his Postum from a China coffee cup. He was seated on a Regency sofa the bluish-red color of ripe plums. A wall mirror told him unequivocally that he was nearly bald. He looked away.

Marjorie paced the floor, occasionally snapping a glance at him. Her dress was a loose smock like a Left Bank painter. Her hair tossed with her movements while long bangs swung over her forehead like a shifting dark cap. Her pouty upper lip was as scarlet as the anger in her eyes.

"Marjorie," he motioned with his half-filled cup, "what other newly-wed young lady has buildings and streets named after her...will inherit ten or fifteen million dollars when...My God, you've sat on Sarah Bernhardt's lap, shook hands and chatted with John Barrymore, and Lillian Russell. You've hummed marches in our own front parlor with the great John Sousa. Not one of your chums can say their papa has taken them along on every serious business trip..."

"Ha."

"...to Europe, the Orient, Texas, to learn about how..."

"Texas. Jesus, what a treat. Thanks very much, father." She shook her head violently. "You go everywhere but you can't make it to my wedding."

He set aside the cup and saucer, got up and went to the double windows, watched people strolling along the sidewalk on their way downtown or returning.

"I'd swear Battle Creek has grown by a thousand population every time I come back."

"Which is hardly ever, father. We should sell this house. Ed and I won't use it twice a year. And while we're at it, please send that damned gun cabinet someplace, to California or wherever you want it, but it doesn't belong here."

"Edward still shuns the midwest life, doesn't he?"

"Don't start up on Ed. He isn't a snob, he's just from a different background. His ancestors came over on the Mayflower or one of those ships. My God, the church where we got married, smack in the middle of Manhattan, sits on land Ed's great grandfather gave to the parish."

"They should have held on to it. They could've used the money nowadays," Post mentioned dryly.

"They are like aristocracy, father. A socially prominent family in Greenwich. He's a graduate of Columbia Law School..."

Post glanced at the tall glass-doored gun cabinet, walked over to it and studied its contents with an odd expression that suggested he was seeing the displayed firearms for the first time. His eyes wandered over the two 12-gauge breech loading shotguns with their elaborately engraved Royal Damascus finish. As for the other rifles banked inside, he couldn't remember their makes or calibers. He sensed, but could not see, a special bore 30-30 Winchester hunting rifle that was snapped into thongs across the inner roof of the cabinet, completely invisible even with the doors open. There were also numerous pistols gleaming in the cabinet, including a Remington derringer in its gold-inlaid box.

"I'll have the guns and the cabinet packed this week, shipped to Santa Barbara."

Marjorie watched him. He was stormy, unpredictable, irritating, but the most exciting, adventuresome person she had ever known, though she had never told him so. She recognized that her love and admiration for him bordered on a mania. And she knew this was a big part of her dislike of Leila Post.

"Father, the sad part of what's going on is how you've changed in the past few years..."

"You mean since Leila," he said.

"Goddddd," she howled, "Yes, since Leila, since everything. Do you know how embarrassing your egomaniac newspaper article was to me and to Edward? I go to lengths to avoid being dubbed a midwest hick by those eastern biddies at the country club and you take up sermonizing in the nation's newspapers."

"I'm not concerned with the small-minded opinions of uninformed people, Marjorie, except to set them straight. I only clarified for that herd of fact-twisting journalists that John Harvey Kellogg was not the single-handed creator of the breakfast food business. And I asked you to meet me in Battle Creek to visit the plant, not to argue. I only want to keep you current on the developments at White City. After all, it will be yours one day."

"I'm not sure the price is worth it, father."

"Dammit, girl, you sound like...like..." faltering, searching for a name.

"Not like mother. She was too easily manipulated for her own good. Do I sound like Leila? Is she less even-tempered than you imagined?"

WALKING through the Post factory with Carroll as a willing guide and Leila a glossy adornment on his sleeve, C.W. was congratulating himself: I wanted an empire and I have it. More than I counted on, bigger than Kellogg's, bigger than anything Battle Creek ever has seen or will again.

"I do wish Marjorie had joined us." Leila wore a gown of green chiffon velvet. Her husky words were full of childish delight. "It's all so fascinating, seeing the factory this way, I mean, with you, Charles."

C.W. squeezed Leila's hand tenderly where it rested on his folded arm. Beyond the rows of windows of the general office area were the terraced lawns of White City, with a contingent of groundsmen laboring in the sunshine. "She said she had already taken the tour."

"Marjorie went through the whole place Monday and again yesterday," Carroll admitted. "Took in the factory, the offices, even the dairy and gardens. Gave it a fine tooth comb."

As they reached the roasting room with its floor-to-ceiling cookers, where dozens of men in white suits moved along a literal wall of glistening metal and escaping steam, Leila remarked, "To think it takes all of this to make those little cartons of Postum." It drew an amused smirk from both men.

At the entrance to the GrapeNuts bakery room, where eighteen brick ovens trundled out 28,000 loaves each day, C.W. said, "I'm glad the cold air pipes are in place and being used."

"The bakers appreciate them, C.W. With those blowers hooked up, every man gets plenty of air, can set the gauge at his station to bring in as much or as little as he wants," Carroll said. "Too bad, though, you and Leila couldn't have been here for the dedication of the new building. We needed the space badly for the flaking room and the packing bins, especially with Post Toasties coming on line."

"The houses up on Marjorie Street and Lathrop Avenue, all goes well?" Post could visualize every foot of the five miles of streets: a thousand trees, miles of sidewalks, hundreds of homes for Post wage earners. Well built, individually designed, one and two story, take your pick.

"You drove through on the way in, C.W. The Addition is full to overflow. Every spot sold and occupied."

"Do we need more houses?"

"We're hiring every month."

"Then contract to build another fifty. And put in a Leila Avenue."

Leila looked admiringly at her husband. "Charles, I've never dreamed...I mean...a street with my name on it. All I can say right now, here in public, is thank you, dear."

"The way you take care of things, C.W., the unions will never get hold of White City, you can bet on that," Carroll prophesied.

"We give our people good pay, good conditions, good benefits, and they give us loyalty and effort on the job. It's a fair exchange." Post was cut short by a thunderstorm of noises from the printing and box making department they entered. He had to shout for Carroll to hear him.

"When we have a shutdown, too many old hands are being laid off, the work going to the new men, a lot of them without families. I don't want our longtime people displaced by newcomers."

Carroll nodded agreement, then asked Leila, "You didn't know your husband was softhearted, did you?"

"I'm learning something new every day," she chirped.

THE Bartlett Street plant was a midget in a realm of goliaths. Mapl-Flak, at the junction of McCamly and Liberty, loomed ten times larger. Flak-Ota, in its brick and concrete plant on Porter Street, or Malta Vita on Angell Street, could have swallowed Kellogg's shabby three-story clapboard operation, including its two-boiler power plant and nine roller mills, and not even burp. Postum Cereal Company could have lowered the collective industry down one of its smokestacks and would not have registered an increase in the fires of its baking ovens.

Shaw had just come through the outer room of the Kellogg factory where cereal cartons were filled by hand from metal bins, then shook down, and conveyed to a gluing contraption that sealed them. He unfurled a roll of paper he carried, laid it atop Will Kellogg's desk.

Kellogg saw a drawing of an eye and large block letters that read: "Wink at your grocer." He read the words aloud, incredulity in his voice. "The advertising man you hired did this?"

"That's the basic slogan, boss. We will hit the newspapers in Dayton with $150 worth of ads. Same in Chicago, St. Louis, Milwaukee. The major cities. Single column 'reader' ads, a new one every week for three months. They say something like 'Give the grocer a wink and see what you'll get,' or 'Have you winked at your grocer? If not, wink and see what you get.'"

"It sounds like it comes from a trashy penny novel." Kellogg's nose crinkled in distaste. "Tell me, if a woman is foolish enough to ask, what *does* she get?"

"A sample box of our corn flakes." Shaw's arms flew up in a hosanna position. "But we don't mention the cereal until the seventh ad. Until then, it's a secret unless they ask."

"A winking campaign. I can't believe it. We'll be the butt of ridicule from coast to coast."

Shaw bent across Kellogg's desk, tapped the unrolled advertising sketch with a finger. "Believe me, boss, this will put your corn flakes on the grocers' front shelves."

"Mister Shaw, you are a counselor, an advisor. You are not noted on my company payroll. I am not your boss."

"You pay me. I work for you. That's a boss to me."

As seriously put as if he were asking Shaw to renounce his religion, Kellogg said, "I'd prefer you call me W.K."

"W.K." Shaw tried the sound. He released the sides of the stiff paper, let it coil over itself. "Just the initials?"

Kellogg stood, walked between desk and files, handed Shaw one of the new cereal cartons. Now it was Shaw's turn to read aloud: "Kellogg's Toasted Corn Flakes. This food is a delicious dish for breakfast, lunch or dinner. Used and recommended by the Battle Creek Sanitarium." He read further, lips moving without sound until he reached the bottom section of the carton's front panel. "Not genuine without this signature: W.K. Kellogg."

Shaw set the carton on the desk. Finally, he said. "I like it. It sounds important. I truly like it...W.K."

Kellogg returned to his chair, jabbed a finger in the charcoal eye on his desk. "You actually believe this is good advertising?"

"I do."

Kellogg's stare drifted from Shaw's face to the closed door that led into the factory, then floated farther away. He spoke as if daydreaming, "We can't afford to be seen as con men. It would ruin us. Swindlers and confidence men have made investors uneasy. They don't trust cereal makers."

And he recalled traveling a long distance looking for someone who would trust. Pittsburgh, Philadelphia, Minneapolis...

Going down Skinker Road early that day, he had glimpsed the limestone art palace through the trees, the sole surviving relic of the St. Louis 1901 World's Fair. He hoped for a spare hour to spend in the Merchandise Mart building, just browsing. But there had been no time for sightseeing. None.

When he had arrived at the iron facade building on Washington Avenue and stepped off the cable car, he looked up at the Eads Bridge ramp that ran above and across the street. Its traffic was a melded stream of color and hurriedness, a city droning in full motion. The downtown's soot-covered buildings were lined with stores, shops, warehouses, decaying tenements, crowded loft factories.

His optimism plummeted. This was no Battle Creek of green and blue, it was a metropolis of rusty browns, Parisian architecture, electric-powered elevators and ten-story skyscrapers. These men he had come to see were not neighbors or lifelong acquaintances. They were hard-driven businessmen in hard driving occupations. His despair had been instant and overwhelming. He forced himself to enter the building and ride to the eighth floor in a black iron elevator.

"This is a risky venture, you propose, mister Kellogg." The heavyset man behind the polished wooden desk spoke briskly, wasted no words. "How many have failed?"

"A few years ago there were forty companies in Battle Creek, sir. Each proposed to make cereals. Today there are ten."

"An honest answer, but not much of a recommendation. How many of those remaining ten are making money, mister Kellogg?"

"I would guess half."

A small twist of the mouth. "So I could easily lose my money if I let you have it?"

"C.W. Post is earning a million dollars a year."

"He is one out of ten, originally forty."

"I know the business. I have the Kellogg corn flake. The reputation is already built. The name is saleable. You won't lose your money."

The heavyset man had leaned back comfortably in his heavyset chair. "You can guarantee that?"

"No. But I know it." W.K. was less certain than he sounded. He wondered, painfully, but briefly, if Post had felt the same degree of apprehension when he tried to connive a partnership with John Harvey some six years ago.

"You have corroborative figures, some documentation to support your contention, mister Kellogg?"

Two hours later he left the office and stepped into the elevator to go back down to the bustling streets of St. Louis. His shirt was sweat soaked. His hands trembled slightly. In his pocket he carried a check for $35,000.

Now, in the Bartlett Street office, W.K. said to Shaw, "Our approach will stay simple. First, we will make the best product. Never stray from the search to improve. Second, we will get our product into homes. That is an absolute condition. You said samples, and I agree. How many sample packages will we have to give away?"

Shaw shrugged. "Four hundred thousand, maybe half a million before we're through, until word gets around that it's good."

The number sounded outrageous to Kellogg but he saved his opinion. "Third, we must get our product onto the grocers' shelves in every state, from Maine to California. That means setting up retail distribution." He paused, thoughtfully. "Several imitations of our cereal are out. Mostly wheat flakes and generally not very tasty. None with our flavor. So we have an advantage."

Studying the unrolled paper, not looking at Shaw, he said, "I agree we must advertise. We'll try the eye idea."

"No one's done anything like it, boss. Not even Post. We'll knock the market for a spin. And wait'll you see the next idea. We're going to ask everyone in Chicago to stop eating Toasted Corn Flakes for thirty days."

"What?" he spluttered. "What..."

"It'll sell ten million packages. We'll ask people to quit eating your cereal for thirty days so packages can reach homes where they haven't been available because they're always sold out. You know, the regular customers buy them up too soon. That's the message."

"That's even worse than the winking ads."

"Wait and see, W.K. Just you wait and see."

48

THE summer cottage on Gull Lake overlooked the water. Ella and Len and Beth sat by an umbrella-shaded table on the fieldstone patio while Hannah unloaded a tray of lemonade and a plate of walnut cookies. The air smelled of sunshine and pastry. There was a stroking breeze off the lake.

"I think you must help your father." Hannah picked up the conversation where it had dwindled minutes ago. "He done for you all them years, now he needs help but is too proud to ask. Listen to your mama, Len." Hannah waggled a finger. "She is telling you the troot."

Ella Kellogg watched the lake, drank some of her lemonade, grateful that Will had bought this cottage. She liked it out here where things were quiet and easy to care for and where a routine order was maintained; not like the hectic pattern in town. And the summer heat was bearable by the water. Without shifting her gaze she said:

"You know your father has put every cent of his cash in the company. Advertising cost him almost forty thousand dollars already this year. Those colored pages in the Ladies Home Journal and then the newspapers."

"He'll make it back, mother," Len said, eating a cookie. "It does pay to advertise. Post has made a believer out of us on that count."

"Will works long hours, son, trying to do too much at his age, going on fifty."

"He's got twenty-five employees," Len defended. "Be realistic. It isn't exactly as if he's doing everything single handedly, even if he says he is."

"The others just work in the plant," Beth mentioned.

Len adjusted his dark-framed eyeglasses and let his eyes walk down Hannah's wide hips, across her thick belly that still retained the weight she had gained before Will Keith II was born a month ago. He wished she would trim back to the size she used to be.

"Father is doing fine without me. The sweetheart of the corn promotion put Kellogg on every shopping list in the nation. He's shipping a thousand cases a day and I know he takes out a good salary, not to mention the twelve thousand he received this year for his part of the Canadian rights to Corn Flakes."

"Mister Kellogg wants none of your money," Hannah scolded. "He needs you, his son, to help him to run his cereal factory. But you got to be the one big enough to say, Father, I woot help you."

His gaze roved from one woman to the other. "All right, mother, I surrender, you tell father I will start with him in two weeks." He noticed a pair of sailboats racing beside each other on the lake, and he wondered why his sudden decision hung like a lead weight in the middle of his throat.

49

JOHN Harvey drummed his fingers on a bookcase, his eyes sleepily half closed. Beside his hand, an iron clock with buffalo heads on its sides ticked softly.

W.K. put aside a book he had lifted from a stack of books on a shelf. "Let's get facts and impressions straight from the beginning, doctor. You've agreed it is no hardship on you if Len leaves your employment?"

"I shall miss his good work." He gave Len a slight nod.

W.K. tucked his hands into his pants pockets, walked behind the battered desk in the one-room office of doctor Kellogg's Modern Medicine Publishing Company. A spot of light glistered on the top of his bald head. When he spoke, his voice was as toneless as a door closing.

"I started the Toasted Corn Flake Company barely a year ago. My only working capital was the $35,000 I secured in St. Louis. Meanwhile, I agreed to go on managing all of your various interests..."

"For a sum."

"...and have done so. The entire reason I started my corn flake company was your unwillingness to do so."

"That's a gross oversimplification."

"Meanwhile, Post and half-a-dozen others like Hornsby Oats walked off with the flake secret. Post was able to buy it from your trusted factory manager, Gibson. Hornsby got it by simply paying a Sanitas employee to take him on a tour of the plant one Sunday."

"I can't be responsible for another man's honesty. We've had strict rules of secrecy imposed from the beginning, but some workers violate it." John Harvey's fingers began to drum on the bookcase. The sleepiness had faded from his eyes.

"Uncle John, why don't you and father sit down. You agreed to talk this out, so why not be comfortable?" Len pushed a wooden chair close to the doctor.

"Thank you Len, but I'll stand. I get restless when Will revisits every hurt or bruise he has ever endured and for which he blames me."

W.K. said, "You're a director of the Corn Flakes Company, doctor. I am its president. The board insisted it be that way. But there have been enormous problems between us. I won't mention your refusal to pay for the Sanitas factory we built. The Peptol issue was something else, though. Your tonic to put weight on underweight people was an outright fraud."

"Another gross oversimplification."

"Since it cost me a great deal, I believe I have the right to such opinion. You persuaded the Chicago buyers to pay $20,000 for Peptol rights. You told them it was a product in demand. A twelve percent return on investment, you said. And you lied. You sold them a broken wheel, worth nothing. They sued us for misrepresentation but somehow you convinced them to drop the suit against you. They continued against me; my suit lost in circuit court. I was fined the judgement as well as court costs. Purely because my name was also on the contract."

John Harvey sat heavily in the chair beside him, profoundly irked. "Will, this spring, when I returned from a trip to Europe, I found you had renamed the corn flakes brand to Kellogg's Toasted Corn Flakes. A fine, impressive name, but you knew very well I did not want our name on a commercial product. It would always be seen as *the* Kellogg of the Sanitarium — me — and it would do me great injury in medical circles. So you see, it isn't I alone who have caused our difficulties."

Turning his back on his brother, W.K. sat on the desk's edge, head up, intently watching the window curtains vibrate weakly from a feeble breeze. Len was close by the office door guarding against anyone entering. "We don't see things the same way, doctor. We are ill-matched partners. I believe we would serve each other best by cutting off any mutual business relations."

He concentrated on the bloated green trees out in the golden light. "I will buy out all of your stock in the Corn Flakes Company, doctor. I will pay you a fixed sum monthly, and a yearly royalty on sales. You can close Sanitas. It's no good to you, anyway. It is failing."

John Harvey rubbed one eye as though it itched. "I suppose the money *would* pay some debts at the San. Affairs have been a little difficult lately."

W.K. lifted himself from the desk, walked to the window, pulled aside the limp curtain. "Len, would you leave us a moment?"

"Father, I think I have a stake in this, too. I'd like to hear it out."

"Let him stay, Will. I don't mind Len hearing anything we say. I've always wanted us to work together and achieve great things. And we have. I never wanted you to leave."

"Doctor, there were times when I used my credit to its limit. I obligated myself for thousands of dollars of debt on Sanitarium paper. Wholly in your interests. I want you now to see that I am released from all obligations on Sanitarium notes. And inform your secretary not to call me for future endorsements as he did only recently. You must take over the management of Sanitas yourself, if you insist on maintaining it. As I said, my advice is to close it down. You no longer have a monopoly on the flaking process. Sturdier competition will drive you to your knees."

For a moment, John Harvey could hear quite clearly the judge's pronouncement in chambers. Just himself, the lawyers, and a stenographer. Brown office with floor-to-ceiling windows and walls of leather bound books. The decision coming after months of legal hopscotching:

"Your flakes, doctor Kellogg, are substantially identical with many foods which had long been produced when you obtained your patent. Your flakes are only different from them in form and degree. You were familiar with the manufacture of Shredded Wheat Biscuits, a patent held by one Mister Perky. I understand you tried some years ago to buy his roller process, so there was no invention on your part in omitting the grooves from those rollers and thereby obtaining flakes. This did not make a new product."

With those words, the casket lid had closed on his precious Sanitas patent. After that, all comers were free to make *any* flaked cereal. John Harvey nodded absently. "You are correct, Will, competition is stalking me from every side."

No one spoke for a long while in the closed, stuffy office. The only sound was the hollow ticking of the iron clock. Clouds drifted past the window and made faint shadowy patterns on the floor. John Harvey pushed away his chair, walked tiredly to the door Len opened for him, and left.

MUNICIPAL court justice Davis had completed the reading of the charges brought before him in the assault and battery trial. Prosecutor Cavanaugh stood far to the side of the accused, showing discomfort for having had to issue a warrant against a man of such immense wealth, influence, and power.

The judge rustled a few papers, adjusted his eyeglasses, frowned at the accused.

"The fact that you have several million dollars makes no difference in the decision of this case, mister Post. Nor does the fact that mister Zuver is editor of the Journal newspaper. Your prominence nor his neither enhances or mitigates the offense."

C.W. and his attorney kept bland faces.

Judge Davis lowered his gaze to the typed document before him. "You struck mister Zuver. If he had been assailed by an itinerant tough, my sentence would be the same for the culprit. Furthermore, I am impelled to tell you that this court heartily disapproves of the way you tried to portray mister Zuver in the subsequent interviews in this city's other leading newspapers. It was nauseating vilification." He looked up sharply, sprayed his denunciation over the entire courtroom.

Prosecutor Cavanaugh shifted nervously from one foot to the other, caught his wife's attention in the back row, compressed his lips to signal her there wasn't a damned thing he could do about the judge's rebuking of Post.

"I want to say for the record that these opinions have in no way swayed my decision."

C.W. choked off a grin. "Of course not, your honor." He frowned almost as gravely as the judge, though he wanted to say, "Yes, your honor, I followed him out by the streetcar tracks. It was necessary in order to tell him if he ever mentioned my name in another of his editorials, I would knock his block off. He claimed he wasn't an anarchist, wouldn't stoop to public brawls. So I gave the bounder a cuff on the jaw, enough to knock his hat off.

"Anybody in Battle Creek can attest, your honor, this renegade came along with a full stomach of hate for every thrifty man, a sneer for every man who tries to build up a community. He uses his newspaper column to slur every act that makes Battle Creek a prosperous place."

Post's lawyer nudged C.W. sharply with a knuckle. C.W. realized the remembering had caused him to smile.

Justice Davis' words were acerbic enough to eat through sheetmetal. "Do you find these proceedings humorous, mister Post?"

"No, your honor, I do not find them in the least humorous. My expression, if it showed cheer, was caused by the thought of something well outside the walls of this courtroom."

Davis grunted, leveled his gavel at Post like a pistol, sighted along its handle with a squinted eye. "Witnesses have testified that mister Zuver conducted his side of the controversy in a most gentlemanly manner. It appears that it was he who kept the coolest head. My decision is in behalf of the prosecution." He rapped the gavel twice on a wooden block. "This court fines you the sum of $14.20, mister Post."

On the way out of the City Hall building, C.W. told his attorney, "Dust off your file of sales contracts. I may need one before long. I think I'm about to buy myself a newspaper."

FROM the vantage of her apartment just off Pennsylvania Avenue in downtown D.C., Ella Post could not see the White House or Ford's

Theatre. She considered it of no consequence because she *could* glimpse the Potomac River and the Washington Monument and the Japanese Cherry Trees when they bloomed along the Tidal Basin. She also could watch the motor traffic as it wended thinly along the tarvia-concrete road below. Someone had told her that the road's surface was partly plastic — whatever that meant — so it couldn't be scraped or gouged by automobile wheels. She had never repeated the tidbit of information, because she couldn't imagine who would care about it one way or the other.

On the tea table in front of Ella and Marjorie, was a 20-ounce box of Whitman's Old Time Favorite chocolates and a package of Nabisco Adora wafers. There was a silver setting with coffee, cream, sugar. A maid brought in China cups. Ella thanked her and sent her away.

"I know it isn't Christmas, dear, a long way from it, but I saw them and just thought you would like them." She beamed at her daughter who wore a gown of London smoke cloth with yellow buttons the size of peaches.

Marjorie held up the practical gift: Paris garters. Made in New York. On the box lid was a picture of a beautiful young lady, all smiles, and the wording, "No metal can touch you."

"I love them, mother. And so will Ed." She inclined out of her chair, gripped Ella's hand with a loving squeeze.

They had been talking for fifteen minutes, going over health, mutual friends, single-breasted overcoats and raglan shoulders. They agreed the weather was hotter, more humid than usual, and the number of deaths by railroad accident — nearly ten thousand last year alone — was surely the result of everyone's growing obsession with speed. They could not decide if Teddy Roosevelt would win the coming election or if his secretary of war, William Howard Taft, might outrun his old boss.

"And, things in Battle Creek, darling, how are they?" Ella poured two cups of coffee. Regular coffee, not Postum.

"Always changing, always the same, like father says."

Marjorie saw the reflexive twist of Ella's head, as if twinged by a sudden ear ache, realized her blunder, said hastily: "They tore down the old Grand Trunk freight house, not much loss if I do say so, and there was a big tussle between the Women's League and the Women's Club over who could use the easy rooms in Willard Library. I believe they divided up the week but I forget who gets the rooms on which days. Then, Upton Sinclair and his wife were at the San the last time I was in town. That's about all the news." Marjorie rested a fingernail on her chin, eyes sweeping the ceiling, pensive. "Oh! Before I forget, everyone is playing Skiddoo 23 all over Battle Creek just as if it were New York or Los Angeles."

"I know of mister Sinclair. He is that socialist who is always running for Congress or some other office and writes those dismal novels. I don't know about your skiddoo."

"Well, it's just a nutty thing going around," Marjorie laughed. "Everybody says 23 Skiddoo instead of Holy Moses or Jim Dandy. It really means to leave, you know, to go, to get moving, skiddoo. It's an expression."

Ella continued to look puzzled. She fussed disconcertedly with the white satin collar of her lacy blouse.

"All right, it's a game too," Marjorie went on. "That's how it got started. You think of a number between one and nine. Try it, mother. Which number do you pick?"

Reluctantly, Ella said, "Five."

"Now add one to it."

"Six. Five and one is six."

"Multiply it by nine."

"Six times nine?" Ella computed. "Fifty four."

"Take away the first number — the five from fifty four — and add fourteen."

"Four and fourteen is eighteen." Ella compressed her lips, patiently waited for the finish to this silliness.

"Now add your original number," Marjorie instructed her triumphantly. "What do you have?"

Ella looked mildly surprised. "Twenty three."

"Skiddoo 23," Marjorie shouted. "That's how you play it. The total will always be twenty three, no matter what number you start with."

Both women took up their coffee and sipped delicately around gentle smiles.

"Is it because she is younger than me, prettier?"

Marjorie dreaded this moment each time she visited her mother. She knew the next line by heart.

"He is old enough to be her father," Ella murmured. "I told him that once, a long time ago."

Ella, a trust fund has been arranged to provide you with more than ample funds. You can buy what you please, travel where you choose, without a care in the world. You'll want for nothing.

Except the family that was mine. Oh, God, Charles, where did we lose what we had? Or did I just imagine we had anything? Was I blind? Naive? Or stupid?

We haven't actually been husband and wife for a long, long time.

Since your illness.

I'm surprised you didn't say since Leila.

You are now a man to be counted, you have the fortune and prestige and the power you always wanted. You're over your nightmare, but mine seems to have begun. You are a different person from the one who came to Battle Creek on a stretcher in a snow storm, pushed about town in a wheel chair. You're also a great many years older...

You keep reminding me. Maybe that has been part of our trouble, you kept reminding me.

Be on guard that your energies don't lag too soon. It may be difficult to keep pace with a woman so young, hardly more than Marjorie's age. Be careful your Leila doesn't wear you down, weaken you, destroy you.

It's odd you should say that. I told her almost the very same thing the first day I...

But then, you needn't worry, Charles, it's fairly certain you will be safe. After all, unlike Samson, you have almost no hair to be shorn.

Her mother's small cry, somewhere between pain and a squeal of amusement, startled Marjorie. Ella said, "I suppose I'm still a little surprised — and disappointed — at aunt Mollie's taking up so easily with my replacement. It's as if I was never there. I thought she was my friend."

"She is, mother. Aunt Mollie goes where Carroll goes."

Eyes bright, lids trembling, Ella balanced her coffee cup on one knee, ritualistically selected a chocolate from the Whitman box, put it on a saucer and forgot about it.

"Mother, maybe you...have you thought about marrying?"

"I've nursed all the adult babies I care to."

"Just father."

"One's enough, dear." Her voice broke. She turned her head and stared out past the curtains at the bruised July sky where heavy clouds had pushed in from the east.

"You can't still love him, mother."

Ella rose stiffly, her spine rigid. She produced a tiny silver bell, jingled it. Its call was so sweet and crisp it seemed to flow in a perfectly straight line to the ear. "We'll have Wanda bring us a fresh pot of coffee."

She adjusted a curl of hair that wasn't out of place. "When enough years go by, the beautiful ones and the plain ones look the same. All that youthful prettiness fades and we all finally look the same."

The window of her face closed down. "Marjorie, I would like to try your skiddoo game once more, just to see if it works the same every time."

50

July 1906

JOHN Harvey, strolling, exercising, running the halls and the inner stairwells of the San, wore only his loincloth and carried a towel to wipe off the sweat. He was sleepless for the second night, his mind occupied with calculations of revenues, considering now the possibility of selling his few remaining shares in the Kellogg Corn Flakes operation to get more funds for his limping San.

Reaching the sixth floor, he passed a window, noticed an unusual glow several blocks to the southeast. At first it was only a pale bud on the clothing of night. At the next window, it became a red and yellow flower of fierce proportion, its fimbriate petals fringing and stretching. Six windows more and it was a brilliant orange coneflower climbing upward on a stalk of smoke, softly touching the white moon's curved chin.

Kellogg ran shouting for the telephone at the nurse's station.

TWO miles outside of Battle Creek the railroad tracks came to an ascending curve. The grade was not steep enough to require a helper engine. The early morning freight train — 70 cars and a 66-ton engine — always approached the hill at forty miles an hour and reached a speed of sixty on the downhill grade. It had just cleared the summit.

A single headlight speared a bright hole through the dark. Bell and whistle split the night with warning sounds that raced ahead of the rumbling chuga-chuga power of the iron hulk, this moving, squealing, thundering, coal-burning factory.

Beyond the base of the hill, where the land flattened out for a half-mile, Loony Lew Reesner leaped and cavorted between the rails in a farcical, uncoordinated jig. He halted momentarily, swayed back at a hazardous angle, swigged from a whiskey bottle. His bare head, criss-crossed with scars and trenches of hardened skin, was outlined by the beam of enlarging light that raced at him from behind. He dipped forward woozily, saw nothing except the wooden crossties at his feet, a gauge for every lurching step. He heard only the burble of his own delirious giggling.

"Burned, burned, burned," he howled. "Whomp! Whole damned factory. Heeeyahh!" He didn't know where he was or where he was headed. Purposeless and ecstatic. In thirty seconds he would be dead.

The pilot — a wedge of protruding bars at the front of the train's engine beneath the coupler — was an immense prow that jutted ahead to clear the tracks of any obstruction. This "cowcatcher" struck Loony Lew first.

It scooped him up like meat on a spatula. The impact cracked both legs at the knees and ankles. His whiskey bottle sailed into the trees, shattering unheard, while he spun in the headlight's beam. The train shot forward and the circular front of the hurtling smokebox caught him broadside in mid-air with the force of a cannon shell. Loony Lew's head burst into geometrically exact halves, flinging coils of gray matter, splinters of bone, dense splatters of blood. His body was hurled into the bushes fifty feet beyond the tracks.

51

"YOU refuse to sell me any rollers, mister Lauhoff?"

"I said I can't sell you any, mister Shaw, because I don't have none." His voice was spare and crackly, coming over the telephone line from Detroit. "They are spoken for."

"Then we'll take your next shipment. The delay isn't welcome but it won't be disastrous. How soon can we expect word from you?"

"About next February, sir."

"Don't joke with me, mister Lauhoff. That would be an eight month wait."

"No joke, no sir. A company contracted for them every one. Complete supply."

"What you're telling me can put the Kellogg company out of business permanently, Mister Lauhoff. Surely there is some way I can appeal to you for four rollers, six at the most? Who bought you out?"

"I wish I could oblige you, believe me. But a contract is a contract and if I don't honor it for one, how could I be trusted to honor it for others? It'd ruin my name in the industry if I reneged. I'm sorry, mister Shaw, I can't let you have even one roller. They're all sold, and it don't matter to who."

W.K. KELLOGG realized how John Harvey must have felt when he had stood in the ashes of his San. W.K. had twice circled the smoking, cindered remains of what used to be his factory.

"I called two out-of-state foundries." Arch Shaw carried his suitcoat over one arm. "They won't give us credit or ship to us without money up front. Worse, the earliest we can get our order is November, maybe December, even if we pay now. It's a maybe at best, not a certainty."

W.K. had not removed his gray suitcoat though the afternoon temperature was eighty-five degrees. His eyes skipped across the incinerated lot as if they might singe if they hesitated. "We've been in business a year. Now we're out of business overnight. We were 300 carloads behind on shipments before the fire. Grocers, brokers, they'll flock to other suppliers." A sigh, a grumble of stomach. "The land and building lease was valued at $64,000. I'll get that much from the insurance. Still have a little money in the bank. I calculate we have to borrow $50,000 more to rebuild, equip a new factory."

Shaw chewed on his thumbnail, wanting to help but uncertain how. The possibilities seemed to be closing down very fast.

"I might find a financier. It would be pointless. Without rollers we couldn't fill orders. We're stalled. Finished."

Len Kellogg parked his quarter-top buggy, newly purchased for $45, on the edge of the gravel road. He stepped out of it and called:

"Have you made a decision, father? What's your first move?"

Shaw answered, "We were going over the options."

"We eliminated them," W.K. said. "Did you just leave your mother? I haven't seen her since morning. Is she all right?"

"Resting. Beth and Hannah both are there."

"She is so lifeless since...I worry about her..." W.K. coughed self-consciously. "Hannah is a splendid woman. A good wife, an excellent mother, Len. A welcome addition to the family."

Len did not remind him that he had refused to speak to Hannah for two months after the elopement. "Anything I can do here, father?" He removed his coat, folded it over his bent arm. Like Shaw. "Hannah and I have a few dollars we've put away. You're welcome to..."

W.K. waved him off. "Funds are not the immediate problem. I thank you. It's thoughtful."

"Your father means we can't get new water-cooled rolls. Some smart shuffler has cornered the market, bought them all up."

Len lowered his chin to his chest. "Maybe we should do some quiet freebooting."

"I'll wager I can guess the plant you'd like to rob, Len."

"Probably could, Arch. It's big and white and..."

Shaw was matter-of-fact: "You wouldn't get within a hundred yards of the place before their security grabbed you."

W.K. dug his shoetips into the burnt grass, let his eyes zigzag again over the field. "I won't consider theft. Even if it is regularly done by some so-called businessmen."

"Father, did that same shuffler of rollers have a hand in setting fire to the plant?"

"No," Kellogg said flatly. "Chief Weeks and four of his best men searched every inch. They found pieces of firecrackers out there." He pointed to the distant line of the property.

"Weeks' conclusion," Shaw explained, "was some kids probably were playing back of the building and sparks from their fireworks set off the blaze. I'm not so sure."

W.K. studied the floating strand of a spider's web dangling from a nearby bush. The silky filament drifted, seemed to disappear, then become visible as it wafted back into the sunlight. Suddenly he announced, "Len, get word around to the employees. Have them report here tomorrow morning. Tell them they are not laid off." He removed his glasses, waggled them at the smoldering heap of blackened timber and machinery. "They have work if they are willing to do the clean up."

Arch Shaw and Len Kellogg looked uncertainly at each other. Finally, Shaw phrased their question: "If we're going to clean up this site, does that mean we're going to rebuild?"

"Lauhoff said he could sell us no new rollers?"

"He was emphatic about it, W.K."

"And Len has suggested we obtain used ones from someone else's factory?"

"He was joking, W.K. No one would loan them to help us. We're the competition."

"So we will borrow our own." Kellogg sensed the tingle of anticipation he used to get when ordering a bowl of oyster stew in Webb's diner.

"I don't understand." Len wondered briefly if the shock of losing his factory had unsettled his father's mind.

"Lauhoff said nothing about reconditioning rollers, did he?"

A long, drawn out "No" from Shaw.

"Then we will send him a freightcar of rollers to be reconditioned. The ones we need are right down there," he announced, pointing at the charred debris.

"My God, that's right, W.K." Shaw was hustling into his coat. "I'll have Lauhoff on the phone before you can spit. Len, I need a fast ride downtown in that fine looking rig of yours."

52

OCTOBER 1907

THE AIR was rainwashed. Time was music.

John Harvey felt good about dumping a big block of his Corn Flake Company shares. The money was needed for expenses at the San, and the economy was dangerously foundering, and Will had been foolish enough to pay $6 a share for stock that might be worthless in a few weeks. W.K. might be in business again but everyone knew he was straining to stay afloat.

The doctor signed a letter he had written, sealed it in an envelope and asked an employee to deliver it to Will at work a few blocks away. The message was unequivocal.

"Dear Brother Will. I have decided to manage the Sanitas food holding groups myself. I intend to close Sanitas as a named enterprise but I have other plans which I have faith in and must at least make an effort to work them out. You are already overloaded so I do not ask your help any longer.

"You will soon learn that I have adopted the name Kellogg Food Company for my products, now that the Sanitas label is being retired. I will market Kellogg's Toasted Wheat Flakes and Kellogg's Toasted Rice Flakes. I disliked abducting the name, as it were, knowing you are using it, too. But I have heard that a patent medicine man, one Frank Kellogg (no relation), intends to organize a food company. To forestall his use of our name, and to preserve the food business for the purposes I built it up — that is, support for the philanthropic intent of the Sanitarium — it is the only thing for me to do.

"On advice of legal counsel I am adding a line to my cartons which will read, No Connection with the Toasted Corn Flake Company, Makers of Kellogg's Toasted Corn Flakes. That should satisfy your distrust of my purposes.

Your loving brother, John Harvey."

When W.K. read the letter his neck turned purple and he kicked his desk so hard he limped the rest of the day.

"CONFOUND you, doctor, you are plundering the company. I've spent thousands of dollars advertising. The trade and the public now know the Kellogg name because I've placed it in front of them. Then you rise up like a pike and snap up the june fly I have patiently enticed at great cost."

"I don't see why you resent my profiting by your advertising, brother. It's narrow-minded of you. But, I've said several times, I desire above all else to work out our differences in a peaceful and fraternal way. You told me your company has no intention of making a wheat product. I don't understand why you complain if I do it."

"There seems to be no orderly way to resolve this, doctor. It seems I must tolerate the fact that you are intolerable." Will slammed down the telephone.

AN AUTUMN world cool and lazy. Trees, hills, fields, like a spread of brown cereal flakes.

C.W. looked out of his Post Tavern apartment. His arms were stretched wide, a crucifixion against the window frame. Below him and sweeping outward like semi-precious stones spilled from a jewel box were the shops and factories and homes of Battle Creek. How it all glistened with sweet energy. The sight made him catch his breath and swallow hard.

"I can't really ever leave this town, Leila. It has a hold on me I can't explain or be rid of. I feel the attachment no matter where we are, even overseas. Is that ridiculous?" He was outfitted in a flannelette night-shirt, buttoned to the throat, and had on stiff leather easy shoes with wool lining.

"Charles, we can talk about Battle Creek in the Tavern dining room just as well. I want to get out this morning, see people today." She thumbed through a magazine she had already read. "Besides, you know I dislike it when you work in your bed clothes."

C.W. did not turn around. "Not working, just thinking. Thinking there is a covenant I have with this city and as long as I return to it, sip its waters, wash in its sunshine, scrub in its snows, I'll be all right." He chanted playfully, remembered words from Lewis Carroll:

"Who are you, aged man? I said.
And how is it you live?
His answer trickled through me head,
Like water through a sieve."

He placed his full attention on her face. "If I abandoned this odd little looking-glass city, everything would just trickle out of my head." He grinned. "Sound melodramatic?"

"Yes." Slightly curt. Wanting him to do his ablutions and take her out of the apartment, into the warming day, before the skies shifted and turned leaden.

"Unbutton your dress. Let me look at you."

She acted startled, was not. She wrinkled her nose, thumbed quickly past three pages of the magazine, seeing none of them.

"Take off your dress and come here to the window." The smile was gone. He was earnest.

"I can't do that, Charles. Don't ask me." Watching him for a sign he was joking. She felt chilled, as if a cold wind had entered.

"You did last night."

"I'd had a glass too many of wine last night."

"You were stunning. I'll call down right now, have a bottle sent up." He winked, disappeared into the bathroom. "Is it better here than Texas?" He called out to her. "The ranch, I mean." The foreplay was forgotten.

"Different than," she answered, unthawing, feeling relieved.

Wiping his mouth with a towel, head protruding into the bedroom, he said, "I'm sort of glad that little runt, Kellogg, has his corn flakes plant cranking again. I believe I'd actually miss his sniping if he weren't around."

She smiled and her eyes were black agates with stains of amber. "Is that why you bought up all the rollers in the state? You did, didn't you?"

"You're very lovely this morning," he told her, meaning it, drawing back into the bathroom. "Kellogg is what Rollin called a competitor, spelled f-o-e. Maybe I sensed a possible vulnerable spot. My reaction was purely instinctive, dear, like a mongoose who sees a cobra."

Moments later he came out, all business and seriousness. "I want to talk to Carroll today about replacing those redeemable coupons we've been issuing. When we started putting them in packages it was a runaway scheme, but now everybody does it. We want something new, unique, something the rest of the trade will scramble to match. Remind me."

Fully dressed, he sat in a chair, began to buff his already brilliantly glossed leather shoes. The telephone rang and C.W. signaled her to answer it.

"It is Joe Cox. He wonders if you can meet him at noon. Something about buying his newspaper?" Her nostrils flared, lips parted to show a slit of white teeth. "Don't you have enough to do without going into the publishing business? I never imagined you had a yen for it."

"Tell Cox I'll meet him at noon. At the Enquirer."

"And our lunch with mister Montgomery?"

Post continued to polish his shoes. "You can entertain him until I join you. Would you mind?"

Her heartbeat quickened, her lungs seemed short of oxygen. "No. I'm sure we can find something to discuss." She paused, added: "I mean, if you promise not to be too late."

POST was pleased with the deal. Cox had put a fair price on the Morning Enquirer, didn't try to gouge him for more than it was worth just because he could afford it. Tomorrow they would sign the sales contract and he would be a player in the newspaper game.

At the Tavern's arched entrance he surveyed the dining hall before going in. It was one-quarter filled with patrons. He located Leila easily. She was laughing and he simply let his gaze follow the sound. Across the table from her, Lawrence Montgomery appeared pleased and proud, apparently the cause of her merriment. Soft colors of light from the stained glass window behind them painted the couple's faces as though they were going to a masquerade ball.

They were inclined toward each other, Leila's left hand on the table, her arm extended. Montgomery's right hand was reaching out, but a floral centerpiece of roses and baby's breath from the greenhouses at White City blocked further view. Post couldn't be certain their hands were touching.

His stomach whirled with nausea, jaws clinched, eyes squeezed shut. If not for the cane, he would have lost his balance. Through slits he saw Leila and Montgomery drinking from wine glasses and they were sitting well back from each other. The dizziness subsided.

My God, I'm starting to imagine things, he told himself. Conjuring up visions like a degenerate Mesmer...

"Mister Post, I'm terribly sorry I didn't see you waiting. May I show you to your table?"

"No, thank you, Annabelle." He gave the uniformed hostess his hat. "I know the way quite well."

Leila discovered him walking toward her and waved a graceful white hand, her face yet contoured in mild laughter. Lawrence Montgomery rose to shake hands with his employer.

53

JULY 1910

IF it had four wheels, a steering wheel and carried passengers, it probably was built in Detroit. It was ten years into a new century and

Flint's population out there on the edge of that spreading industrial phenomenon in Michigan had accelerated to 25,000, and every man in the vicinity was involved in building those gasoline-powered wonders. So, too, were half the women.

C.W. Post had three touring cars.

John Harvey Kellogg's vehicle had a revolutionary sliding gear transmission.

W.K.'s choice of automobile was a brown air-cooled Franklin. It cost him $1,650, and would travel 30 miles on a 25-cent gallon of gasoline. His only complaint was that the gear shift had been mounted outside the car on the driver's side which made it, he said, "a pain when it snowed or rained."

It was 1910. The year Mark Twain died and Halley's comet passed across earth's view just as it had in the year he was born.

The common drinking cup and the old oaken bucket were under indictment by public health officials as being public menaces, spreaders of disease.

Heavyweight champion Jack Johnson knocked out James Jeffries, the great white hope, in a fight that was supposed to "prove a white man is better than a Negro." Blacks celebrated across the nation, singing, dancing in the streets. Race riots erupted, hot as the July weather, raw as a fresh incision. Hundreds of people hurt, eighteen killed. The ring slugfest was nothing compared to the street brawls.

Prohibition was traveling a bumpy trail. In local elections, Michigan's voters changed their minds a lot. One year they threw rum bottles in the rivers and lakes, demanded dry counties. Next year their thirst prevailed and they went for wet counties. Crusades by the Anti-Saloon League and the Women's Christian Temperance Union were picking up recruits. But brewers and saloonkeepers studied the stars or the drippings of bacon fat and proclaimed "this too, shall pass." They couldn't know statewide prohibition was just six years away.

"I WANT the Kellogg name to be the only one people think of when they think cereals. It must become so familiar, so popular, Post will be a forgotten name."

W.K. was in a rare, expansive mood. He reclined in his office chair, fingers laced across his belly, legs crossed at the ankles. Arch Shaw stood beside the desk with several advertising sheets in his arms.

"We'll start the best-ear-of-corn contest next week," Shaw commented. "Take it into every county and state fair in the country. There won't be a farmer or gardener anywhere who isn't buying our products." He, too, felt jubilant. Business was booming. "You still want the winner to get a thousand dollar trophy?"

"The national winner." W.K. sat up straight, began cleaning his thick-lensed glasses. "Make sure those kids booklets, what are they called..."

"Jungleland Moving Pictures."

"...are shipped before the month is over. A full carton to every grocer."

Shaw nodded. "I'd bet a dollar to a nickel those booklets will be a champ with the kids. And the kids sway mom's decision when she goes to the store. We're taking the giveaway ink blotters to printing next week, too. Fifteen million of them scheduled, and the baseball cards as well. Hell, W.K., you won't be able to look anyplace in this business without seeing the Kellogg name."

"I suppose so," Kellogg said, his attention reverting to an old theme. "Keep the pressure on. I want to hear Post yell 'Uncle'. He thought his cornflakes brand would knock us off the shelves. Openly admitted his intent. All it did was cut into his own Post Toasties market, not ours."

He stopped just short of grinning, put on his eyeglasses. "We'll see who finally does who in."

"I WOULDN'T have taken the job, mister Post, if I stood opposed to most of your views. It would be a bad trade for both of us. I'd be giving up a newspaper in a town I like; you'd be stuck with the wrong manager for your own newspaper."

"I wanted to be certain there were no misgivings or second thoughts, Albert. Care to meet the staff now?"

"Yes, thank you. But first, if you don't mind, I'd like to eliminate any chance of second thoughts on *either* side, I mean, before I meet the staff."

Outside the new publishing offices of the Enquirer on north McCamly street, Albert Miller removed his hat, ran a long-fingered hand through his brown hair, thick, parted in the exact middle. He was slightly shorter than Post, thinner, with questioning eyes that drooped down at the corners to give him a melancholy expression.

"I take it you approve of the building?" C.W. gestured to the two-story brick structure with its plate glass windows and framed alcove entry. On one window, in large white letters: "The Morning Enquirer." The stretch of concrete sidewalk along the front was chalky fresh.

Miller said, "I do."

"The equipment is just as you specified. I don't believe we salvaged a thing from the old Enquirer operation. The staff, too, was chosen as you recommended but you are at liberty to release anyone who doesn't meet your expectations. Every one of them knows that."

"Thank you. I'm confident it is a qualified group." Miller said, "I hate to bring this up, but those four points we agreed on when I was first here..."

"Speak your piece, Albert."

Miller coughed nervously. "Just to clear up any second thoughts." He was silent for a moment, then said, "First, the Enquirer will openly denounce misconduct and public dishonesty wherever, whenever it is found."

Post's eyebrows raised and his expression was amused. "Such as the $50,000 libel suit Collier's Weekly has thrown at me? They claim I engaged in untruthful advertising, deadly lies I believe they called them. Mister Collier charged that I lashed out at his Weekly because he tried to make an example of me."

"I mean, sir, the Enquirer won't engage in scurrilous or unfounded reports about people, businesses, or politics for anyone's personal gain or to satisfy anyone's personal animosities." His tone was courteous but growing in resolution.

Post kept his amused look.

"Second, I recognize that the Enquirer is your newspaper, mister Post. You own it. As manager and editor, I will print any statement you choose to write over your own signature, within the bounds of decency, and run it as an opinion piece. I won't represent it as news or fact unless it is undeniably one or both."

"I've heard nothing disagreeable or unexpected so far, Albert, nor unacceptable."

"Third, sir, I ask for your word once more that you intend to provide necessary financing until the paper has had a reasonable chance to establish itself. It's up against formidable competition. There may be no profit for the first full year or so."

"Mister editor, you run the damned paper as though you were flat broke, but remember there is a hell of a long pocketbook in back of you. You'll hear no complaints from me for one full year."

"That's fine, sir. The final condition, you may easily recall, but may want to sleep on it before..."

"I sleep little."

"...you decide if it is truly digestible."

"Albert, you want the option to buy up to twenty-five percent of the newspaper, such option good for thirty-six months, providing you remain with the Enquirer. Am I right?"

"And..."

"And," Post interrupted, "you want first privilege to purchase the paper entirely, as long as you are connected with it, if I should ever decide to sell it outright. Have I covered the particulars correctly?"

"Yes."

"Would you like to have your four conditions put into writing? A formal contract we can each sign?"

"I would appreciate it, mister Post.

"It'll be drawn up tomorrow."

Post tilted his gold-handled cane at Miller.

A HANDMADE sign dangled on the glass door of the Enquirer's front office: Closed Until Nine.

Albert Laird Miller sat on a four-legged stool by the counter just inside the front doorway. He looked around at the expectant faces, two reporters, four machine operators, a bookkeeper, a proofreader, and an office girl. He saw the anticipated gamut of mild fear, uncertainty, and challenge, even haughtiness. In the hand posited on his knee, he held a pair of eyeglasses.

"I thought it would be a good idea if we became acquainted before we begin working together. I'm sorry mister Post left but he wanted to give us the freedom to learn a little about each other.

"I have some ideas about how newspapers ought to be run and how to organize them to get the job done, efficiently, smoothly, professionally," Miller said softly. "Those of you who come to know me will realize I make a lot out of the notion of professionalism. That's what journalism is to me. A profession. I have little patience for professionals who aren't profes-sionals." He nodded, agreeing with himself, then went on: "I think of a news-paper as a factory. We manufacture and package reading material...."

He told them he was raised in Kansas, worked at the *Ottawa Journal* when Henry J. Allen was its editor, later paid down on a small newspaper with a partner and was well along toward making it into a success when C.W. Post wired him.

"You may know," he concluded, "mister Post was my mother's cousin." As an afterthought, Miller quickly added, "My wife, Louise, comes from Kansas, too. We've been married seven years and have one son, Robert. I hope you'll have a chance to meet them soon."

"MISTER Roe, when you were a patient at my Sanitarium, were you treated well?"

"Yes, thank you, doctor Kellogg. Very well, indeed."

"Am I correct, you are no longer employed as business manager of the American Baptist Publication Society?"

Roe was portly with a handsome fleshy face, straight graying hair and full moustache. "I am seeking other opportunities."

The two men sat at a small circular table on the veranda of John Harvey's mansion. White clouds were reflected in the table's glassy sheen.

"Did you enjoy the food while you stayed at the Sanitarium?"

"Reasonably so. It was very nourishing, no doubt."

"It is also representative of a line of foods I have developed over the years which enjoys an international reputation for both quality and flavor."

"Certainly, doctor."

"Mister Roe, you mentioned on more than one occasion that you know a great many people in the, shall we say, upper echelons of business and capitalism of New York and Philadelphia and other important eastern cities. I want to put a position to you that may be quite lucrative for you."

"I'm flattered, doctor Kellogg. I do, in fact, acknowledge my acquaintance with numerous leaders of the banking and commercial world." A persuasive smile pulled his moustache into a straight dark line above his straight white teeth.

"Very good, mister Roe. Quite simply, I intend to develop a series of companies which will each handle one or more of my food products, products with the Kellogg name on them. After I have developed them, I intend to sell those companies individually to the highest bidder."

"I see." Roe's eyes grew shiny. "And you want bidders?"

"Can you deliver them?"

"It's a fascinating concept. I would want a bit of time to think..."

"While we think, others act. I offer you the potential of $5,000 a year for managing and selling businesses I will establish, finance, and stamp with the world famous names of Kellogg and Battle Creek."

Roe's eyes surrendered him. The money was five times what he had made at the Baptist Publishing Company.

"You've found your man, doctor Kellogg."

JOHN Harvey lifted the telephone, glanced back at Ella where she sat before the blazing fireplace in their library. "That will be mister Roe, darling. I can tell by the way it rang."

Watching her, he said into the instrument: "Yes, this is doctor Kellogg."

From hundreds of miles away, Roe's words sounded metallic. "I've located a buyer, doctor Kellogg. He's interested in the Rice Flakes option and he has the necessary connections to put the deal together. He can bring several other monied men in to tie this up in a pretty bundle, if you get my meaning."

"That is good news, indeed, mister Roe. Make arrangements as soon as you are able, and inform me as to when and where we must meet." After he replaced the receiver on the hook he went to Ella's side, put a hand on the back of her neck, rubbed it gently. "I can expect a telephone call or visit from brother Will the moment he learns of this. I'm confident he will threaten to make mincemeat of me if I don't withdraw."

Ella closed her eyes, enjoying the massage. "We so seldom hear from your brother anymore."

"Puss isn't doing well. Her strength and vitality are draining away as if she has a wound we can't find. I think Will doesn't believe I'm doing all I can for her. Frankly, the woman works too hard, for her age and condition. Even with all the help around her house, she seems determined to exhaust herself. I've about given up prescribing rest."

"The last time I saw her was at the church three weeks ago. She has aged, John. Her eyes were empty, turned inside. She's very sick, isn't she?"

"No better or worse than a year ago." He moved to a chair across from Ella, sat heavily. "Doctor Keim reports regularly to me since Will doesn't want me to handle her case."

"Will probably thinks you have too many patients under your care as it is."

"Well, I do have enough to keep me quite busy. I performed six operations this morning before my ten o'clock calls."

"Six? And yesterday morning?"

"Six."

"And tomorrow?"

"Only five are scheduled."

"I'm glad to learn you are taking your advice about easing off on the work load." She clucked her tongue in admonishment.

His thickening face opened into a grin, folds of flesh doubling up around his eyes. Nimble fingers played a thumping march rhythm on the leather arms of the chair. A foot tapped silently and swiftly in the softness of the rug. "You are my forever love, Ella, darling. When all the world is wiggly and wavy, you show me a straight, firm path."

The telephone sounded again. John Harvey said deploringly, "That is Will. I can tell by the harsh way it rang."

54

OCTOBER 1910

TABLET in one hand, pencil in the other, Albert Miller wrote slowly, knowing he could fill in later from memory. Nearby, the rows of wheat tanks outside the Postum Company formed a 200-yard steel wall of giant cylinders stocked with wheat. They lined the railroad tracks, dwarfed the waiting freight cars. The morning was very cool. Trees were leafless, the sky leaden.

Facing Miller, the attorney for Collier's Weekly — fortyish, with a large belly well disguised by his tailored topcoat — said, "Mister Post went too far in the cause of money-earning mendacity. We deemed it advisable to indicate to him that his grossly false assertions must stop. It is our magazine's policy to do so."

"Uh huh," Miller acknowledged. "And mister Post disallowed that he ever claimed medicinal effects for his products?"

The lawyer scoffed. "Mister Post's brazenness is extraordinary. He believed he could benefit from a lie so easily disproved." The attorney adjusted his stiff black hat against the breeze, then rested a gloved hand on his hip, arm cocked proudly. "Post retaliated by publicly asserting that we attempted to coerce him into advertising with us, that he never intended to place ads with us."

"And you've sued him for those allegations?"

"Certainly. The man posits that GrapeNuts is a brain food. He blatantly says that various experts show one-half of the cereal's mineral salts are phosphate of potash. Admittedly, that mineral *is* an important brain food. On that flimsy connection, Post proclaimed that GrapeNuts is an important contributor to the health of one's brain." His pinched face wiggled. "GrapeNuts contains *no* brain food nor heart food nor shin-bone food nor any other such nonsense."

LATER, in the Post Tavern, Miller still wore his heavy overcoat as he sat across the table from his employer. Beside Post, Leila looked as though someone had brushed her with glazed sugar and it had hardened. She stared at the glass of unchilled pink grapefruit juice she had ordered but left untouched.

"Collier's Weekly attacked me. I struck back. They didn't like it that I dared to counterattack so they filed a libel suit." Each time C.W. lifted the Postum-filled cup with the Tavern's crest, crisp white cuffs shone three inches beyond his suitcoat sleeves. "Expert surgeons attest to the fact that many cases of appendicitis are healed without operating. Often it is sufficient alone to get rid of the cause which, frequently, is undigested food. So, our advertisements point out, when food is ready to be taken again after an operation, the use of a predigested food will not overtax the weakened organs."

Leila reached for the juice glass but did not drink from it. "And, of course, GrapeNuts is partly digested. It says so on every lovely box."

Post said, "Leila, why don't you go up to the apartment and freshen yourself. I'll be along in a few minutes."

She didn't move. Miller tried to smile reassuringly.

Post spoke slowly, precisely, as if he feared even the shadow of misinterpretation. "For years we offered prizes to people who used GrapeNuts and Postum if they would write to us with an honest statement about the value of the foods. Testimonials came by the hundreds of thousands. Those letters will be produced as evidence if there is a trial."

Miller closed his notepad. "One last question. Not for publication. Are the letters authentic and unedited?"

Post didn't hesitate with his answer. "We received carload lots of them. Most were ungrammatical, far too wordy. They had to be edited for our advertising."

After Miller left them, Leila turned sharply toward Post, intending to suggest he should not be so free with information about a pending law suit. She was startled by his bloodless face. His teeth were clinched, his eyes had turned to paste.

"Charles?" She touched his hand, jerked back from its iciness. "My God, you're freezing cold."

"Dizzy. Help me upstairs, Leila. Need to lie down." His voice was the croak of a swamp animal.

NEWS ITEM

AP Wire Service. December 10, 1910 — A jury today found in favor of Collier's Weekly in the publication's libel suit against cereal magnate C.W. Post. On hearing the verdict, the court awarded $50,000 to Collier's, whose managing editor said, "Justice has been done." Mister Post was unavailable for comment.

55

AUGUST 1912

BATTLE Creek's population reached the awesome height of thirty thousand in the year 1912. Railroad tracks crisscrossed the town like tic-tac-toe games marked on brown paper. There were twelve colleges and training institutes — from the Bryant School of Piano Tuning to the St. Philips Convent. Publishers aplenty: The Enquirer, the Moon, the Journal, the Dog Fancier, the Poultry Breeder, Post's Square Deal newsletter, and so on. The town had sixteen saloons, and the doors on every one of them swung constantly, much to the dismay of the more temperate citizens, many who preferred to nip in the privacy of their homes.

JOHN Harvey was dressed in a white Panama suit, white shirt, white tie. His beard was gone, replaced by a Vandyke goatee and moustache as white as his shoes and socks and cane. He looked like a chrysanthemum planted in his brother's frontroom floor. Beside him, Ella was cocooned in a long white cape.

"Puss is very, very sick, Will, but I think she could improve with sufficient rest, and if she would follow the diet we prescribed. Does she take her yogurt?"

"She doesn't like it."

Will would have preferred to sit down but he did not want to signal his weariness or give his visitors any incentive to remain. So he stood, stiff-legged and rooted. A chiming clock on the mantle near the hall door informed him that the conversation was ten minutes old and going nowhere.

John Harvey raised his face to the ceiling. "Yogurt has remarkable antitoxic qualities. The Europeans have long recognized it as a superb remedy for intestinal disorders. I believe autointoxication is the cause of most chronic maladies in humans, and the lactic acid-forming fermentation of yogurt defeats the growth of those resultant germs that come from ingesting impure milk and flesh foods."

"Thank you for the discourse, doctor. Puss won't eat the yogurt."

"Try not to blame John," Ella interrupted. "He truly regrets the recent confrontations over your cereal products. His chief anxiety is caused by seeing how it distresses you, Will." Nearing fifty years, her once dark hair now contained wide swathes of white. "Your lawsuit against him nearly devastated him."

W.K. blew out a huff of air. His hands were dug into his coat pockets. He gave John Harvey his full attention, as though Ella wasn't present. "Doctor, you set up your Riceflake and Kellogg Biscuit Company. Then you tried to sell the companies outright. Your scavenger, mister Roe, failed to deliver buyers..."

"Because you ran them off or bought them off, Will."

"...so you gave the companies to the American Medical Missionary Society. Donated them out of spite. They, then, could sell Kellogg products. Under the Kellogg name. Next, you filed to enjoin me from using my own name on my own products. Doctor, I think you are a scoundrel."

John Harvey's face darkened. "Look here, Will, you hired away my sales manager the very next day after you and I signed our agreement to keep our products separate. You forced me to find a new manager at a most difficult time..."

"Whitmore was ready to leave you. I didn't seek him, he came to see me about a job." Will switched to another sore point. "Our purchase agreement and your stock liquidation forbid you to market corn flakes in the United States. You did it, anyway. Over one hundred invoices were wrongly billed to me. Hundreds of letters of protest flooded in from salesmen, brokers, retailers."

"The San was faced with temporary financial problems," the doctor offered weakly.

"You talk of your San as though it were sinking in quicksand. Why then did you recently add a 300-room annex? Did you build it because you wanted more empty rooms?"

John Harvey slumped unbidden into a chair, dabbed at his bald dome with a white handkerchief. "Will, let me ask you something, one brother to another. Give me a truthful answer. How many cartons of corn flakes did you sell last year?"

Frowning, "I don't carry those figures in my head, doctor."

"Approximately."

"Andrew Ross believes our output this summer was sixty million packages. Something near 250,000 packages a day."

John Harvey whistled softly through his teeth. "That certainly must have been like a bumblebee inside C.W. Post's armor."

"Yes," W.K. said flatly. "You can calculate the dollars yourself. When you do, deduct my advertising costs. You wouldn't know about that expense, since you ride free on mine. Last year that expense was two million dollars."

Ella gasped at the enormity of the figure and John Harvey mournfully shook his head.

"Will, the San's annex amounted to nothing. You added a building to your own plant just months ago. You yourself are the money interest in Michigan Carton, and its new paper mill. You admit you spent two million on advertising. You furnish your salesmen with fine automobiles. You have this magnificently furnished home, undoubtedly mortgage free. All of this, and you begrudge me the right to use my own name on products of my own initiative." He wiped his head again with the handkerchief.

W.K. strolled to the hall door, looked up the wide stairway toward his wife's room. He listened intently. "Puss is ill. I want to be with her," he said. "Please let yourselves out."

The doctor gained his feet, balanced on his cane. "Mother would roll over in her grave if she knew what you were doing to your own brother."

W.K.'s anger gorged into his throat like vomit. He took three quick steps, grabbed the doctor's chin whiskers and yanked them, throwing John Harvey into a stumble, reeling across the floor, collapsing again onto a stuffed chair. Ella jumped to his aid, glaring at W.K. as if she thought he had gone mad. John Harvey's eyes were huge and as white as his clothing.

"I'm going to outlive you, doctor Kellogg," Will challenged, his chin jutted on a stretched neck. "I'll outlive you and your sick fixation on bowels and enemas and meat and damned near everything else. I'll eat oysters and bacon and beefsteak and I'll outlive you. You go to 65, I'll go 65 and one year. You go to 85, I'll go 85 and one month. You go to 100, I'll go 100 and a day."

The threat befuddled John Harvey, submerging any natural reaction to strike back. "That's senseless, Will. What difference would it make if I'm already dead? I won't even know about it."

"No," Will said, reverting to instant calm. "But I'll know. That's the point."

56

PUSS wore a soft gown, buttoned to her chin. On her head was a sleeping bonnet that almost succeeded in covering her sheer white hair. The iron bed's heavy posts were gilded with decorations. The 45-pound cotton mattress she lay on was only forty pounds lighter than her own weight. Except for one sleeved arm, she was covered to her shoulders with layers of woolen blankets.

When W.K. tipped the carved oak rocker lightly with his toe, it swayed squeakily against the floor rug. His eyes were darkly pocketed above a tight mouth. In the sun-speckled room, he listened to the sounds of commerce and casual passers-by on Van Buren Street: occasional automobiles, wagons, the whinny of horses, the call of human voices.

"Skimpy news in today's papers, Puss." He turned the front page, carefully folded it over, scanned the columns. Not reading, he said, "There now are two penny arcades downtown. When you get well, I'll take you to one. But don't expect very much."

"Len tells me they show some motion pictures of scantily dressed women." She shut her eyes, frowning.

Color touched his cheeks. "I don't think there'll be much future for such gimcrackery." He doubled the newspaper onto his lap. "Most of the flicker films are just fast little melodramas or a prize fight."

"I've been sick for so long, you've had that to worry about..." She lifted her hand a few inches. "Did they find any of the poor people from that terrible shipwreck?"

He started to ask which shipwreck she meant, then he remembered her horror over the sinking of the ocean liner, Titanic, back in April. More than 1,500 lives had been lost. She anguished about the disaster for weeks, shaking her head and asking repeatedly, "Why did so many have to die?"

So he said, "Yes, Puss. Hundreds got away on lifeboats."

She smiled, satisfied. "I know Karl and Len are able to look after themselves. They're men. Tell me about Beth and Norman. Do they seem happy? Is Beth going to services regularly?"

A few blocks away, in the upstairs hallway of her house, Beth Kellogg told the nurse she would be back from shopping in an hour. The nurse said don't hurry, I'll keep an eye on things. Beth kissed Kenneth Stanley Williamson on his blonde head and instructed him to mind nurse Weber while mama was gone. He held tightly to her, his small arms encircling her neck, clinging, until she unlocked them and smoothed his hair lovingly. He asked when daddy would be home and she answered it would be a few days because daddy was on the road, selling for the Morton Salt Company and making lots of money for Kenneth Stanley to buy a new toy. The answer satisfied the boy and he turned away and climbed on his tricycle. There was a horn attached to its handlebars. He squeezed the rubber bulb twice, honking it the way he had seen Grandfather Kellogg's hired driver, a black man named Spech, honk the horn on that big air-cooled Franklin. Then he peddled the bike down the long hallway, going away from the safety gate at the stairs. He drove relentlessly toward the open door of the far bedroom, hooting the horn, warning make-believe pedestrians out of his way.

W.K. rocked gently in his chair, talking to Ella. "I don't know what it is about our children, Puss. All that elopement. It was wrong to run off, get married. Us not even knowing about it. Is that what we taught them? First Len, then Beth?"

"Karl never eloped," she reminded him, her memory serving up unarguable logic at times, failing her totally at other times.

"He might just as well have. Married out in Montana. We never met the girl."

"Karl needed a dry climate, Will..."

"I know. His lungs." Kellogg shrugged broodingly. "I had counted on him practicing in Battle Creek. My wishes didn't mean a thing. He barely got out of medical school, then left town."

Ella closed her eyes, a tender reproof. "You hear me, Will Kellogg. Karl has two beautiful sons, little Karl and little Will Lewis. It's a blessing that wouldn't have happened if he hadn't gone where his lungs could heal."

W.K. changed the subject. "You asked about Beth. She's fine. She was here this morning. Do you remember? She brought Kenneth Stanley."

"I think I do." Puzzlement wriggled over her face. "It's easier to see things that happened a while back than what happened this morning. Isn't that silly? Did we talk about her and Norman?"

"The man's lazy. Always saying what he plans to do, never doing it. His sales job is a farce. Doesn't earn enough to pay the electric bill. Expect that's why they still use those kerosene lamps. If we didn't help them, give them a place to live, they'd be down and out. He probably cuts some shenanigans when he's on the road. I know about salesmen. Work with them every day."

"Oh, Will," she cried softly, "Norman loves Beth. He wouldn't do anything to disgrace her or hurt her."

"He ever shows he isn't on the straight and narrow, I'll see he gets his comeuppance." Then, as if debating with himself, "I've thought of hiring a detective to check on him."

Her hand tensed in his and he forced an unaccustomed grin. "I came to cheer you up. I'm doing a poor job."

Beth Kellogg adjusted her bonnet. Nurse Weber was putting the bed in order where Beth and little Kenneth Stanley had slept last night, straightening the dark green comforter, brushing out the wrinkles, pulling it tightly over bulging pillows. Directly across from the doorway, in a straight line with it, a tall window was opened into the warm September air. The window reached nearly to the ceiling and extended down to within two feet of the floor.

I'll be going in just a minute, Beth said.

At the other end of the hallway, Kenneth Stanley ran his tricycle, speeding down the hardwood floor, pulling up just short of his mother's bedroom door, then turning and peddling furiously back the way he had come.

W.K. sat up straight in the rocker, making a great deal of fuss about it, resolutely squaring his shoulders, still holding Ella's hand. "A postal letter came from sister Laura yesterday. She and hers are grateful for the money we send every month. And aunt Cordele has herself a housekeeper by now. We've provided."

"That would please Ann Janette," Ella ventured, squeezing his hand with a marshmallow grip. "Aunt Cordele was her favorite sister."

Kenneth Stanley's tricycle almost collided with nurse Weber as she came out of the bedroom into the hall. She caught the handlebars, turned them, spatted the boy on his rump, told him to stay at the other end of the house while she straightened things in the bathroom. He asked when his mother would be home and nurse Weber said she just left a few minutes ago and it would be at least an hour before she returned. The answer satisfied him, an hour being no different than a minute. Nurse Weber went to her work and he wheeled around and again raced from one end of the upper hall to the other. He did not bother now to stop at the door of his mother's room. Instead, he spun through it, executed a daring horseshoe turn near the wall and the tall open window, and fled back into the hallway, gathering speed.

"Len is coming along at the factory," W.K. announced as if Ella didn't know it. "A good worker. Creative mind. Flighty at times. Have to remind him of his place. I hope a little growing up will settle him."

"He is grown up, dear, with two strapping boys. I expect you don't give him enough credit." She attempted to focus her gaze on W.K., but it failed to hold, drifted off and swept along the patterned wallpaper. "Or is it Karl with the two boys?"

"You're right, Puss. It's both. Hannah was just telling you today that Will Keith is five. John Leonard junior is over a year. A little man already. He can nearly talk. I don't understand what he says, but Hannah does."

"I love you, Will Kellogg. Do you know that?"

"Yes, Puss. You always showed your love for me, the boys, for Beth." His throat felt tight and dusty. "We should have done a better job of returning it. Especially me."

She grinned. "I like these afternoons when you come and sit and we talk like this. The sun warms the room and makes things so cheerful. It's like we are young, younger than Len or Karl or Beth." Her grin faded. "We thought we'd never get old. Now look at us. We get older and don't even know it until all of a sudden..." She stopped abruptly. "You didn't have a beard, then, did you? I can't remember if it was you or John Harvey, or both of you."

"No, Puss. I didn't. I never had a beard. But it doesn't matter." His throat muscles were knotted. He swallowed several times.

"I love you, Will Kellogg. I want to tell you that before I go to sleep. I'm so drowsy and I might go to sleep while you're here. I don't mean to..."

He sat by her bed until her breathing was regular. Then he lifted his hand from hers and left the room without disturbing her.

Nurse Weber noticed the silence at almost the exact instant it settled. She was folding towels for the bathroom linen closet when she realized she did not hear Kenneth Stanley playing. A bubble of panic rose and stuck in her throat. She stepped into the hallway. It was empty. Her vision followed along the floorboards to the door of the far bedroom and beyond to the open window. At its low shelf was the overturned tricycle, a back wheel still spinning. She hurried frantically to the window, one hand clutching the collar of her uniform, the other grabbing at the wall for support. She looked out and down to the concrete walk two stories below. Her scream could be heard far beyond the neighborhood.

57

SEPTEMBER 1912

"PLEASE come in the house, father. Hannah has fixed some things to eat."

Len wanted to tug W.K.'s sleeve, pull him away from his dark mood, but decided against trying. His own cheeks were tear marked, eyes raw and veined, as he stared at the grass around his shoes. It reminded him of pasture land he had known as a child, very green but snarled with dried leaves the wind had shook down early from the trees.

Hannah yelled from the back porch, "Mister Kellogg, please come to have some food. Beth and me we have put out the fixings on the table."

W.K. motioned he heard her, but he did not stop staring at the Sanitarium building rising in the warm sky less than a city block away. He made a quick, high noise like laughter.

"Karl thinks you should eat," Len offered. "He's a doctor, he knows about these things. Mother's gone. She's out of her pain, father. Making yourself sick won't help now." He looked back at Hannah, shrugged his shoulders. When she went inside the screen door banged shut with a sound as hollow as an unkept promise.

W.K.'s voice was a whisper. "All those days and nights, over there working. Work so important. I thought of nothing else. I gave you so little time, Puss. My long hours and piddly pay. And I left you to care for the house, the children, everything. It wasn't just the San, though, was it, Puss? I had to build my own company. Work was the beginning, the middle, the end. Even when I was with you I grumbled about business."

"Father, you did everything possible for mother. You hired the best doctors in the world. You took her south for the warmer weather. She had special nurses with her every minute. Uncle John's staff was on call. Quit knocking the stuffing out of yourself. She's at peace."

The moaning, metallic note of a train whistle came on the morning air. Kellogg straightened, gave the Sanitarium another glance. He thought to himself, there is a hurt that no amount of rest or medicine will cure. That pain filled him to choking, reaching a point at the bottom of his lungs where it lodged and intensified. It raised awareness mercilessly, heightening the loneliness and the wretchedness.

W.K.'s eyes searched Len's face. "Little Kenneth Stanley has a metal plate where part of his brain used to be..."

"Please, father."

"...he's blind in one eye, nearly blind in the other. His right arm flops out of control. He barely can move his right leg. He will be a cripple all his life. Money has done nothing for him. The best specialists and treatment gave us no improvement whatsoever." His eyes turned glassy. "I traded you, Puss, for the money and the power. Now they can't even help our grandson."

He made the quick high noise again. Len realized it was a whimper of desolation.

58

OCTOBER 1912

OH hell, oh damn, Post cried in the dream, feeling the slam of his heart in a contracting ribcage. Oh hell, it's come back...

The nightmare had been inching its way into his sleep for more than a year. A mere moment had intruded the first time: just a glimpse of a dirt road rushing away under him like the current of a flooded river. Larger pieces had taken form in the following months.

The buggy was soaring, its wheels barely skimming the ground. Horses screamed and snorted, eyes bulged, their ears were laid back, manes and tails stiff in the wind. Fire and lightning. His grandfathers howled toothlessly at him as he raced away from them.

Except this time it was different.

He was a grown man, not a child.

The old men were calling more directly to him: Sixty! No mares! We're waiting!

Waiting for what, for God's sake? Rollin and Carrie weren't there any more on the roadside by the picnic blanket with the spread of food. Now there was another person...a woman in a white sleeping gown, but her features were blurred.

The ringing telephone woke him.

"Yes," he hissed into the mouthpiece, gripping the neck of the telephone in a sweaty hand, fitting the receiver to his ear. A glint of moonlight from an open window lit up the bedside clock. Nearly five a.m.

"Father?" Her voice was tinny, filtered through the cables from Washington to California.

"Yes, Marjorie. It's me." His tongue felt as thick as a skid of cardboard. He glanced at the other bed, relieved to see that Leila was still sleeping.

"Mother died."

The telephone line twanged with electrical pops and pings. C.W. thought he heard his daughter snuff as if from a head cold. He peered down the unbroken length of the hall outside the bedroom, his gaze reaching at last the balastraded balcony of the villa. Tacked above the balcony, the moon was a garish crescent of blood-red linen. His arm jerked involuntarily.

"I thought you ought to know," Marjorie said.

"I did know," he told her, watching the profile of mountains on the horizon but seeing the woman in his dream.

"Are you still asleep, father? You're not making sense. Mother died just minutes ago."

"Of course," he stammered. "I meant, it was right for you to let me know." His hand was trembling so he set the telephone on the table, stretching to speak into it. "I hope there was no suffering."

"She wasn't even sick. She went to sleep last night. She didn't wake up this morning. That's all it was." The sob was distinct this time, not imagined. "We will take her to Springfield to be buried."

There was another silence. Then, "Father, you will come to the funeral?"

His nightshirt was sticky against him. "I'll try to be there, Marjorie," he lied. "I'll honestly try."

59

MARCH 1914

THE SANTA Barbara meeting hall was filled with hundreds of people waiting to hear the announced speech, every chair occupied. Spring breezes drifted in through open windows, spilling the aroma of blooming jasmine and the piquant fragrance of an orange orchard in the courtyard by the entrance.

Post came to the microphone amid sustained applause loud enough to be heard thirty miles away in Ventura. He smiled, waited, looked over at his wife, caught her wink.

It was the last public speech he would ever make.

"The Postum workers gave me a testimonial dinner a few years ago. One of the men who spoke was a worker in the plant. I want to share his words with you tonight because I believe they epitomize the sentiments of most hardworking men of dignity. I believe, too, they represent the thoughts of our National Association of Manufacturers, you gentlemen out there.

"He said to me, 'mister Post, we've read about hate and murder in the air, and good workers chased through the streets by mobs of strikers. We've heard about workmen no longer able to draw wages because the factories were burned down, families going hungry, cities at a standstill. We want no part of that kind of labor union rule. In Battle Creek, all across the city, you'll find the highest wages and the best conditions,' he said. 'That's why it's called the Free City.' He looked me in the eye and said, 'captain, we thank you for leading the way. You're a friend and benefactor, and the great Postum Company is a happy and contented family'."

Applause rattled the hall like an earthquake. C.W. drank some water, replaced the glass on the table, but his hand trembled badly and he spilled part of the liquid. Leila's eyes widened. She whispered, "Charles?" but he already had returned to his speech.

"The public doesn't need, nor want, a leach-like power that controls workmen and dictates the conduct of human beings. No working man should be forced out on strike, sacrificing his pay envelope, losing his home. A few pennies of pay raise achieved this way only result in dollars added to the costs of commodities. In the end, the worker has less money in his pocket than he had before.

"But we at the helm of businesses and industries also have a deep responsibility we must not shirk. It is our duty to provide our workers with fair wages and the best of conditions."

He paused long enough for the direction he was taking to catch hold in everyone's mind.

"I believe workmen live on too narrow a margin of safety. If sickness or accident lays them low, their reserves are generally too small to tide them through. That's why industry should set aside an amount each year to cover the unexpected that befalls its employees. And the employees should have wages raised enough to warrant their contributions to this fund along with their employer. At Postum, I can tell you, any worker injured on the job is cared for and paid in full during disability. Furthermore, to make sure the worker has funds of his own at his disposal, any Post employee who stays with me for two years gets an amount equal to five percent of his salary deposited in a bank account in his name. We add ten percent each year thereafter."

Post was perspiring heavily under his coat. His throat felt too dry and the endless rows of faces were faded and blurry. He moved several pages of his speech aside.

"I am not a warm advocate of a lot of foolish, misapplied maudlin sympathy that has passed under the name of welfare work. The welfare that I believe in is that which makes it possible for the man to help himself. It does not include the holding of a milk bottle to his lips after he is weaned."

Post tried to clear his throat, felt a razor-slash pain in his right side as though he had run too hard and too long. He drew an extended breath.

"Every American workman wants an honest, first-class prize for his labor, and then he wants to be left alone."

His voice had dropped to half its volume. "If men are paid the highest standard wages, they will pretty well take care of themselves."

The pain eased for a moment. "I admit, if I were a competent workman and employed in an industry that is run on the grind principle, I would join a labor organization to defend my rights against tyranny. But I should be an active opponent of violence and tyranny, whatever side might move to use it. Thank you, ladies and gentlemen."

With Leila and two of his assistants helping him, C.W. was bustled from the hall to his waiting touring car. When he reached the leather interior of the automobile, he crumpled onto the seat. A hot needle was stitching his right side.

"God almighty," he gasped, teeth clenched, eyes tear-filled. "Get doctor Leslie. I think I'm dying."

"EVERYBODY in town really likes the Enquirer having a morning and evening paper every day, mister Miller, except the Moon and the Journal, they don't like it." The office girl's face was cheery. She picked up some AP press fillers from the out basket. "How is mister Post's condition?"

"Mister Post is fine, Susie. His special train took him from California to the Mayo Clinic in Minnesota in sixty-six hours. That's speed by anybody's definition. The Mayo doctors removed his appendix. He's mending nicely. Missus Post told reporters her husband's condition was, and I quote, greatly exaggerated."

"I don't see how she couldn't go to the hospital with him," the girl said. "He's her husband."

"But she's no physician," Miller grunted. "Besides, she came to Battle Creek to visit relatives. A sensible thing to do, I'd say."

The girl headed toward the composing room with the copy sheets. "Those rich people sure live different than most of us," she commented.

"IT'S GOOD to have you home, Charles. The California climate will-work its magic for you, darling, plenty of sunshine and fresh air..."

"Leila, you sound like John Harvey Kellogg. This isn't Battle Creek, so please shut up." Raspiness. A grinding of vocal chords, noises from out of his past. He heard and it made him feel as if he had just peeped through the streaked window of an old house and witnessed a transparent, dark vision of himself at the San waiting for treatment twenty-three years ago.

Damn you and your dictatorial ways, she thought, and felt an instant jolt of guilt. She smoothed a blanket around his thin chest. "You'll soon be doing everything for yourself, completely healed in another week or two."

Her optimism drew the corners of his mouth together like strings on a tobacco pouch. "Don't be so full of glad tidings, Leila. Your mock enthusiasm isn't pleasing to me."

She had inured herself to his increased outbursts. Each time he berated her for something trivial, she reacted with a wan smile, a touch of her hand. Each time, he fumed and jerked away as if she had pricked him with a pin. Each time it seemed to her that his faultfinding grew daily instead of diminishing as doctor Leslie had predicted.

"The operation didn't cure my stomach pains. They're worse than they were before. Why do we pay those damned doctors' fees when they just give us one inept diagnosis after another?"

She partly closed the arched window's striped drapes, lessening a western sun that was heating the room. On her way out she said, "I'll bring you something cold to drink." He paid no attention to her.

"*Build yourself a house in Jerusalem,* it says in Kings." It was an old man's voice, wheezing along the tapestried walls of a million dollar villa in the late afternoon heat. "*And you must dwell there and not go out from there to this place and that. And it must occur that on your day of going out*...damn," he blurted, "what the hell is the rest of it? Going out, going out," he primed his memory. "Yes, yes...*when you do pass over the torrent Valley of Kid'ron you should unmistakably know that you will positively die.*" A trickle of bitter laughter spilled out of him as rattly as pinecones in a basket. "I left Battle Creek. That's why I'm sick. There's your reason, you bunch of Hippocratic quacks."

After a few minutes, Leila eased the door open and looked in. Post's head was tilted sharply onto his shoulder. He was dozing, his body twitching every few seconds with the old nightmare.

HE was shouting in a voice remarkably strong for someone whose physical condition had worsened steadily for two months, ever downward like a stone dropped into a bottomless well. The words were baffled by the walls, tossed and bounced, made incomprehensible.

Leila and Carroll and Mollie could hear him ranting from the edge of the villa's tiled entrance. The iron-ribbed front doors stood open and their luggage was being carried by a chauffeur to the waiting limousine.

"Would you like us to stay longer?" Mollie's question was ripe with dread. The two days had been hellish, witnessing C.W. swinging like a pendulum from brilliant, opinionated debater — the old C.W. at his best — to demoniac child, rife with fits and tantrums and hurling baseless accusations, even against Carroll. Mollie yearned for the normal, frantic activity of White City and the Postum plant and the tranquility of Battle Creek.

Dark smudges seemed permanently dyed beneath Leila's eyes. "C.W. has these moments of anger when he can't remember something he wants to say, but he gets over them quickly," she said.

Mollie's lips kept coming together and parting. "We can stay longer," she muttered, climbing into the limousine, tugging Carroll after her, then reaching across him and closing the automobile door.

Before they were driven away, Carroll said from the lowered window: "Call us if there is any change, good or bad."

When Leila went back to the sitting room, Charles was pacing, moving brokenly, supported by the gold-topped cane he once carried like a rapier. "Are they gone?" An agitated growl.

"Yes. They sent you their love."

"I heard you and Montgomery whispering about me on the veranda yesterday. Didn't know that, did you?" His expression was childishly menacing. "You don't fool me one iota."

"Charles, I'm really tired of your insinuations and imaginings and your disgusting suspicions. Since you became sick..."

"It's made it easier for the two of you, hasn't it?"

"Mister Montgomery came at *your* insistence. He left almost a week ago, do you understand?"

"I didn't ask him out, dammit to hell. Don't try to confuse me, Leila. It's for goddamn sure I don't want him back. And you are not to go to Battle Creek until I'm able to travel with you."

"I had no intention of going..."

"You've traveled the world with me, stayed in the finest resorts. We have villas, mansions wherever we go. You have an army of servants jumping to your command, plenty of hired help so an invalid husband isn't too great a burden on you. What else do you want?" He glowered at her, his eyes yellow and unsure. "Is it worth throwing it away for a hotel clerk?"

She bit back a reply. Her jaw muscles ached from clamping her teeth together. He saved her from answering.

"My guns, Leila, where are they? The cabinet is empty. What have you done with..."

"I told Julio to put them away for safekeeping."

"Safekeeping? What in hell's half acre does that mean? They were safe in the cabinet. It was made for them."

"The doctor gave orders for us to put the guns away, out of sight, Charles."

"Oho! The doctor handing out instructions again, eh? Who the hell does he think is in charge around here?" Post spoke levelly, uncompromisingly. "See that the guns are put back in the cabinet."

"I won't do that, Charles. I'm sorry."

"CHARLES, do you want your father and me to come to Santa Barbara and see you? It's hard to believe you are being mistreated but..."

"No, Carrie." Abrupt as a door buzzer.

They had been talking by long distance telephone for ten minutes. A wriggling, tottering, waddling conversation. Most of it so convoluted and mazy that Carrie could not follow it.

"Then I'll call Carroll, he and Mollie can..."

"No. The company needs Carroll more than I do. Besides, I have Leila..."

"I can't hear you, son. Why are you speaking so low?" Her own voice, after more than 70 years, was nearly worn out.

Hand cupped around the mouthpiece, his lips pressed against the black metal, he whimpered, "They listen in on me, Carrie."

"I can't hear you, Charles. Please put Leila on."

A mournful humming sound bubbled up inside of him. "I'm lost, Carrie, so damned lost. Nothing means anything to me, not my work or friends or White City. Not anything. God, oh God, what is wrong with me? I hurt in every bone, every nerve."

"Where is Leila?" she asked again.

He began to cough, managed to choke out a nearly soundless plea: "Why is this happening to me, Carrie, what is the reason? Tell me, please, Carrie..."

"Charles, can you speak louder, son? Is Leila there?"

C.W. hung up the telephone.

THERE'S a stranger living inside me, he won't go away. I can't control whoever has hold of the damned steering wheel.

I talk jimjam. Only a minute ago Quanita asked politely, very politely, mister Post would you like to go out on the balcony for some sun? And I told her I couldn't stand the digging. What in hell was I thinking? No one is digging at the back of the house. Nothing but the mountains, small over there, far away. Gibberish. That's all I'm good for. That, and peeing on myself in the toilet.

Food tastes worse than medicine.

God almighty, I'm always so tired. I've been away from people too long — real, live, do-things people. I'm losing my balance, that's what it is. No wonder. All I see are nurses and yessir servants and the damned doctors. I should get back to work, start pulling my own weight, making the serious decisions about the company. Carroll does an adequate job. But he isn't me. He can't think like me. Who am I kidding? I'm getting worse every day. Just a question of time.

HE quietly, slowly, turned the brass handle, eased open the empty cabinet's doors. A faint odor of oil and cedar drifted to him and he sniffed it hungrily, then reached in and angled an arm upward, holding firmly with his other hand to the wooden frame. His fingers rubbed the grainy, rough underside of the cabinet's roof, an area dusky and out of view, recessed ten inches higher than the peak of the double doors. He explored the dark area, feeling only sanded boards. Futility coursed through him. They had found it and took it, too, damn them.

He started to withdraw his arm. His thumb bumped cold metal. He touched it hesitantly, then more boldly, gripping it there in the box of shadows. A lift, a pull, and the object came free of its restraining thongs. C.W. extracted the hidden treasure, his special bore 30-30 Winchester hunting rifle. He opened one of the cabinet's side drawers, drew out a box of cartridges, inserted a shell in the rifle's magazine.

He straggled toward his bedroom down the hall. The only sound was his moccasins pushing along on the shiny floor. In his room, he perched on the edge of the bed. The coverlet was turned back. Two round pillows lay like giant toadstools. The sheets were freshly changed, cool to the touch. A mimosa tree's branches outside the latticed window caused pale dancing images on the white walls. C.W. positioned the rifle across his knees. He cocked the lever easily, pleased and surprised at his own strength.

"Nothing endures," he murmured.

He stretched out on the bed, jammed the rifle barrel under his chin.

"Forgive me, Leila. Forgive me, Carrie. Forgive me, Rollin. And Marjorie, please forgive me, little sweetheart."

He did not hear the explosion of the 210-grain, metal jacketed bullet, did not feel it rip into his brain. He was a boy again, in his old nightmare, but no longer frightened by it. The racing carriage was overturning, dislodging him. Both of his grandfathers waited beside the road while he tumbled through the air to arrive unharmed on the waving grass. The two old men smiled. They had their teeth in place and looked very dignified: hair combed, clothes spotless. They had truly spruced up to come and meet him. Even as he drifted toward the ground he heard their words, faint and broken: Sixty!!! No mares!!! Then the gaps filled in as his hands touched the grassy mounds, his body still twisting in a wonderful, grass-cushioned somersault: You didn't live to sixty! But there's no more nightmares, Charley. Welcome, boy!

He rolled onto the green carpet of clover. His grandfathers each took an arm and lifted him to his feet. He was so very glad to see them.

60

AT ten p.m. Albert Miller sat alone in the Enquirer newsroom. The presses were idle on the first floor, waiting for early morning when they would come thunderously alive, churning out the sunrise edition. He scanned the copy he had just composed.

"May 25, 1914. Battle Creek, Michigan. The last will and testament of Charles W. Post, a resident of Washington, D.C., was made less than one year ago on November 3, 1913, at Battle Creek.

"To his wife, Leila, went all real estate at Battle Creek except the Marjorie and Enquirer blocks; all real estate at Santa Barbara, California; one half of all real estate in the state of Texas; one half of the common stock of Postum Cereal Co., Limited; and one quarter of all personal property."

He skimmed past the details about an administrative cabinet for the Postum Company to be led by Carroll Post. He glided over the provisions for C.W. Post's parents.

"To his only child, Marjorie Post Close, now residing in Greenwich, Connecticut, the will bequeaths that property in Greenwich which was owned by mister Post, one half of the Texas land, all of the Marjorie and Enquirer blocks, one half of the common stock of Postum Cereal Company, Limited, and one fourth of all personal property wherever situated. Missus Post Close is the owner, too, of all the preferred stock of Postum Cereal Company, Limited. The estate's value was set at $20,552,380.00."

He reviewed the laudatory comments made by local and national figures eager to praise Post posthumously. At least there was no hypocrisy by W.K. Kellogg, he mused, thinking of the unpublished interview.

Miller: "You don't care to comment, mister Kellogg?"

Kellogg: "The man was a scourge. A philanderer. A thief. In the end he proved a coward, taking his own life."

Miller: "You surely can offer a compliment for the gifts he bestowed on Battle Creek."

Kellogg: "Post was a slick operator. He could dish the applesauce. His gifts to this city were by motive of profit. I didn't like the man. I won't degrade myself by pretending I did."

Miller took up a pencil and marked an insertion after "a resident of Washington, D.C.," adding "and formerly of Battle Creek." He clicked off the office lamp, walked to the stairway, paused.

"Mister C.W. Post," he said to the darkness, "maybe you were a man who loved this town more than it ever loved you."

NEWS ITEM

Battle Creek, Michigan. December 9, 1915 — Nineteen months after the death of cereal food multi-millionaire C.W. Post, his widow, missus Leila Young Post, has agreed to accept a cash settlement of $6,000,000 for her rights in the Postum properties. According to the agreement made public today, she will withdraw absolutely from the cereal company. Control passes entirely to missus Marjorie Post Close.

Missus Leila Young Post told the Enquirer, "There is no trouble between Marjorie Close and myself. This action is a peaceful settlement without litigation."

The settlement followed a suit recently filed to determine ownership of the Postum properties...

NEWS ITEM

Battle Creek, Michigan. April 8, 1916 — Missus Leila Young Post, widow of the late Charles W. Post, was married today to Lawrence J. Montgomery, manager of the Post Tavern...

PART SIX

"Do not measure another's coat on your own body."

Malay Proverb

61

DECEMBER 1919

IT had been a war of unprecedented mayhem and destruction. Poison gas. Liquid fire. Winged engines stocked with machine guns and bombs, instant death plunging out of the sky. Belgium to Italy, a landscape pocked with craters and trenches, each swabbed by human blood. More than eight million men had been killed, another twenty million slashed, exploded, ruined. The heralded unbreakable Hindenburg Line finally shattered in late 1918. Armistice, November 11. The Treaty of Versailles. Paris. Woodrow Wilson, Orlando, Clemenceau, Lloyd George. Names, promises, hopes, and the order of the day was a simple one: back to life in the normal.

Women's skirts hiked six inches off the ground. A male ogler said, "The female gender is going to get the vote, so it might as well show something for it."

July 1 had arrived with its gift to Carrie Nation: prohibition.

Mister Ty Cobb led the American League. A new boy named Ruth was showing some promise. Twenty homers wasn't anything to pooh-pooh.

Hudson sedans were nearly $2,000 each; a Buick Six coupe was tagged at $1,425. Ford's Model T sold cheaper.

The stock market climbed fifteen, twenty points a month.

Battle Creek built itself a new jail and a statue of C.W. Post was erected in Post Park. The fire department shed its last horse and carriage, like the Post Office which had also gone mechanized, putting spavined old "Dollie" out to pasture. Movie theaters nearly outnumbered grocery stores. The road to Goguac Lake was paved by state money and the city commission gave it the snappy, imaginative name of "Lake Road." Streetcar fares were five cents, up from three the year before. By contrast, the nation's cost of living had climbed 88 percent in less than five years.

Battle Creek's employment outlook was excellent. There were more than enough jobs for skilled workers; plenty of openings for the unskilled, too. Camp Custer, on the edge of town, was busy demobilizing the doughboys. Enlistees had come from Michigan, Illinois, Wisconsin, over 40,000 in those sixteen months America took to win the war. Quite a few settled in Battle Creek after mustering out of the army. Population up.

JOHN Harvey Kellogg's attire was so white it looked holy. The chalky accouterments emphasized the ruddiness of his cheeks and nose and the cavern brown of his eyes.

He went to the front door of his house when he heard the chimes because no one else was close by. On the wide porch, Len Kellogg stomped his snowcaked shoes and brushed flakes from his coat. He carried a small, brightly wrapped package and grinned winningly at his uncle. At age 36 he was three inches taller, thirty-five pounds leaner than the older man. They clasped hands, the doctor using the greeting to tug Len into the foyer.

"Ella and I were just talking about you the other evening. What in the world brings you here?"

"To wish you a merry Christmas, uncle." Len pushed the red and green package at doctor Kellogg who accepted it clumsily, trying to help his nephew off with his wraps.

"What's this? A gift?"

"It's only a fountain pen set."

"How thoughtful, Len. But absolutely uncalled for. Still, I'm touched by it and Ella will be. She's upstairs doing some sewing, come up and chat a while."

When they entered the library, Len was shaken by how drawn and lifeless Ella appeared. She sat in a dark upholstered chair that intensified her colorless hair and pale skin. On her lap was a little heap of cut cloth; her sewing basket waited uselessly atop a low table at her side. Her eyes crinkled recognition as Len moved toward her, but it was obvious she had not been stitching anything and did not intend to.

He kissed her cheek. It was like kissing parchment. She asked about Hannah and the children — Will Keith and John Junior — and Len informed her they were well. He shouted his words because her hearing had all but failed.

She inquired about Beth's children — Eleanor Jane and the three boys — mainly to find out how Kenneth Stanley was doing. Len replied that Ken was coming along, though the boy had not improved, despite

W.K.'s having spent hundreds of thousands trying to undo the damage of the fall from the second story window. The eight year old remained a cripple: blind in one eye, barely twenty percent vision in the other, a metal plate fixed forever in his head where part of the concussion-damaged brain was removed in desperation surgery. Doctors had finally, forlornly, surrendered, saying they had done all they could for him.

John Harvey was grateful when Len didn't explain, but he clucked his tongue dejectedly. "Beth's brood all were a sickly lot. No doubt, your father blames it on Norman, never forgave him for marrying Beth, did he?" And he lateraled the conversation over to the moment at hand. "See what Len brought us, dear? A present to go under the tree."

"We have something for you, too, Len. John, do you remember where we put it?"

John Harvey looked despairingly at Len, indicated he knew of no present they had for him. He said loudly, "How is your stepmother, Len? Is she pleased with being the wife of the famous and very wealthy cereal mogul?" A nugget of tactile bitterness embedded in the question, as he led Len to the couch and they sat down.

"Carrie Staines Kellogg is a nice, quiet lady, never intrudes in family matters, uncle John."

"She was my best diagnostician in female diseases. It's a shameful example of a woman with education, professional skills, a promising career ahead of her, throwing it in the trashcan for a marriage of convenience. Will only did it, you know, to get back at me. He wanted to pique me by stealing away one of my doctors in the night, not a hint of warning, not a word of her intentions. Just up and gone."

Len said, "None of the family knew about it until the marriage was done. I guess father wanted no advice or second guessing. I was surprised, maybe more than you, when I heard doctor Staines had eloped with him, because father said after mother died that he would never remarry."

"Surprised? That's hardly the word for it," John Harvey puffed. "I was shocked that Carrie Staines even knew your father, let alone knew him well enough to skulk away and marry him like..."

"Like a couple of school children? Like Hannah and I did?" Len finished the sentence for his uncle, smiling. "I remember how father raked me over the coals for that very same act. But at least, he has companionship. He's been lonely."

John Harvey glanced at his wife who concentrated on her scraps of cloth. "It's a stabilizing gift having someone to share things with, to talk with, just to take walks with. I can't fault Will for wanting those simple pleasures." He changed the topic again, as a maid entered with a pitcher of hot fruit punch and served it in cups adorned with a large blue K. "How are you surviving at the plant? Remember, you can always come back to work for me."

"I may take you up on that," Len said. Then, plaintively, "So help me, I've worked my butt off."

"I ought to be angry at you, nephew. If I'm correct, it was you who set off this infernal five year court fight over bran."

"If I'd been on your payroll, uncle John, I'd have done the same thing in your behalf. We couldn't sell our bran. Yours was beating our ears off, ten to one. Father agreed to let us produce a cheaper priced package, but that didn't boost sales, either."

"So you came up with that blasted All-Bran, didn't you? Swept me right off the market with those ads poofed up to read like patent medicine copy. People thought they were buying a prescription, not a food." No malice. If anything, grudging admiration for a winning scheme.

Len sipped his fruit drink and passed back the compliment: "Learned it all from you, uncle John."

"No, you more likely studied Charles Post. He even claimed his GrapeNuts would cure rigor mortis."

Len was glad he hadn't offended the doctor. "I don't mean to blow my own horn but I've done a lot for father's business," he said pensively. "But I like inventing and solving puzzles. That's how I developed Puffed Rice and Wheat Krumbles. And I saved us a small fortune by converting the printing of our cartons from roll presses to rotary. I spread out our advertising, moved a big share of it from magazines to newspapers, about 1,200 ads. I wrote most of the ads myself, and they've paid off damned nicely in sales, if I do say so."

He looked sheepishly at his uncle. "Lord almighty, I sound like a conceited ass. Sorry I got carried away with my own self-importance."

"Don't be modest. I fervently wish I had dreamed up the Waxtite idea." John Harvey set aside his cup and stood up, paced around his chair. "It was worth its weight in gold, that little trick of yours, sealing the cereal in wax sheets instead of paper bags."

Len explained, "The plant draftsman told me over and over it couldn't be done. He said no machine in the world was set up for it. I finally showed him you could actually seal the waxed paper with a hot iron, using two fingers and a thumb. Anything that simple, I told him, could be done by a machine. Today we're running *eighteen* folding and sealing machines."

"You designed those, too, am I right?"

"Yes."

"I expect the number of patents you hold now, my boy, may exceed my own."

"Counting machinery and processing," Len answered shyly, making quick mental calculations, "and a few on packaging, I guess about 150, more or less, but in the company's name, not my own. They're all owned by the company."

"Well, if you want my opinion, I think Will ought to step aside, let you run the company."

"Not likely. If I tear down a wall to enlarge a work area, uncle John, it isn't the wall he wanted down. If I change the order of crating and shipping he changes it back. At the company picnic last summer, Gene McKay and I rode out on burros, and we wore some old Mexican costumes we'd bought, thought we'd liven things up. Father got boiling angry, said our behavior was undignified. Now he's threatened to stop the picnics and office parties because of the friction he claims they create. Truth is, those picnics are pretty dull affairs for most of us, anyway. I'm not sure there would be much grief over their loss."

The two men lapsed into silence. Len finished his drink, doctor Kellogg fingered the skin beneath his chin and circled the couch like a skater in a rink.

"In my estimation, your father has never forgiven himself, or the whole world, for allowing me to become a physician while he became a grain merchant. Since he felt denied, he realigned his sights, set them on you and Karl, convinced himself you both would redeem him by joining the lofty ranks of doctors. Karl performed according to dictates, earned himself a medical degree, but then moved away so fast old Will couldn't gloat over it. You, my bright inventive nephew, you turned out to be a man of your own mind and talents and an inconceivable disappointment by proving yourself an industrial genius. That's why your father is such a prickly cactus, takes me to court every time I cough."

Lawsuit. Filed in 1914. John Harvey remembered waiting out the court's decision. A decision in the judge's chambers. Judge Walter North had listened with a certain amount of uninterest to counsel for both sides, keeping the proceedings isolated by holding them in his office. He said the rancor of two brothers, their willingness to parade such apparent loathing for each other, did not merit public display. Nearly eighteen months of anticipation curdled like sour milk into a single declaration by North who ruled entirely in W.K.'s favor. The doctor had appealed immediately.

"The state supreme court will make its judgement sometime next year," John Harvey announced to Len, coming out of his reverie. Then, "Your father attempts to atone for his bitterness and hard-headedness with great spurts of generosity from time to time, but a donkey is a donkey even if he does occasionally prance like a show horse."

"If he only would hear my side on an issue once in a while instead of making up his mind before I get a chance to say a word."

"You can't reason with someone like that, so don't try. Go home, Len, hug Hannah and the boys, take a warm enema, get a good night's sleep, and quit worrying about it."

Ella called to them when Len stood up: "You aren't leaving are you, Len? We haven't visited." He promised to come back soon and that satisfied her.

JOHN Harvey watched from the upstairs window as Len waded through the six-inch snowfall to his Model T coupe and began to crank its engine.

"A group of carolers is coming up the block, dear," he shouted back to Ella. "Would you like to come over to the window? I'll raise it and we can listen to them singing."

Ella moved the pile of sewing material from her lap to the side table, positioning it painstakingly, as though the colored scraps had to maintain a specific order. He guided her carefully to the draped window, keeping a supporting arm around her waist. They watched Len drive away.

Holding firmly to John Harvey's arm she asked, "Have you finished your article for the Surgery Journal, the one you were doing on antisepsis?"

"I'm very encouraged," he thundered, "about a natural way of combating sepsis with protective bacteria. I think you'll like what I have to say on the subject."

"I've never read anything you wrote that wasn't excellent." Her strength suddenly escaped and she began to slump. "I believe I'm too tired to wait for the carolers, John. I'd like to sit down again."

While she rested, he poured her a fresh cup of hot juice. "You're my darling," he told her loudly. "If I ever lost you, Ella, the world would end for me, you know that, don't you?"

She patted his hand, this woman who had been his helpmate, companion, inspiration for more than forty years, and he wished they had made love a million times and had produced a dozen children of their own blood. It was too late now. She was dying; he had seen the familiar, unyielding signs. That was the penalty for being a doctor. Doctor Dunston had told him exactly that, long ago.

62

IN the perfect stillness of a winter evening, W.K. lingered on the open front porch of his two-year old house. The residence was finished just after the wedding, barely in time to be occupied by himself and doctor Carrie Staines — missus doctor Kellogg as he called her, without a trace of amusement in his voice. It was a well planned building with an entrance directly into the large living room that spanned the width of the structure. Plenty of east and west windows and a fine, big fireplace. Dining room, sun room, kitchen, pantry. Four bedrooms upstairs. More than enough space for a married couple and a cook-housekeeper.

His eyes flitted from barren tree to snow-covered roadway to the black, low-lying sky. There was no wind so his suitcoat provided enough warmth. He was restless and enervated with a pointless energy. Inside his home there were festive activities: tree decorating, cooking, last-minute touches of pine wreaths above doors and red ribbons on window sills. Beth and her four were there: Norm Junior, John Harold, and Eleanor Jane who had a chronic chest cold and fever. And Kenneth. In his wheelchair. W.K. wondered sometimes if he would ever be able to recognize the boy without it. Len and Hannah were there, too, with their boys, Will Keith and John Junior. Karl and Etta had called earlier to say they couldn't manage the trip from out West with their three. Clara would stay until after the meal and the opening of presents, then she would go to her other brother's home where doctor Kellogg hosted his staff each year. He would host without Ella whose health was very bad, W.K. thought, as I must do in this house without Puss. Thank God Beth's wastrel husband, Williamson, won't get into town until later, possibly even tomorrow morning. And thank God Clara's no-account husband chose not to tag along after her. Those were two reasons for a little cheerier state of mind, he told himself.

The war was over, Congress had finally passed prohibition, the company was thriving. I'm a rich man, W.K. recalled. Yesterday he'd boosted Len's salary to thirty-five thousand and nice increases to Shaw and McKay and the others. There was nothing wrong that he could get hold of. It was just that nothing was quite right, either.

He touched his paunchy stomach delicately, feeling the scars through his clothing. Cholecystostomy, two of them. Then under the knife to patch a hernia, and once more to remove stones in his bile duct. Now he had insomnia. Every night, every rotten night. He asked the darkness, "What can they cut out of me to cure that?"

The door behind him opened. There was a burst of light and warmth. Beth reached out to him.

"Father, come inside, it's too cold on the porch. Besides, it's time to hand out gifts, everyone is waiting for you. Doctor Carrie was concerned, she didn't know where you'd gone."

"Not very far," he said as Beth closed the door, leaving him alone.

Missus doctor Kellogg. Yes, there was certainly missus doctor Kellogg. Ironic, he thought bitterly, so many doctors in the Kellogg family. At least, he conceded, she is someone to play cards with on winter nights. He cleared his throat and spat forcefully out into the snow, barely clearing the porch banister. A trickle of spittle clung to his lip. He wiped it away with a stubby finger. He'd never been able to whistle through his teeth or spit across a river. Little shortcomings, how they gnawed.

In the carpeted, splendidly furnished basement room was a smaller version of the nine-foot Christmas tree that ruled in the living room. Around it and spilling out over the floor were the presents, a landslide of ribboned and decorated packages. A mild aroma of burning logs wafted from the fireplace of imported tile.

W.K. assumed his traditional position in the leather armchair at the edge of the tumbled packages. He lifted each gift ceremoniously in its turn and read the name on label or tag before passing it along. Even Kenneth Stanley, his body warped to his wheelchair, laughed and clawed eagerly for parcels which Beth carried to him and stayed to help him tear away the wrapping. In one large box he found an Atwater Kent radio with its detachable speaker and a set of Burgess A and B power batteries and he began to cry in satisfaction, tears edging out of eyes that too often rolled uncontrolled or unfocused.

The toys seemed to appear endlessly. Baseball gloves, roller skates, cameras, scooters, dolls, books, rubber stamping kits. The room soon took on the appearance of a madcap toy shop. For the adults there were engraved gold rings with diamonds and garnets, all from a collection of jewelry once owned by Russian nobility.

Packages unwrapped. Punch poured. Handsful of sweets, nuts, popcorn, and sliced fruits crammed into hungry mouths. The children lined up to pass by grandfather Kellogg, hug him or kiss him or shake his hand, thank him for the gifts.

Carrie Staines — missus doctor Kellogg — waited next to W.K.'s chair during the ritual. Exactly as tall as her husband when he stood, she was 58, stockily built, with a pleasant, thoughtful expression that rarely changed. She placed her hand tactfully on Kellogg's shoulder but when he did not acknowledge it, she finally let it fall back at her side.

One by one the grandchildren stepped up before W.K. and thanked him. He anchored each child at arm's length, holding the youngster's shoulders lightly, and asked "What did you do today?" After they told him, he asked: "Do you like my new bran cereal?" knowing they would snicker and wrinkle their noses. It gave him a moment of amusement. Finally, he always inquired, "What is it you want to be when you grow up?"

Answers were sensible. A scientist, good mother, judge, even an artist. W.K. listened carefully, signifying that the ambition was all right — the important thing just being to *have* an ambition.

"And you, John Junior," Kellogg had come to Len's youngest. "What is it you would like to be? A professor? An engineer?"

The darkhaired, nine-year old boy wore knickers with buttondown pockets and a tailored coat. "I want to be like you, grandfather," he said with the perspicacity of Solomon.

"Whatever for?" W.K. fussed at adjusting his thick spectacles, peered at the boy, searching for a hint of duplicity.

"Because it's all I have ever wanted. I love you, grandfather."

"Our lad is nobody's fool, is he, Len?" Hannah's loud whisper was as audible as a whipcrack to everyone except W.K. whose hearing, like his eyesight, grew more defective each month. "Your fodter, he loves to pretend at Santy Claus. He dotes on all his grandchildren, don't he?"

Len covered his mouth with cupped fingers. "They're the only ones he can order around who don't resent it."

Hannah laughed brassily and squeezed against him. She guided his hand from her waist to the thick swell of her hip, and he thought with sudden uneasiness that she had too much flesh still stationed there.

63

JUNE 1920

"WHEN it is summer and a circus comes to town there is nothing you can do except stop your work and go to the main tent and plop down your fifteen cents and buy a ticket," Albert Miller contended. "Come on, Louise," he said, bursting unexpectedly into the kitchen of their Garrison Avenue home at one o'clock in the afternoon. "Round up Bob and get your parasol and let's catch the next streetcar."

Louise didn't pause from drying and stacking dishes on the cabinet shelves above the sink. She wore a blue percale ankle length dress and her brown hair was bunched into a soft knot at the neck.

"What about your morning paper?" she asked.

"I'll shape it up tonight, Louise, the way I always do. The parade is coming through town in an hour. They're already unloading the boxcars out by the switching station. Where is Bob?" He opened the icebox, removed a bottle of milk, poured a half-glass, drank it in an uninterrupted swallow, wiped his mouth with the side of his hand.

"Besides, the biggest news of the moment is the city council's vote to put a motorcycle policeman on duty to catch automobile speeders. They're doing some fast driving on Upton Street and out Lake Avenue, thirty miles an hour. That's worth about one small paragraph."

"It sounds like a take-on job, being a motorcycle policeman." Bob Miller said, coming in at the tailend of the conversation, adding his two cents with uncommon certainty. Thin and wiry like his father, he had his mother's features, especially the small mouth and quick eyes.

"Maybe I could get that cop job in a few years. I hope they put him in plain clothes, the policeman I mean, or he'll stick out like skeezicks in church. He'll never catch you, anyway, father."

Louise said, "Of course not, your father won't even buy an automobile to drive to work."

"I don't know how to drive."

"You can't learn by walking everywhere."

"Yeah, father, a car would be terrific..."

"A benzine buggy for us would be a very unnecessary expense, Louise."

"Oh, and you wanting to buy the whole newspaper from Marjorie Post Close, go into that much debt, I can't believe it, Albert Miller."

"The Enquirer will be a good investment," he said. "Hawk agrees."

"H.C. Hawk has his job at Postum to see him through if the newspaper doesn't make any money."

"The Enquirer is already successful, Louise." He patted her on the shoulder, gave a wink to Robert. "And Hawk is the most astute businessman I've met in years. He can smell out a winner in a half sniff and be ten steps ahead of the pack all the way. He believes we'll beat the

Moon-Journal before they know we're on the move. And don't forget, I've put in nearly ten years publishing here, and I know our chances better than anyone does. It's a sound, money making investment."

"*If* Marjorie Post Close will sell it."

"She has no real interest in managing a newspaper. Hawk and I have been buying up shares of stock when they can be had. We've gathered in about fifteen percent so far and we're still buying. Being part owner puts us in a good position to buy her out."

Louise turned to her son: "I think you have enough to occupy you with your part-time work at the newspaper, Robert, without dreaming of being a motorcycle policeman." His mother called him Robert when she intended to make her point and wanted to hear no argument about it. "Your father says you don't exactly show a burdening ambition to be a go-getter."

He lifted both shoulders, turned his palms up in futility. "Sorting type and plugging in wires at the switchboard isn't very exciting, mom, you have to admit."

"He's coming along, he's learning." Albert allowed. "Now let's get cracking or the whole show will be over."

"What show, dad?"

"The circus. We're going."

"Hotdog! Can Sid come?"

DOWN McCamly street came the circus parade, led by six elephants in single-file and decked out with banners, each with a maharajah riding in bright costume under a yellow umbrella that resembled a toadstool. The train of delights traveled under the elevated crosswalk at the Post Tavern and swung onto Main street, past the Security Bank, Preston's shoe store, the Montgomery Ward store.

There were trained mules and albino camels and dancing dogs who leaped among the scores of painted clowns as if they had springs on their paws. There was a silver calliope on a truckbed pulled by eight black horses, its steam-powered whistles sounding out the tune of a familiar march, the sun ricocheting off its sides, blindingly. There were barred wagons with lions, tigers, black panthers, all roaring ferociously, sending small children into fits of laughter or crying.

The Millers stood at the corner of Main and Maple, by the savings and loan building. Bob and his friend, Sid, edged into the street for a better look. Bob, though, was watching the man and boy directly across the street He nudged Sid. "Who is the boy over there with mister Kellogg?"

A quick answer: "His grandkid." Sid's eyes darted back to the circus float rumbling by. "Name's John, I think."

W.K. Kellogg, short and thick, was wearing a dark suit and hat and round spectacles. He held a long, narrow cane in his right hand. The boy next to him was pudgy, with a serious face, almost stern.

"They look alike," Bob said, "except one's older."

"Yeah," Sid smirked, "a pair of salt and pepper shakers."

IT DID not seem fair to him that the June sun was so bright while the room was shadowy.

He sat by his wife's bedside in the mansion they had built together 31 years ago, ten years into their marriage. His alabaster suit was a dusky gray in the half light. Children were riding bicycles and rolling hoops in the street, shouting and squealing with a zest left over from the circus parade.

He continued to squeeze her hand tightly between his own as he had done since sunrise. She had died an hour ago but he refused to let her go or leave her. She cried out a great deal at the end, the pain intense, the medicines powerless to relieve. Now all of the pain had shifted to him.

His head drooped close to his knees. A nurse entered the room, approached, stood dutifully by him. "Why don't you come out with me now, doctor? We have a sedative prepared for you. You can rest. It's time to let her go...please."

To her surprise, he rose slowly, painfully, as though his body was crippled by arthritis. He bent across Ella's bed, pressed his lips to her forehead, whispered: "I have to leave, dear. You understand, don't you?"

When he straightened he was shocked to see a tear on her blanched cheek. "My God, she's crying," he exclaimed, hope rising in him, only to sink heavily, brutally. He numbingly realized the tear had come from his own eyes. Shoulders slumped, he shambled to the door, the waiting nurse, his worldly duties.

"It seems as if life is a constant series of letting go," he told the nurse, his voice sighing like a crypt just opened. "Someone always is leaving. How will I ever carry on now?"

"The way she would want you to," the nurse said.

He looked at her as if she had just uttered the most wonderful thing imaginable. He stiffened his spine, skimmed a shaking palm across the remaining strings of his white hair. "Of course, nurse. You are exactly correct. Unquestionably."

64

THERE was a popular saying: when matters run amuck, keep your pecker up and sit tight. That is, keep up the courage, wait for the next move. Things may get better.

And, again, as John Harvey learned, they may not.

Robed, dignified, a body of men empowered by the state with the awesome might to interpret and penalize, the eight justices in their black garb surveyed the courtroom from their paneled aerie. Fewer than twenty spectators occupied the stands. At two long tables down front were the attorneys for W.K. Kellogg and John Harvey Kellogg, though neither brother was present.

Judge Stone, the centralmost figure on the bench, bent forward and began to read sonorously:

"The justices of the Supreme Court of the State of Michigan are unanimous in their decision in the case of Kellogg vs. Kellogg. The writing of said opinion fell to me and, as author, I will read said judgement into the official record."

A court stenographer's fingers flew so rapidly and lightly over the keys of the silent, miniature typewriter, that the movement of his fingers could hardly be seen.

"We have devoted weeks to the examination of the immense record in this case, all 1,996 pages of it. We have scrutinized and analyzed the numerous exhibits and the lengthy briefs. It would be idle to attempt to set out in this opinion, within any reasonable limit, even an abstract of the pleadings or the mountains of evidence. The mass of data was unduly lengthy.

"We are of the opinion that the statements contained in these affidavits before the court disclose a situation which was anticipated by all parties concerned and by the court at the time of the initial hearing. Annoyance and contention cannot be avoided so long as these parties are each marketing products of such similar character and on such an extensive scale. No one doubts that each party experiences inconvenience and financial loss."

Justice Stone turned a page of his document, marked his place with a pencil. The Kellogg attorneys on both sides sat transfixed in their chairs. Stone read again:

"Judge North who originally heard this case in the lower court presented his findings so clearly and thoroughly that this court can do no better than to quote him. He wrote:

"'The details and events are confusing and contradictory. Missus Collier, a demonstrator for the plaintiff testifies that she saw mister W.K. Kellogg's bran product willfully substituted for doctor Kellogg's product at a demonstration held in the Schnitzler Store in Chicago. Mister Schnitzler testifies that he believed all along that the demonstration was sponsored by mister W.K. Kellogg. Miss Greelee, another demonstrator claims that her orders for doctor Kellogg's bran from the National Tea Company stores were substituted with mister Kellogg's product.

"'In further affidavits the claims are set forward that doctor Kellogg's salesmen misrepresented themselves to grocers and distributors as being from the Kellogg Corn Flakes Company in order to market their product.

"'For this court to issue a temporary injunction even as to marketing the one product, Kellogg's Bran, is to decide in advance which of these parties is invading the rights of the other. This is the very question which must be adjudicated upon the final hearing. The record is in such a state that no one can tell which of these parties is right and which is wrong.

"'I must add, however,' judge North went on to comment for the record, and I am still quoting, 'that the court is troubled by a most noteworthy consideration. If doctor Kellogg expected to claim commercial rights from the prestige of the Kellogg name which had arisen from the doctor's reputation as head of the Battle Creek Sanitarium, it seems passing strange that, prior to 1908, he never attached his name to any of the various food products in such a way as to identify him and his product with doctor John Harvey Kellogg of the Battle Creek Sanitarium. This fact is inconsistent with the present claim that the word *Kellogg* as used incidental to these manufactured products necessarily means doctor *John H. Kellogg*. Letters by doctor Kellogg, as well as other items of evidence in this case, show quite conclusively that the name Kellogg was commercialized not by doctor Kellogg but in spite of him.'"

Justice Stone paused, leafed another page. He glanced at his fellow jurors appraisingly, then concluded his remarks.

"The 1911 agreement, as argued by doctor Kellogg's counsel, stipulated that he would not use the name 'Kellogg's' on cereal foods and it is acknowledged that he was duly compensated for this accession. However, as judge North ably pointed out, while the doctor retained the right to use his name as part of the corporate name on cereal foods, the unrestricted use of the name was conceded to the Kellogg Toasted Corn Flake Company. The Supreme Court of the State of Michigan hereby upholds the decision of the lower court ruling in favor of the defendants,

W.K. Kellogg and the Kellogg Toasted Corn Flake Company."

JOHN Harvey said morosely, "This seems to be my season for losing. What are the damages?"

His attorney rationed some time by shifting a leather case from right to left hand. "I wish it could be better news, doctor. There's little I can say that will blunt the facts. It could have been worse. Your brother waived any settlement, I'm pleased to say. You must, however, pay all costs of the litigation, both your own and his."

The two men were meeting in the San's annex, built to handle the more recent overflow of patients from the main building across the street. The structure resembled a huge country house.

Wistfully, Kellogg said, "You know, counselor, I find it very difficult to go to the dining hall and look up at that tremendous rectangular dome, all the murals along the walls, everything flooded with sunlight, I can hardly bring myself to go there because Ella helped to plan it and she should be there with me, but she isn't." His voice trailed to nothingness.

The attorney gripped John Harvey's sleeve just below the black band of mourning silk. "Doctor Kellogg, are you sure you are all right?"

"How much must I pay?" A hard-soft coil of tension was gnarled in his voice.

"It comes to a total of $225,000." The attorney lowered his hand from Kellogg's arm as he told him the figure, expecting a shocked reaction. When John Harvey gave no response, neither a blink nor a shudder, the lawyer wondered if he had misunderstood the meaning of the doctor's question.

65

AUGUST 1924

THE Kellogg Company's executive dining room was furnished in the style of an expensive restaurant. Tables for four, white linen, centerpieces of fresh flowers, chandeliers and large windows for bright lighting, well-cushioned chairs for the weary buttocks of busy managers whose work involved a lot of sitting. The menu changed daily and wasn't especially lengthy but the choices were excellent and the food was prepared to perfection by a talented chef and staff.

Helen Flanner greeted Len Kellogg at the entrance. She wore a white uniform and a blue perky hat that resembled a soldier's cap except for its color. It was the prescribed garb for hostess of the dining room and it set off her coal black hair as if she had designed it herself.

"Your table is ready for you, mister Kellogg." A hint of playfulness in her heavy lips. Dark eyes under dark brows pierced and held him.

"Thank you, Helen." He adjusted his glasses, self-consciously. "Lead on. We'll follow. Right, Gene?"

McKay, a stocky man with a pleasant face that could twist itself into seething anger if something went wrong in his plant, nodded at his companion, winked, fell into step behind the swaying hips of the hostess. Gene McKay had been the production supervisor of the Kellogg factory for more than five years. His friendship with the owner's son had nothing to do with opportunism. If he hadn't liked Len, he would have stayed away from him regardless of the consequences. But the two men had a fairly similar outlook on running the plant and they shared a sameness in their sense of humor and their inclination to occasionally bust loose from work and "take a romp."

When they were seated, the hostess remained at the table, near Len. "I'll be pleased to take your order, mister Kellogg." She lifted a pencil and a pad of paper into view. "I could send over a waitress but you'll be served faster if I turn it in personally."

Her eyes bolted themselves to his. He couldn't break the stare, didn't want to. It warmed him down through his chest and into his groin. Her nose, he thought, is so narrow and the nostrils are lifted up and flared. Sensuous. That's what it is. Never knew a nose could be sexy, it makes me want to...

"I'll have those salmon croquettes," McKay announced, "if they aren't all cracker crumbs. And green beans, spinach, some of that fig bread and black coffee."

Helen continued to stare at Len while she wrote McKay's order. "What do you recommend, miss Flanner?" Kellogg asked.

"How hungry are you, mister Kellogg?" She unrelentingly held his gaze, her full lips lifting into a complete smile.

"Very."

"Then let me surprise you."

"How do you mean, miss Flanner?"

"Let me choose your meal and bring it to you."

"What if I don't like what you bring?"

"You can have it taken away."

"Wouldn't it be safer if I picked out what I want?"

"Maybe. But I think you will like what you get."

"Is this a new service?" McKay asked, only half serious.

Helen Flanner said, "We're trying it out today, mister McKay, on a selective basis, a sort of end-of-summer special."

When she was gone, McKay whistled softly and thumped Len's arm. "She thinks you are a basis for selection." He whistled again. "I'd watch myself if I were you. You'll find yourself stuffed and mounted and hanging over her mantle. Or Hannah's, if she hears about it."

A SQUARE clock with an illuminated face indicated it was eight in the evening. A colorful calendar printed by the Gage Printing Company hung behind the bar next to the clock. The days of September were crossed off with black ink, except for the final four.

Len Kellogg and Helen Flanner occupied a booth away from the solid oak door where a broadshouldered giant kept vigil on a four-legged stool and peeped out of a tiny hole whenever someone knocked.

In front of Len was a bootleg scotch and soda; in front of Helen, a bootleg gin and bitters. Neither drink had been touched. Their wet raincoats were draped on hooks at the side of the booth.

"There is something I'd like to ask you, Helen. A bit touchy, maybe even a little embarrassing, but I'd appreciate having a woman's view on it. I don't know who else to ask. That's why I invited you to have a drink at the club."

"I'll help if I can, mister Kellogg."

"Well, first, the situation. Then the question."

"All right."

"A married man, a friend of mine who has a family, wants to speak candidly with a married woman he only met weeks ago. He has an uncomfortable — for him, that is — desire to tell her things he certainly has no right to say."

She skimmed a fingertip around the rim of her highball glass. "I must admit, this isn't what I expected when you asked me to meet you."

"You were warned it might seem a rude subject."

"Mister Kellogg, if anyone should see us..."

"Please don't call me mister Kellogg, Helen. It's Len." He sipped his drink, pushed the glass aside. "And we're doing nothing to be seen at or criticized for. We're talking."

"In an illegal saloon." She laughed and he wanted to reach across and touch her. It was the sort of urge people have when they see a polished stone or a painted canvas: just looking isn't enough.

"Helen, we're discussing my friend. I have to tell you he wants to say to the woman that even her voice does things to him, suggestive things I won't phrase for you, of course. Its sound tempts him in strange ways. You might say it seduces him."

Helen hoisted her eyebrows quizzically.

"He wants to ask her if she realizes how much he wishes to put his hands on her, on her hair, her lips, say unthinkable thoughts out loud that are stuck inside him." Len dropped his gaze to the table, coughed nervously. "At least, that's what my friend told me."

"This isn't a discussion we probably ought to be having, Len. Your friend, whoever he is, should take a strong purgative and attend church more often. What you've described isn't a healthy way for a married man to feel, although I admit I'm no judge of how a married man is required to behave. You did say he is married?"

"His marriage is almost undone. Sort of fallen apart. As it stands, he would tell you his wife thinks more of her father-in-law than her husband. Most of his feelings for her are gone. He used to have them, but the years have messed them up."

Then, abruptly: "How old are you, Helen?"

"You're very bold, Len. That is a strange question. I don't see what it has to do with..."

"I just suddenly wondered how old you are."

"Not so old as you, but nearly." She grinned winningly. "I'm 38 if you must know." She pointed a shapely, ice cream finger at him. "I think you'd be smarter to talk to a priest about your friend's situation. I don't pretend to be an expert on these things. You say the object of this poor fellow's attention is also married?"

"No. I lied about that."

"She isn't married?"

"I believe she is a widow. You are, aren't you, Helen?"

"Yes," she answered simply.

A quartet of revelers was allowed in by the giant doorman. A rap of thunder from the storm followed them in. They had unquestionably visited another club or two or three before arriving here. All were cackling at once, shrugging out of raincoats, yelling hellos to the bartender between bolts of laughter.

Len watched them settle in, then he faced Helen. "You'd be foolish to take me up on anything I offer. You know that, don't you?"

Their ankles touched, pushed gently against each other, leg pressing leg. The heat beneath the table was becoming extreme.

"Your father will string you up, you know don't you?"

"Let's get out of here," Len suggested sternly.

Without a word of objection or the faintest show of reluctance, Helen stood and gathered her coat, as Len did, and they went out, holding close to each other, not speaking, but hurrying into the rain as though any delay would be intolerable.

66

DECEMBER 1924

THE detective who entered Albert Miller's office was medium height, with undistinguished features, though very thin and bony as if having just recuperated from an illness. He had manicured nails and a tweed topcoat. He took the leather chair directly in front of Miller's desk, lifted a plain notebook from a patch pocket of his coat, slid a pencil from the inside pages, and checked the time by Miller's desk clock.

Miller patiently watched the man prepare for notetaking, thinking how primly this stalker of men went about his business. "You won't mind if my son, Bob, remains during our talk, mister Fortney?"

"No objection, mister Miller. It's your office."

Bob Miller had moved to the edge of another leather chair at the left of his father's desk. He laid aside the copy sheets they had been red-pencilling when Fortney arrived. The young man had on a suit and tie, as well as a grave expression, practiced for its solemnity because it added the impression of a few years to his eighteen. He looked as though he was displeased with the interruption by this pseudo-policeman. In truth, he was thrilled over the unexpected visit from an out-of-town detective.

"Mister Miller," Fortney's voice was as narrow as his size twelve neck, "I hope you can spread some light over my limited search and research. I've been hired to look into the doings, if you will, of one John Leonard Kellogg, generally known among his acquaintances as Len Kellogg. It has been my practice at the outset of my investigations to talk with the publisher or editor of the city's foremost newspaper. It almost always proves to be a good starting point, meeting with one who has his finger on the pulse of the community's affairs, if you will."

"I don't know Len Kellogg all that well, mister Fortney. I understand he pretty well runs the Kellogg Company, he's president of our Chamber of Commerce, he's active in most of the city's interests, but we aren't chums or business colleagues." Miller angled forward in his chair, elbows on his desk, chin parked insouciantly on his fists. "I'd go so far as to say, he doesn't subscribe to this newspaper. I believe he reads the Moon-Journal."

"All the better," Fortney said. "I'll try to be equally frank with you, sir. In my investigations, I've learned that persons in the know can offer more useful information if they have some inkling of the broad nature of my inquiry. I ask only that what I divulge must stay within this room."

"I understand an off-the-record talk, mister Fortney. And, I'm confident Len Kellogg has done nothing he needs my protection for." On the floor below and to the rear, the presses kicked into motion, rolling out the evening edition.

"Very well." Fortney wrote unhurriedly in his notebook, closed it on a delicate finger, looked up at Miller. "I've been retained to determine if John Leonard Kellogg is engaged in what can only be described, if you will, as an extramarital affair."

Bob Miller thought the detective's use of "engage" and "extramarital" was a bad juxtaposition of words. He couldn't decide if the man was trying to be clever or snide.

"Who employed you?" Albert Miller was a picture of patience, as if he knew the answer before it came.

"I'm not at liberty to tell you. Confidentiality, if you will." A silken grin. "Requirement in my line of work."

Miller smiled bitterly, plowed a hand through his thick hair, messing up the sharply defined part in the middle. "You're an odd man, sir. You come here for information, you tell me you routinely go to local newsmen for the details on libelous or slanderous accusations you are tracking down, then you offer no information yourself. Confidentiality, you say The Enquirer and News doesn't need a tight-tailed private cop dragging dirty linen into our newsroom."

Unperturbed, Fortney smiled conspiratorially. "According to my investigation, John Leonard Kellogg is married 23 years to Hannah Kellogg, two children of the union. A chief executive with the multimillion dollar Kellogg cereal company. A man whose personal, professional and civic responsibility demands of him an untarnished character, unblemished behavior. During the past few months he has been unexplainably and repeatedly absent from work for as long as three days at a time, leaving no word where he can be found or when he will return. He also has failed to appear at his home at day's end on countless occasions, giving his wife the excuse, if you will, that he stayed at the plant throughout the night and did not remember to call her.

"Witnesses say Kellogg prefers the companionship of one Helen Flanner, a hostess in the company's executive dining room. Flanner claims to be a widow, has a son twelve years of age. She lives with her father. Her ex-husband is dead or gone away. No one seems to know." Fortney closed his notebook, gazed at the ceiling, taking thought cues from the wallpaper. "My own observations, discreetly conducted if you will, confirm these reports." He inhaled a long breath, blew it out, cheeks puffed. "Your turn now. What can you add to that, mister Miller?"

"Nothing."

"What do you mean, nothing? We're off the record. Are you saying you won't give me a particle of information in exchange for what I've told you?" Fortney got to his feet, his face slowly slipping, jowls sagging, eyes becoming desperate.

"I can't."

"You won't?"

"I mean, mister Fortney, I can't. I don't know a thing about this so-called affair. I've heard rumors, most assuredly, but I don't trade in rumors. At any rate, none of it is news and I sure won't editorialize about it. I'll leave that subject to the ministers in the pulpits of our churches across our fine city. And since you're such a reputable sleuth, see if you can find your way out to the sidewalk, sir."

When the detective had slunk from the office, Bob's eyes were alight and his brows were clinched over the seriousness of what he had just heard. "It sounds like mister Kellogg is in trouble, doesn't it, dad?"

"Do you know what it means?"

Apprehensively the boy said, "Nothing? Like you said?"

Miller clapped Bob on the shoulder. "Right. Absolutely, firmly, unequivocally, irrefutably nothing. Not to us, anyway."

67

MAY 1925

THE Kellogg plant dominated the entire east end of the city with its metropolis of brick and steel buildings. The structures were four and five stories high and they stretched a mile in every direction. It was a province of 3,000 workers, watched over by supernal smokestacks and gleaming water towers. And one man.

"Mister Kellogg, the international division is a huge success. Mexico, Brazil, all across central and south America we're selling corn flakes like tamales. You can tell from these columns here, we're in fine fettle. Canada and Australia are doing as well or better." Gene McKay pointed a pencil at entries in a ledger. W.K. hardly noticed them.

"And we're on schedule with our review of sales potentials in Denmark, Sweden, Germany, France, Spain, and so on." The production supervisor located a colored world map among the papers on the conference table, brought it to the top, speared his pencil into one of the large block "K" letters stenciled over various land masses. Beneath each K was a small number, like a footnote, going from one to thirteen in order of importance. "The figures were shown on the listing you looked at last month."

W.K. gave no reaction, which wasn't unusual, so McKay continued his briefing.

"Buying out the Quaker plant has proved to be a smart investment, sir. It gave us the capacity for our Bran Flakes and when Post company tried to undersell us we met the competition, beat their price, and surged ahead of them."

"We spent half a million patching up Len's follies," Kellogg interrupted. He moved heavily — for he had gained considerable weight — and lowered himself into his armchair. He hadn't looked at the reams of documentation McKay exhibited, not altogether because he wasn't interested, but because undetected glaucoma had thickened his eyeglasses while reducing his vision each year. Reading anything that was smaller than bold headlines had become a tiring if not impossible chore. He exuded gloominess. "Len cost us a fortune."

"It wasn't so much his fault, sir," McKay offered. "Some of our investments went sour. At least, that's what George tells me." Referring to his brother who was the company treasurer. "The paper shortage hurt us, too, with magazines cutting down on advertising space and raising their prices."

"Investments. Paper. They had nothing to do with buying that blasted oatmeal plant in Iowa. Hot cereal. Cook it in one minute. Bah! Len's folly."

"Ralston took it off our hands..."

"At our loss. We never should..."

The office door abruptly swung wide, cutting Kellogg off in mid-sentence. His son was framed in the opening, his hair wild, his rimmed glasses outlining hot eyes, his necktie twisted as though it had been put on by a man wearing mittens. His jacket hung open. He was breathing heavily as if from running.

"What the hell do you mean siccing a detective onto me?" He hurled the words like punches.

"Good morning, Len." W.K. spoke evenly and quietly. To McKay he remarked: "Gene, leave us. We'll talk later."

"What've you got a goddamned detective following me for?" Len insisted, still blocking the doorway.

"Pardon me, Len," McKay said, squeezing past him, face flushed, arms cradling the rolls of maps and charts he had brought in only ten minutes ago. "Take it easy, pal," he whispered.

"Lower your voice if you want to speak to me, Len," W.K. ordered sternly.

"I'm going to get a whole lot louder if I don't hear some answers damned quick, father. I want to know why that private investigator is dogging my steps like I'm a bandit. What the bloody hell are you up to?" He kicked the door shut behind McKay, using his shoe heel as a ram.

W.K. could barely see his son's features across the office, though the bulk of the figure was clear. He made a mental note to have his eyeglasses strengthened again. "It's plain and simple. Your affair with this Flanner woman must stop."

"Well, that's too bad, father. I'm going to marry her."

"You *are* married."

"Hannah and I intend to get a divorce."

W.K. switched his gaze to a painting on the wall at the far side of his desk. He had purchased the landscape from a street artist on his last trip to Europe because the vivid colors were soothing. "Hannah needs you and she is your children's mother. You will come to your senses. Stop your despicable affair with this Hell-en woman. She will bring you grief. If you persist, I will disown you. There will be no place in the company for you."

Len took a long step forward, arms hanging loosely at his sides. "Father, you're a royal pain in the ass. You tried to ruin Beth's and Norm's marriage, hired a detective then, too, to snoop around and get something on Norm while the poor bastard was out on the road working like a madman to prove himself worthy of marrying the great W.K. Kellogg's daughter. You had men trailing him from Indiana to California and they came up with nothing. You wasted your precious money. Well, you've lost again because I won't knuckle under to you, not even if you threaten me."

"It's no threat. It is an absolute condition." Now that Len had moved closer, W.K. tried to focus on his face but could only pick up shadowy contours of nose and lips and hooded eyes. "Tell me, does her father still send her out to the saloon for his nightly bucket of beer?"

"My God, you've been spying on her, too. You're so high and almighty, I'm surprised you don't sprout wings and fly out of the room on a shaft of blinding light."

"This may come as news to you, Len. You have an inflated notion of your value. The company can survive without you. Just as it is doing without Hell-en Flanner since I had her dismissed. Quite well, I might add." He returned his attention to the painting. "You have made some worthwhile contributions. You have also made some unforgivable blunders. Many of them very costly."

"You'll never quit bitching over the change I made from cast iron to stainless steel, will you? Because you didn't think of it. But it was smart, it boosted efficiency..."

"Our funds were low. It was bad timing."

"Oh, hell yes." Len waved his arms as if fighting a swarm of insects. "How about your big strikeout with Kaffee Hag? Talk about a blunder piled onto a classic case of bad judgement. You were so wrapped up in crowding uncle John's Caramel Coffee off the market, you grabbed up Gund's first offer for the Hag franchise, didn't even question it, just paid three times what he would have settled for. And the customers ran from Kaffee Hag like it was made of horse manure. When you found out you couldn't give the stuff away, let alone sell it, you let the smart boys at Post's buy you out for pennies on the dollar. C.W. Post must've rollicked in his tomb, watching you lose a small fortune on the decaffeinating process. You couldn't have made Kaffee Hag saleable or drinkable even if you'd mixed Postum in it."

If W.K. heard Len's recount of the botched gamble, he refused to show it. "You cheat on your wife, Len." Kellogg's words were flat, unemotional. "In doing it, you cheat your children."

Len's moan sailed, fell, a cry of disbelief. "You are really so self-centered you don't know how much you robbed your own family. Let me tell you, father, cranking out money sure as hell wasn't a good enough reason." His lips were clamped, his skin was chlorotic. He swallowed a fist-sized rock. "It's always your way or nobody's, your opinion or no one's, isn't that what it boils down to, father? You've fired Helen, but that's better than the god-awful treatment you gave Caplin, your inventory controller. Remember how you forbid everyone in the factory to speak to him after he ran afoul of you? You stopped all his mail, every scrap of correspondence from touching his desk. You even took away his parking space. You stole his dignity, his self respect, you left him nothing."

"He was an opinionated troublemaker. He should have resigned when I gave him the chance."

"No forgiveness. No understanding. Just unerring judgements by his royal and holy highness."

"Len, you hold 63,000 shares of company stock. The value on today's market is more than three million dollars. You are rich because of me and this company. Are you willing to throw it away for a lunch hall tramp?"

"Watch your words, father. I said Helen will be my wife."

"Your model assuredly was C.W. Post. A philanderer." W.K.'s face twisted into more lines than a geological map. "Hear me well on this. If you leave Hannah and marry your black widow, you leave the company forever. It is a one-way door."

"I intend to marry her."

W.K. extended his arms, fingertips holding at the desktop's edge. He glanced out of the office window. Between heavy velvet drapes the distant skyline of low buildings that formed the downtown part of Battle Creek was hazy blue. "Then, for the sake of the company we will minimize the true reason for your leaving. I will personally make the announcement. You will be promoted to president of the company just before you leave for Europe."

"Why am I leaving for Europe? Since when?"

"You presumably are going there to explore new markets for the company. You will stay for at least six months. Have your ill-begotten honeymoon if you want. The dust and the gossip will settle here. On your return you will not live in Battle Creek. You will not ask for reinstatement in the company. You and your Hell-en will find your futures elsewhere."

When he finished speaking, W.K. slumped in his chair, feeling tireder than he could remember. For the first time in a long while his stomach rumbled and stirred. His head throbbed and there was a dull ache in his chest.

Len's voice was soaked with loathing. "I agree to your conditions, as you say, for the good of the company. But let me tell you one thing more before I leave. You have spent your life sticking your dictator's nose in other people's business. You have stirred up trouble for everyone you've ever known, frightened them, tyrannized them."

Not looking up, W.K. heard Len's footsteps retreat to the door, heard it scuff open.

"You may be my father, but you are a dangerous plague. From now on, I want you to just leave me the goddamned hell alone. It will be like a breath of pure fresh air to be as far from you as I can possibly get."

68

MAY 1930

THE stock market crashed in 1929.

Investors saw their paper riches turn to trash. Unable to face the disgrace of being broke, not a few formerly affluent speculators who had climbed too high, jumped out of high office windows. Or blew out their brains with a pistol. Or slashed their wrists in their bathtubs after drinking a pint of gin they had stirred up in that same tub a week earlier. The Great Depression had arrived.

Barely two years before the crash doctor Kellogg made the serious error of adding a 14-story tower section to his San. Just when patients were about to decline in great number. He didn't know it then, but the "tower" would tumble his empire.

By 1928, Albert Miller and H.C. Hawk of Postum Cereals had managed to round up the majority shares of *Enquirer* stock and bought out the newspaper. Marjorie and her current husband had wanted to dump it anyway, so it was a fairly easy negotiation. Miller quickly purchased two more papers, the *Lansing State Journal* and the *Grand Rapids Herald*. Together, with the *Battle Creek Enquirer and News* the three organizations combined into a chain called Federated Publications. In the midst of a Depression, Albert Miller from Kansas was on his way to becoming another Battle Creek millionaire.

Edward F. Hutton, Marjorie's second husband, had guided Postum since she married him back in 1920, and he had quadrupled its size and reach. The company headquarters were permanently ensconced in New York but the Postum site in Battle Creek expanded yearly in goliath proportions. As though enjoying a Monopoly game, Hutton also bought the Jello-O Company, Swansdown Cake Flour, Minute Tapioca, and Log Cabin Syrup. Then he paid twenty million for Birdseye General Foods. Right after that, with Marjorie's admiring approval, he reformed the entire conglomeration and titled it the General Foods Corporation. Few people in Battle Creek paid much attention, though, since Marjorie had moved away so long ago.

Also, before the market crash, Ralston Purina out of St. Louis snapped up the defunct Mapl-Flake factory on McCamly street. The maker of Purina Wheat and Ry-Krisp tiptoed into the ready-to-eat cereal business with its Ralston wheat flakes and Ralston corn flakes. No one at Postum or Kellogg's huffed or grumbled or asked "who needs another breakfast flake manufacturer?" There were customers enough for all. Even a financially crippled nation is full of hungry people.

LEN'S absence from the Kellogg Company stretched to five years. He tried twice to change W.K.'s mind, get himself reinstated in the kingdom's official books. Neither attempt worked. He gave up, changed directions, and opened a business in the Chicago area, a seed company. It flopped. So he optimistically attempted a new cereal company. It failed. Later, he bought a paper mill to manufacture wax paper for cereal containers. With the help of his son, Keith, they pulled a modest profit, especially after Keith landed the Cracker Jack account. But, when creditors became too many and too insistent, Len signed over his small remaining cache of Kellogg stock to Helen, putting it out of reach of everyone, including himself, resigning himself to her control. Though times were God-awful across the nation, Helen nursed their funds and guarded against extravagances, so they lived well enough.

The Depression had done almost nothing to slow the growth of the Kellogg company. Corn flakes, Rice Krispies, Shredded Wheat had a market, apparently, in good times or bad. Outbound shipments increased every month. The Battle Creek plant was a thriving rail center of packed freight cars headed for the world's grocery shelves. Another overseas plant was opened, this one in Sydney, Australia.

SINCE 1925 W.K. had been giving away money. A ten-acre park in Battle Creek, a bird sanctuary at Wintergreen Lake, an experimental farm and reforesting station near Kalamazoo. He handed his hometown a civic auditorium, new junior high school, and an agricultural school. Dismayed and bewildered over grandson Kenneth's crippled mind and body, feeling helpless, he funded the creation of a school especially equipped and staffed to work with handicapped children, the first of its kind in the nation. He christened the school Ann Janette Kellogg, in memory of his mother; all other donated monuments he named after himself.

He traveled to Hawaii, Europe, Africa, China, the West Indies. Wherever he had not been, or where he had been and wanted to go again. Sometimes he took missus doctor Kellogg with him. Usually he didn't.

The Kellogg Hotel was completed, the finest and newest of its kind anywhere within two hundred miles, a great satisfaction to W.K. Now he no longer scowled at the Post Tavern each time he passed it, yearning for a way to compete with it, exceed it, put it out of business if possible.

The six-year old, seven-story Kellogg Inn, another structure he felt compelled to build, had a waiting list for each of its seventy-two apartments. W.K. and missus doctor Kellogg allotted themselves four apartments on the top floor. They didn't stay there very often, but it was theirs when they wanted it.

"The old bird's aerie, his perch," John Harvey once said.

W.K. bought an 800-acre ranch near Pomona, California, with a nineteen-room villa and a fancy row of stables where he bred Arabian horses. Rudolph Valentino dropped in one day for a visit, appraised the mounts in the Kellogg stables, then persuaded W.K. to let him ride one of the stallions in the movie, *Son of the Sheik*. He said: "Having been privileged to become slightly acquainted with Jadan, I am now anxious to show this marvelous stallion to the world through the medium of an Arabian motion picture which I am now making. We will give you tremendous clear advertising and publicity campaign through magazines, press, and film, and sincerely believe this will help Arab horse cause in America."

Valentino was true to his word. The ranch became a magnet for movie stars and political figures, though it was well known that W.K. enjoyed the company of the first and generally disdained the latter, even if he was an unabashed admirer of Herbert Hoover. Hundreds of thousands of spectators came weekly to see the horses or the stars in the outdoor arena down the hill from the villa. They were treated to the sight of Tom Mix or Will Rogers on the scene, or Mary Pickford, Marlene Dietrich, Gary Cooper, casually chatting and smoking near the arena entrance. W.K. pretended never to notice their cigarettes. For any of the celebrities who preferred flying instead of driving, there was a decent airport on the grounds not far from the stables.

Kellogg, the magnate, divided most of his time about evenly between the Pomona ranch and his three million dollar Gull Lake estate outside of Battle Creek. He wintered at one, summered at the other. He owned a third retreat from the world, a villa in Dunedin Isles, a few miles from

Clearwater in Florida, but it had never quite caught on with him as a favorite so he seldom stayed in it. At any rate, like his apartment, it was there when he wanted it. He had come a long way from his old job at the San.

69

AUGUST 1930

LEN exited the Kellogg Inn, his face flaming, but a wide grin on his mouth. His hat was mashed in one hand, his suit coat was unbuttoned and flying open in the summer wind. He bounced into the back seat of the taxi parked at the curb.

"The train station, Floyd, but drive us around by the Kellogg plant first. We've got time to spare."

"I take it he told you no again?" Helen blew a stream of cigarette smoke out of the car's open window.

"He did," Len laughed and arranged his glasses. "But the amusing part was seeing John Junior sitting beside his grandfather there in the living room at the big desk, sweating over those damnable business receipts. He looked like a regular high roller, fine business suit, the requisite reading glasses, the serious expression, the perspiration on his upper lip, the disdain for being interrupted while counting the take."

"I don't see any humor in it, Len." She took a final pull on the thin cigarette, a bleached bone against her emerald green glove, flicked it into the street as the taxi turned south onto Washington and picked up speed. "Your son has your job and he will inherit the company and it won't do you a bit of good. I imagine your father will make him sign an agreement never to let you set foot in the place."

"You're probably right," Len said, leaning into the car's coarse wool seat, watching the recognizable streets of Battle Creek glide by the window like a false background in a motion picture at the Bijou.

W.K. AND John Junior finished their accounting, then neatly put the reams of records into sturdy envelopes and squared them on a corner of the desk. They pulled chairs to the front window and sat side by side, idly gazing out at the vivid green trees six floors below. In recent years, W.K. had found something soothing about a seat before an open window in an upper office or apartment. The view seemed fresher, less encumbered when taken high above the world. He would have been mortified to know C.W. Post had felt the same way about watching life from an elevated vantage point.

Traffic on Van Buren and West Michigan was light. Only a few people were on the sidewalks. It was a drowsy afternoon under a clear sky and hot sun, the day's earlier breeziness gone.

"Hasselhorn will be putting in a new work week," W.K. said offhandedly. "This economy is throwing men out of work. The new schedule will help spread the jobs among more employees."

John stiffened. "You're having Walter Hasselhorn implement it? Surely not Hasselhorn, grandfather. He makes an ordeal out of everything, uses a cleaver when a paring knife is needed." He tried to snare the old man's attention by pulling his own chair forward a few inches.

"Walter has made a mistake or two but he has streamlined our accounting." W.K. closed his eyes behind the thick glasses, choosing his words with forethought. "He keeps me informed of details. I appreciate that."

"Hasselhorn tattles. Tells you only what he thinks will further his career around here. Ask McKay or Freeman or Adams, ask any of your best people. They will tell you he has a reputation for a heavy hand and faulty judgement."

"Nonetheless, I've given the task to him. We're eliminating the eight-hour shift. We'll have four six-hour shifts every twenty-four. Plant workers will make a bit less salary but the trade-off is worth it. We can hire several hundred additional people."

"But, why Hasselhorn? I'm the vice president." Stocky and short, John had the Kellogg build. His face was squarish and his grin, when he used it, was lopsided. Straight dark hair combed flat on his head, a full nose supporting gold-rimmed glasses that enlarged his already large, unsettled eyes. He struggled to mask his displeasure. "I should be the one to tell the employees."

"I think not," W.K. said.

LEN reached across Helen, rolled the taxi window almost shut, cutting down the wind and noise. He pressed the lapels of his coat with both hands, sucked in his cheeks, mildly satisfied about something. "Father is twirling John in circles, the way he tried to do me, the way he does everybody."

Her glance was accusing, "Have you lost your mind?" Her long narrow nose twitched, the nostrils flared. "You sound as though you're glad to see John Junior tormented. I assure you, if my son, Tommy, was being short-circuited, I'd hate it and I'd say so."

Len cupped his chin, fingers across his mouth, speaking through them. "As the two gray mares said when the roan frisked by, that's a horse of a different color. The whole scene reminded me of what I used to put up with, the badgering and embarrassment I tolerated for a place at the top. When I asked father if his attitude about me working for him had changed, I felt like I was crawling again, and I was actually glad when he said no. He walked me out into the hall and talked about John Junior being a great business leader, said he has the makings of a first rate executive. I guess he was telling me I don't have."

"John is a lot like your father, you must admit."

"I don't think so at all, but father must. John is on every committee, even the budget committee. He attends board meetings. Barely twenty years old, no real experience, and he's already a crown prince."

"DID it bother you to have your father drop in on us, John?"

W.K.'s head was up, chin out, eyes yet closed. His gray suit was buttoned tightly across his paunch.

"I felt like I wasn't his son. I have to admit, I didn't like the feeling."

"I'll restrict him from coming here again."

"No." Abruptly, too loudly. W.K. swiveled and glared sharply at him and John stammered, "I mean, don't do that. It would make me feel worse."

"All right." His grandfather continued to stare, though he could see little, then finally returned his concentration to the window. "Do you want some juice or a soda pop?"

"Grandfather, can I speak openly to you about a matter of importance?"

"If it isn't the Hasselhorn matter."

John shook his head, stood, leaned his forehead against the window pane. "It's about McQuiston. I wanted to..."

"First, though, tell me something, young man. What is your assessment of my instructions to McKay and Selmon? To move ahead with setting up a foundation to carry out several projects I have in mind. Carnegie has a foundation. Rockefeller, too. People think well of a man who helps others. And I've found it is pleasurable on those occasions when I've given donations to causes that came calling."

"It sounds fine if it's what you want, grandfather."

"I want your opinion, John."

"I don't have one. I know nothing about foundations."

"You certainly have sentiments about Walter Hasselhorn and the revised factory schedule." W.K. sniffed. "What did they teach you at Babson? Only to disagree or keep quiet?"

John Junior reseated himself in his chair. "I heartily approve of the six-hour schedules. It is the decision to allow Hasselhorn to handle it that I don't care for. As for Babson college, most of what I learned was the very sort of skills I hoped would benefit you with your business: finance, marketing, distribution, production."

W.K. took out a handkerchief, began wiping the lenses of his eyeglasses. "That education of yours cost me quite a sum."

After a moment of silence John said, "Thank you for hiring Jim McQuiston, grandfather. He's a good friend."

"He has some qualities that might rub off on you."

"Was that why you sent him with me on my trip?"

"My company's vice president could hardly take a voyage around the world, fresh out of school, without a companion, could he?" Kellogg returned his glasses to his nose. "If he gets the chance, McQuiston will do a good turn for this community if I don't miss my bet. I hope I can say as much for you, John."

THE taxi hit a hole in the road. The impact tossed Helen against Len, and they grinned at each other foolishly, righting themselves, finding an unexpected pleasure in the momentary contact.

"Sorry," Floyd called out.

"How's business?" Len asked the driver.

"Slow, mister Kellogg. Wasn't for your pappy's place and the Postum outfit I wouldn't have none at all. They got salesmen and them executives coming and going. I make a buck." He raised a fist, thumb erect, and gave the "okay" sign.

Len scooted deeper into the taxi's tufted-hair seat. He felt lethargic, wondered if he was catching a cold, attributed it to a drowsy afternoon. "Families are living on a bag of potatoes and a loaf of bread a week. People sit down to dinner with nothing but cornbread in a glass of milk, Helen. I read about it. Maybe we're like Floyd, we've no room to complain."

"I'm not complaining, Len." She exhaled despondently. "It's just a shame, after all you did for the company, you'll never get another penny out of it."

"You're probably right. Screw it." To Floyd he called out: "Never mind the run out to the company. Just take us to the station."

"YOU'VE read all of these, grandfather?" John Junior removed a book from one of several full shelves.

"Yèars ago. When I could see the print."

John's head bobbed in admiration. "You've probably got a better education than I have."

"I'm still waiting for your thoughts on my foundation idea. I intend to call it the Child Welfare Foundation."

"I told you, sir, I don't know anything about foundations so it's difficult for me to offer any real insight." He shoved the book into its slot on the shelf and clasped his shaking hands behind his back.

"If I leave my money to my relatives, most of it will be piddled away." The old man chewed the idea as if it were sour rhubarb. "They wouldn't know what to do with it. If it didn't corrupt them, it would make fools of them. I won't have my memory linked to a bunch of neer-do-wells or my name and my fortune would turn to dust when I'm dead. But a foundation, properly directed, could provide benefits after I'm gone." He made a noise that sounded as if he was spitting something off of his tongue. "You know I don't approve of some of your activities. You're high strung. Going out on the town..."

John's startled expression flashed like a neon light but W.K. missed the reaction.

"I'm aware of your escapades, John. Girls, wine, cigarettes."

"We just have fun and laugh and..."

"You can't manage a company on a laugh. Especially if your tail is dragging from cavorting every night. Some mornings I can smell the cigarette smoke on you, it stinks in your hair, your clothes. You are spoiling precious energies. You and your merrymakers parties. A waste of your money, having those freeloaders into your house every weekend for whatever it is you do." He glowered. "You'll be financially set, of course, considering you'll take over for me one day. If you watch your health a little better. And you don't die before I do."

70

JANUARY 1933

"MUST be the year of the woman," John Harvey quipped, giving rueful glances to his two female companions. He tossed the Detroit Free Press atop the Battle Creek Enquirer, and sat lamp post stiff on an upholstered footstool in the library room of the mansion he and Ella had built a half century ago. He was whiter than the snowdrifts on the frozen lawn: suit, tie, shoes, fringe of hair, moustache, goatee, all perfectly colorless. Perched on his shoulder was a white cockatoo that squawked reproachfully when Kellogg moved quickly or unexpectedly.

The room's original furniture remained but a magnolia wood davenport had been added, as had an Air Castle seven-tube radio. Its bright dial glowed while low, bouncy music leaked out of it: a number by Paul Whiteman's orchestra. There was a new indirect ceiling light of cut-glass. An ebony finished miniature Musette piano, two feet by five feet in size, now resided elegantly by the large east window.

Kellogg accepted a cup of Caramel Coffee from Angie. As she poured, her breast flattened against his shoulder, the one not occupied by the cockatoo. John Harvey watched her until she looked at him, then he grinned knowingly, causing her face to redden. She hastily drew away, her small, round lips pinched to puckering.

"Year of the woman, you say? It's more than past the time for it," Angie's sister, Gertrude, suggested from across the room. "We've been voting now for fourteen years." She sat at a mahogany desk, busily checking pages of a manuscript containing the doctor's most recent writings, ensuring that each was in order and the pencilled edits had actually been made.

Kellogg had hired the two women as companions and secretaries when he realized one day how lonely he had become and how difficult it was to care for his own endless array of needs and wants. The sisters came with high recommendation from a trusted acquaintance. Both were mid-fortyish, minimally attractive for their years, though Gertrude's nose was too long, while Angie's eyes were set so close they occasionally crossed.

"The way politics and the economy are trying to do the backstroke in five inches of water, I can't see where suffrage has brought any especially laudable benefits to the women of this nation, Gertrude, or vice versa." He pretended to shudder. "We've a national Depression no one knows how to solve and my Sanitarium is being shunted into receivership; that's the extent of the ballyhooed advances of the last ten or fifteen years."

Gertrude flipped another page with a tongue-moistened thumb.

Kellogg felt talkative and he had a willing, if not always acquiescent, audience. "Every so-called liberated woman in America thinks its smart to puff cigarettes and abandon all vestiges of decorum over that silly MahJongg game or some caterwauling singer like this Vallee fellow." He thumped the mess of newspapers with a balled hand as if the printed sheets harbored a responsibility for the way things were.

"Gertrude and I never smoked cigarettes," Angie corrected in a tone of personal injury.

Kellogg ignored her, lifted a newspaper and flourished it. The cockatoo flapped its wings, raised hell, repositioned its clawed feet, and dug in for a better hold. Chunkier than a parrot, but from the same family, its erectile crest looked like a backward horn atop its head.

"That bird is going to drop something unpleasant on your coat," Gertrude warned, openly bossy.

"Never has." He read again from the newspaper. "At the Bijou they're showing 'Registered Nurse' with Bebe Daniels; the Strand has 'Little Miss Marker' with..."

"Shirley Temple," Angie provided. "I would like to see that one. She's a darling."

"Don't interrupt me, Angie, I'm making a point. At the Rex is 'Spitfire' with that skinny Hepburn woman, and at the Regent they've booked a thriller-diller called 'Operator 13' and its star is another woman, of course, Marion Davies."

"They all sound entertaining," Gertrude said.

"Good lord, ladies, every one of them has a woman's title. That's what I meant about it being the year of..."

"Operator 13 isn't a woman's title," Gertrude argued.

"Did you girls have your enemas this morning?" he asked suddenly.

"Doctor, please," Angie stuttered, blushing again and backing farther away from him, straightening cups on the serving tray she still clutched in her hands.

"You know that kind of personal talk embarrasses my sister." Gertrude tossed a handful of manuscript sheets on the stack in front of her. "Yes, doctor, we had our enemas, just as we do each and every day; if you'll allow, as regular as clockwork."

When Kellogg stood up, the cockatoo repeated its hop-and-grip routine, then lifted off with a murderous cry and sailed to the corner where it climbed into a gigantic silver cage. John Harvey went to the desk, tapped a fingernail on its waxed surface. He winked at Gertrude.

"I take two a day..."

"We know."

"...and have taken two a day for sixty years. I am eighty-one and in perfect health." Kellogg ran in place for half a minute, knees lifted high to his waist. When he stopped, he was barely winded. "I still perform three to five operations a day. Hands are as steady as they were when I was thirty." He held them at arm's length. Not a hint of a waver. "Brother Will, who never followed my instructions, ate the most vile foods, refused to take enemas..."

"He's alive and robust," Gertrude injected matter-of-factly.

"He's seventy-three and a long way from robust," Kellogg countered. "Five major operations — cholecystostomies, hernias, gall stones, intestinal blockages. My God, he's walking scar tissue."

"Very rich scar tissue," Gertrude reminded him.

John Harvey deflated. "Yes," he muttered, "rich. While my San, my life's work, is threatened with extinction."

Despite the doctor's melodramatics, Gertrude felt genuine sympathy. "Let's not dwell on that, doctor."

He wasn't dissuaded. "Mister Joe Enright of Ohio wants his $4,200, dear ladies. We have eleven million in assets, a payroll that yet exceeds eight hundred employees, and our liabilities are scarcely three million. But, we have no cash. Our creditors say pay us right now, doctor Kellogg, or we'll close your Sanitarium and sell it stone by stone." He jabbed a forefinger several times into his other palm like an icepick, emphasizing the iniquity of the demands. "They are shortsighted men."

"The Depression, doctor. They are worried they will lose their investment, or not get paid what is owed them." Gertrude scanned another manuscript page. "They are scared people."

"Everyone said Judge Tuttle hated having to make any ruling against you, doctor," Angie remarked, trying to find a bright side, finally sitting expectantly on the piano bench.

"He is an estimable man," Kellogg agreed, "but he had to put the San in receivership. The worst of it is, we've started to show a profit these last few weeks. People of renown have practically flocked to us — Eddie Cantor, Amelia Earhart, Henry Ford, Pavlov, Admiral Byrd, even that young swimmer..."

"Mister Weismuller?" Angie said and her eyes nearly touched.

"Eleanor Roosevelt is supposed to be planning a stay," Gertrude encouraged, not looking up from her work.

Kellogg's grumpiness persisted. "This negative publicity will no doubt bring a raft of cancellations. Impossible to fill all the rooms."

Angie naively asked, "Wouldn't your brother loan you enough?"

"He claims he put everything into a trust for that foundation of his."

Gertrude changed the subject, having heard enough of the San's gloomy financial mess. "The Century of Progress in Chicago is expected to be the best world's fair ever when it opens in June. If we can afford hotel reservations, doctor, I could write ahead and arrange..."

Kellogg watched the fireplace logs slip and settle with an upgust of sparks. His face was like raw dough poured from a mixing bowl. "I saw the fair once in Chicago. We rode the ferris wheel and we walked through the exhibits and marvelled at enough sights to last for a lifetime." His voice cracked. "I couldn't go back now." Then he added, "It's beyond our financial means, anyway."

WINTER finally turned its breath in another direction. At least, for a day. After three weeks of sub-zero temperatures, there came welcome medicines: thirty degrees and sunshine.

In the cemetery on the east side of town, at the foot of Ella Kellogg's grave, W.K. and John Junior snugged their collars against the chill. They wore hats and scarves and had their gloved hands tunneled to the bottom of their overcoat pockets.

W.K. purposefully chose the late, vacant afternoon for his visits. On a wire stand lodged in the wet ground by Ella's headstone, a fresh wreath of flowers wiggled in the wind. The two men had picked twigs and leaves off the grave and deposited them in a black metal barrel by the edge of the gravel access road. Now there seemed to be nothing left but to remain staring at the tombstone as if the information chiseled on it — her name, birth and death dates — would clarify its recondite message.

"You would have liked Puss."

It was the litany they followed each time. John Junior answered with his standard response.

"I don't really remember grandmother Kellogg, but I wish I'd had the chance to know her. I've heard only praise for her from everyone, even missus Carrie."

"Doctor missus Kellogg is a sturdy woman." W.K. raised his eyes over the treetops, responding to the jibes of a flock of crows lazily struggling to propel themselves aloft, moving upward in dips and sidedrifts, as if fighting their own slipstream. He could barely make out their black shapes.

"I suppose we've stayed long enough." He turned toward a waiting automobile, driver behind the wheel, motor still running.

John Junior fell into step. "A long while ago, grandfather, you asked what I thought about your starting a foundation. Do you still want my opinion?"

Kellogg grunted, "A little behindhand, aren't you? It's three years old."

"The grants are spoken of in high praise," John Junior said, "and, of course, everyone wants to get one. Bringing all the county health offices together was an impressive piece of work, it's getting national attention. And changing the name from Child Welfare Foundation to the W.K. Kellogg Foundation was a wise decision, no reason you shouldn't receive credit for your generosity, your name deserves to be known along with your foundation's good deeds."

The tip of Kellogg's cane sunk into the mushy earth with every step so their progress across the cemetery was slow. He halted and looked at the ground. "I sense a 'but' coming from you about my foundation."

"Only in regard to doctor Pritchard." He waited for his grandfather to move again. "He is, in my estimation, grossly overpaid. His salary is unjustifiably exorbitant when contrasted with his duties and responsibilities."

"It's less than I pay you." The tone was harsh. His face was as immobile as a hood ornament.

"There is a big difference, grandfather. I'm a vice president of your company, I help you to run your entire business. Pritchard sits and waits for us to hammer a profit out of the market, then deliver the money to him so he can give it away like Santa Claus."

A gust of chilly wind washed around them, pinned their coats to their bodies, urged them toward the promised warmth of the waiting automobile. Kellogg's driver, dressed in black overcoat and chauffeur's cap, held the car door open but W.K. did not step inside.

"Doctor Pritchard is not a tittle-tattler. Nor a magpie. He is a reasoned man." He glowered at his grandson. "You will do well to show him proper respect."

John Junior's shoulders narrowed as something went out of them. He dug his chin into his upturned collar, tightened his hat brim lower on his forehead. "All right, grandfather. But I warned you, too, about Hasselhorn and I was proved..."

Kellogg silenced him with a gloved hand extended before his face, then he entered the automobile, hesitated, looked back over his shoulder. "Pritchard has a low evaluation of your judgement. It may be valid. What in hades did you intend by resizing the All Bran cartons? Dropping them to fifteen ounces but retaining the sixteen ounce price. A stupid blunder. Made the eight ounce package cheaper to buy. That lowers profits."

John Junior stammered, caught off guard, lost for an answer, trying to remember his rationale for the change in carton size. His mouth drained dry; a knot coiled and tightened in his stomach.

71

APRIL 1934

THE horse had small ears set apart on a broad forehead, a lean face, a neck long and trim, joining up with withers and shoulders that were neither bulged nor slinking. John Junior appraised the animal's straight back, its moderately sloped croup, and grudgingly admitted to himself that Pritchard knew his equines.

"You sure your granddad don't mind you going out this early by yourself, mister Kellogg?"

"Pritchard knows I ride his horse."

The stable man accepted the evasive answer, exhaled white vapor nearly as dense as if he had just drawn from his pipe. The sun had not appeared, though its crimson messenger had colored the low horizon through dungeon-black treelimbs. The man concentrated on his job, doing it well, checking the girth, tightening it, then letting his fingers explore the saddle flaps and skirts to ensure neither horse nor rider would get pinched. He moved aside and John Junior took up the reins, grabbed a fistful of the horse's mane, put a foot in the stirrup, hoisted himself into the seat. The chestnut moved its broad-heeled feet only an inch or two.

Astride and comfortable, John Junior noticed the misty scene beyond the stables, the silent lake an eighth of a mile down the steep embankment at the estate's water boundary. The lake was dark, motionless, with a haze hanging over it. He forced his attention up along the dirt road, past the gray plank fence that twined back to the mansion at the top of the hill. There was a light in W.K.'s upstairs window. He wondered if his grandfather was watching him but he didn't actually care one way or the other. He was belly-full of the old man.

"Take notice of the hedges and fences, mister Kellogg. It's hard to see where you're going at this hour..."

"I know the grounds. So does this horse."

A shelf radio played a recorded transcription of an earlier newscast. President Roosevelt's lofty voice was telling the nation: "...foreign war is a potent danger at this moment to the future of civilization...in the face of this apprehension, the American people can have but one concern...the United States of America shall and must remain...unentangled and free."

He heard none of FDR's wishful words. He nudged his mount with both knees, whacked it behind the girth with his crop, and the animal bolted forward. It settled to a trot on its way out of the stable grounds, but he spanked it into a canter, enjoying the damp air that plastered itself against him, bringing tears to his eyes. By the time horse and rider cleared the top of the first small hill, they were in a gallop.

Only three minutes into the ride, running full out, the animal's left front foot descended with piledriver force into mushy loam that sunk instantly downward as though breaking through to an underground cave. The horse's speed was chopped short in full stride, its heel and fetlock gobbled by the crumbling earth. The horrified creature lunged to its right, struggling for balance, its eyes peeled in terror.

John Junior pitched from the saddle as if he had just hit a concealed wire stretched across the path. His yellow snapbrim hat sailed away like an injured pheasant — twenty, thirty feet — then toppled to the hard-packed meadow. His head struck the crusty ground with the whack! of a steel-edged ax biting into timber.

The unnerved horse recovered, tossed its mane, then complained loudly in a series of deep coughs. At last it settled down and for a few minutes it intently watched the man's motionless body. Finally, it pawed the earth, tossed its head, and trotted away toward the stables.

72

JULY 1936

THE game was a sizzler in every way.

With the score up for grabs, the odds were lengthening badly for the losing team. And, the temperature for the third day in a row was 103 degrees. Both teams looked as though they had stood under the faucets in the shower rooms with their uniforms on. White material was sweat gray, blue was sweat black. Sitting in the bleachers watching the Postum team battle it out with the Negro All-Stars required a lot of spectator fortitude, a big umbrella, and a constant supply of liquids. Postum Company had financed the ball park back in '22 for semi-pro industrial teams. A six-acre diamond, canvas covered infield; grass topping that was watered bright green even during the hottest, driest times. Like now. A truly splendid ball park. The stands could hold five thousand fans and had about half that number today.

In the top of the ninth, Benson was at the plate for the All Stars, but the odds were just no good. The black players knew only a homerun would win this one. The loud crack of his bat came on the pitch, so solidly you could feel the reverberations in your own arms. The baseball spun into the parched sky, Benson flew across first base on his way to second, the man at first now headed for third. The center fielder's glove was casually raised. He caught the high fly easily. Game over.

McKay said to Bernie Angood as they shuffled along in the crowd leaving the grandstand, "Did you take notes?"

Angood looked at him and they both laughed. "Sure. I wrote down every Postum play and signal. We'll give it to the coach Monday. Should make a Kellogg win a sure thing next week." He and McKay waved a hand at a knot of businessmen headed out of the park — Lassen, Stetler, Shaw, Franklin, the latter who ran an iron and sheet metal company and had made some frames for Kellogg ovens.

"W.K. believes we really do influence the outcome by watching the games, reporting what we see," McKay muttered. "More like spying, but if the results please him, they please me."

"Me, too," Angood was thin, tall, had dark receding hair, and wore rimless eyeglasses. Like McKay, he had on the required dark wool business suit of a Kellogg Company executive.

"W.K. approves of your interest in the town, Bernie. You know, being on the Y board, that kind of thing. Keep it up."

"Sure. But you have to admit, it didn't do John Junior any good."

McKay turned to face Angood. "No, Bernie, it didn't." There was a flicker of sadness in his eyes. "But that was a different thing altogether. John tried to do too much, couldn't keep up with his own pace. He wouldn't admit he had limits. More than anything, though, he wanted to satisfy his granddad. He wanted W.K. to approve of him."

"Sounds like a tough goal." Angood moved out of the sunlight and under the overhang of the grandstand. The crowd had cleared, leaving a few lingerers here and there like bread crumbs on a table after an enjoyable meal.

Remaining in the sun's heat, McKay stared across the playing field. "John couldn't sleep worth a hoot, spent half his nights prowling around, looking for things to take care of at the factory. Or sometimes, just any activity to get his mind off whatever was prying at it. That's how come he was riding Pritchard's horse practically in the dark. And racing it, naturally."

"Gopher hole, I heard. A wonder it didn't break the horse's leg."

"Pritchard would've preferred to shoot John if there came a choice. He was in the hospital quite a while and he never was the same when he came back to work. The spark was gone. A light had been turned off up here." McKay tapped the side of his head. "Funny thing, W.K. started that school on Champion street for handicapped people, already has itself a national reputation, and his foundation was meant to help just about everyone, so you'd think he would be one hundred percent sympathetic to any person with an affliction, especially his grandson. But it was as if he just turned away."

"Mister McKay," someone called out.

"Hello, Paul," McKay greeted the thirtyish man who came toward him. "I didn't know you were a baseball fan. Bernie, do you know Paul Tammi, our high school's master of music?"

Angood laughed, stuck out a hand and he and Tammi pumped away at each other. "We were roommates at the same boarding house in the poor old days," Angood joked. "Those Band Follies of yours have made you the toast of the town, Paul."

Tammi's round face glowed all the way to his balding head. He squinted behind rimmed spectacles and nervously tapped his right foot to some melody he was tuning in his head. "You just think the Follies are special because your son's in our band."

Angood clasped the shorter man's shoulder. "Art probably will never make it big in the concert world, even with your help, teacher."

Tammi had a deep, mellow voice. "Did I overhear John Kellogg's name when I approached you? Have you had word from him?"

"Only what we get from the salesmen now and then. He's in Chicago, you know, working with his father on the puffed corn cereal John tried to sell to W.K. before he went west."

"He tried to sell cereal to W.K.?" Tammi's ice blue eyes enlarged. He blotted his forehead on a crisply folded handkerchief embroidered with his initials

"I heard the gist of it," Angood admitted, "but I never understood what took place."

McKay eased under the bleacher roof at last, getting out of the sun. "No secret about it. Bill Penty and I knew W.K. was pressuring John after he came back from Wisconsin where he'd been working and recovering from his fall. Everyone knew he wasn't well, everyone except W.K. It was plain that John was about to go off the deep end, but the old man seemed to be onto him about every stitch and stone. It was hard to understand why he ragtagged him. John spent every waking minute trying to do what he thought his granddad wanted."

"I've heard," Tammi put in, "mister Kellogg can be an uncompromising soul if you land at odds with him."

McKay dangled his hat on his knee. "I won't argue that with you, Paul." A discussion with W.K. popped into his memory, W.K. telling him:

"After Len left the company, I looked forward to the time when John Junior would be my successor. Even though John was always a nervous child. He has long shown symptoms that all is not well with him. But I kept my hopes."

McKay had wondered at the time why he was being told those things. The unasked question was never answered. He surmised it was simply because he was on hand and the old man had felt an urgency to explain his actions and search out his own justifications.

"I took him into the business. Taught him myself. You probably don't know it, mister McKay, but I was informed by someone that John nearly had a nervous breakdown while he was enrolled at Babson."

"I never heard that rumor, sir. I wouldn't give it much due. Schools are full of rumors."

"I shouldn't have refused to see what was coming. Closed my eyes to it. After his accident he was in the hospital. Then he went to a recovery home in Wisconsin. Doctors advised he spend a winter on a ranch in Montana. So I sent him there to recuperate. When he came back to the company this spring I was told he was all right. He wasn't. Didn't have to be a physician to discover that. He couldn't get anything right. So I gave him an outside job. Sent him out to do field work. For his own good."

McKay ruefully remembered the letter W.K. dictated to John, could even hear the scratch of the stenographer's pencil on her notebook...

"...I hoped you would curb your enormous energies, John, and concentrate on getting well if you had business away from the company. You insist, though, in carrying on in a rather active way. I dislike very much being a party to these activities. I fear I am indirectly aiding and abetting you in such matters by allowing your salary to be continued at its current level. I have given the matter considerable thought. I have lost much sleep over it. My conclusion is that the Kellogg Company had better discontinue paying your high salary. It doesn't occur to me that it is good business, or even good sense, to furnish you with funds to carry on as actively where you are as you would if you were here at home."

"Demoted from vice president at $25,000 a year to salesman at $50 a week," McKay said out loud in the settling quiet of the Postum ball park. "I'm afraid that is enough to crush the spirit of any man."

He saw Angood and Tammi listening attentively and he cleared his mind of old thoughts. "Just reminiscing. Anyway, as I was saying, Penty and I were fiddling around in the new products lab and we found a way to make corn grits pop up like crisp, hollow little balls. It looked perfect for a new cereal product. So we fixed it up that John Junior would get the credit, thinking it would put him back in solid with his granddad. Problem is, W.K. didn't buy it. He wasn't impressed with the corn puffs and he didn't believe John Junior had discovered them. Bad matters turned worse, John convinced himself he alone *had* made the discovery, so he figured it belonged to him. He tried to *sell* the idea to W.K. More to the point, W.K. said even if John had single-handedly created the corn puffs, he did it on company time and the company wasn't about to pay for what it already owned.

"I wasn't there when W.K. and John went at each other but they must've had some mean words. John took the puffed corn grits and his personal belongings and stormed out and that was the last W.K. Kellogg has seen of his grandson."

"So he's in Chicago with his dad?" Angood inquired.

"They've organized a company, small one, getting by, I understand. They call it New Foods, something like that."

73

FEBRUARY 1938

"ARE things going well for you, John Junior?"

"Reasonably well, grandfather. We aren't setting the woods on fire or anything like that, but there are some very promising signs. The corn pops cereal doesn't have the potential we hoped, but father's frozen coffee is another matter..."

"I thought he wrote me it was dehydrated?"

"Yes, grandfather, it's both, you see, a dehydrated frozen extract. There are encouraging prospects since the George Washington coffee company and even Nestle's has been asking around about us."

"Your father also wrote that you intend to be married."

"That's actually why I called you. I wanted to let you know about it, wanted you to hear it from me. I didn't know father had told you. Mary is a firm-minded girl, knows her way around, and can give as good as she gets. You will like her."

"That is the name of your bride-to-be? Mary?"

"Mary Muench, grandfather. She's an airline hostess, that's how I met her, on a flight..."

"Mary is a good name."

"Yes, I'm glad you think so. How is your health, grandfather?"

"As well as it might be for a man near eighty, though I can't see my hand in front of my face. I think I'm destined to spend my years watching little pinwheels of light in my head."

"I hoped you could come to Chicago for the wedding next month. I can tell you the exact date..."

"It isn't likely I will be able to attend, John Junior. I will send my wishes for your future, though. And an appropriate gift."

"No need for a gift, I mean that isn't why I telephoned. I just hoped, well, uh..." There seemed to be no logical end to the thought so he abandoned it. "We see your advertisements everywhere — the stores, magazines, the newspapers. We listen to your radio programs, too. We enjoy *The Texas Rangers*. We tune them in because, well, the company sponsors them and we still feel an attachment to..."

"John Junior, the economic chaos of America is far from settled. The jubilance of New Deal politics is unmerited. And I am deeply worried about the situation in Europe. Hitler is a maniac. He will bring great harm to the entire world, mark my words. Nevertheless, the Kellogg company is keeping its head comfortably above water. I am glad to learn that you and Len are doing likewise. Is there anything else we need to convey to each other?"

"Father wanted me to mention that if you need either of us to assist..."

"I don't believe that would be in anyone's best interests."

"No, you're probably right. Father just thought I should mention it..."

FROM his Buenos Aires hotel room, W.K. watched the evening sun ooze behind the buildings across the wide boulevard. Pale blue sky, darkening high up where clouds hung gray and heavy. Late shoppers and homeward-aimed businessmen moved briskly on their journeys; the sidewalk restaurants were mostly empty.

He could discern only splotches of color and motion. But, seated in front of the open window, he could hear the honking of auto horns and the husky whine of the buses as they labored from low to high gear, and he was content with that much of what there was.

It had been a particularly good day. In the coolness of morning he had been driven over gently rolling slopes and long stretches of flatland that reminded him of Indiana. His automobile had bounced along dirt roads that were little more than footpaths winding through shady groves of Eucalyptus and long gum and hickory trees. The driver, a Kellogg employee, took him past farms where electricity and indoor plumbing were unheard of, and where the campisinos tilled the fields with their fingers and toes. Soil and water conservation were equally unknown in the poor, beautiful countryside. Kellogg had wondered if his foundation might find some way to help.

The noon mail brought an awaited sample of the latest innovation: a variety pack, an assortment of twelve small single-serving boxes of Kellogg's cereal. An ingenious sales item. And an early morning telephone call from Michigan had confirmed that the newest addition to his worldwide chain of plants opened on schedule in Manchester, England.

A knock at the door called Kellogg's attention away from the open window. Drake, a company man, came into the brightly lit room. W.K. could see him well enough to distinguish that he carried a yellow sheet of paper. He accurately guessed it to be a cablegram from the States.

"I was listening to the street, mister Drake. Daydreaming, you might say. I'm fond of this Latin city."

"Yes sir," the man answered, his voice thin, his face anxious.

"I was reflecting on the various events of today. Our plant in Great Britain, the new variety pack."

He did not rise though he had one hand balanced on the handle of his cane. Drake moved closer, the cablegram held out before him like an offering.

Kellogg said, "I shouldn't admit this, I suppose, but I am glad doctor missus Kellogg did not make the trip. I am not much used to traveling with her. I don't think I will ever form the habit."

"This message, sir, it just arrived." Drake's voice quivered. His hand shook as he extended the cablegram toward his employer. "Your grandson killed himself today."

"What?" Kellogg's head snapped up as if he had been jabbed with a hatpin. "What did you say, Drake?"

Rattling the cablegram, "This arrived minutes ago. His father sent it. It says John Junior shot himself."

Kellogg did not wince, did not move at all. He only blinked several times as if to clear his eyes in the hope of improved vision. The ceiling fan's long wooden blades revolved in a slow hum, stirring the air negligibly.

"John Junior is dead?"

"In his office at their plant in Chicago. He was at his desk when he shot himself." Drake's shoulders sloped as enervation replaced tension, arms hanging listlessly at his sides, one hand holding the crumpled cablegram. He felt as if he had run a mile uphill with a cannonball in his arms. "Do you want to send a response, sir?"

"Did John Junior leave a note? A message of any kind?"

"I don't know, sir. The wire doesn't mention it."

Kellogg faced the open window, noticed the lamps were lit on the boulevard. He thought the bright bulbs made the street look festive.

Softly, into the evening street sounds, he said, "He was no coward, mister Drake."

"I'm sorry, sir, I didn't catch that."

W.K. tossed a hand in dismissal of his employee. "Leave me alone, if you will."

Drake moved to the hallway door, asked quietly: "Do you wish to send a return message, sir?"

Kellogg did not answer.

74

MARCH 1941

BATTLE Creek continued to accumulate people. At the beginning of 1941 it had a population of 64,000, if the myriad little townships clustered around it were counted. The Enquirer and News bought out the Moon-Journal and now stood alone as the city's only daily. If he had lived, C.W. Post would have clapped Albert Miller on the back and exclaimed, "Well done, mister publisher." *Camp* Custer, out on the western reaches of the town, was renamed *Fort* Custer, as if anyone really cared except the army; the change of title proved to be like most changes of title: it altered neither the pay nor the job. Nichols Hospital was torn down. Leila Post Montgomery died in California. Her final request was to be buried in Battle Creek in the Post mausoleum.

A federal court approved the Sanitarium's reorganization. Bondholders and creditors were notified so they wouldn't file any fresh claims against the San to add to the hundreds already on record.

Radio competed with movies for the nation's attention. It had one big advantage: it was free. In the Sunday funnies, everyone was fighting: Li'l Abner fought marriage, Alley Oop fought typhoons, and Boots and Her Buddies fought the heartaches of being young.

There was another kind of fighting. Germany had become a weapon of destruction, methodically crushing its neighbors — Poland, Denmark, Norway, Belgium, the Netherlands. Then into France, paralyzing and occupying the country instantaneously. Only Great Britain was left to hold alone against the Berlin-Rome axis.

The United States was sending supplies and armaments to its British cousins even while Adolph Hitler, the goose-stepping killer, jigged in his black knee boots and spewed vitriolic warnings of repercussion:

America, stay out of the line of fire or face the consequences.

President Franklin Delano Roosevelt's response over every broadcast network was optimistic. "We must be the great arsenal of democracy," he said in a *fireside chat*. "There will be no 'bottlenecks' in our determination to aid Great Britain. No dictator, no combination of dictators, will weaken that determination by threats. I believe the Axis powers are not going to win this war. We have no excuse for defeatism. We have every good reason for hope."

JOHN Harvey wore a white nightshirt and sat propped against a pile of pillows in his bed, throwing pages of the Enquirer and the Detroit Free Press onto the floor as soon as he scanned them. While Angie picked up the papers, Gertrude leaned across him and wiped bread crumbs from his lips, his silver moustache. Then she removed the breakfast serving tray that straddled his shrunken stomach, placing it on the table by the front window.

"How's our doctor today?" Gertrude inquired.

"I can't stand any more of this impending war news," he growled in a voice no longer commanding or lively. "I feel well enough, though, to beat you at a game of cribbage if you dare." He grinned mischievously with eyes that receded in a thinning face. "Then I shall pop out of this bed and get over to the hospital and make certain no one except the patients are lying down on the job."

"It's Sunday. You will stay here and rest," Gertrude instructed. "That is what doctor Leffler recommended and it is what you agreed to do." She exhaled mightily. "Ever since that parrot of yours died..."

"Cockatoo," he said.

"...you are impossible. I'm going to buy you a dog or a monkey, so help me."

"No dogs, please. Will would swear it was because he has that big German shepherd."

"It's his seeing eye dog," Angie chimed.

"No, it isn't, Angie, even if that's what everyone thinks. It's just a wolf-size Alsatian, a gift from Lee Duncan out in Hollywood for some kind of favor, heaven knows what. An offspring of Rin Tin Tin, like the one he had before, grandson or grandpup or something like that."

"I'll bring the cribbage board for you," Angie said, undaunted. She hurried out of the room on her self-appointed errand.

"I should be at the hospital." He sighed long and noisily. "Lord, how disappointed Ella would be if she were still alive, seeing what is happening to our hospital. Condemnation proceedings underway, a federal district attorney telling us our indebtedness is too large so Uncle Sam will take over and straighten things out. Ha!"

"It will take months," Gertrude said. "The government delays forever unless it's something that ought'n be done, then they rush it through in a day. So don't try to wiggle your way around doctor Leffler's instructions." She snugged the bedcovers under his arms decisively.

"Tell me about my brother and his wife." Kellogg smirked. "Or should I use past tense, his used-to-be wife? Are Will and doctor Carrie divorced or just not living together?" John Harvey spoke into his bed-covers, his chin supported against his chest.

She beamed as if he had just told her to take a paid vacation. Gertrude loved the prospect of sporty diversion, tattling and prattling. "They aren't divorced, doctor. I explained to you yesterday everything I know."

She plopped on the edge of the bed, folded her arms across her breasts. "I don't know why you get such joy out of your brother's misfortunes." She baited him. "After all these years of feuding, it looks like you'd both be worn out with behaving like spoilsports."

He scratched his goatee thoughtfully, using a withered hand that had entirely lost its firm fleshiness. "Spoilsports? It's almost become a sporting thing with me and Will. Sometimes, though, he went too far, hurt other people while he tried to win a decisive point against me."

Gertrude leaned into John Harvey's face and whispered to him, though no one was in the room except the two of them. "They had trouble when mister Kellogg wanted to spend last summer out at his Gull Lake home and she wouldn't go, she stayed right on at their apartment in the hotel. Then, I guess, after he had his glaucoma operation..."

"The second one."

"...he couldn't read anymore, they say he's almost completely blind, and he couldn't play card games with her and he didn't like going on rides, so there wasn't much for them to do together. At least, that's the word that's around, though I wouldn't know personally."

"And she has gone from Battle Creek?"

Gertrude bobby-pinned a strand of her grayish-brown hair that had fallen loose. "Doctor Staines-Kellogg went to live with her sister in Ohio or Indiana. I told you that yesterday, too."

"So you did," he smiled as Angie came in with the cribbage board.

75

DECEMBER 1941

"YESTERDAY, December seventh, 1941, a date which will live in infamy, the United States was suddenly and deliberately attacked by naval and air forces of the empire of Japan..." President Roosevelt intoned.

In every front room in every home in all forty-eight states, radios glowed while anxious families circled the talking mahogany boxes. Fingers reached forward and adjusted radio dials, trying for the clearest reception. A nation of people listened with dread and sinking hearts.

"No matter how long it may take us to overcome this premeditated invasion, the American people in their righteous might will win through to absolute victory..."

Hands touched, then held tightly. Children smelled and tasted the ominous atmosphere as palpable as the odor in the room of a dead man, and they said nothing, just watched their parents stricken faces and felt an uneasiness wriggle its way beneath the doorsill of their minds.

"With confidence in our armed forces, with the unbounding determination of our people, we will gain the inevitable triumph, so help us God."

NEWS ITEM

Battle Creek Enquirer, May 15, 1942 — A transaction in which the U.S. Government took over the main buildings of the Battle Creek Sanitarium was completed this afternoon. The government will take full possession August 1 and is expected to use the properties for a general hospital similar to the Walter Reed hospital in Washington, D.C.

The price paid, $2,251,100, will enable the Sanitarium to pay off all bonded indebtedness and to start anew on the other side of Washington avenue, reestablishing itself in the John Harvey Kellogg hall, formerly the Phelps sanitorium.

Doctor Kellogg reportedly is looking forward with enthusiasm to his new Sanitarium. He intends to continue its functions without interruption and build even greater prestige in the new, smaller quarters. He regrets that the 187 tenants now occupying the Halls' 225 rooms will necessarily be displaced to allow for current patients. There were times, prior to the Depression, when the Sanitarium's patients and guests exceeded 1,300...

"CHRIST almighty," the army colonel said leadenly, "we not only have the whole goddamned Japanese empire to fight and the goddamned Nazis, now we have some pisspot old doctor who thinks he's Don Quixote in a white cotton suit." He lifted his arms, let them drop with a smack against his sides. "Jesus Christ almighty."

John Harvey had defensively positioned himself in front of the main door of the San's twin towers. Onlookers were lining up to watch the proceedings, partly out of curiosity, partly from a sense of being present at a special moment in the city's history. An army colonel, two city councilmen, and a policeman advanced up the steps passing between a pair of the entrance's forty-foot columns. Each man was uttering what he hoped was soothing advice.

"Doctor Kellogg, let's go inside and discuss this matter like gentlemen." And,

"Sir, you have no right to bar the door to the U.S. Army but I assure you, under the circumstances, we will not press any charges if you move aside without further delay." And,

"Doctor Kellogg, this can come to no good. Please think of yourself and your reputation."

John Harvey was a Grizzly guarding its lair. His teeth and claws were a single hunk of ash wood, tapered, brown stained, weighing about two pounds with a taped grip and an oval imprint that proclaimed, "Regulation Louisville Slugger."

"You're not coming in." He wiggled the bat menacingly, daring the trespassers to advance on him. "I built this sanitarium, designed it, oversaw every detail, made it what it is. It belongs to me, no one else. You'll not get past me."

While the officials huddled in conference, two women parted from the crowd along the street and walked directly up the steps and stopped not twelve inches from the combative doctor.

"Go away, Angie," Kellogg said with uncertainty. "Go away, Gertrude."

"If you will come with us, doctor." Angie's crossed eyes glimmered as though she might begin to cry any minute.

"They're already inside the building, doctor." Gertrude's approach, as usual, was practical, direct. "The San is theirs, it belongs to them now, it's no longer yours and Ella's and nothing will change that. She isn't here anymore, she doesn't mind if you let it go, she's only concerned about your welfare. You must come away before someone gets hurt because then the consequences would be severe. There is much work to do at the hospital and no one will really get started unless you come with us where you're needed. At the hospital."

For several minutes she talked with him. The officials waited and watched. Finally she reached out, gently seized Kellogg's white suit sleeve and eased his arm down, catching the end of the bat in her other hand, slipping it entirely from his grip and handing it to Angie who simply dangled it at her side until the policeman, in turn, took it without her even noticing.

The half hour siege of the Sanitarium had ended.

76

DECEMBER 1943

DOCTOR Leffler remained calmly by the closed door, toying with the stethoscope hanging around his neck. He was tall, bony, with bushy gray hair and spiritless eyes that came alive only when he was tending a patient or operating on living flesh. He wore a white jacket and trousers in the San's prescribed mode of dress but with brown shoes.

Across the room, John Harvey occupied his desk chair in the relocated Sanitarium. His secretary, a middle-aged man with cheeks so red they appeared rouged, sat plumply in a straightback chair, alert for the doctor's dictation.

Kellogg coughed a rattling, mucous-filled cough, and doctor Leffler stepped toward him, but was signaled to remain where he was.

"You should be in bed," Leffler said dully.

"I haven't time for bed," Kellogg announced. "I've several articles for Good Health to put on paper, a hundred letters to answer, many business matters to put in order."

"You have pneumonia, doctor Kellogg, among other maladies which you know of as well as I. If you persist in working eighteen hours a day..."

"I know, I know. It will kill me." He moved some papers aimlessly on his desk. "I have a secret for you, doctor Leffler, I am already dying."

"That's nonsense," Leffler replied, avoiding eye contact with Kellogg. His instinct to comfort caused him to add, "You could go on for years if you would conserve your strength, take better care of yourself, as you are always instructing our patients to do."

"None of our patients are ninety-one years old, doctor Leffler. I read that the war casualties are arriving at the San daily — I mean, the federal hospital — by rail and being brought into town from Fort Custer, too." He smiled wanly. "My Sanitarium is continuing to do what it was built to do, provide healing for the sick and damaged, isn't that right?

Before Leffler could respond with another bit of medical advice, Kellogg slapped his desk loudly and said, "Last night I thought of the most unusual thing. In another hundred years I will have been dead for at least 95 years. Imagine that." He slapped the desktop again. "Apply it to yourself and you will find it very sobering." He looked from Leffler to the secretary and smiled weakly.

Leffler knew further argument would be pointless. He removed his stethoscope, slid it into a side pocket, his hand remaining there. "I'll look in on you this evening," he said and left the office immediately.

"Now, " Kellogg proclaimed, going back to his desk, perching on its edge, picking up a wooden pencil and tapping it in a bizarre, unrhythmic clatter, "I wish to dictate a very personal letter to my brother, Will."

WHEN John Harvey arrived at his mansion it was early in the evening. An icy December rain was falling, the kind that would freeze solid on tree limbs and streets and porch steps by midnight. He endured the expected scolding from Gertrude and the fussing by Angie as she helped him out of his wet coat and hat. He instructed them to tell doctor Leffler when he arrived that his patient was in bed, sleeping soundly and should not be disturbed.

"You ought to be in your own hospital, soaked to the skin the way you are," Gertrude reproved him again.

Kellogg was too fatigued to joust. He was tireder than he could ever remember. "You know," he said, loosening his tie, "it's funny about rain, the way it knocks down everything except itself. It pelts leaves on the trees, beats a cigarette snipe to pulp, pushes grass blades down flat, but big clear drops hang on the bare limbs of trees or on clothes lines or telephone wires, they just hang there, they don't get knocked off. Sometimes they fall off, but that's gravity at work. I wonder how the rain recognizes its relatives so it doesn't knock them down?"

Gertrude helped him enter the elevator and they rode up to the third floor. Kellogg was grateful that he did not have to climb any stairs. When he finally was bedded, Gertrude tiptoed to the outer room. On a table was an envelope he had dropped off on his way to the bedroom. It was addressed to W.K. Kellogg. She saw that the flap was not sealed. She hesitated, then took the letter with her. Downstairs, she opened it, despite Angie's scorching disapproval, and read it aloud, her face growing stormy as she proceeded through the paragraphs.

Finally, Gertrude said, "This letter is degrading. Doctor Kellogg makes himself sound like a common servant, practically begging that old fool of a brother who doesn't care spit for him." She returned the pages to the envelope and sealed it with a swipe of her tongue. "If he wasn't too sick to know what he's doing he would never have written it."

She went into the library and jammed the envelope out of sight behind a photograph of John Harvey and George Bernard Shaw on the fireplace mantle.

SOMEHOW, he had seemed indestructible. The headline that morning told otherwise. KELLOGG IS DEAD AT 91 it announced in 120-point boldface type. There was a three column photo of him so the readers would know which Kellogg was meant.

The rest of the Enquirer story told how he had passed away peacefully in his Manchester street residence after a three day struggle with pneumonia. He had worked in his hospital until late in the afternoon, seemed improved, talked energetically for an hour at home with doctor Richard Kellogg, one of his adopted sons, who was leaving the sanitarium's dental staff for war service. Then, according to the report, he sat in his library and corrected Good Health articles as they were read back to him. He consumed a light meal at five o'clock. The severe bronchial attack hit him around seven. By ten o'clock he was dead. He was a man who had never slowed down, the newspaper said. He would be buried at Oak Hill cemetery next to his wife, Ella.

77

ALBERT Miller entered the sitting room of W.K. Kellogg's apartment and had to feel his way along in the darkness. The brocade window curtains were closed, only a sliver of gelatinous light slipping between, and only one dim floor lamp was lit in a corner. The maid shut the door behind him as he bumped into a footstool. His clumsiness brought the snarl of an animal where Kellogg was cushioned in a deep, upholstered mohair chair by the low-burning fireplace.

"Quiet, Rinette." Kellogg yanked at a leash and the head of a German shepherd raised into view beside his chair. The dog eyed its master, then dropped back onto outstretched paws as the leash was loosened.

"It's Albert Miller, mister Kellogg." He did not step any closer.

"I was told you were coming up." W.K.'s doughy face floated in the room's underwater gloom, his head devoid of hair.

Miller said uncomfortably, "I trust your dog won't bite."

"She bites. If you are reaching to pet her, don't." He jostled the leash. "Wouldn't own any other canine breed. This one suits my temperament. Doesn't like for people to get too close to me."

Hearing the intended message, Miller sensed, more than felt, a seat by his leg. "May I sit over here?"

Kellogg extracted his other hand from under a patterned blanket that engulfed him from toe to neck, gestured with twittering fingers, a flash of fish-belly white.

"I can't rise to greet you. I'm blind."

"Yes, I'm sorry, mister Kellogg."

"No need. I've had the life that was cut out for me. Some blessings, some curses. Good luck and bad." The hand drifted back under the blanket.

Miller opened a pocket in his heavy wool suitcoat and found his pencil, note paper, and a sealed business size envelope. He placed the items beside him on the davenport and let his eyes adjust to the faint light. He could discern furniture — a library cabinet, two occasional tables, a grandfather clock, armchairs and side chairs, a sideboard with brass railings. Overhead was an unlit crystal girandole.

"I suppose you'll soon be going back to California?"

"Is that why you asked to see me, mister Miller?"

"No sir, just making small talk."

"I'm not fond of small talk," Kellogg answered captiously, admitting, "I leave here on the twentieth. I was told you wanted to talk to me about John Harvey's death." A distinct lack of enthusiasm in his tone.

"There has been a national outpouring over the loss of your brother, mister Kellogg. The Enquirer is preparing a follow-up memorial section." Miller picked up his pencil and paper, temporarily disregarding the sealed envelope. "Herbert Hoover has suggested donations be sought to commission a statue of doctor Kellogg, a public monument."

W.K.'s mouth scarcely moved. "I think my brother has had enough written about him. You should be writing about the war. It is *today*, John Harvey was yesterday."

"We *are* covering the war. My son, Robert, and half of the staff spend most of their time doing exactly that..."

"I'm aware," he broke in. "My secretary reads the daily papers to me. When Beth is here from California, she reads them. So did her son,

Norm, but they've drafted him in the Navy, even with his bad back." Kellogg uncovered his free hand again, rubbed his crinkled lips. "You live through a war, a national depression, it colors how you think the rest of your life. Things that happened stay inside you. Sounds or words can set you off years later, make you think of the war."

"You've contributed your share to the victory effort, mister Kellogg. It's common knowledge your Gull Lake estate is used by the Coast Guard for an induction center and a rehabilitation center for wounded service men. The Army uses your Pomona ranch for a remount station."

"No more than anyone else is doing."

"It's a great deal."

"I have more to give away than most people."

In spite of himself, Miller laughed.

"Wasn't trying to amuse you. Never developed much sense of humor. Wish I had. Wouldn't live longer, maybe just better," Kellogg mumbled. "Only time I ever allowed myself the luxury was in the motion picture theaters. Chaplin was funny, Our Gang, Laurel and Hardy. Harold Lloyd did wonderful gags."

W.K. paused to search his thoughts for another comedian's name and Miller said, "Sir, our readers would like to hear some words from you about doctor..."

Kellogg interrupted with surprising volume. "I had not talked to my brother for more than a month before he died. Knew only remotely of his illness." A half-hearted shrug. "Should have guessed that at his advanced age some mechanical thing inside him would skip a cog. Being old myself, and loathe to idle chatter, I did not call him. So I've nothing to tell your newspaper."

Miller supposed the interview was ended. His hand touched the sealed envelope on the davenport and he raised it, juggled it in his palm, extended it toward Kellogg. The dog growled threateningly and Miller drew back.

"I have an envelope addressed to you from John Harvey."

The only sound in the room for a long while was the sputtering of log fragments in the fireplace. Finally, "How could that be?"

"I don't know why it hasn't already reached you, but I was asked to deliver it. I stopped at doctor Kellogg's house on the way here, to talk with the two ladies who looked after him..."

"Those two," W.K. tongued the notion bitterly. "That's another reason I did not visit my brother. His keepers, they hovered. There was an unsavory aspect to that relationship."

"Mister Kellogg, it wasn't my intention to upset you. I'll give the letter to your maid on my way out." Miller stood.

"How did you come by such a letter?" Grudging curiosity stirring the old man's interest.

"As I left the doctor's house, the woman named Angie gave it to me. She said the doctor dictated part of it and wrote out part in his own hand. She was troubled that her sister mislaid it and it hadn't been delivered to you."

Kellogg's face was as stolid as sheet metal. "Could I impose on you to read it for me?"

"Perhaps your secretary or a relative..."

"Mister Miller, Beth has taken the train back to California. You are here, my secretary is not. I ask you to be my confidential eyes. Read the letter."

"Aren't you afraid I might publish its contents?"

"No. That isn't your way."

Miller sat down once more, then ran the point of his pencil under the envelope's gummed flap and opened it. He removed a cluster of folded sheets, flattened them, angled them to catch what little light there was.

"Dear brother Will. This letter is being written at my dictation since, as I am confident you are aware, my hand is no longer sufficiently steady for anything more than the very briefest bouts with pen and ink. Who ever would have imagined that the renowned doctor Kellogg, surgeon of repute, would be unable to control the scribblings of a fountain pen, let alone the blade of a scalpel?

"Some months ago you apparently received letters from senator Davis and from mister Hegate of the Wall Street Journal expressing concern for the Sanitarium's financial difficulties. Those well meaning gentlemen suggested that you might do something to help.

"I want you to know, dear brother, I only lately learned of their correspondence to you. I never suggested they write to you. I want very much for you to recognize my distance from their well meaning intrusions."

W.K. stirred in his chair, made disparaging sounds, disconnected syllables. Miller waited until he was quiet again.

"I have often thought, Will, about how your patience must have been tried by my demands on you. I remember as a boy, father tried to break me of the habit of becoming so absorbed in things that I overlooked the relative greater importance of other things. If I had the opportunity, I think I should be glad to change my life program over almost altogether. I trust it is never too late to mend one's ways. I recently began doddering when trying to walk so I have commenced to do systematic pedestrian exercises, returning to many of the health duties I promoted all my life but lately neglected."

Miller took up the next page.

"Our beloved sister Clara tells me that you cannot read because of blindness. Please know that I appreciate deeply what it means to be deprived of sight, except in one's memories. I can read with difficulty, if I wear strong magnifying glasses, and I can make out people in a good light, but I seldom find a picture in the newspaper which I can unravel. My eyes create all kinds of hobgoblins, and it will not be long before I shall have to have a constant attendant. I suffer steady pain, but none from my eyes. Worse, though, I find my memory failing, especially when I do not sleep well. I am glad I do not have so many years ahead of me to live with a failing body and mind."

W.K. verified: "John Harvey seldom slept. It's a Kellogg curse." Then, more subdued, "I didn't realize he was in pain. He never sent word."

Miller continued reading. "Will, some people have accused that I am an agnostic, not a believer in the Supreme Being. I assure you, they are wrong. I've seen a hundred thousand bodies, all shapes and weights and lengths, and I've looked inside them all, seen the blood, veins, and bones of each. I am forever amazed at the complexity and perfection of the human machine. All those marvelous parts covered by a seamless skin, no loose edges, no upturned corners. Sometimes I wonder if it is because I violated that perfection, cut into it, scarred it and left it less than it was, that God penalized me. But I ever operated to save lives, though not always successfully, and I hope He will take that into account when I stand before Him. I pray, too, that you might be equally generous."

Kellogg's sightless eyes pushed at the darkness. "Here it comes. The doctor intended to ask for money for his San after all." Disappointment was mixed with a touch of self congratulation.

Miller read: "You once made a remark about unbrotherly treatment which struck me forcibly and, I confess, unfavorably at the time. Since then I have tried to put myself in your place, Will, and look at it from your standpoint. I know now I have done many things which, without explanation, would appear inconsiderate and worthy of criticism. Now I am exerting desperate efforts to put all my affairs into order to preserve as much as possible what good they may represent, and to make amends for any injustice I have done to you."

Kellogg spoke hesitantly, "I thought this was a dun for money."

Miller turned another page. "I earnestly beg you, Will, to give me a frank expression of anything I have said or done which you see as unbrotherly or even unjust. I do this not to invite discussion, but to allow me a chance to obliterate, as far as possible from your memory, any unkind action of my doing. I ask you, please, allow me the opportunity to heal any wound I have made.

"I look back upon that period when you were closely associated with me as the most important and successful of my life. It was the greatest possible misfortune that circumstances led us in different channels and separated our interests. But now I can only congratulate you on the splendid work your foundation is doing along scientific and philanthropic lines, and I can only speak with admiration about your own balanced judgement that has led you to great achievements in the food business. Well deserved, dear brother. I envy you and I admire you."

The fireplace logs were gone to embers. W.K. sat motionless, his useless eyes fixed on some inner vision.

"Are you all right, sir?"

A tip of the head.

"There is a closing." Beneath the typed sentences, was a single paragraph scratched in a wavery, inky scrawl. Miller touched the lines with his fingertips. "I humbly ask your forgiveness, Will, and your love. I need both more than I can possibly describe at this time, and I pray that I may tell you in person. I will wait with much anticipation, hoping to hear from you soon. I am your apologetic and loving brother, John Harvey."

Miller stood and folded the several sheets of paper. He stuffed them back into the envelope and handed it to Kellogg, guiding it into his hand. The dog watched him, but made no noise.

"Thank you, mister Miller." The old man's voice was as soft as wine fermenting.

"You're welcome, mister Kellogg. I'll be going now."

"If you please, mister Miller. Tell my nurse I don't want to be disturbed until I ring."

Miller saw tears freely coursing down Kellogg's crumpled cheeks. Just before he closed the thick oaken door behind him, he heard a single desolate sob, forlorn and heartsick. "Puss. John Junior. Now you, John Harvey..."

78

BATTLE Creek's first radio station, WELL, had been brought to the city by Albert Miller in the 1920's. A quarter of a century later, in the middle of Kitty Kallen's suggestive warble, "It's Been A Long, Long, Time," the musical program was interrupted for an announcement by President Harry S Truman.

"Men and women of America, this is a solemn but glorious day," proclaimed the Missouri haberdasher-turned-politician. "I only wish Franklin D. Roosevelt had lived to witness it. General Dwight D. Eisenhower informed me shortly ago that the forces of Germany have surrendered to the United States. The flags of freedom fly all over Europe..."

Joyous as the news was, men still died and families still mourned and the empire of Japan fought on against mounting odds.

On Saturday, August 11, 1945, while lawn sprinklers doused grasses in Louisiana, and tomato vines ruptured with redness in gardens all over New Jersey, and Bingo games were played with dedication in church basements across Texas, the atom bomb ended World War II.

Events rolled on like the gummy floodwaters of the Missouri and Mississippi rivers that came and submerged two million acres of farmland from Topeka to St. Louis, and exiled 200,000 people from their homes. On capitol hill in D.C., it was argued that the assassination of Premier Ali Razmara by Arab nationalist groups might have been prevented if the United States had acted more forcefully toward Iran. The war over and old allegiances forgotten, the USSR raised up on its hind legs, a communist beast bent on shredding the heart of democracy. Scandal burst in the U.S. Treasury Department like a blister; bribes, illegal gambling, theft, shakedowns.

THE THREE of them were in the wood-paneled main room of the Gull Lake manor, making intermittent conversation, long gaps between fits of general sentences. Beyond the picture windows a stone patio reached out to a stone retaining wall that overlooked a sloping bluff. Below and beyond the bluff, Gull Lake's green waters shimmered in the April sunshine. It was April in the year 1947, too early and too cool for boats, so the lake was uncluttered and flat, like a freshly mowed lawn.

"If the years can soften you, dull you, I'm a prime example," W.K. said. "At age 87, the only thing that hasn't entirely failed me is my hearing."

Len turned from the window where he had been watching the lake.

He studied his father's face for a double meaning, found none, looked out again at the water. Beth was seated on a leather couch, her attention drifting over the rug at her feet. She wore a floor-length dress of the Dior style.

"I'm just fed up with not being able to see anything that goes on around me." Kellogg's robed arms rested on the padded arms of his wheelchair. A pair of canes lay at his reach on a Chippendale table. "It affects my taste. The cook fixed a grand meal, I'm sure. Tasted like burned cabbage to me."

"One thing you have not done is become dull," Len laughed lightly, raised a cocktail glass in half salute. He was drinking a scotch and water, mixed from a bottle he brought along from California. He wore a blue doublebreasted suit and a striped tie. His hair, like his face, was very gray and very thin.

"It's wonderful to have you back for a visit," Beth said for the tenth time. "I wish Helen could have come with you."

"The postwar economy is booming," Len said, choosing not to discuss Helen's absence. "Houses and buildings going up everywhere you look. Aluminum, copper, all the materials available again. The '47 Studebaker is stunning, looks like a Buck Rogers space car."

"Our company is on top of it all, always ahead of the pack," W.K. replied defensively. "Nearly six thousand employees worldwide, about four thousand of them right here in Battle Creek. We built that new warehouse last year. Cost one million dollars, mind you. Can hold half a million cases of cereals. A good investment." His voice shook. "We're first in cereals and we'll always be because that's what we do. Post had to branch out, try to get their fingers in everything from jello to syrup. Bad move, getting all strung out."

"They're a corporation," Len reminded. "General Foods. Post is just one unit."

W.K. scoffed, shifted loudly to high gear. "And old C.W. is getting lost in the process. Just what he deserves."

A scowl drew deeper creases across his lined face. He said quietly, "I stay out of the company's way, and my foundation, too. The men in charge know what they're doing. I only upset them, confuse them when I show up at a board meeting. I blow my nose or clear my throat and they stop in their tracks and try to figure out what I meant by it. Didn't mean anything, so I stay away." He coasted. "How is your business doing, Len?"

Len did not say, "You've asked me that question twice and I've told you I'm no longer in business." Instead, he shrugged, finished off his drink. "The shares of Kellogg Company stock Helen squirreled away for us have done well. They give us a comfortable living." For the third time, he told W.K., "Helen sends her best wishes to you," and watched the old man wince.

Beth left no space for W.K. to speak. "Father, there is a camera on the market that develops a picture as soon as it's taken. Develops it right inside the camera box itself."

W.K. barely nodded. "Polaroid," he announced. "Probably a half-decent stock to buy. After Kellogg."

"And he says he's going dull," Len chided, walking out to the kitchen for a refill of scotch.

"One of missus Allen's boys telephoned earlier to ask about you," Beth said.

W.K. looked quizzical.

"Missus Allen worked at the company," Beth reminded him. "Her husband was shot and killed by an FBI agent who mistook him for a moonshiner."

"I remember," Kellogg said. "The FBI man killed himself when he found out what he'd done. Tragic thing." He brightened. "Missus Allen was a fine worker. She had four children, two boys, two girls. Her husband's death nearly did the poor woman in but she was made of stern stuff. Kept going."

"Her son sent his thanks again for your help, giving them clothes, paying their food and rent bills."

Kellogg tilted his head disparagingly. "Nothing."

Beth smiled. "He thought it was a lot. He said you supported their family two entire years after the accident. You never mentioned it."

In silence, W.K. simply stared at nothing, his mouth tight like a stretched string. Then he announced, "I am leaving my estate to the foundation. Everything I have. Len knows that."

Beth stirred on the couch. "Len doesn't want anything from you, father. Except maybe your approval."

"There will be a small trust fund for each grandchild. You have your house and whatever else I've given you, some company stock..."

"We'll be all right, father." She went to him and cradled one of his brittle hands in her own. "Besides, this kind of talk is silly. You've a long life ahead of you yet."

Len entered and asked, "Okay, you two, what're you cooking up?"

W.K. answered, "Beth is filling me with fairy tales about living happily ever after."

79

AUGUST 1951

WITHIN A half-dozen years after the end of World War Two, yet another conflict rumbled into sight, cannons thumping, men dying. The politicos dredged up a softer sounding tag for War in an obscure country like Korea, calling it a "police action." But, whatever they named it, it had all the earmarks of a real sonofabitch.

Though *wars* arguably might never become extinct, there was a notable disappearance of kings and tycoons in Battle Creek.

THROUGHOUT the summer of 1951, W.K. Kellogg drifted between coma and dim awareness. An irony he would not have appreciated was that he was confined in a hospital built with money donated by Leila Post Montgomery from the estate of C.W. Post.

People who passed along North avenue or Emmett street no longer looked up at the second floor, trying to guess which window belonged to the ninety-one year old cereal magnate. For the most part, they had forgotten he was there. He had gone in on the first of July, initially for treatment of anemia, then complications and collapse of the circulatory system. A team of doctors had worked on him for six weeks, kept him alive. Barely.

"Beth?"

"Yes, father, I'm right here." She placed her hand on his hot forehead, looked hopelessly at the other woman in the room. "Elsie is with us, too."

"Thirsty." His voice was soft and apologetic.

Elsie Hoatson, who had nursed his wants for eight years, came to his bedside. She wore a fresh white uniform and newly polished black shoes with low heels, attire she had put on before returning at noon after a dash home for a bath and a meal of cold leftovers. She pressed a damp cloth against W.K.'s mouth. He sucked it hungrily, pulling at its meager wetness.

"Is it daytime?"

"Yes, father. Afternoon. A bright day with the sun out and there is a nice breeze, perfect for short sleeves this time of year." Using the cloth Elsie handed to her, she fanned it in the air to cool it, then laid it across his brow.

"What's movies?"

Beth smiled. "I knew you'd ask so I looked them up in the paper last evening. At the Bijou is a football story but I can't remember who is in it. The Rex has a musical with Betty Grable. The Regent has a very funny Cary Grant with him doing a spoof about being a doctor..."

"Wouldn't care to see," W.K. whispered. "Enough doctors."

Elsie sat on the cushioned chair by the foot of the bed, folded her hands in her lap. "The Tom Corbett television show is doing very, very well with the young people, mister Kellogg. The company officials are pleased with the boost in sales. Everyone gives you credit for suggesting it."

"Don't want their applesauce."

"I'll tell them," she said dutifully.

"When will Len come?" Less of a question than an insistence.

Elsie lowered her eyes and anyone walking into the room might have thought she was praying. It fell to Beth to explain again what he had been told a dozen times during the past month.

"Len isn't coming, father."

"Knows I'm sick?" Surly voice rising a half octave, flutey and angry. A frown wrinkled his brow, his cheeks bulged, and color crept high up on his neck, like a child holding its breath before a tantrum.

"Father, try to understand, I know it's difficult for you, but please try. Len is dead. A year ago this past April, after his visit with you in Battle Creek." She glanced out the window, watched two sparrows chase each other across a tree limb, fly out of the foliage and shoot away like little charcoal lumps thrown from a sling. Below, on the street, an automobile backfired as though someone had sighted a rifle on the birds when they took wing. "You two had a wonderful visit, shook hands, and you told him you would pay his way back as often as he could come."

"No..." he began, hesitantly. "Saw him. Yesterday." Then, because he feared the answer but didn't understand why, he asked, "Yesterday?"

"Len is dead, mister Kellogg," Elsie raised her head, speaking with an authority meant to close the subject. "He went back to Chicago and then he went to California to see Karl and he died out there of a heart attack."

W.K. huffed defensively. "Know that. Meant Karl."

"Karl is too ill to travel," Elsie continued instructively. "He is staying in touch by telephone."

"John Junior?" The question was an open petition: no more bad news, please.

Before Elsie could answer, Beth hushed her with a wagging finger. She touched W.K.'s cooling cheek. His fever had fled, the chills would enter next. "John Junior is taking the train," she lied, "he might be here tomorrow or the next day."

"I want..."

The word dangled on an extended silence. His mouth shut ever tighter and crawled inward, lips disappearing, while his eyelids agitated as if he was following the action of something that moved with great speed. Elsie sat forward, touched the bedclothes where his foot peaked the coverlet.

"Tell us what you want, mister Kellogg."

"...bowl oyster stew. Webb's Diner."

"Yes, father, we'll send out for it," Beth replied instantly. She did not mention that Webb's had closed forty years ago and the corner where it stood was now occupied by a three-story brick building full of self-cleaning stoves, six-slice toasters, and other shiny work-saving appliances.

His stern expression relaxed, as though a heavy concern had been satisfied. He whispered, "Will Bev come?"

The question surprised Beth. She had never heard her father mention anyone named Bev.

"Black hair," he said dreamily, from the distance of a star. "Loved her, didn't tell her. First love. Never told Puss." A frothy gibberish. "Bev. Pretty Bev. Copelund. Made my heart happy. Her father said no, can't go to tent show."

Beth was confused by the confetti of words. "Where did you know Bev?" Her question crackled with dread. "Where did you meet her?"

"School. Third grade. Black hair." A shiver ran the length of his body. "Loved Puss most. Longest. Bev first."

Beth's face softened. "She will be here, too, father. Maybe John Junior will come with her on the same train and walk through the door at the same moment."

W.K. beamed with believing her, though he was chilling fast. "Outlive him?" he asked spunkily. "Outlive John Harvey?"

"Yes. Uncle John has been gone nearly ten years."

"Told him so." Spoken with satisfaction, while faint shadows moved beneath the skin of his face like changing colors of ocean currents. "I won."

"Won what, father?"

"Something..." His face contorted as he tried to find an answer. Futilely, he replied, "Won...something."

He shook suddenly and so forcefully the bedcovers shimmied as if a strong wind had entered the room. Elsie brought a woolen blanket from the closet and spread it over him. When he succumbed to sleep, his thoughts tumbled drunkenly, tipping one by one over the edge of a precipice into a depthless canyon of insensibility.

An hour later the doctor arrived, checked his patient. The examination required less than a minute. He straightened, removed a stethoscope from around his neck, double-checked the time on his wrist watch, and said to Beth and Elsie: "I'm sorry, ladies."

Epilogue

ALBERT Miller waited on the steps of the Enquirer offices while Bob held the door for an elderly woman to enter the building. Across State street, the sandwich shop enjoyed a vigorous business for a Friday evening. On either side of the shop, the cigar store and book store were clotted with customers. It was that way all over the town: busy.

The weather was warm and the Millers had loosened their neckties, unbuttoned their shirt collars. They were wearing identical lightweight tan business suits, Albert's somewhat more crumpled than Bob's.

"A dreary week finally ended," the older Miller replied, shifting a folded copy of his newspaper to a coat pocket. "Schools closed, stores locked up early, the Kellogg company dark and empty as an alley at midnight."

Bob said, "The saddest part for me was the flags at half mast. Everywhere you looked they hung like sick creatures, not a breeze to stir them the whole time. Nobody outside. It's been like a ghost town." He extracted his car keys from a tangle of coins and pocket ravelings.

"Well, the ghosts are gone tonight." Albert gestured at the endless convoy of automobiles that crept end-to-end on the brick street, hundreds of headlights glowing in the assembling darkness.

The sidewalks thronged with people, the way a city emerges from hibernation after a severe winter, except that it was still only August. A block away on Main street, the crowd was even more densely packed — shoppers, movie goers, late diners — moving in great masses before the brightly lighted store windows of Cole's clothing, Godfrey's jewelry, the Owl drugstore, the Lantern Gardens Chinese restaurant. Neon marquees crackled above the Regent, Orpheum, Strand, Bijou theaters. Tin-eared critics by the hundreds hurried along toward a concert at Kellogg Auditorium.

"Mister Kellogg is dead," Bob muttered philosophically, "and the city is alive." He surveyed the street in both directions, nodded acceptingly, and followed Albert through the streaming crowd. "I don't think there's a Kellogg left in Battle Creek, certainly none with the company or the foundation. And C.W. Post's name is just a vague memory that shows up on cereal boxes. The tycoons all are gone. Will that be good or bad for us?"

"Battle Creek will survive, Bob. We may even grow a new crop of tycoons, as you call them, but different from the Kelloggs or C.W. Post."

A sign at the entrance of a dirt lot, fenced in, read "Reserved Parking

Only." They walked to a roadster automobile at the rear and Bob opened the unlocked car door. He rolled down a window to let out the day's heat, waited beside the car to learn if Albert intended to ride home or walk.

"That was a pretty fair editorial you wrote, dad. I heard someone in advertising describe it as tasteful."

Albert took the newspaper from his pocket, hummed indistinctly over the sentences. His glasses caught splintery glints of light from a street lamp as he read, "W.K. Kellogg was the last survivor of that notable list of home residents who built our basic industries, each from primitive beginnings. Wherever the fact of his death is told there will be comment on the passing of a great industrialist and public benefactor."

The paper went back into a pocket. He surveyed the parking lot. "It's a nice evening. I'll walk."

Bob got into the car, started it, shifted into gear without grinding. He waved to Albert, then drove out of the lot, leaving a trail of white dust spinning off the ground like angel breath.

Miller ambled to the entrance of the lot where it met the sidewalk. He rested one arm atop the private parking sign, a man in no hurry and uncertain which direction he preferred to go. He pondered a half-dozen routes while a languorous breeze trifled with his hair, fluffed it, passed on. Finally, he whacked the wooden sign with his fingertips, a neat little smack, and decisively marched east on State street. He slowed. Stopped. People coursed around him the way water parts for a rock in a river bed.

He knew Louise would have his meal on the table and would be watching for him, but he wasn't hungry yet, and it was an inviting summer twilight under the soft circles of street lamps and the shadowy trees. So he turned and walked westward to McCamly, then north to VanBuren where the houses were close and each had a brightly lighted front room that cast rectangles of silver onto the street.

He crossed over to Washington. As he passed the old Kellogg Hotel he paused only a moment, the duration of a deep breath. But when he reached the Sanitarium he lingered to let his eyes scale its sixteen floors of windows and columns and cornices. He heard Bob's words again, "The tycoons all are gone," and he nodded to himself. He drank in the San's timeless design and grandeur, and before he moved on, he felt a small sweep of satisfaction for having decided to take this longer, less traveled way home.

Robert E. Hencey has worked as the publications director for a university, and the communications director for a worldwide private foundation. His background includes a stint at the Kansas City Star, and he is the co-founder of an electronics firm in the Silicon Valley of California. Mr. Hencey is a graduate of the University of Missouri. He is married, has three children – Dawn, Mark, and Justine. Mr. Hencey currently lives in Battle Creek, Michigan.